Emily
ever
after

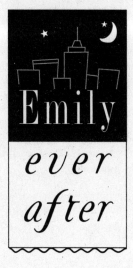

Emily
ever
after

Anne Dayton and

May Vanderbilt

Broadway Books
★ · New York ★

This book is a work of fiction. Names, characters, businesses, organizations, places, events, and incidents either are the product of the author's imagination or are used fictitiously. Any resemblance to actual persons, living or dead, events, or locales is entirely coincidental.

PRINTED IN THE UNITED STATES OF AMERICA

BROADWAY BOOKS and its logo, a letter B bisected on the diagonal, are trademarks of Random House, Inc.

Visit our Web site at www.broadwaybooks.com

First edition published July 2005

Book design by Donna Sinisgalli

Library of Congress Cataloging-in-Publication Data

Dayton, Anne.
    Emily ever after / Anne Dayton and Mary Vanderbilt.—1st Broadway ed.
      p. cm.
    ISBN 0-385-51463-8 (alk. paper)
    1. Publishers and publishing—Fiction. 2. New York (N.Y.)—Fiction. 3. Women editors—Fiction. 4. Young women—Fiction. I. Vanderbilt, May. II. Title.

PS3604.A989E45 2005
813'.6—dc22

2004061939

10 9 8 7 6 5 4 3 2 1

ACKNOWLEDGMENTS

A very special thanks to all the good people who helped us out, from encouraging us when all we had was an idea to spying for us at meetings: Dudley Delffs, Trace Murphy, Claudia Cross, Kate Prentice, Joan Biddle, Margie Barritt, Trish Medved, Beth Meister, Laura Welch, Kate Harris, Charlie Conrad, Becky Cole, Beth Haymaker, Tracy Zupancis, Christine Pride, Rakesh Satyal, Laura Marshall, Nina B., Jenny Cookson, Allison Mooney, Beth Buschman-Kelly, Allyson Giard, Ursula Cary, Sarah Rainone, Maria Meneses, and Michael Windsor.

Anne Dayton: Heartfelt thanks to Mom and Dad. Sorry about the tuition bills. Thanks to Nick for showing me how to beat Super Mario Brothers that one time, and to Peter for letting me dress him as a girl for so many years. Maybe someday one of you will actually read the book. And thanks to Wayne.

May Vanderbilt: Thanks to my parents, Larry and Laura, for raising us in a permanent episode of *The Cosby Show*, to Matt and Diem for their prayers, and to Sandy for being my baby sister, whether she wanted the job or not. A big thanks to the Bransfords for reading *Emily* right away and for providing lots of almonds. A special thanks to Bob Darden for being the first to believe in me. And to Nathan. For everything.

Emily
ever
after

new york, new york

★

The last thing my parents wanted to see before they left New York was a museum, so here we are at the Met. We did the whole museum in about forty-five minutes—they aren't exactly art collectors—and now we're up in the rooftop sculpture garden, and I'm taking a moment to watch the sun stain the green treetops orange in Central Park. It's just like a postcard.

I turn and see my father lumber over to a pop art sculpture, a metal garden spade fit for a giant, and rap his knuckle on it. I take off at a tasteful—well, as tasteful as I can manage in my new strappy sandals—sprint to try to stop him. He rubs his hand over the textured paint job, scratching the metal with his fingernail, manhandling the thing. It's too late. Two museum security guards in blue blazers beat me to him.

"Sir, do not touch the sculpture," the shorter one barks.

I am at my father's side in an instant. He looks at me, wounded and confused, and then back at the men.

"This is the only warning you'll get, sir. Do not touch *any* of the art," the other one says.

"He didn't mean to, he . . ." I sputter, simultaneously embarrassed by and aching for my poor confused father.

"Sorry about that. It won't happen again," says a deep voice behind me. Uncle Matthew is striding quickly across the roof on his long legs, his brown hair mussing in the wind, his confident demeanor and calming intonation setting the guards at ease. "I'll make sure he behaves," he laughs, winking at them.

They look at each other and, wordlessly, turn away. They walk back to the other side of the roof, stepping with almost military precision. I imagine sticking out my leg to trip them, but I control myself.

I turn and shake my head at my father. I feel how hot my cheeks are, and I glance around to see how many people have noticed. Everyone is staring at us.

I thought it was bad when my parents started singing "Give My Regards to Broadway," in harmony, in Times Square, but this is far worse. We stick out like sore thumbs. The Clampett family in New York. *Green Acres* all over again. Except that this isn't an old TV show. It's my actual nightmare come true. The Hinton family in New York.

"Daaad . . ." I whine a little. I can't help it. Please God. Please just let my family act normal. Oh please. I count in my head the number of hours until the Hinton family goes home, and Emily Hinton stays behind. Five. I can make it five hours. At least Uncle Matthew is here.

Mom comes up behind Dad and puts her hand on his shoulder. "Honey, Dad just wanted to see what it was made of. He wasn't going to hurt something as big as that." And then she turns around and with her third-grade teacher's voice belts out a warning to my twin brothers, who are currently across the rooftop garden trying to spit on the people below. God, just take me now, I say to myself. Take me now.

I always knew I'd get out of Jenks the first chance I got. Yes, Jenks, like jinx. It's a fitting name actually, like a curse. But technically the town is named after the man who founded it and has nothing to do with how you feel when you live there. Jenks, California. A regular old California suburb, with its regular old identical houses and regular old cars and regular old families. It's just north of La Jolla, the trendy suburb of San Diego with gated communities and a Banana Republic on every corner.

My parents are ex-hippies who "got saved" during the Jesus Movement. You'd never know it now, but they used to have long hair, trendy hip-hugging jeans, and weighed a combined total of 225 pounds. Now my mom's hair is a nondescript color, neither red nor brown, and she wears denim jumpers with wooden-bead necklaces. Essentially, she looks like every third-grade teacher in America. My father is your basic T-ball dad. He's got brown hair, a brown mustache, a barrel chest, and a basketball stuffed in his stomach. They're sweet and I love them, but they're definitely not New York. They're, well, Jenks, I guess.

I knew I wanted to live in New York ever since I saw *When Harry Met Sally* during my Meg Ryan phase. (The Hinton Family Council, of which there are exactly two members, approves of the entirety of Meg Ryan's film work.) There Harry and Sally were on New Year's Eve at a glitzy party on the top floor of some gorgeous skyscraper reaching toward heaven, and I knew someday I'd be a well-heeled, clever, and sassy New York ingénue myself. I'd find my Harry, and we'd buy a Christmas tree on the street and crunch, crunch, crunch our way back through the fresh snow to my apartment. That night I announced that I was moving to the "Big Apple." My father told me to remember to write.

I had originally thought college would be my chance to finally transplant myself to New York. By then my room was cluttered with fashion magazines and I had read every book about New York that I could get my hands on. I even had a poster of the skyline at night hung on my wall. Unlike my best friend, Jenna, who would probably end up teaching physical education just like her mother someday and only attended school to keep up with gossip, I got straight A's. My parents worried that I studied too much and always encouraged me to take up sports or join clubs. My mom even suggested I play the handbells with her at church, which was all fine and dandy if you were over forty or married or both, but not fine for a girl like me. I had different things in mind.

I knew my parents wanted to help send me to college, but they just couldn't. My dream had always been to go to NYU, to be right there in the heart of Greenwich Village. I felt in my bones that I would someday go to parties and mingle with art students and attend fashion shows and book signings. Everyone said I was a shoo-in with my grades and my test scores. Jenna and I were already planning her sightseeing visits, during which I planned to whack her over the head with a frying pan and drag her into A.P.C. in SoHo, the shopping capital of the world, and buy her some basics. And even though I needed a hefty scholarship to make it happen, I wanted to only apply to NYU.

At the last moment my mom forced me to apply to San Diego State University as my safety school. The possibility of my staying in Jenks seemed so absurd at the time that I didn't fight her on it too much. I had been saying I was moving to New York the first chance I got ever since anyone could remember.

When I got the letter from NYU saying I had been wait-listed, I didn't immediately lose hope, but the more I looked at the math with my guidance counselor, the clearer it became that it wasn't going to work out, even if I did get in. They allotted 85 percent of their scholarship money to non–wait-listed applicants. I was crushed. My parents tried to make me feel better, pointing out all the positives, but I was inconsolable. I actually began to pray that I didn't get in at all, just so that I wouldn't be tempted to take out loans that I would never be able to pay back. But I did get in. I got off the wait-list in late May. I just threw the giant manila envelope in the trash and never told my parents. By doing essentially nothing, I found myself attending classes that fall at San Diego State University. Go Aztecs.

If in high school I had wanted to get out of Jenks in some idle way, the way most teenagers dream of distant shores, then in my college years, it became an obsession. School was a breeze so I got a job in the dining hall to make extra money. It wasn't a glamorous job, but it paid well because no one else wanted to do it. I slaved away, saved every penny, and lost myself in books. And even though I loved Jenna and we'd been friends since second grade, I became obsessed with the people I knew who had gone away to college, not stayed at Jenks and attended SDSU. In particular, I was dying to see what those who left were wearing, saying, and reading. The Berkeley students were always the best. You could take an average girl from my high school, give her one year at Berkeley, and she would return the following summer to Jenks a fascinating person with her own sense of style. One girl came home wearing a dog collar. She somehow made the dog collar look like a Tiffany choker. But all the time, I was making plans. Plans to get out.

"Is there going to be food at this thing?" Jenna asked, staring at herself in the rearview mirror.

"I don't know. Maybe. Please don't stick your feet out the window." She pulled them in slowly. It was toward the end of our junior year of college, and I was getting excited about spending the summer reading. Jenna was getting excited about catching up on her TV and her surfing.

"So who is this guy we're going to see?" she asked.

"James Collins. My favorite contemporary poet. He's one of the best people writing today." I looked at her hopefully. "He's won all kinds of awards. And he's only in town one night, which he chose to spend at a book signing so people like you could be turned on to the world of literature," I said. She yawned.

"Don't you want to know something about this guy before you hear him speak? Come on. Please pretend to care a little. Just for me."

She looked at me sideways, pasted a fake smile onto her face, and said through unnaturally bared teeth, barely moving her lips, "Just for you!"

I sighed. She was hopeless. She had on a pair of acid-washed jeans, a Coca-Cola T-shirt, and a miserable kelly green and black checkered flannel shirt tied around her waist. I wondered if I could knock some fashion sense into her if I pelted her with *Vogue*. Sometimes I swore she intentionally dressed cluelessly to get under my skin. Still, she had given up her evening and the season finale of *The Bachelor* to come with me, and I knew she wouldn't find it at all exciting. I had to give her that.

We pulled into the parking lot of the Barnes & Noble in La Jolla and walked to the store. Stepping inside, I took a deep breath. It smelled delicious, divine—like paper, coffee, opportunities.

I led Jenna to the rows of chairs. We found seats in the back and waited for the presentation to start. The bulk of the audience was older than we were, though there were a few other student types, and they all seemed to be immaculately dressed. Several people had notebooks out, and almost all clutched a copy of Collins's book. I wish, I thought to myself, I could be around people who care about books all the time.

While Jenna fidgeted, I paged through my copy. When James Collins finally came out of the back room and was introduced by the manager of the Barnes & Noble, I was enraptured. He looked a little older than he had in his author photo, his hair grayer around the temples, but he looked dignified. As he stepped up to the microphone, I clapped politely, and Jenna put her fingers in her mouth and let out a loud whistle and clapped enthusiastically. I glared at her, and she shrugged, whispering, "Just for you."

I turned back to the front, and he started to read, his voice low and soothing, a poem about looking at the surface of the water from underneath. The rhythm and cadence of his words came to life as he read. My mouth was hanging open. Jenna was playing a game on her cell phone.

He read several poems, and then asked if anyone had any questions.

A woman in the front row asked where he found his ideas, enunciating every syllable carefully.

"From the world," he replied slowly. "From nature. From children. Music. Art. Democracy. My inspiration is life." He paused, letting us absorb what he said.

"What is he babbling about?" Jenna whispered in my ear. "He didn't say anything at all."

"Shh . . ." I hissed at her. I was trying to ponder the profundity of his statement. I was sure if I just thought about it, it would become clear.

"Who has the greatest influence on your work?" a guy about my age asked.

"Without a doubt, that would be my editor, Roger Cole," he said. "He understands my poems and shapes them more than I like to admit." He laughed. What power, I thought. "For his wisdom I am undeniably grateful." It had never occurred to me that someone did that; that someone made the artist's raw work into art. I was intrigued. How did one become an editor?

After the questions, almost the entire crowd got into line to have their books signed. I waited patiently, while Jenna hit the complimentary refreshment table. I watched her skip over the baked brie and crudités tray and go straight for the potato chips and sodas they set out in case any children came. I groaned inwardly. I looked around at my fellow poetry lovers. These people were educated. They cared about literature, and they saw beyond their own private world. Jenna, over there now browsing the fitness magazines, well . . . as much as I loved her, she was a part of the world I wanted to leave behind. These people represented what I wanted to grasp. "I need to get out of here," I said under my breath.

"And whom shall I make this one out to?" I heard. I turned quickly. James Collins was reaching to take my book from my hand, smiling.

"Emily," I stammered.

"Emily, what do you do?" he asked kindly, looking up at me. Does James Collins really care what I do? Probably not, but he did ask.

"I'm a student," I said.

"What do you want to do when you get out?"

"I want to . . . get out of here, I guess. I think I want to work with books." I didn't know. I wanted to get paid to read, to work with literature. "I want to . . . be an editor maybe?"

"That sounds like a plan to me," he said. "There could be no more noble calling," he said dramatically, taking up his pen with a flourish. He scribbled something, blew on it to dry the ink, closed the cover, and handed the book back to me. "Good luck," he said, winking at me. I walked toward chairs and sat down in the first row. I opened the cover slowly. "To Emily," he had written. "Make it happen. James Collins." I will, James, I thought. I will.

Jenna saw me sitting down and came over. "Did you get it?" I nodded. "Cool. Can we go to In N' Out now? I'm dying for a milkshake."

I sighed. "Yeah," I said. "Let's get out of here." Someday, I couldn't help thinking, I really will.

"Emily! Emily! Come quick!"

I left my Psych 101 homework and ran into the living room

at my father's frantic call and found the TV tuned to the evening news. A picture of the New York skyline flipped on as a national news story broke. My father had the volume up so loud that my ears were starting to hurt. The anchorman spoke. "When we return from our break, we'll take you to the streets of New York where today a man jumped from the top of the Empire State Building."

As soon as it cut to a commercial, my father turned to me. "You see, Emily? It's a really dangerous city."

I knew the drill. Mom and Dad did not want me moving to New York. They didn't know the city and didn't trust it. Anytime they caught wind of something bad happening there, they played it up.

"I understand Central Park is littered with used needles and all the kids your age are starving at miserable jobs. *Plus . . .*"

I knew where this was going. My father had once visited his brother in New York in winter. It always came back to this.

"*Plus*, it's so *cold* there. Snow everywhere. Snow's not like you see it on TV. It's dreadful stuff. Like rain, only dirtier. And it's so cold—"

"That you'll think you have an iron lung," I finished off his classic condemnation of my city.

He laughed. "That's all. Just want to make sure you have all the facts since you think you want to live there. I mean, I'm happy to identify your body when they thaw you out come spring. Believe me, California girl. You won't like that weather."

I rolled my eyes as the news came back on.

"Many New Yorkers were disturbed today to see what looked like a man jumping off the Empire State Building. Fortunately, it wasn't the tragedy many assumed—it was a stuntman taping a scene of what is expected to be this summer's big blockbuster." My father quickly turned the volume way down, embarrassed. He said, "It's still really dangerous."

"I promise not to hang around any movie sets and try to meet cute young actors. Oh wait! No I don't!"

We chuckled, and I went back to my homework. As I left the room, he yelled behind me, "Twenty degrees in the winter! You'll see!"

But I knew it wasn't just my safety they were concerned about. They told me they worried I'd forget who I was out there, lose my faith. I knew they were right that Christians were few and far between in that coursing metropolis, but I insisted they needed to trust me. What they couldn't understand, no matter how many times I tried to explain it, was that I was going to change New York. I would be the salt on its pretzels and the light in its subway tunnels. I'd make it a better place. And once I'd made up my mind, there was no changing it. As graduation approached, I began posting my résumé on every job board I could find online. I sent résumés to every publishing company in the city. Just the addresses were enough to make me excited: What would Seventh Avenue look like? I'd heard Park Avenue was nice. Central Park West—could I sit in the sun on my lunch break?

When I didn't find a job right away Mom kept encouraging me to look at some companies nearby. Why not San Diego, if I had to live in a city? she asked. Even Los Angeles? Jenna suggested I should stay right here in Jenks and get a job at the public library if I had to work with books. Mom reminded me how much money I'd save if I lived at home. But my mind was made up. Stubborn as a mule and twice as foolhardy, she mumbled under her breath more than once.

When Uncle Matthew, who'd heard about my job search, e-mailed my dad to tell him about the opening at Morrow & Sons, my father almost didn't tell me. He was just looking out for my best interests, he confessed later. But I think he felt sorry for me when he saw me trot earnestly to the post office with another batch of résumés, and he told me to go ahead and give Matthew a call. When I accepted the job, my parents tried to resign themselves to my inevitable departure, but they reminded me more than once of all that I would be missing—free cable, clean laundry, and family dinners. I yawned. The twins' first day of eighth grade? I would have none of it. My dream was coming true, and I couldn't wait. The funny thing is, I would have cleaned the sidewalks by eating the gum off the pavement just to live in New York. Even now, I can't believe it's happening to me.

We arrived Monday in Manhattan, the whole family present and accounted for. My father had insisted on taking time off work from the concrete plant and driving with my mother and the bratty twins all the way to New York. He wanted to make sure I got there safely, he said, but I think he was really almost as excited as I was.

Since I didn't go away to college, I didn't really own anything *to* move. I packed up a few boxes, and my dad put them in a cartop carrier. We drove all the way like that, stopping every hour to feed the gangly goons or let Mom and me out to go to the rest stop. It was kind of fun, like my last moments as a child, driving straight into adulthood, where there would be no more boys and grades and football games. Welcome to New York, where there were responsibilities, and actual dates, and fabulous parties. Where I would finally fit in, even if it killed me.

But as we left New Jersey and entered Manhattan, the car fell silent. Mom turned off the radio, and we glued our faces to the windows until Dad barked at her that he could, very well, use some help navigating, thank you very much. Eventually we found my new neighborhood. Tall apartment buildings faced the street, which was narrow and lined with parked cars. I had never even been in buildings this tall, let alone lived in one. After circling a four-block area for half an hour my dad finally found a place to park the old Volvo station wagon, which never seemed like a big car until we entered Manhattan. I got out and read the tiny print on the parking sign. Even after I had read it, it still didn't make sense to me. I looked at my dad in the driver's seat and just shrugged. My mom rolled down the passenger's side window. "What's it say, Emily?"

"Monday and Thursday eleven to two. No standing ever. Don't litter."

My dad turned off the car and rolled down his window. "We're fine."

I eyed him. "Are you sure?"

He got out of the car, went around the back to the popped trunk, and grabbed my IKEA lamp. "Sure," he said.

"I guess we'll find out," my mom said. She got out, and then opened the back door to get Craig and Grant out of the car. At twelve, they should have been able to do this by themselves, but getting them unplugged from their Game Boys often took some persuading. Not today, apparently. They bounded out of the car, practically falling onto each other. Then they took off down the sidewalk at a run.

Craig yelled back at me, "Is it this building?" He pointed straight up at the high-rise in front of him. Grant stopped on the sidewalk and looked up, staring with his mouth open at the building Craig pointed at. Before I could answer yes, Craig said, "Hey, Buttface. Shut your mouth or a pigeon will fly by and poop in it."

I lifted my hand to my face in shame. "That's the building but *do not* go in there yet." As soon as I said this, I knew it was a mistake. The boys ran for the lobby, straight into the open door that the suited doorman was holding open for them.

I turned back to the car. My mother's derriere was stuck out of the street-side passenger door, straight into traffic. She was digging through some of my stuff in the backseat. "Mom, can you please keep those two on a leash? They're going to horrify my new roommate."

"Emily, those are your father's sons."

"Funny, Mom," I said. "Can we just go and catch them?" What in the world was she looking for? I didn't have the heart to tell her that people in their cars were giving her bottom-in-the-air routine raised eyebrows.

"I'm just trying to find your comforter, Em. I thought it might be nice to get your bed set up for tonight."

I met Brittany through a New York online community bulletin board called www.nycconnect.com. It was recommended in *Start Spreading the News*, my "move to New York in order to follow your dreams and fall hopelessly in love" how-to book that Jenna picked up for me the day I sent Uncle Matthew my cover letter and résumé. I had the laptop computer I had saved up for and bought in college, but we didn't have Internet connection at my house, so I had to go up to San Diego State to send them to him. Luckily my student ID worked after graduation. I'm not sure how I would have made it until August without the Internet to dream with. Jenna and I would go up to SDSU and spend untold hours researching cafes in the Village where I would drink coffee and clubs where I would dance the night away.

Nycconnect.com was a godsend. You could sell your exercise equipment or buy a papasan chair, you could find out about an art opening or promote your concert, and you could find a roommate. Brittany's posting made her sound perfect for me. Maybe not the Emily Hinton that I was when I read it, but the one I would soon be.

Young, hip professional seeks same—no men or smokers
I am a young professional female who works in finance. I live in a doorman building on Park Avenue South, below 42nd Street. The apartment is small but clean and bright. I

have the bigger room so you pay less. Please no pets, messy people, live-in boyfriends, or smokers. I will conduct interviews and will require personal references. You must sign legally binding lease and pass landlord's credit check. E-mail me to get in touch.

B—

Brittany and I hit it off on e-mail right away. She was actually originally from San Diego and her mom was also a teacher. After a few interactions she agreed to take me on as her roommate without interviewing me in person, but only after I sent her my picture. She joked she just wanted to make sure I didn't have two heads. She never sent me her picture back, and I was too embarrassed to ask. Besides, I kind of liked not knowing what she would look like. I was an English major in college and spent most of my life with my nose in a good book. I had fun imagining her all summer long.

I thought I had a pretty good idea of who she was. I knew, for instance, that she had attended Berkeley and was a Women's Studies major. If anyone knew what a Berkeley student looked like it was me.

I pictured Brittany all the time. I guessed that she would be tall and thin with jet black straight hair. She'd enjoy eating soybeans out of the pod and reading art history books. She knitted her own purse and had a cat named Einstein. Plus, I added with a final flourish, she ran marathons.

My dad cleared his throat nervously, and the boys jostled behind his big body. My mother stood next to me with my bedding, smiling. I rang the bell. Instantly the door flew open and we saw the chaotic scene inside. There was loud electronic music pouring out and a girl with brown, very curly hair standing in the doorway on a cell phone. She put up her finger, with orange-crush nail polish, to her lips and gestured for all of us to be quiet. My mother turned around and shushed my brothers. Then the girl turned her back and walked into the apartment, leaving the door open.

I guess we all just stood there in shock. The girl came back and waved us in with a half-annoyed look on her face. She then disappeared into a room, presumably her bedroom, and shut the door.

We walked in tentatively; even Craig and Grant were tame. I poked around the tiny apartment and found my bedroom. It came with a twin bed that her previous roommate had left. The bed was all that was in it, which was good, because little else would fit in there. I wanted to sit down and sob, but I wouldn't. I was on my own now.

I put a smile on my face and turned to my parents. "This is great, huh?"

They nodded.

I added, "I think she's got a phone call from work or her parents or something."

They nodded again. My father must have sensed my fear. He came over, kissed me on the head, and said, "I'm sure you're going to change the world again this week."

Even though he'd been saying it since I was a little girl, I'd never needed him to say it so much as right then.

CHAPTER 2

morrow & sons

★

Morrow & Sons will take your breath away. I knew from reading the *New Yorker* that the building was brand-new and being hailed as "a monument to publishing," but I was not prepared for the glistening tower that housed the largest book publishing company in the United States. Five years ago, Morrow & Sons had purchased a choice plot of land abutting the south end of Central Park and hired the world-renowned avant-garde architect Rem Koolhaas to design the new building. Standing before the building, my back to the park, staring up at its endless stretch into the sky, I instinctually place my hand over my wide-open mouth. It is imposing, sublime, a temple for the written word. Twenty-five glistening floors of all my dreams come true.

Realizing I am gawking, I join the army of women entering the building. They all seem to have just stepped coolly down from a runway, wearing smart fall suits and sculpted heels. After the revolving door spins me out onto the noisy marble floor, I stop dead still—that is until a shoulder bumps into my back, and I realize I am clogging up the excited flight of these gorgeous creatures. They are like bees back to the hive, nervous with energy and most likely hopped-up on caffeine.

The lobby is decorated in the only fitting way. From the stone floor to the ceiling several stories up hangs a long, uninterrupted glass display case of books, chronicling Morrow & Sons' proud history. A whole library of first editions. Probably worth more than I'd make in my life. Aside from a few sleek benches, there is nothing in the lobby except intimidating men in blue coats with badges behind a tall desk at one end. The women in suits, and the occasional man, are all using ID badges to admit themselves through some futuristic-looking turnstiles on the right. I take a deep breath and approach the security guards behind the front desk. It takes a little while, but I eventually get my temporary ID badge and am prompted to make my own way into the body of this terrifying, glistening hub.

Stop looking at your feet, Emily Elizabeth. Look alert. Look excited. Look confident. I am perched lightly on the edge of an overstuffed leather chair that is so soft it feels like silk. The receptionist on what will be my floor has called someone to announce my arrival, and I try not to fidget while I wait.

I look at my watch and then realize the receptionist has seen me. I act like I am trying to see the books in the display case by her desk. I've been waiting five minutes, but I don't want to be rude or act bored. Finally, I glance up at the glass doors, pretending to smooth my hair, and suck in a deep breath when I spot a girl with long brown hair approaching. She is clearly here to collect me. I try not to look too hopeful as she opens the door with her ID badge and walks toward me. I meet her eye, lift my chin, and try to look pleasant.

"Hi, I'm Helen," she says, thrusting her hand toward me. She is efficient and businesslike, already ushering me back through the doors. "We didn't know you were going to be starting this week. Xavier is on vacation."

"On vacation?" I stammer. Why would they have me start

work when my new boss wasn't even going to be here? "I'm sure this is the day they said I was supposed to start . . ." I say uncertainly.

"It probably is. Someone must have gotten confused in Human Resources. It's fine. Somebody will show you what to do." Her serious demeanor isn't exactly unpleasant, but she comes off a little cold. "Xavier's in his house in the Hamptons for the week," she continues.

I make a mental note that I don't need to call him Mr. Weir, but just Xavier. I had been obsessing over that all last night while I couldn't sleep and the cars honked their horns below my window.

She rounds the corner and points at the women's bathroom as we pass. "Bathroom's in here. And don't worry. We'll help you figure out what to do until he comes back," she ends, trying to hide her irritation at being stuck with a shadow for the next five days. She almost succeeds.

"Your job will be largely administrative. You'll be answering Xavier's phone and making his appointments. You'll have to read some manuscripts, of course, and mail packages to authors, but a lot of the time you'll be taking notes at meetings and things like that. It kind of stinks, but everyone has to put in their time," she says as she leads me down a hall lined with cubicles. My cubicle is at the very end, straight across from Xavier's corner office.

"Here's where you sit." She gestures at the empty desk, the blank gray walls, the black chair on wheels. "Let me know if you need anything. I'll introduce you around in a little while, when everyone is here. For now, make yourself at home. I have a meeting to prepare for." She vanishes into the office next to Xavier's.

I look around slowly. A pencil holder with two red pens and a broken number two pencil, snapped off at the head. A half-used pad of yellow notepaper. A stapler. An office phone with tiny little buttons. Oh God, I pray, don't let it ring, don't let it ring. At least not for another hour.

Then my eyes sweep over to my sleek, flat-screened, state-of-the-art, chrome-colored computer. This is more like it. Quickly, I reach over and switch it on, almost greedily, like a child given a present with a giant bow. Nothing sounds better than my old friend the Internet, a high-speed Internet connection to a world beyond this scary place. I hope Jenna wrote. If not, I'm going to kill her.

As the computer warms up, I glance at the shelf above my new desk. It is lined with chubby paperbacks that have an alarming amount of neon-script and silver-foil writing on their spines. I chuckle a little, thinking of Jenna on the beach reading what she calls "throw-away" books. I am glad I won't be working on fiction like that. In our phone interview, Xavier casually mentioned that he worked on *Darkly Cometh*, by William Finneran. He kept referring to him as *Liam*, saying how much I'd like working with *Liam* and what a good head *Liam* had even after winning the Pushcart Prize for First Fiction.

Unfortunately, my computer isn't as convinced as I am of my bright and promising future. When it finally warms up, the screen that pops up asks me for my password. PASSWORD, I type, but it gives me an error message. XAVIER, I try. No good. What would the password on this computer be? EMILY. MANHATTAN. BLOOMINGDALES. I decide I can't keep guessing all morning, and, uncertainly, I get up and poke my head into Helen's office. "Helen?" I ask, timidly. She sighs, puts down her pencil, and comes out to help me.

I finally connect to the Internet and check my free e-mail account. Jenna *had* written me, but then, I don't know why I even doubted her. My whole life Jenna has been the first to know everything about me and takes great pride in this. She loves nothing more than to call and yell at me, mock-indignantly. She is the loudest person I know. I chuckle thinking about the time I picked up the phone only to have her yell, *Aren't you worried about me?* when in high school she had gotten into a fender bender in the parking lot after basketball practice. My mother had already told me everybody was fine.

> Emily E. Hinton,
>
> How are you? How's New York? Argh!!! It's killing me. The supense is killing me!!!
>
> I didn't think it was appropriate to call you and yell at you for not checking in with me yet so I settled for this e-mail. Do you know it's 9:40 in New York as I write this? I woke up at 6:30 to check my e-mail and hear from you!!!
>
> You'll be dying to know that life in old Jenksy is the usual. I went for a swim the other day, came back, made some huevos rancheros and coffee, and missed you! Who's going to join me for my morning ritual now that you're gone? No one, that's who.
>
> Sorry this one's so dull. So far, that's how stuff is without ya, kid. Call me? How's Britt? Fallen hopelessly in love with a man in a suit yet? Better not forget your little Jenna, stuck in paradise!
>
> Jenna
>
> PS I'm clearly going to need your work phone number for future calls. Kindly pass it along.

At the end of the e-mail, I'm chuckling quietly to myself, but my eyes are a little watery. I never thought I'd miss Jenna forcing me out of bed early on Saturdays to join her at the beach. She loved to lose herself in the rhythm of the waves as she swam back and forth across the water, hundreds of yards out from the beach. She always said she needed me to come along in case she started to drown, but we both knew that I would be no help if she ever did. I liked to think she really just wanted the company once she emerged. Jenna was definitely the brawn, and I was the brains. I usually read on a towel as the sun came up, and she slowly moved back and forth. Then we'd go back to her house and make huevos rancheros and drink coffee. I'd tell her all of my dreams, and she'd tell me why I was insane and start talking about the apartment in San Diego we'd get together someday. I always thought it was weird that she didn't seem to have any dreams or goals of her own. But she said she loved living in Jenks and just wanted a job that kept her outdoors and gave her summers off. Me? I planned on changing the world.

What I loved most about Jenna was that we shared the same burden. Saturday tradition dictated that at some point in the morning over our coffee, after we had greedily polished off our huge breakfast, we'd drift to the same topic. The one thing that made us identical. Boys. By fourth grade, we had dated or ruled out all of the members of the dating pool in Jenks, so it was largely theoretical, but that didn't stop us from dreaming. And neither of us ever met anyone at SDSU. It's hard to meet boys when you don't live in a dorm. Not to mention we both wanted the Holy Grail of all boys. We wanted—needed, really—Christians. We often joked that we were the last two Christians on the planet in our age bracket. Maybe it wasn't true, but it felt that way. The few male Christians we knew were nice but, uh, not exactly our type. They would have liked girls who baked and played the handbells. Not a girl who wanted to move to New York and attend fashion shows or a girl who had a permanent freckle colony sprinkled on her nose from all of her sunrise swimming. I wasn't sure how Jenna expected to meet the man of her dreams by sitting around in Jenks, but she said she trusted God's timing. Well, so did I, but that didn't mean I was going to just sit around and wait.

A phone ringing at the cubicle next to me makes me realize I'm getting nothing done with all of my pining for home. I close out my e-mail and thank God that my phone still hasn't rung. I look around again and am almost surprised to find myself in this glittering corporate world. I wiggle my toes in my high heels and feel a little giggly. My first day at a real publishing company. At Morrow & Sons, the largest publishing company in the country. Despite my less-than-welcoming reception this morning, I can't stop feeling excited. I am finally here—working for a real editor, making real books, in New York City. I smile broadly and slide back a bit in my rolling chair to peek beyond my cube walls. If I look through Xavier's open door and out his window, and if I crane my head a little, I notice I can see a part of Central Park. I have made it.

I look at the clock: 10:45 Monday morning. Who knew making it could be so boring? The next hour drags by as I try to peek at what other people are doing, alternately hoping that someone will come talk to me and hoping that I have somehow become invisible. I spend my time trying to teach myself how to use Outlook so that I can start e-mailing within the company. The scary thing is, I keep receiving e-mails from people with cryptic titles about page counts and copy requests. For the time being, I don't open them.

I am relieved when the clock in the corner of my computer screen finally rolls over to 12:00. I spent the morning mostly organizing my desk drawers and perusing the files in the long cabinets right outside my cube. I wrote the computer password (YUMPUS, Xavier's dog's nickname, as it turns out) on a Post-it and hid it in my top drawer. I even hung up a Bible verse on my corkboard, against my better judgment. I just couldn't resist. Jenna gave it to me for my going-away present. She's very crafty and wrote Philippians 4:13 in calligraphy on faux parchment. It looks cool, or at least not overtly like a Bible verse, and I certainly could use a little convincing that I can do anything, much less *all things*, because at the moment, I feel like all I can do is weigh down a little black chair on wheels. Besides, it reminds me of home. It will have to do until I get some pictures of myself with my new friends. At this rate, it may be a while.

By 12:30, I am ready to go somewhere, anywhere, that isn't my desk, and I decide to go for a walk outside, figuring I can find a bench to eat my lunch on. As I am pulling my purse out from under my desk to get my sandwich out, though, a petite dark-haired girl with clear brown skin and warm honey-colored eyes, about my age, pokes her head into my cube.

"Umm . . . Emily?" she asks. She comes around the short wall and stands in front of me. I hope that the gasp noise I hear is only in my head and that I didn't actually utter it aloud. It's Beyonce. A thinner, darker Beyonce. No, I think as I scan her face, it's not her, but the girl before me looks like she has walked straight off a magazine page. As if her glossy long black hair and perfect teeth aren't enough to make you take immediate notice of her, she is the most immaculately dressed person I've ever seen. Her charcoal gray pants, obviously very expensive, gleam; her purse is marked with a label I've only seen pasted on the knock-offs they sell on the streets in San Diego; her chunky silver choker looks similar to my mother's hippie junk jewelry but I instinctively know it must be the latest thing; her top somehow manages to be appropriately demure for the office and extremely revealing at the same time. And her shoes . . . they were the high-heeled pointy kind I'd been coveting in the store window just yesterday. I decide immediately that I want to be just like this girl. Or at least *look* like her.

"A bunch of us are going to lunch. Would you like to come?"

"Sure," I stammer, clutching my purse tightly and following

her, blessing her and every grandchild she'll ever have for such kindness.

"We're just going down to the cafeteria," she says. "It's pretty good food, and it's not too expensive."

I nod. "That sounds great," I say a little too enthusiastically.

She looks at me, staring me up and down. "I'm Regina, by the way," she adds. "We knew Xavier had hired a new assistant, but we didn't know you were starting today." Apparently no one did. "We assistants usually have lunch together every day. We have to stick together, you know? Our daily gossip sessions are sometimes the only thing that gets us through. The others are already down there," she explains as she hits a button in the elevator. "The lines at the cash registers get so long at lunchtime that they went down to get a head start."

"Does everyone buy their lunch?" I ask, glancing into my purse at my sandwich in a little plastic baggie.

"Pretty much. Sometimes when money gets tight, someone will bring in something for a few days, but it's so much easier to just buy it here that it doesn't really make sense to brown-bag it," she explains as we exit the elevator and emerge into a busy, crowded room with every kind of food imaginable. I look around helplessly. Regina shows me where the sandwich station is and where they serve the soup, and I nod as she goes off to put together what looks like the largest plate of lettuce I have ever seen, but still I wander around aimlessly. I need time to think.

I look at all of the different stations and down into my purse at my sad, soggy little sandwich. I don't feel right wasting it—we never wasted anything growing up in Jenks—but I don't want to be the only person eating a packed lunch at the table, and I sure don't want to be known as the office cheapskate. Slowly, I walk to the pizza counter, where I can get a piece of almost nutritious pizza for $2.50—by far the cheapest thing in the cafeteria. I quietly ask for a slice of cheese and tell myself I'll eat the peanut butter and apple-jelly for dinner tonight.

Regina is right—the cash register line is eternal. I spend the entire time focusing on keeping my tray level. After about ten minutes, I hand over my money, noting that my pizza is now cool, and wander into the crowded dining room.

If only I knew who I was looking for. I wander around, threading through the tables, hoping I'll be able to recognize Regina again. Please God, I pray, just let the floor swallow me up.

Finally, I spot Regina in a table way in the corner of the room and smile thankfully as she waves me over. The next thing I know I walk right into a table. Not bump into it. Walk directly into it. *Bam*. Hitting my right leg on the corner and accidentally letting out an "Oof."

I stop to recover and make sure I haven't spilled anything on the two guys whose conversation I have just abruptly ended. They stare at me. The blond one smiles, a little too much, and starts a slow clap. His friend punches him in the shoulder, tells him to grow up, and asks, "Are you okay?" He then touches my leg and adds, "I think you're going to have to get this replaced." I can see he is laughing a little, in a good-natured way, but he's also genuinely concerned. All I am concerned with is his hand touching my thigh and making sure nobody saw what happened—a rich fantasy indeed, as I look around and see my whole table of girls staring at me—so I just mutter, "I'm fine, thanks," and turn away before he can see how red my face is. It doesn't help that he is flat-out gorgeous. Big blue eyes, strong cheekbones, curly brown hair falling over his forehead—he is definitely the most attractive man in the room. At least as far as I can see as I bore my eyes into the floor, trying to disappear.

"Emily, middle name Grace," I mutter under my breath as I walk toward Regina's table. There are two girls with her, one on each side, and an empty seat across the table. Taking the last empty chair, I gratefully put my tray down.

"Girls, this is Emily," Regina declares proudly. "She's Xavier's new assistant," though they clearly know who I am since I've been sitting outside his office all morning. They smile and say hi. They're pretending they didn't see me almost fall on my face.

"This is Lane," Regina says, gesturing to the girl with short brown hair on her left. "And this is Skylar," referring to the girl with long, fine blonde hair all the way down her back. Was I the only one that worked here who wasn't gorgeous?

My thick mane of strawberry blonde hair, usually my proudest feature, suddenly feels unruly and much too pouffy. My nose is too big. I have a zit on my chin. And I am clearly the largest person at this table. I feel decidedly like an Amazon warrior.

"How do you like it so far?" Lane asks politely, her soft Southern accent catching my attention.

"Well," I started, "I haven't had much to do yet, but I think—"

"Oh, you should be *so* grateful," Skylar interrupts. "I've been swamped. I feel like I'm *drowning* in manuscripts. I was here until seven o'clock Friday! I'm about ready to have a nervous breakdown."

"Is that normal?" I ask, choosing to ignore the fact that she has interrupted me.

"No. Since Xavi's out, I have to read everything agents send him," she says. Although she is complaining, she is obviously pleased with this responsibility.

Did she just call my boss "hah-vee"? I had been pronouncing it like "X-savior." I must look surprised because Lane touches my arm and says, "Reggie made it up. We call him that behind his back. Don't do it to his face." I nod. Skylar continues.

"He gets a lot of bad manuscripts, *let* me tell you. This will probably be your job soon—since Helen just got promoted again.

But since no one knew you were going to be here this week, he asked me to handle it. I mean, it is a nice change from the proposals I normally read—I work for an editor who does parenting books, and she's really great, but all I see all day are books about why time-outs don't work and how to get your crummy kid to eat his vegetables—but I am not sure I can *handle* all this stress. I can't *wait* until Xavi comes back. Have you even met him yet?"

As she finally breaks for air, I grin guiltily. She may be beautiful, but at least she has nothing on me intellectually. I immediately feel bad. I try to think kind thoughts about her but come up with nothing, unless you count the idea that it's good to have her around because the rest of us will surely get promoted faster. I don't count it. I just answer her instead.

"Actually, I haven't met him yet," I say. "I have an uncle who went to school with him at Notre Dame. When Uncle Matthew heard Xavier needed a new assistant, he gave him my résumé. We did a phone interview, since I was home in California, and he offered me the job the next day."

"But you know what kind of books he works on, right?" Reggie asks.

"Well," I begin carefully, "He said something about William Finneran."

The girls all look at one another.

"Corpses," Skylar says. "If there's a corpse in it, it's his. He edits thrillers. Lots of blood and violence."

"Which is okay, if you're into that," Reggie adds quickly, pulling on an imaginary noose.

"I thought—" I begin, but Skylar starts again.

"He'll be a great boss to *have* worked for, don't get me wrong. He's one of the hottest young editors in publishing today. A lot of people think he's an absolute genius—he manages to buy books that make a lot of money. He probably keeps the company in business with the number of best sellers he publishes. But there's not exactly any, well, *literary merit*, shall we say."

"He did work with Finneran," Lane manages to interject, swirling cheese grits around on her plate. She sees me staring. "It's Southern Day at the Global Cuisine station," she says, laughing. "My favorite!"

"Whatever," Skylar says. "Can you say fluke?"

"He only did that because he grew up with *Liam*," Regina says. She does a good impression of Xavier saying *Liam*, and all the girls laugh. "He was lucky to get such a good writer. It's usually just hacks."

"Oh, and, Emily, I hate to be the one to break it to you, but Xavi is nuts!" Skylar says. She clearly does not hate to be the one to break it to me. "He drove his last assistant out of publishing with his erratic moods. Remember that day she left in *tears*?" Skylar practically yells, getting really worked up now.

"But she was a little incompetent. I'm sure he'll like you because of your uncle," Reggie says.

"Yeah," I sputter, wondering if my connection makes the other girls wary of me, wondering if this whole New York scheme was a bad, bad idea. "I sure hope so."

"As long as you keep his wife and his girlfriend straight when you answer the phone, you'll be okay," Skylar says.

I gasp and look at Lane. She shrugs, a little embarrassed. I poke my cold pizza with my fork, and it almost pokes me back. I have no appetite.

"Ooh, there he goes . . ." Reggie gasps. Following her eyes, I see that she is watching none other than the guy whose lunch I almost landed in. We all turn and look immediately, and for the remainder of his walk to the exit, he has four pairs of eyes fastened on his back.

"I still think he's so hot. I don't care what you say, Skylar," Reggie says, wiggling her eyebrows up and down, trying to get a laugh out of Skylar. I have to laugh myself. Regina seems to love to be the center of attention, but I notice no one minds. She's really over the top, her face is always contorting into hysterical shapes, and her jokes are pitch-perfect.

"Bah. He's hopeless," says Skylar. She puts up her right hand to shield her face from Regina's eyebrow routine.

"Hopeless?" I can't help but ask.

"A waste of such a handsome man," Lane says.

"A handsome man who works in the finance department," Reggie says.

"You don't mean he's . . ." I say.

"No. But just as tragic. He's a *church* boy. Won't get drunk with us. Gets up early Sunday mornings. A total goody-goody," says Lane.

"He only wants to date Christians," Skylar says flatly, staring at her fork.

Had I heard that correctly? Hot Table Boy was a Christian? Looking to date another Christian? My heart starts pounding, and I think it might possibly end up on my tray. I lower my chin and smile to myself. Maybe this place isn't so bad after all, I think as I start back in on my pizza. Things are definitely starting to look up.

"What's his name?" I ask.

"Bennett," Reggie says. "Bennett Edward Wyeth, the third."

"Bennett," I say to myself.

love and soup

★

A*fter lunch, the* phone starts ringing off the hook. Agents call about projects I've never heard of. An author calls, asking me something about dummy pages. I have to stifle a laugh as I write down her phone number and make a mental note to find out what a dummy page is. A man with a thick Southern accent calls to say he has written a political book that we'll definitely want to buy as soon as we read it, since he guarantees it will be bigger than Harry Potter. He offers to fly up to New York to tell me all about it in person. I spend half an hour trying to politely decline. Finally at three, I get the first call I know what to do with.

"This is Emily."

"Em?"

"Uncle Matthew?"

"Hey there! I can't believe it's you. Listen to that professional voice of yours."

"Hah, er, yeah. I've been working on it all day. How are you?"

"Great. I can't tell you how excited I am to finally have a family member over on the wrong coast. I always knew you'd be my little convert. Good for you, Em. And now, I've got to start really showing you New York. Forget all that tourist stuff."

"I'd love that," I say, trying to keep my voice low. I wonder if it is okay to talk on the phone at work. I reason that Xavier is not here, and, well, Matthew is his friend anyway.

"I know it's kind of sudden, but I'm rotten with plans. What do you say about hanging out with your fusty old uncle tonight?"

"Great," I say, not able to hide how thrilled I am at actually having somewhere to go other than my apartment after work.

"I don't know how exciting it will be, but I could use another set of hands down at the Locus to help serve dinner," he says, referring to the mission he founded and is hopelessly wed to. "I thought after that I could take you out for dinner to this great Middle Eastern place around the corner. The owner's a friend, and I've been talking you up."

Walking from work to the mission center, I can see the lights in Times Square from ten blocks away. It looks like a circus after the corporate calm of work. As I negotiate the busy sidewalks, I think about my uncle and his fascinating life. Sometimes when I was growing up, it seemed impossible that Matthew and my trusty old dad could have had any DNA in common. On the other hand, I had always felt that Matthew and I shared more genes than were scientifically possible for an uncle and niece.

When I was a small child, Matthew, my father's much younger brother (my grandparents always call him their *pleasant surprise*), shocked the family by announcing he was moving to New York. Matthew was fresh out of Notre Dame with a business degree, and he'd just come through a tragedy of the worst kind. Autumn, the girl he had dated all through college, the one everyone expected him to marry, died in a car crash their senior year. My grandparents knew he was upset, and they were really worried about him moving, half-expecting him to return to California the prodigal son in just a few short months. But eventually Nanna and Pops gave him their blessing, worried sick though they were, and some phone numbers of friends he could call once he arrived. What no one realized was Matthew had decided to stay in New York no matter what happened.

He got a job on Wall Street immediately, buried himself in work, and very quickly began living the high life. He bought a fancy apartment in SoHo, which in those days was just starting to become trendy, and lots of expensive suits. He bought art and nice furniture. He dated some pretty women, but none of them ever lasted very long. He always gave lavish gifts at Christmas and tithed generously to the church, but he also managed to save a lot. Then, as he tells it, he just got bored. He had everything money could buy, but he wasn't happy. The girls, he said, were just gold diggers and arm warmers, and his friends started to seem like strangers, chasing after riches and power. He toyed with the idea of going overseas to do mission work in places where it was forbidden or smuggling Bibles into Communist countries, but he wasn't sure he was ready to just leave it all behind. He agonized over what he was supposed to be doing with his life: on one hand, he was able to fund a number of missionaries in the greater New York area and live quite a comfortable life to boot, but on the other hand, he felt like he was digging a hole in the ground and burying his talents.

One day, he says, he decided to take a stroll to clear his head. He ended up in Times Square, which at the time was the seediest corner in New York, full of prostitutes, peep shows, drunks, and drug addicts. He didn't even know why he wandered over there that day. He usually avoided it because it was dangerous and depressing, but suddenly, there he was, hands stuffed into his pockets, whistling a chewing gum jingle, when he looked up and saw a flimsy, handmade *For Sale* sign in one of the dingy front windows of an enormous ramshackle building. Without thinking about it, he called the number and said he was going to purchase the building.

When he came home at Christmas that year, he told us he was selling his apartment and cashing in his savings to start a mission in Times Square. Nanna was worried about him giving up everything, but he spoke movingly of the people hunkered down on the streets of Times Square who had nothing and talked about their collective hopelessness. He envisioned a center to get these people off the streets and into rehab, counseling, and job training. It would be completely operated by the people who lived there, swapping services for food and shelter. And now, seven short years later, the Locus serves over two hundred people a day. Unfortunately, I think to myself, Uncle Matthew still hasn't looked up. When he gave it all up, he gave it *all* up. He now lives in a rent-controlled apartment, I can't remember the last time we've seen him out in California or heard him speak of time off or a girlfriend, and the only new clothes he gets are what Nanna sends him for Christmas, which, with Nanna's love of the JC Penney's catalog, is a mixed blessing at best.

I find the Locus without much trouble—just beyond the Broadway show discount ticket booth, like he told me, below the wall of moving fluorescent billboards, across from the Naked Cowboy (who isn't completely naked, thankfully)—and enter a brightly lit room with long chains of empty tables and chairs. Walking uncertainly to the back of the room, where I see another group of tables set up with food in serving stations, I realize how awesome what he has accomplished truly is. All these chairs will be filled by people who would otherwise have no dinner tonight. A surge of pride rushes through me, but my contemplation is interrupted. *"Emily!"* he yells, running toward me.

It doesn't take long for Matthew to introduce me to the ten other volunteers—lawyers, teachers, hair stylists, plumbers—lending a hand and the permanent staffers overseeing the evening, who were once homeless themselves.

And then Matthew introduces me to Josie, his second in

command, who scampered up to us the minute she laid eyes on me. I had heard her name before because she is one of the few people on staff full time at the Locus. She is blonde, short, and very slight with tiny eyes, a jutting chin, and a sharp little persnickety nose that makes her look very unusual. I realize immediately this is the kind of tireless woman who runs on Dr Pepper, two hours of sleep, and overinvolvement. There were always women like this at our church back home. Publicly, they're called saints.

"Matthew's niece, Emily, right?" she smiles and asks. I nod. She reaches out her hand, and I take it in mine, only to discover it's a bony rattrap. She clamps on with a death grip and pumps my hand up and down vigorously a few times. I pull my hand back as soon as I can. "He's told me practically *everything* about you. I'm so glad you're here now."

"Yeah," I return. I don't like the way she's insinuating that she knows *everything* about Matthew as well.

"Josie? Would you mind rounding everyone up please?" asks Matthew.

"Sir, yessir!" Josie barks like an army recruit. I forcibly stop my eyes from rolling into the back of my head. "Rolls," she says inexplicably, pointing a knotty little finger at me, and then hurries off across the room.

She climbs on top of the chair, but is still only a little taller than me. She puts both her pinkies in her thin, tight mouth. A shrill whistle peals through the air, sending a shudder down my spine. We all fall silent. She reads aloud from a clipboard everyone's assignment—aha! I am serving the rolls—as I look out the window. People are impatiently pressing up against the side door, hungry for their meal.

After Josie is through, Matthew ushers me over to the serving line to the rolls station. I assess my spot. I'm next to a nice staffer named Samuel who is quiet and elderly. I smile at him, and he smiles back and offers me his hand. "The boss's daughter, right?"

"Uh," I laugh. He smiles and winks so I know he's teasing. "No. His naughty niece." Samuel nods. And then I turn to my right only to see Josie switching with someone else to have the spot next to me. Great, I think, I'm going to spend two hours on my feet next to this little yappy Chihuahua of a woman.

I look across the room and see Matthew unlocking the heavy doors to let in the line, which has been forming since early this afternoon, Samuel tells me. Matthew comes alive, and I can see this is his true passion. He greets many of the regulars with a familiar handshake and asks the old ones about their children. Somehow, with the help of some staffers, they are able to get everyone inside, lined up in an orderly fashion, and relatively quiet before Matthew picks up a microphone to welcome everyone. He explains how the serving will work, for any newcomers, and then discloses the menu. It's spaghetti night. Many of the customers groan, and I giggle, thinking of my own dislike for Mom's spaghetti night. Then Matthew asks for a volunteer to say grace. The next hour and a half rushes by as we load up plates for the people who shuffle by. Josie annoys me with her church jokes.

"Hey, what's God's first name?"

"Um, I don't know . . ." I say. "Yahweh?"

"I guess you don't read your Bible," she says, snorting. "It's Howard. You know, *Our father, who art in heaven, Howard be thy name!*"

I keep silent.

"What's the name of the most famous virgin in the Bible?"

"Mary . . . ?" I ask, placing a roll on a plate. I try not to look at Josie.

"*The King James Virgin*," she cackles. "How do we know God loves baseball?" she continues without pausing. I shrug, turning away. "He started the world *in the Big Inning!*"

Samuel proves to be a great resource for help when I'm in a pinch. I am allowed to serve only one roll to each person. The patrons know I'm new so many of them pester me for an extra. One woman even tries to steal one when she thinks I am not looking. Samuel pipes in to help me. "Now, now. Leave some for the folk that come behind you."

"Hey, tough guy! Lighten up!" Josie says. She even snorts a little.

I watch Samuel give the lady in line a stern look, daring her to join Josie in laughing at his following the rules, but she moves on, ignoring Josie, like I have been all night. I try to be vigilant about my post, but when one man insists on singing "Love Me Tender"—in what I have to admit is a good imitation of Elvis's voice—as he makes his way down the serving line, I can't help but slip him an extra roll. Josie elbows me. "I saw that. I'll tell your uncle."

"Hah," I say, trying to laugh along with her and resist my fantasy of cramming a roll in her mouth to keep her quiet.

The Elvis fan smiles, winks at me, and continues on down the line, crooning as he goes. I try to smile at each person, joke with those who are willing, but I am exhausted and glad when the line is closed down and we begin cleaning up.

Getting out of the door at the Locus with Uncle Matthew by my side proves to be an almost impossible task. He seems to know everybody, and everybody loves him. I think we're finally leaving, and my stomach is grumbling, clamoring for some hummus, when Josie calls to him. He turns back, telling me he'll just be a minute.

Standing by the door with purse in hand, I am making a mental to-do list for tomorrow when I happen to glance at where Uncle Matthew stands. I watch as he speaks with Josie, patiently answering, it appears, her question. I can't hear what they're talking about, but I see her lean in to hear him and notice she's looking at him very intently. He turns from her, gesturing to where I'm standing, and she smiles, waves at me, and leans in to say goodbye. It's painfully obvious that she wants him to stay, and equally as clear that he doesn't have a clue. I decide not to enlighten Matthew; maybe it's best if he stays clueless.

Getting seated at Ali Baba's is also difficult, even though there is only one other couple in the restaurant, because Matthew introduces me to the owner and his entire family, most of whom are the cook and waitstaff, and each one has to shake our hands and welcome me to New York. Finally we sit down. As soon as their gorgeous younger daughter, Jihan, puts the complimentary hummus and pita on our table I practically dive in. Matthew thanks Jihan in Farsi, making her giggle, and then opens his menu. I already know I want falafel, and so I study Uncle Matthew instead. I've never noticed, but he isn't a bad-looking man. He's more than ten years younger than my father, so he's only in his early thirties, and has thick, dark hair and extremely warm brown eyes. Hmm . . . He has a kind face, and though he has a bit of a broken countenance, he is an attractive—if I weren't related to him, I might even say sexy—man. Sexy, yes, if you look past his clothes. They appear to be stuck in a time warp. Who wears button-down flannel shirts anymore? In New York? In August? And his goatee looks like it might have been cute when he was still a twenty-something but needs to go now. I decide right then to give him a makeover. In fact, I think, already getting excited, I'll make him my project. I'm not just going to give him a makeover, I'm going to get him a girlfriend.

"What are you mugging about over there, eh?" he asks over the menu, his eyebrows pulled up high.

I laugh, and luckily Jihan comes over and interrupts us. He orders baba ghanoush, and then confesses after Jihan walks away that he's suspicious it's his favorite dish just because he loves to say it. We laugh. His eyes crinkle in the most adorable way, and I notice he's not the least bit balding. This will be easier than I thought, I tell myself.

"So, how was your first day?" he asks.

"It was good," I answer, I realize, truthfully. "The people there seem really nice." I tell him about lunch, though I leave out the part about walking into the table, and how I finally mastered the company's e-mail system, and even learned a few editors' names. "Xavier wasn't even there, though," I say. "It was kind of weird that they told me to come in and start when he wasn't even going to be around."

"Ah, he must be out at the beach with the little lady." He winks. I start to open my mouth, dying to know if he actually has more than one little lady, but I can't bring myself to ask Matthew about Xavier's possible infidelity. "I'm sorry you didn't get to meet him," Matthew continues. "He's a trip. Hall of Famer at Notre Dame. But I guess you'll meet him soon enough, and there's no going back then."

I start to ask him more, but then Jihan places our dinners in front of us, and I forget about Xavier in my haste to devour my meal. After a few minutes of satisfied silence, Uncle Matthew looks up from the brownish-purpley mess on his plate.

"So, what'd you think of the mission center?" he asks. His eyes sparkle, but he looks almost pleading.

I shake my head from side to side, at a loss for words. "It's truly incredible."

He nods. A crooked smile creeps up slowly on his face, and then he adds quietly, "Thanks."

A silence settles on us, and I notice he looks over my shoulder at nothing. I feel uncomfortable with the hollow look in his eye and decide to put an end to it. "It must be hard to find enough volunteers and bring in enough food every night to feed all those people . . ." I venture, but he waves my question away before I have a chance to finish it.

"People are generous. Churches in the area give more man-hours and food donations than we know what to do with. City Harvest picks up leftovers from restaurants around town and brings them to us. We practically have to throw away food every night. The Lord provides. The hard part," he says, taking a sip of water, "is trying to figure out how much my faith can play a role in what goes on there. Our primary purpose is to feed, clothe, and rehabilitate the needy, provide job training and beds for those who can use them. But our underlying motivation is obviously much deeper than that. We want the people we serve to know why we're serving them, and who it is we're ultimately serving. But we can't say that explicitly—preaching goes in one ear and out the other, and very often turns people off altogether." He tears off another piece of pita.

"These people don't care about the bread of life if they don't have bread here on earth. They don't want to hear about it. It's tough—how do we show them that this is a Christian ministry without doing more harm, spiritually, than good?"

He's gotten so serious, and I don't know how to respond. I shrug.

He looks up, and I realize the last question was rhetorical. He dips the pita in hummus, looking at it intently, then slowly lifts his eyes to mine. "It's a tough line to walk, especially in a big city. This is not a spiritual town, and very few people will agree with your morals or understand why you do, or don't do, the things you do. You'll see—it's a fascinating place, full of life, full of fertile soil, but it's a hard place to live out your faith and still be accepted as a normal person." He looks up at me and grins. "But I know you'll be fine."

I stare at my plate, drinking in his speech, wondering what I have gotten myself into.

When I get home, Brittany is nowhere to be seen. I work on unpacking, trying to make this place feel homey. Then at about nine thirty she comes home. We talk for a moment about the correct temperature to keep the thermostat at—who knew there was a correct temperature?—and then she announces she is jumping in the shower. She comes out of the bathroom in a robe with a big towel-turban on her head and disappears into her bedroom for an hour. I keep hearing the hair dryer turn on and off. Brittany finally comes out of her room at about eleven o'clock. Her hair is stick straight now, and she is wearing a tight black leather skirt, a sparkly tank top, and two-inch heels.

"I'm going out," she says as she moves toward the door. When she reaches the handle, she turns back. Her eyes flash toward my bedroom door, where I am hovering anxiously. Our eyes meet, and I follow her stare to the end table, where I have placed a photo of my family. "Please ask me before you decorate in here. I kind of like it the way it is," she says, almost apologetically. She turns the doorknob, gets halfway out the door, then turns back. "Oh. And I labeled my food in the refrigerator and cupboards. I figured that way it'd be easier to keep straight what's yours and what's mine."

"Sure. Sounds good," I say.

"Cool. Laters," she says. Jerkily, she turns on her heel and, door slamming behind her, is gone.

Going out on a Monday night? I am shocked—doesn't she have to work in the morning?! She must not need very much sleep, I tell myself as I carefully arrange my new lavender chenille pillows on my comforter and pick up *Vogue*. I wonder if I will do that once I get settled into my new Manhattan life. "Probably not," I say aloud to no one. My father always joked that to get me up in the morning he just opened the door, threw in a raw steak, and came back in a half an hour. I need my beauty rest.

I flip through the glossy pages for a while and try to read the articles, but my mind just keeps skipping off the page. This isn't going exactly how I'd planned. There is no giggling with my new best friend as we share a tub of Ben & Jerry's and our deepest secrets. There is no get-to-know-you toenail polishing session. I am alone in an apartment full of food I can't eat.

A tear leaks out of the corner of my eye. It isn't that I am mad, I decide. I am not disapproving. I am not even really disappointed. I am, it occurs to me, jealous. I want to look fabulous (if a bit scandalous) and go out on a Monday night. I want somewhere to go, and friends to go out with. And I want this little red dress on page 201 for that matter. I've never owned anything like it.

I can't wait for my life in New York to begin.

My first week passes with lightning speed. I have figured out the best route to the office from my apartment, learned the names of almost everyone in my department, though what they do all day is still somewhat unclear, and have begun to overcome my terror of the phone. Even though I usually didn't know the answer to anything people called to ask, I was becoming an expert at filling in the little pink slips that the company uses to take phone messages and hauling them all over the company to find what the person needed. I have pretty well taught myself the job. I guess I could have asked Helen for help, but she seemed very busy and standoffish. Her door was often closed.

I am glad when five o'clock rolls around on Friday—I am ready for the weekend. Not only am I looking forward to sleeping in on Saturday morning, but I have my first real night out planned for that evening. On Wednesday Reggie, who I had begun to realize was the group's social planner and all-around instigator, had sent around an e-mail asking if anyone wanted to go out for drinks, and I wrote back right away with an emphatic yes.

When I get home Friday evening, all I want to do is sleep, but instead I make myself a plate of pasta and a cup of coffee and try to stay awake until it is time to get ready. I try on about ten different outfits but finally settle on my stretchy pink sweater and khakis with my chunky black oxfords. I straighten my hair, even though it takes almost an hour to blow it completely dry. I put on eye shadow, eyeliner, a touch of dark lipstick. I look in the mirror, frown, and head back to the closet. On my way though I glance at my watch and realize it is almost eight thirty. I panic. We were supposed to meet at nine, and it will take me almost a half hour to get to the bar—a trendy new place downtown, hung floor to ceiling with surveillance cameras taping everyone and displaying them on big screens, Skylar told us—and I don't want to be late. The outfit will have to do.

I come up out of the subway at the stop, only going the wrong way once—a huge victory, since the streets all look the same, and I can never figure out which way is uptown or downtown—before I find the address. It is 9:05. Good, I'm not too late, I think as I take a deep breath.

I push open the doors and scan the room for a familiar face. The bar isn't very crowded, and I can tell right away that the girls aren't there yet. A little flustered, I turn back to the door and step out into the warm night air. I will just wait here, I decide. They will be here any minute.

Forty-five minutes later, Skylar shows up. She gives me a quizzical look, but as I am explaining that I was waiting for someone else to come before I went inside, she asks why I haven't snagged a table. I am saved from having to try to explain that I didn't want to sit in a bar by myself by Reggie and Lane's appearance. Skylar gives them both a big hug.

"It's probably mobbed *now*," Skylar says. I feel bad. We open the door, and indeed the place is crawling with beautiful, shimmering people. Skylar looks back at me and smiles. "Let's spread out and look for a table. I'm usually pretty good at getting something. Years of practice, you know."

We disperse. I realize that earlier, in my awkwardness, I hadn't even thought to look around. The bar is something out of a sci-fi movie. The milky white plastic floor glows green from underneath. All over the bar are large screens showing different scenes from within the bar—people kissing, dancing, talking. I look for the cameras themselves but don't spot any. Duh, I realize, that must be the point. They are hidden.

I weave meekly through booths cluttered with raucous groups of guys and girls using the handheld controls mounted on the tabletops to change the views of the screens around the bar, to seek out people in corners. Sometimes I catch a boy looking at me as I pass, but instead of being excited I just feel nervous and twitchy. Maybe it is the notion that I could end up on one of those screens at any moment. Finally I spot Lane, Reggie, and Skylar at a booth. I let out a sigh and walk over quickly, glad to be done with my tour, making a mental note about the unspoken-yet-understood-by-all rule that an *actual* meeting time was an hour later than the *specified* meeting time. Good to know. I sit down and Reggie hands me the drink menu.

"Oh yeah, we found a table," Skylar says. As if I hadn't noticed they are all cozily seated without me.

"Cool," I say, grabbing a menu. I pretend to be looking through it but instead am sneaking glances at the other girls. I appear to be the only one not dressed almost entirely in black. Regina, fashionista extraordinaire, looks stunning in a short black skirt, a tiny black tank top, and a pair of red sling-backs. Skylar is wearing a tight black dress with a lace trim around its deep V-neck that makes her shiny blonde hair shimmer, and Lane has on a tight black T-shirt and skinny dark jeans with high-heeled black shoes. The black lights scattered on the ceiling of the bar make my pale pink sweater glow like a dork beacon. My stomach cramps. I toy with the camera controls at our table that are linked to a screen in front of us. I don't find anything interesting around the bar.

"What'll you ladies have?" the waitress asks, interrupting my thoughts.

"I'll have a Diet Coke," I tell her, and out of the corner of my eye I see Reggie and Skylar exchange a glance.

"Gin and tonic?" Lane drawls, almost apologetically.

"A glass of red wine, please," Reggie says sweetly.

"Cosmopolitan," Skylar says.

The waitress nods and walks away quickly. It's not that I don't drink. I have wine with dinner on special occasions, and Jenna and I even went to the bars in La Jolla sometimes, mostly to look at the boys we'd never go out with. (Boys taking shots and yelling at the game on TV rarely want to roll out of bed Sunday morning for church.) And of course I've never been drunk and would never *be* drunk, but I have no problem with a little alcohol. It's just that I'm not ready to drink in front of these girls yet—I don't want them to see me get even a little tipsy before I have a chance to convince them what I am really like. I tend to be very chatty and confessional after even just a small cocktail. Unfortunately, there is no good way to tell them that. I consider changing my order, but after glancing down at my glowing pink sweater and judging the distance between the bar and our table, I decide to just order a cocktail next time and act like I didn't see that look from Skylar.

"So how was your first week, Emily?" Lane asks.

"Good and over," I say. Reggie laughs raucously, as if this were a really funny joke, and I start to feel a little better.

"Let's just wait and see how week two goes," Skylar says. "Xavi's back."

"Do you really think he's all that bad?" Lane asks diplomatically.

I turn and stare at Skylar's perfect face, her cold crystalline blue eyes. "I guess not. But he's no bed of roses either."

I don't want to talk about this again and think this might be the perfect time to try to get a read on Helen. "What's the story with Helen?" I ask.

Instantly, all three girls have their eyes on me.

"Was she mean to you?" Lane asks, worried.

"No . . ." I can't put words around it. She is just removed, distant, an ice queen.

"Oh, Lane, I don't think she'd be mean to Emily. Emily wasn't even here during all of that," says Reggie.

I cock my head a little, hoping they fess up.

"Have you heard what happened?" Skylar asks.

I shook my head. "I just heard she has been promoted and that she used to be Xavier's assistant."

"She deserted us," Skylar says.

"Skylar, not really. Emily, what happened was that Helen was hired just a few months before us. She has been promoted a couple of times, and now we don't see her as much. She's very, uh, ambitious is all," Reggie says.

I look at Lane, the one who usually speaks the truth even if it kills her. She shrugs at me. "I just started a few months ago and was never very close with her so I don't notice it really. She doesn't come to lunch anymore. That's all."

I nod.

"I don't really care all that much either," Skylar says. "I still see her on the weekends. It's just weird." Somehow it makes sense to me that Skylar and Helen are friends.

There's a moment's pause and then Reggie screams, "Skylar! That's, um, your, your . . . It's *you*." She is pointing at one of the biggest screens in the bar. On it is Skylar's ample chest. My mouth falls open, and Lane winces. "Here, quick, slide this way," Lane says, thinking on her feet, but Skylar isn't listening. She is smiling from ear to ear and looking around the bar with a mock-accusatory look on her face. She stands up from our table, tilts her head to the side, and plants her arms akimbo. Across the bar, a group of guys burst out laughing, and she shakes her finger at them and then sits back down, still laughing. "Boys will be boys."

She clearly loves the attention. I wish that the boys would have chosen anyone but Skylar to single out. Reggie and Lane are also gorgeous but, alas, not the blonde busty beacon that is Skylar.

We spend the rest of the night talking about Reggie's future career as an actress. "I'll only do *artistic* nude scenes," she declares, making me swallow my Diet Coke down the wrong pipe. "Just like Halle Berry." We discuss Lane's crush on the security guard who works in our building, a tall Puerto Rican man with a cute accent and *a smile that would melt your heart*, and how she can get him to ask her out. And by the third drink, we're all chummy and cracking ourselves up. Okay, *they* are chummy and cracking *themselves* up. I am feeling pretty left out. They didn't say anything, but it is clear they think I'm not quite, well, cool. I vow next time to have at least one drink. Maybe that will prove that I'm not an utterly hopeless dork.

I try my best to fit in anyway—we end up talking about the sneaky things we've all done to get a guy's attention, and I gladly share about the time I pretended to drown at the beach because I thought the lifeguard was cute. I added a few embellishments to the story. Okay, so maybe my bathing suit wasn't *quite* falling off, and my drowning was not totally an act, since I was actually having a hard time getting out of a riptide—but no one notices, and they all chuckle as I recount how I burst into laughter when he started to give me CPR.

I start yawning about twelve thirty, but I'm certainly not going to be first one to leave, so I am pretty grateful when, not too long after, Lane signals for the check. "I've got to get up early to meet up with a friend who's coming into town tomorrow," she explains.

"What's everyone else doing this weekend?" I ask.

The girls all look at one another, and Lane stares at the table. Skylar pipes up. "Nothing much."

Reggie nods and adds, "Some laundry. Whatever." And then I catch Skylar give Reggie a wink. Reggie quickly asks, "And you, Emily?"

I am about to mention the church I want to try out Sunday morning—hey, at least I have plans of some kind—but then I decide that what with the Diet Coke blunder, I should keep quiet. "I . . . oh, you know," I continue, hoping desperately to seem nonchalant. "Not much. I might hang out with my uncle." Even though we don't have plans and this last part verges on being a lie, I want them to know I'm not totally alone. In fact, I want myself to know it also. Besides, we might hang out.

"Your uncle?" Skylar asks. "I'd never hang out with any of my uncles voluntarily."

I immediately switch on my computer when I get home. All I want to do is talk to Jenna, but it is too late to call, even with the three-hour time difference, so I e-mail her instead.

Jenna,
   I just had my first night out on the town as a young urban professional. Didn't go as well as hoped. The girls at

my office are nice enough—heck, they didn't have to invite me out with them—and they are very funny, but I'm just not sure I have much in common with them. Honestly, Jenna, I know it's only been a week, but I'm afraid I'm not going to find anyone in this city to hang out with. I have this whole empty weekend in front of me, and I almost wish I had to go in to work, just to have something to do. I miss you.

Em

I read it over quickly, but can't hit send. It sounds so . . . pathetic. I'm not ready to let anyone, even my best friend of eighteen years, know how much I want to fit in, and how bad I am doing at it, so I make a few changes.

J-Dog—
    I just had my first night out on the town as a young urban professional ☺. The girls at my office are nice, and they have really tried to include me in everything. They are very funny. I'm not sure I have much in common with them, but it's only been a week. I'm having a good time, but I sure do miss you.

Emily

That is much better, I think, as I hit send. I will make this all true soon enough. Things are going to change. Either that or *I* am going to change.

CHAPTER 4

bennett

★

I *am feeling* very proud of myself Monday as I wait in the endless line to pay for my lunch. Things *are* changing. After nearly breaking down out of loneliness in church yesterday, I had decided I would do just about anything to lift my spirits and my status, and ended up downtown, on a street lined with little high-end clothing boutiques. My budget wasn't very high-end, but I managed to control myself, mostly. At first. Initially I was shocked by the prices I saw on the dresses and tops, and vowed I would only be window-shopping.

The clothes, though, were beautiful. Silky fabrics, well-cut patterns, intricate beadwork, carefully stitched seams, unique designs—these clothes would make even plain old Em into a hip young New Yorker. I could definitely see Reggie wearing them, which seemed like the ultimate test. And I found a skirt on the clearance rack at the back of a boutique called Veronica's that I fell in love with. It was made of a light blue filmy fabric and came down just past my knees—long enough to be office-appropriate, but sexy enough to double as a night-out skirt. It sure beat the pink sweater. I fingered the material carefully. It was fabulous. There was no doubt about it. It fit beautifully, too. I hesitated a long time, turning around and around in the dressing room, watching the way it swooshed around my legs, the way it fell gracefully when I stopped moving. It was, I rationalized, fifty percent off the sale price. It was still more than I had ever paid for any article of clothing in my life, including my prom dress. But that dress was ugly, I told myself. I would never wear that now . . . and this was divine.

Quickly, before I could change my mind, I pulled my jeans on and ran to the front counter, handing over my credit card. I would pay it off later. Now, I needed some clothes for my job, I reasoned. I had always heard that you were supposed to dress for the job you wanted, not the job you had, and the job I wanted involved wearing skirts like this.

I felt a twinge of guilt as I imagined what Jenna would say if she saw the receipt, but I pushed the thought aside. Jenna didn't understand what it was like here. People dressed well and had to dress well, I had already learned, to be accepted. These clothes were gorgeous, and as soon as I could afford it, I intended to buy more. What I was most afraid of was not the credit card bill that would come in the mail, but that I was going to get addicted to really nice clothing.

Now, as I inch closer to the cash register in the cafeteria, I am glad I did. I am feeling pretty smart in my blue skirt—I couldn't wait to wear it—and a tight white V-neck tank top. Pretty smart, that is, until the woman at the register finally rings up my lunch.

"Five seventy-five," she bellows.

"Sorry? I thought the pizza was $2.50," I say, confused.

"You got the thick-crust kind there, with toppings, and that sauce on the side is extra," she says, pointing to the little container of garlic butter I had on my tray.

"Oh, no," I mutter, digging though my wallet desperately. "I don't think I have enough." I am mortified. "Can I leave the sauce? I'll go put it back," I say, praying in my embarrassment that no one will notice why I am holding up the line.

The cashier rolls her eyes dramatically. "Just leave it here," she says, tsk-tsking me under her breath and subtracting the price from my total. I hand her a five and shake my head as she gives me a nickel in change. Maybe I shouldn't have spent quite so much on accessories yesterday. Once again looking at nothing but the floor, I weave my way through the tables and sit down with the girls.

". . . I couldn't believe how gross he was, and he fully expected me to go home with him," Skylar was saying. "I was like, ew, maybe if you didn't have sweat stains all over your pits and reek of beer. I mean, I let him buy me some drinks but that does not mean that we are *together*. Ugh! Thankfully Reggie came up to me, crying, and saying that she needed me because her cat had gotten out of her apartment."

"I was practicing being able to cry on command! Do you think he believed us?" asks Reggie.

"Totally. It was hilarious. If you hadn't rescued me then I don't know what I would have done. He was making me so crazy."

I was slowly gathering that they had gone out and had a wild time on Saturday night. Without me. I look at Lane, but she won't look back at me. I look down at my tray, trying to pretend I don't care. My pity party is interrupted by a long shadow falling on me from behind. I turn my head to the right and try to see who, or what, it is, but all I see is a smooth arm just by my cheek. A big hand places a small container of garlic butter on my tray.

"Uh, here you go," the voice says. I look straight up. Bennett Edward Wyeth, the third, is already turning away from our table, blushing.

The girls are all staring at me, open-mouthed, and I manage to call out a weak thank-you as he walks to the door. My face flushes as I realize he must have seen the debacle at the cash register, but my stomach turns with excitement as my head processes what he has just done. I can't help but feel pleased at his gesture. Or, if I am honest, at the look of envy that each of my companions is giving me right now.

"Shut up!" Skylar says. I've learned she means something like "Incredible" or "No way" when she says this. I giggle. It's such a funny thing to say when no one's talking. And, hey, I'm giddy anyway.

"What happened?" Lane asks. I tell them about being short on money.

"That's so dashing," Lane sighs.

"Somebody's got an admirer," Reggie says and winks at Skylar.

"Oh, it's just a thing of butter," Skylar says.

I don't care what Skylar thinks, I must be the happiest girl on the whole island.

How can I thank Bennett? Sadly, this is what I spend the hour after lunch thinking about. My first instinct was to e-mail him, and as soon as I got back to my desk I composed a heartfelt and self-deprecating yet witty message, expressing my sincere thanks and my willingness to accept any more free food he was ready to give me. I looked up his e-mail address in the corporate directory and was about to hit send when I realized that I am not supposed to know who he is. Of course I know all about him, but he doesn't know I know. He would think I was a complete stalker. I minimize the window, deciding to deal with it later.

Today is, after all, Xavier's first day back, and I have more important things to be doing than e-mailing. Mostly I have been trying to decipher his handwriting so I can type up the letters he is sending out to literary agents. Xavier apparently has a real aversion to technology, so most of the things other editors would do themselves get sent to me to handle. I am realizing slowly that I work for a man with many quirks.

For instance, this morning. For all I know, the man lives in the building. I came in at eight thirty to get a jump on my first day with a boss, and he was already there and, judging by the three empty cups of coffee, had been for a long time. I heard him as I was coming down the hall to my desk—he was muttering about gravity—and stacks of paper were flying out the door to his office, landing loudly, one stack at a time, in a pile in the hall. I put my purse down, switched on my computer, and leaned timidly toward his door. He didn't seem to notice me and, with his back facing me, sent a giant manuscript flying out the door, just past my right arm. I decided to speak up quickly.

"Xavier?" I said. He looked up sharply, and his dark eyes fastened on mine. He had dark, slightly out-of-control curly hair and an aristocratic chin. He wore modern light-framed glasses and a heavy tweed coat, complete with professorial elbow patches. He was young and, despite the crazed look on his face, startlingly attractive. He stared at me, his face completely blank, for several seconds, long enough for me to wonder if he had any idea who I was and whether I should remind him that he hired me.

"Ashley!" he finally exclaimed loudly, his face breaking into a wide smile. "You must be Ashley."

"Emily," I said, politely. He didn't even remember my name? This could be a long morning.

"Yes, of course. That's it. Time off kills the brain." He walked around his desk to me. I assumed he wanted to shake my hand, since he put his out in front of him, but as I reached out to take it, he suddenly turned, stretched his arms straight out. "How do you like it?" he asked me. He turned in a slow circle gesturing toward the tall, dark oak bookshelves crammed tight with books, to his big broad desk of matching wood to the long panel of a glass wall that showed a million-dollar view of Central Park.

"It's great," I said. "And I'm really glad to finally meet you."

He had finished his revolution and was facing me again, eyeing me up and down.

"Likewise," he conceded, then lunged, almost violently, really, toward the chair in front of his desk. "Have a seat," he said, picking a stack of manuscripts off the chair and throwing them in the hallway with the rest. He grinned at me.

Uncertainly, I sat down, and he raced back around his desk to sit in his chair.

"Tell me. How's Matthew?" he asked.

"He's doing really well," I said. "He seems to be very busy with his work at the Locus, but he's happy. He promised to show me Chinatown sometime this week. He's been such a big help with this whole thing."

"Did you get a chance to familiarize yourself with the books I work on?" Okay, so he's done talking about Uncle Matthew. I nodded.

"I'm really excited to work with William Finneran," I said.

"Glad to hear it. His new book will be out soon. There's a big book release party for him coming up. That will be big. You should plan on coming to that. Do you want an autographed copy of his first novel? I have a whole stack in here somewhere," he said, looking at his wall of shelves. "Maybe under the printer or something . . ." He turned around to look. "I don't know." He was looking under his desk now, then sat up and began lifting up papers as if he might have missed a stack of books hiding under his thin calendar.

"Um, sure, if you have one, that'd be great," I said.

"Take whatever you want," he said, looking up and gesturing to his gigantic library. "They're all up for grabs."

"Anything? Free?" That couldn't be right. Books were expensive.

"What do you think this is, a tuna factory? We make books. We read books. We like it that way." He started tapping his desk with a pen. "Take anything you want, and if you want something you don't see here, we can order it. I'll get you the company card. Let me know." I was stunned. This was a nice perk. "And there's a champagne toast in the conference room at four on Friday. We have one every Friday if we make the number-one slot on the *New York Times* best-seller list. Just send up for the stuff from a caterer around the corner." He grinned boyishly. "Turns out it happens quite a lot around here," he laughed. A little too long, rather maniacally. "Go to that little shindig, and I'll introduce you around. In the meantime, you might start shopping for another big book party we're having. It's for Madame Castadot of Plum fame. You've heard of Plum? Michelin Guide–starred restaurant? Anyway, she's their celebrity chef, and we're fêting her at the Peninsula just after the president blows through, so you'll want to look nice. The whole thing's being sponsored by Veuve-Clicquot."

I nodded, now dumb at the opulence of this industry, and Xavier turned his head to look out the window. "Was everything okay last week?" He could not maintain eye contact, which instead of seeming rude just made him all the more eccentric. "I hear there was a mix-up in Human Resources," he continued. "I trust Helen took care of you?"

"Oh yeah, things were great. Helen showed me around, and some of the other assistants helped me out. I think I have an idea what I'm supposed to do," I said, aware that I was babbling because I was nervous.

"Really?" he asked, raising his eyebrows. "Good. Very good." He nodded, almost to himself. "Then why don't you go log all those manuscripts in," he said, pointing to the mess he created outside his door. I turned my head to where he was pointing, but when I turned back he had already started reading something on his desk. Was that it? He looked up at me quizzically and then said, "Thank you, Emily." I popped up from my chair and exited. I was dismissed.

Hello, corporate life, I thought, as I trudged uncertainly back to my desk. At least that time he got my name right.

At about two thirty a group of five men, all in dark suits, goes into Xavier's office and closes the door. There had been streams of people coming by his office all day. Apparently the whole company has wanted to talk to him about something while he was gone. At first I tried to keep up with who went in and out, listening to how he greeted them so I could figure out their names, but by midafternoon I gave up. Sometimes there were even people hovering by my desk, waiting for him to finish talking to whoever got there first. I made a mental note to buy a bowl and fill it with candy to make friends with the people who come by to see Xavier. But this particular group of suits looks especially intimidating. I crane my neck to try to hear what they are saying. Maybe Xavier's in the Mafia, I think, then shake my head as I hear one of them say something about sixty-pound paper. They must be talking about books, I think sadly. Right about now I wouldn't be surprised by anything I heard about Xavier. This morning I answered calls for him from two different women, both saying they were looking forward to seeing him tonight. I wonder why Xavier's tomcatting around doesn't upset anyone here.

"Excuse me?" My thoughts are interrupted by a voice behind me. It is deep and masculine. A rarity around here. I turn quickly, trying to pretend I was thinking about something important, and freeze when I see Bennett there. I smile and say hello. I throw a quick glance back at my computer screen, praying the e-mail to him I drafted isn't on display. It isn't. Whew.

"Is Xavier busy?" he asks, a stack of stapled papers in his hand.

"Yes, he's, uh, in a meeting. I'm not sure how long he'll be in there, but I can give him something for you if you want. Or, you know, give him a message or whatever," I stammer.

He's laughing, but he smiles at me very kindly. "Maybe I'll just hang out here and wait until he's done," he says, his eyes traveling down my body to my legs, which are partly hidden under my desk.

He comes to stand next to my chair. "I'm Bennett," he says, holding out his hand.

"I'm Emily," I say, grasping his hand firmly. "Thanks for the butter."

Thanks for the butter?

"Oh," he says, turning red and lowering his eyes. "It was my pleasure. I hate to see a good container of butter go to waste."

"Yeah, all those starving children and all that," I laugh. He even smiles back.

"So, you're Xavier's new assistant?" he asks. I nod. "How do you like it so far?"

"It's been going well."

"Xavier's a little, uh, bizarre," he says, lowering his voice conspiratorially, "but I'll tell you a little secret. He loves peanut butter. If you remember that, you'll be fine."

"Peanut butter." I nod. "I'll try to keep that in mind."

He leans back. "I like what you've done with the place," he says, gesturing at the bookshelves above my desk. I've separated the books by height and alphabetized them by author's last name within each section. "Neat freak?" he asks, laughing.

"Clutter can be toxic," I laugh guiltily. I look at the blank walls of my cubicle. "I've been meaning to bring in some stuff to put up to make the space a little more homey, but I haven't really gotten around to it yet,"

"Oh, it looks great. Sleek and sparse. Some people pay thousands for designers to come in and give them this look." He meets my eye, then looks down at my corkboard and leans in to read the writing on the parchment Jenna made. "And what's this?" he asks.

"Oh, it's nothing," I say, trying to shoo him away from it. "It's just something a friend made for me."

"That's my favorite verse," he says, looking up at me. "I can do anything through Him who gives me strength."

"Really? I mean yeah, heh, it's one of my favorites too." He is silent, thoughtful. "It's a nice reminder of home. That was the first verse my friend Jenna and I memorized when we were in Sunday school. I think we won jelly bracelets for our hard work," I explain.

"Jelly bracelets, eh? I'll have to hear more about that sometime." And then he drops his voice a little. "Do you go to a church here in the city?"

"Not really. I mean, not yet. I just moved here. I went to one on Sunday, but I didn't know anyone and it felt kind of weird. I'm not sure if I'll go back to that one or not."

"Why don't you come to church with me?" he asks. "I'd love the company."

"Wow, that would be great," I answer, trying to keep my voice calm. "That would be really cool." I want to jump up and pump my fist back and forth saying, Yes! Yes! Yes! like the twins do when their favorite football team makes a touchdown, but I control myself.

"Great," he says. He smiles at me, and I can see his square white teeth. He looks ruddy and boyish, like he just came in from a rugby game. I'm out of intelligent things to say so I just smile back. Just when the silence gets awkward Xavier's door opens, and the men in suits pour out.

"I'll e-mail you," he mouths toward me as Xavier sweeps in on him, loudly saying, "Bennie, my main man! Good to see you."

Dear Jenna,
I'm in love. You can be my maid of honor. He bought me butter.

Em

Five minutes after I send this e-mail, my phone rings. I can tell by the caller ID that it's Jenna's home line. I am greeted by her incredibly loud voice. *"You're in love? You didn't call me first? What's his name? Is he totally hot?"* I crack up and talk her down. I whisper just the most basic details into the phone and thank God Xavi and Bennett are keeping each other busy and out of earshot at the moment. When Jenna finds out that we're going to church together she says, "Emily. I just got chills." She's so dramatic, but it's hilarious.

We walk down the side aisle and have a seat. Bennett's church meets in a building in Greenwich Village (or Green-Witch Village, as my dad called it on his visit). It is called, cleverly enough, the Greenwich Village Church, and it's an offshoot of a larger church uptown. He nudges me and gestures at the woman wearing torn jeans and the man with a clingy orange paisley shirt and tight red pants in the pew in front of us. "It's a little more relaxed than most churches," he says.

The worship band plugs in their guitars and microphones while the congregation seats and quiets itself. I look around, noticing the high stained-glass windows, the dark red velvet pew cushions, the formal high-back chairs on the traditional stage. "This place belongs to a congregation of Seventh-Day Adventists—all that stuff on stage is theirs," he says, following my eyes. "They don't need it on Sundays so we rent it from them on the cheap. We can't afford much. Most people here are pretty artsy. We've got painters, photographers, dancers, actors, you name it—'starving artists.'" He makes quote marks around the last phrase, and I giggle.

Artsy is definitely the right word for the people I see around me. I've never seen so many pairs of dark horn-rimmed glasses in my life, but I like it. It feels comfortable, laid-back, welcoming.

"It's possible I'm the only one in this whole church who has a real job, but let's just keep that between you and me," he says, turning to me. "I don't want to be kicked out." At that, a couple passes us holding hands. The woman has a small infant secured to her chest in a colorful silk scarf and the man's forearms are covered in tattoos. "I'm not always sure I belong here, but the people are nice, and I figure we're all outcasts in this city," he says. "At least at church we've all got one thing in common."

My eyes lock with his. I try to think of something witty, even something borderline intelligible, to say in response, but as long as he is looking at me like that I can't think about anything but how much I would like him to lean over and kiss me. Luckily, the worship band starts up, and I turn forward—he didn't break eye contact first, I note approvingly—to sing.

The service isn't nearly as *out there* as I would have guessed from looking at the people sitting near me, but the offering time takes me a little off guard. As the plates are being passed, a man does an interpretive dance while he chants Psalm 23. Bennett meets my eyes and laughs. Good, I say to myself, he thinks this a little weird too. I like the service, though, and I especially like that Bennett's leg is touching mine. When we first sat down we had several inches between us but with the ups-and-downs of the greeting, the Confession of Faith, and Worship Time we moved into each other. I like sitting so close to Bennett's side. I like pretending that I'm with him. That he's my boyfriend.

Once the service is over, the minister tells us to "Go with God."

Bennett leans over and whispers in my ear, "He means go with God and Bennett downstairs to get the free bagels and coffee."

I try to laugh quietly, but the worship team starts playing a song so I just let it out. "Really? God likes bagels?"

"He *is* Jewish." Bennett leads me downstairs to where there are tables crammed with bagels, muffins, doughnuts, and oh my favorite, coffee. He ushers me around with my coffee and bagel in hand to meet some of his friends. Am I imagining things or do some of the girls look at me with envy? Finally we stand by ourselves in one of the corners.

"So are you too freaked out, or will you come back?" he asks, slathering cream cheese on a sesame bagel (my favorite kind!). He wraps it in a napkin.

"Do they serve free bagels every week?" I ask, being as flirtatious as I can while trying to remove the cream cheese I have managed to get in my hair.

"Of course," he says, narrowing his eyes as he looks at my face intently.

"Then I might be persuaded. But only for the bagels," I laugh.

"Good. Though I hope to see you again before then," he says, leaning closer to me. "I would try to trick you into hanging out with me this afternoon, but I promised a friend I would help him move."

He puts his free hand on my arm, and I get goose bumps, although I am a little startled by his announcement that he's taking off. I try to recover quickly. "Trick me some other time then." I look at him. He breaks eye contact first this time, but only after several seconds.

"I should get going," he says, turning toward the door. "I'm glad you came."

"Me too." I watch him maneuver through the wad of people at the door. Once outside, he looks back and waves. I wave back. Hmm. That was a little weird. I suppose I had been hoping there was going to be more. Lunch with his friends? A stroll? Nope. Probably a moving truck is waiting on him. I know how that can be. Too bad I didn't think to ask where the subway was.

I look back at all the strangers walking around with coffee and bagels and shrug. Here goes.

friends

★

"S*top it,*" I whine. "Nobody likes you."

My alarm continues to wail at top volume. It's seven in the morning.

"Mmph." I say to it. It continues. *Whaah. Whaah. Whaah. Whaah.*

Last week I placed my alarm across the room from my bed for mornings like this one. Snooze-button mornings. I finally drag myself over to the alarm, telling it what an awful machine it is on my trek over there and then fall back into bed. The worst part? It's only Wednesday. How did my poor mom and dad do this working thing their whole lives? Getting up early and spending all day in an office is going to be the end of me.

I pull myself out of bed, thread my arms into my robe, and try to run my fingers through my hair. They stick halfway through in a tangle. I sigh and stumble over to my computer. I didn't want to get DSL here, but I'm now glad Brittany insisted. I need to check the weather. The weather website has a little cloud icon over today with thunderbolts sticking out of it. What a shock. It's always raining here. I wince, and then rub my eyes to try to read the small numbers. Ninety degrees with 100 percent humidity. I groan. My hair is going to look like a madwoman's today. I decide to check my e-mail, hoping some kind soul will turn this morning around.

My face breaks into a weak smile when I see a whopping three new e-mails in my inbox. The first one isn't from an address I recognize. It says *hinton@northsideelementary.edu*. Northside Elementary? Mom. But she can't e-mail. She can't even type. I open up the message.

dEAR hONEY,

tHIS KEYBOARD IS TYPKIING VERY FUNNY. aNOTHER TEACHER SHOWED ME HOW TO USKE THE EMAIL EARLIER TODAY BUT i FORGOT SOME PARTS i THINK. iWANTED TO LEARN HOW BECAKUSE i MISS YOU VERY VERY VERY VERY VERY MUCH!!! sO DOES YOUR DAD. wRITE ME BACK. iSAW jENNA TODKAY, BY THE WAY. sHE WAS HANG-ING OUT WITH SOME KIDS I GUESS YOU KNOW AND SAID TO SAY HI.

XXXOOOO LOVE YOUR MOM

I am laughing and crying all at once by the end of it. I decide to call her tonight and explain about the caps lock key and other e-mail etiquette. If only she knew that she yelled her entire e-mail at me. I vow to write her back later.

I am glad to see the second one is from Jenna.

Dear Em,

I've thought a little bit about your new love, uh, Benjamin? Is that what you said his name is? I couldn't quite hear you with all that whispering you were doing. Is he tall or short? Is he athletic or bookish? Is he funny? I need details, girl. Give me details!!! Nothing new on the boy front here, sadly.

I saw your mom outside the supermarket today. She was trying to fit a lifetime supply of toilet paper in the back of your station wagon. That's a big car, Emily, but she had so much it wouldn't close. There was either a big sale on toilet paper, or she's going out with a bunch of junior high girls tonight. I love your mom, but sometimes I do think she's a little bit crazy.

Oh, guess who I ran into? Remember Jacob Keller from church? He graduated from UC Davis and moved back home. He is looking for a job in the area. He asked me about you and seemed impressed to hear you're out in New York. I said I'd say hi for him. So hi for him.

Time to go make some dinner. Have a great night.

Jenna

Jacob Keller. I haven't thought about him in ages. He asked me to be his girlfriend in first-grade Sunday school and, for lack of anything better to say, I said yes. We ended up going to the same high school and though we were never really close—he was actually a big geek by ninth grade—we saw each other at church all the time. Come to think of it, we never actually broke up. I guess he's technically still my boyfriend. Maybe I'll ask Jenna to remind him so I'll be sure to get a present on Valentine's Day.

I am aware of a shadow in my doorway and look up. Brittany comes into the room in rollers and pajama bottoms. "Emily, I bought some cleaning supplies and some paper towels for the apartment, and I split the cost in half," she says and hands me the receipts. She has very carefully circled every item we are to split and written how much each of us pays in two columns on a separate piece of paper. I owe one cent more than she does. "I'll pay the extra penny next time," she says.

"Uh, gee, Brittany, thanks." Has she really split the cost of cleaning supplies down to the penny? Does she really expect us to alternate paying the extra penny every month? "I'll get you a check tonight."

"No problem." She puts headphones in her ears and sashays out.

I shake my head and turn back to my computer. I am about to hit reply to Jenna's e-mail when I remember the final message in my inbox. It is also from an unfamiliar e-mail account. By the address, I can tell it's one of those free ones, and it looks like spam. But I don't see any obscene references in the subject line, so I open it anyway.

Emily, it begins, *It was great to see you on Sunday*. This can't be from . . . I look down to the bottom of the message. It is. It's from Bennett. My heart actually falters inside my chest. I didn't even know that could happen.

> I'm sorry I had to run out on you like that. Let me make it up to you by taking you out to dinner this week. Are you free Thursday night?
>
> Bennett
>
> P.S. Sorry about the strange e-mail address—I try not to use my work e-mail for personal matters.

Personal matters? I take in a big breath, thinking about being called a personal matter. This one I reply to right away.

Okay, so maybe I should be apprehensive that he's inviting me out for the following evening—Nanna would raise an eyebrow at that—but the date of the e-mail says he wrote it late Tuesday; I just didn't get it until today. Good enough, I think, that's technically two days' notice. But I hint to him that it just so happens he found a hole in my busy schedule, that he's got good timing. I keep the e-mail quick and nonchalant. "Aloof," I say aloud, pronouncing it like a little gust of wind.

I run a spell-check and hit send. I glance at the clock on my computer. Seven thirty. Oh no! Late. Move, Em. *Move it.*

I scramble around my room, worrying *not* about how late I will be for work, as I should be, but about my date tomorrow. What will I wear? In my head I start to plan my outfit, while blindly dressing for work. By the time I'm sliding on my socks, I decide nothing I have will work. I run to the kitchen, pour a glass of juice, and sigh. I see why people always buy new clothes here. I have big plans to make. And fast.

Sitting in Xavier's office, I am ostensibly helping him revise a speech he is to deliver at a writers' conference in Berlin next week, but mostly I am listening to him tell me stories about all the trouble he and Uncle Matthew got into in college. I have been trapped here for nearly an hour when Helen pokes her head in, sees that we were talking, mumbles that she is sorry for interrupting, and goes back out to wait for Xavier to finish with me. Xavier, always oblivious, doesn't seem to notice she is hovering outside his office door, and launches into a lengthy list of the attributes of the girl Matthew set him up with once in college. *Tall? And how, she was tall. Two inches more than me. And some people said she was related to the royals. But man oh man, her breath. Hal-i-to-sis!*

Out of the corner of my eye, I see Helen pacing by the door, but even though he is facing her direction, he doesn't seem to notice. I begin to fidget in my chair. It's not like I need more enemies in this place. I try to wrap up the conversation, but he just keeps going and going. Finally, his phone rings. He ignores it at first out of habit and keeps talking to me. Finally a light goes on in his eyes—realizing that I'm not at my desk to answer it, he picks it up.

"Xavier." There is a pause. "Charlie!" he suddenly exclaims. "So good to hear from you. How have you been?" He looks at me and nods. This is one of his ways of saying goodbye, so I get up and walk out of the office.

Helen is leaning against the wall of my cubicle when I get there. "Who's the little favorite now?" she says, laughing a little.

"I was just . . . he kept talking," I try to explain.

"Oh, I know," she says. "He used to talk to me too. But I guess he just likes you better now." I don't know what to say. What does she want me to do? Stop paying attention to my boss? "Just kidding," she says, standing up straight. She walks to his door and, frustrated to find him on the phone, turns back. "I'll just come back later." She glares at me as if it is my fault before slamming the door to her office.

I get out of the shower, my skin finally cool after a sticky, sweltering day. Thank God the New York weekend unofficially begins on Thursday so that I was able to quietly slip out early with the rest of the people who had plans. I made sure to give myself two entire hours at home to relax and get ready for my date with Bennett. My *date*, I think, combing the water out of my hair. I love the way it sounds bouncing around in my head like a frantic Ping-Pong ball. I never really went out on dates in California, first-grade boyfriends aside. Jenna and I had known all the boys since we were sitting next to them in Pampers on the beach. Sure, I reason, I occasionally got invited out in groups to go bowling, but rented shoes don't compare with a new dress and dinner. I plug in the hair dryer for the half an hour process of straightening my hair.

Last night in a panic I went shopping and came back with a new black dress from a boutique I read about in *Vogue*'s "Hot Spots" column. I'm not sure how my parents would feel about the thin spaghetti straps or the slightly plunging neckline, but it's so hot out, I reason, that it only makes sense. And besides, I can't expect them to understand. They don't even know what humidity is. The way your hair wilts and your skin just puddles as you stand there. I get it now.

Bennett and I arranged to meet at a bar for a drink and then move on to dinner. I am a little uncertain about the first part; I don't particularly want to start drinking recreationally, but I reason that Bennett is a Christian too, and he must think it's okay. I will go with it just this once. I am also a little nervous about meeting him since I don't know if he really means seven or if he means *fashionably-seven*. I hedge my bets, hop on the subway a little late, and walk up at ten past. He is waiting patiently outside the bar, leaning against the stone building. My heart jumps into my throat at the sight of him there, leaning, and I give a little cough to steady myself. As he sees me approach, he smiles and stretches out his arms. I fall willingly into the hug he gives me. I am tall, but he is taller and built like a man in a magazine ad. He has a strong jaw and big arms that cover my ears during the hug. He is the perfect height! And when I nestle in the space between his chin and chest, just for that wonderful split second I can smell him. He smells like a mixture of soap and warm, musky cologne.

"How are you?" he asks. He pulls back a little and looks into my eyes. I give him a goofy, toothy smile and nod. He smiles too and without a word leads me to the door, keeping one hand on my lower back, past the host, to a table in a dimly lit corner.

"I'm fine," I finally say as I sit down. I am recovering from the sight of him. "What have you been up to?"

He starts to tell me about a problem at work and then wrinkles his nose as if he smelled something rotten. "Please stop me when I do that." He puts his finger in the air. "I declare that there is to be no talk of the office tonight." At that, he stands up. "I'll think of something witty to say while I'm at the bar. What can I get you?"

"Um, a red wine, please," I answer, smiling. Red wine seems pretty safe. Sophisticated.

"Merlot? A Cab? Beaujolais? Bordeaux?"

I stare at him for a moment. Why is he speaking French? I panic, and then it hits me. I try to recover and act casual. I only remember the first choice on his list. "Merlot's fine."

I sigh once I see him leave and look around. This is nothing like the bar with the video screens. It is dark, quiet, lit almost entirely by delicate sconces and red lamps. I am sitting on part of a long ledge, cushioned in crushed red velvet. Bennett's chair, across the dark wood table, is ornate, like something from my grandmother's attic. The bar itself is beautiful—one massive piece of highly polished dark wood. Mahogany? I glance at Bennett's back at the bar. My date. Bennett Edward Wyeth, the third.

He turns, sees me looking at him, and smiles. He walks back holding my glass of red wine in one hand and a very blue drink in the other. He places them on the table and sits down.

"What is that?" I ask. "I've never seen a drink that color before."

"It's called a Yale Cocktail. It's made with gin and vermouth, but they add blue Curacao to make it Yale's color. They're not very well known outside the family, I guess," he says and laughs.

"Yale cocktail," I say, repeating it just to get a handle on it. "That's . . . um, Ivy, right? I didn't know you went to Yale. Wow." I realize he's smart on top of everything else. I no longer stop myself from thinking he is perfect. He *is*. He is my soul mate.

"Yeah, it is. Let's just say I've spent a lot of time in New Haven."

New Haven, I think. Remember that. Look it up on the Internet when you get home.

He chuckles and waves his hand in the air. "It's not that big of a deal. So where did you go to school?"

"Nowhere like that." I know I don't measure up, but he is looking at me so reassuringly that I continue. "San Diego State. I'm from a small town called Jenks that is nearby, and I couldn't really afford to go anywhere else, so it just made sense. Plus, I couldn't leave the perfect weather," I say, trying to convince him (and maybe myself) that it was a good place to have gone. "You know, the sun shines more than three hundred days a year there."

He looks at me with an eyebrow raised. "If that is true, dear Emily, what made you leave paradise to come out to this stormy coast?"

"I heard there were lots of attractive men out here?"

"I hope you haven't been disappointed." He leans toward me.

"Not yet." I look at his chest, the outline of which I can just make out through his tailored black button-down shirt. I lean back and fiddle with the stem on my glass, trying to do something other than just stare at him.

"So I guess that means you didn't leave someone special back in California?" he asks, sliding his hand gently on top of my nervous fingers tickling the glass. My hand freezes. And then I begin to lightly toy with his fingers instead of the stem. I look him directly in the eye.

"Jenks, you mean? No," I answer and stare at him for a few seconds. He stares back. "Not unless you count my dog, Max." I laugh to break the silence. He just smiles.

"I don't," he says solemnly, squeezing my hand. "And I'm glad." We both pause for a few seconds, smiling at each other like a couple of dopes. "Let's have a toast," he says.

I nod and lift my glass, thankful the pause has been dealt with.

"To Max, the only man in your life."

"To Max." I giggle and clink his glass.

"And may there be room for one more." He stares at me, and I turn redder than my wine. I am not sure what to say, and my head is whirling so I can't think straight. Those last words are floating around in my head, and I know I will be repeating them to myself tonight when I can't sleep.

"So have you always gone to church?" he asks.

"From the time I was two weeks old."

"So your parents are believers, then?"

"They weren't raised that way, but they got saved in the Jesus Movement in the sixties. You know, Peace, Love, and Jesus. And I come from a pretty small town where church is the center of life. I was in the nursery with the same group of kids I graduated from youth group with. I can't remember a time when I didn't call myself a Christian."

"The Jesus Movement? That's incredible."

"You'd never know it now. They're standard-issue mom and dad. But what about you?" I ask.

"I am a Wyeth. And the Wyeths have gone to the same church since they fled religious oppression on the *Mayflower*. The whole family, aunts, cousins, grandparents, went every single week growing up. And I did the same until I moved to New York."

"Do you always do what you're supposed to do?" I ask, slyly.

He pauses. "Yes," he says finally. "Which is why I must surround myself with only the best of company." He winks at me. "Come on." He raises his arm and throws back the rest of his drink. "I'm starving you. Let's go."

I gulp the rest of my wine while he laughs at me. He holds his hand out to me as I stand up. I take it, tentatively, and he repositions his hand, sliding his fingers in between mine.

Our fingers interlaced, we walk out the door into the warm night air.

The lights on the street are dazzling—in New York they have replaced stars as the beacons of night and somehow seem even more beautiful—and the breeze wraps itself around my bare legs as Bennett positions his arm around my waist. I am giddy, perhaps from the wine, and certainly from the emotions rushing through me. We don't say anything, each of us drinking in the beauty of the night and the moment as we stroll, until we arrive, a few blocks away, at Les Copains.

"Have you ever been here?" he asks, as he opens the door.

"No, but I've heard about it," I say, recalling one of Skylar's endless bragging sessions about her weekend. "It's supposed to be amazing."

"It is if you like *la cuisine française*."

Bennett walks up to the maître d' and simply says, "Wyeth, *s'il vous plaît*."

"*Ah. Bien sûr*," the host says. He motions for a waiter to come over, they have a whispered conversation, and then the waiter leaves. Bennett leans in close to my ear.

"I have a funny story about this place. I was once here with a friend when I spotted Xavier in a dark corner with this tall blonde. Have you met his wife yet?"

"No," I say. I am incredibly uncomfortable with this topic that everyone in the company seems not only aware of but also very fond of.

"Laura? She's a brunette. Lovely Irish lass." He chuckles to himself thinking of poor Laura. I gulp. Was the blonde in the restaurant this Beatrice who keeps calling, leaving messages about where Xavier is supposed to meet her? Her voice sounds so young and lithe on the phone.

"Why do you think that's funny?" I ask. My voice lurches out of my mouth with more passion than I intended. But really. Doesn't he consider himself a Christian? What can this mean?

He stares at me and doesn't speak. I gulp. What have I done?!

"You know, Emily Hinton. You are absolutely right. It's very sad. But this also means that *I* am right. About you. You're all that I hoped you would be when I first saw that verse in your office."

I blush a little.

"Sorry. It's just such a godless place at work that I think I just got accustomed to joking about Xavier's womanizing too," he says.

I feel a wave of relief sweep over me, and I open my mouth to apologize for snapping at him when the waiter returns, speaks French with Bennett, motions deep into the restaurant, and begins to walk. I just stare at the two of them, cursing my school counselor who convinced me to take Spanish. We thread through the large room, lit by warm yellow light, filled with white tablecloths and long candles. The host pulls my chair back, and I sit down, pulling it forward. Bennett then sits down, and his knees touch mine. "Sorry," he says, "this table is really small."

"I don't mind at all."

"Good," he replies, moving his legs around, trying to find a comfortable position. His legs brush mine a few times as he shifts around. Then he pulls his chair closer to the table and moves his right leg firmly between my knees. "Much better."

I am a little scared and a lot excited by this. It doesn't seem quite right for his leg to be where it is, but having his thigh pressing against mine feels good. Be cool, Emily.

Bennett orders a bottle of wine, and the waiter has him taste it first. He nods thoughtfully about the wine's quality, the waiter fills both of our glasses, and then we order dinner. It is the best meal I've ever had (salad, crusty bread, roasted pheasant in a white wine sauce, a cheese course, and a blueberry soufflé for

dessert) but I can't eat very much. My stomach churns with nervousness so I keep sipping my wine to settle it. The waiter has
filled my glass throughout the meal the moment it got below the
halfway point. I force down a few bites of each dish. The
cheeses, in particular, take a lot of discipline because they strike
me as out of place being served on their own like that, and they
smell a little funny.

I spend most of the meal leaning forward, trying to hear what
Bennett's saying above the din of the crowded room. He talks
about the most wonderful things: the people he met backpacking
around Europe the summer after he graduated from college; the
year he spent at the Sorbonne studying art history; how proud he
was when his mom, just a few years ago, opened her own psychiatric clinic; how the wind felt against his face as he raced in his
family's sailboat. As interesting as his stories are, though, my
mind swims. I can't focus. Between the wine and the way he
keeps running his fingers up and down my forearm, it is all I can
do to keep from drooling. I am almost glad when the check
comes, and he pulls me to my feet.

He leads me out the door, and we pause, turning to each
other.

"How are you feeling?" he asks. He loops his long arms
around my waist. He pulls me closer to him.

"Great," I say quietly. Very warm, a little sleepy, somehow
both relaxed and excited at the same time.

"Me too," he says, his face only inches from mine.

Slowly, he bends toward me. I know he's going to kiss me.
My mind races. I haven't kissed very many people. I have certainly never kissed anyone like this—on the first date, in the
street—and I am not sure it's a good thing (Jenna would certainly
not approve). But he doesn't stop, doesn't ask my permission. His
lips touch mine, very softly. He pulls back, looking into my eyes,
reading my face. Do I ask him to stop? Do I want him to? I hes-

itate. He leans in again, and this time he inclines his head and presses his lips on mine, confidently, and brushes my lips with his tongue. I am thinking of a thousand things at once. Every cell in my body shivers with delight. I relax into his arms, feeling my shoulders ease while I lean into him a little, trusting his stance. But then his hand moves slowly down my back, down my hips, and keeps going down, down, down. I don't stop kissing him, but I open my eyes. He sighs softly and adjusts his body so one leg is between mine, pushing against me. I break away. I take a step back. He is smiling at me, as if he knows he's been a bit naughty, and he's not sorry.

"I need to go," I whisper. He nods and cocks his head to the side, a little concerned. I add, "I had a wonderful time tonight." Even though the last part made me a little uncomfortable, the whole night was still storybook magical. "I hope we can do it again." He just nods again, smiling. He walks to the sidewalk edge and reaches out his arm to signal for a cab. A yellow car screeches to a halt just next to us.

"Good night, Emily, *ma copine*," he says, opening the door for me. "We'll do this again soon."

I climb in. "I'd like that." I smile, give the cabbie directions, and fall back onto the sticky leather seat, exhausted, a little tipsy, and half in love.

"*Copine*," I mumble, trying to repeat his perfect French accent.

The cab speeds down Broadway, and I feel like I'm on a ride at the summer fair.

It's noon on Friday, and I've been checking my computer screen every five minutes or so for the little envelope that appears when I have an e-mail. I am making myself crazy. Why hasn't Bennett e-mailed? Thank goodness I've already gotten the hang of my job. I am able to perform my daily functions by rote memory while I relive the previous evening moment by moment in painstaking detail. The way he smelled. The light on his wavy hair. His big arms around my waist.

I feel a telltale, long shadow fall over me from behind my chair. Of course he didn't e-mail. Might as well come by. I turn around with a big smile. And then jump at the sight of Lane.

"Oh." I say.

"Emily," she laughs. "Sorry. I didn't mean to startle you."

I blush. "You didn't. I was just daydreaming. I'm sort of out of it. Out late last night." And he hasn't e-mailed, I want to add but don't.

Lane nods. "I wanted to see if you wanted to go *out* to lunch today. Reggie's at an audition, and Skylar's having lunch with . . . Thomas? Ryan? I don't remember."

I laugh. "Great. I'll just grab my things. Whoa. I've never done lunch outside the caf. That's allowed, right?"

Lane laughs. "Not really. But I've got a bogus note from my mom."

The restaurant is a sleek space built on the campy notion of a cafeteria, not the sort that we have at Morrow & Sons with fresh sushi, the Global Cuisine food station, and the brick-oven pizza, but the kind that you have in public elementary school. It is called Josie's, and I cringe when I see the name, thinking of the obnoxious woman from the Locus and my Uncle Matthew. Lane sees my scowl.

"Do you hate it here, Em? I'm sorry. I just love to come because they have Southern food. Grits and stuff." Lane frowns.

"No." I say, trying to reassure her. "No. That's not it. I'm making a face at the name. It's kind of a long story."

Lane nods and then tells the hostess, "Two," and we are seated immediately at a tiny table.

I sit down on a long white bench, and Lane sits across from me in a sleek metal chair. Every piece of furniture in the restaurant is a bleached-white or a highly polished silver, but the servers wear retro brown polyester uniforms that make them look like they work at the Waffle Shop in Jenks. It strikes me as very funny to see such a sleek staff dressed like the average, hardworking Jenksian.

Lane looks up. "So, you uh, went out last night?"

I am relieved. I didn't know how to bring up Bennett without sounding like I was bragging, but I wanted to tell someone about it, preferably someone who had seen him, who would know what a great feat I had accomplished. "I had a date. With, uh, Bennett?"

"Bennett? Finance Bennett?"

I am thrilled to hear she's excited about it.

"He's cute. But he's, uh . . . what did you think of him?" she asks.

"I just kept staring at him. I couldn't even concentrate on what he was saying."

She giggles. "I dated a banker like that last year. He was Adonis. He'd open his mouth and start talking, and I couldn't even pay attention. It was awful."

"Is that why you broke up?"

"No. We broke up because he still loves his mother. And try as I might, I could never treat him *that* well."

I look at her. People back home don't talk in this weird Freudian psychobabble.

"Oh." I nod.

"He was an only child too." To Lane, this seems to explain

everything. "But how was it with Bennett? I've never actually talked to him."

I smile. Where do I begin? "It was . . . perfect."

"No. Surely something wasn't perfect. He got his tie in his salad?

"No."

"He slipped up and admitted that he'd never had a serious relationship?"

"Hmm . . . he didn't say."

"He chewed with his mouth open?"

"No."

"Answered a call from a buddy to get the score of the game? Talked about work the whole time? Anything?"

"No." I shrug, beaming. He is perfect. But still there is something inside of me, pulling at the darkest corner of my mind. Something wanting to be acknowledged. I ignore it.

"But, uh, wait. I thought he was real religious and stuff?"

I stiffen up. I hadn't been prepared for that question. "I, uh, don't know. Maybe he is?" I wince internally right when I say it. Why lie? But I sort of like that she doesn't know about my secret. I decide to change the subject. I can't get up the courage to say anything yet, but I start to think that maybe I was brought into Lane's life for a reason. "What about you? Are you dating anyone?"

Lane and I talk for an hour about everything, work and life and New York and roommates and boys and . . . everything. It turns out that she's very unhappy with her boss, the ultra-glamorous cookbook doyenne Susanna Shriver. Susanna did pieces in *Gourmet* magazine about hot cooking trends and restaurant openings and I had been thrilled even to catch the occasional glimpse of her around the building, always immaculately clad in Hermès and Versace with her signature jet black hair wound into a tight bun, but apparently she was a nightmare to work for.

"Skylar started calling her the Death Bun a while back."

I crack up. I hadn't heard that one yet.

"I'm sorry, Emily. I shouldn't be whining so much about Susanna."

"Oh no!" I say. I'm so happy she's confiding in me. "I'm glad to listen. I admire you so much because you never complain about, uh, the Death Bun. You've got to tell someone about your problems, or you'll just explode. I won't spread it around."

"I'm so glad. I can tell you're not a gossip. You're different than Skylar and Reggie somehow. I really like them too, but I don't want to confide too much in them. They'd be sympathetic, but also they'd be ruthless about Susanna. You don't want to get on their bad side, you know? I don't think Susanna means to be so miserable. It's just that she's really out of touch. She just sits in her office all day and is consumed by herself."

"Yeah. It's a tricky situation. You might just start by mentioning that by spending the morning booking a sitter for her French bulldog, you weren't able to complete your other tasks and thus had to stay late and miss your dance lesson. Just make her aware of the problem."

I keep listening as Lane vents her frustration and devour my mac and cheese, noticing that for the first time at work, I actually have an appetite for lunch. The permanent knot that has been tied in my stomach since I first arrived and saw Brittany standing the doorway in her headphones is finally beginning to fray and loosen. Finally.

As we swipe our ID badges and hurry over to the elevators because we are late—not that Xavier would notice—Lane asks if I want to hang out over the weekend. I say yes, and we make tentative plans for a movie and drinks on Saturday. We scurry quickly down the long corridor to get back to our cubes without being noticed. I am almost sitting down when I turn the corner and see Helen standing by my cubicle with her right eyebrow raised high.

"Nice lunch?" she asks. Then she looks at her watch and walks back to her office.

Lane,

Hiya. Thanks so much for lunch. I think getting out of the office did me good. I wanted to ask you . . . did you take French? I think you said you did. What does "copine" mean? The online dictionary seems to think it means "friend" but that can't be right.

Emily

CHAPTER 6

much better

★

"Mom?"

"Sweetie! I'm so glad you called! Preston? Turn it down, honey. It's Emily." I hear the TV in the background quiet and then a booming voice yell, "Hello Manhattan!" I laugh. Dad hasn't changed. "That's your dad's nickname for you now," she says.

"Manhattan?" I ask. "I don't know. I'm sure going to miss 'Shovelhead.'"

I can hear him singing, "Bup-bup-buhduhdaah-bup-bup-buhduhdaah" from "New York, New York." My mom joins in for a moment so that in unison they are singing at the top of their lungs, "I want to be a part of it. New York! New York!"

I guess they're starting to accept the fact that I moved to New York.

I laugh. "Mom? Mom?"

"Sorry. I'm back."

It is great to talk to them. I am surprised that they haven't called me since my first night alone in the city. I mention it to Mom, but she makes an offhand remark about how I am probably busy now. I shrug it off and assure her that she should call whenever she likes. My father and I talk for five minutes about the weather and my safety. And even Craig and Grant take a turn on the phone, which is interesting because I didn't know that they knew how to use the phone. I mention this to my mom once she gets back on, and she gets very serious and says that the boys are finally growing up. Something to do with my departure, she thought. Little girls had started calling the house asking for them. I ask which brother is getting the calls. Both, she informs me. The girls would talk to whichever one was home. A lump finds its way into my throat. I hate to know I am missing this part of their growing up, pests though they are. We chat a while longer and then Mom says, "You should go, Emily."

"No. Not really. I'm fine. Brittany's out. She won't need the phone."

"But, um, honey, isn't it Friday? Aren't you going out? With friends or something?"

My cheeks flush. I can't tell her that actually having plans on Thursday *and* Saturday with two separate real live people is such a *huge* accomplishment for me that I haven't even worried about not having anyone to call on Friday night. "No. I, uh, thought I'd stay home and relax. That sort of thing."

"Oh," she says. It was a sad sound. "Maybe you should relax for a while and then go see your uncle. I'll bet he needs some help."

I convince her that relaxing is all I ever wanted for the night, but after we hang up I look around Brittany's apartment—as I've come to think of it—and my chest tightens. I feel like I can't get enough air. Long streams of tears begin to pour out of my eyes. I climb out onto the fire escape. I look up and see clouds. I miss the stars. I look down. Dumpsters. I miss the grass. Suddenly it all feels like a foreign country, one where my passport home is lost and my return ticket is void. I sigh and cave in. I duck back inside the apartment, dash over to my closet, and throw on a pair of jeans and some sneakers. I gather my bag, throw in a book for the subway, and head out.

It'll be nice to see Uncle Matthew. He'll be a face from home, from a place where people behave as I expect, and love me, and watch out for me. Where I am someone I recognize.

Sunday morning, and it's raining. Again. It's time to get up to go to church, but I can't make myself climb out of bed. I'm exhausted. Lane and I certainly didn't go crazy last night—we just went to a movie and then retired to a cafe nearby—but since everything starts later here and places never seem to close, I didn't get home until three in the morning. Is it bad to ditch church? Just this once? I have never really skipped just because I didn't want to go. But that's not really what's happening, I reason. Bennett *is* visiting his family this weekend, and I don't *really* know the people yet. This would be a replay of the first time I went to church alone in New York. No siree. Not again. If Bennett was going, there would be no question about it, but since he's not . . . I roll over. But I should go. To avoid forming bad habits, I decide. I'll just sleep for a few more minutes and then get up and go.

I wake up at one and look around my room. A soft light is falling in from the alleyway window, and the room is completely still. It's serene and relaxing. I smile like the Cheshire cat. I feel rested and rebooted. Where is the guilt that I am supposed to feel? I move my covers back and place a foot on the hardwood. The chill of the wood sends a shudder up my back and causes goose bumps to jump up on my arms. Why is it so cold in here? Brittany and her temperature edicts. I cringe when I think of how high the electricity bill is going to be this month. At least she'll be forking over the extra cent this time. I grab my sheet around me and stumble over to the window, dragging it off the bed.

I peek into the alleyway. Still raining. I glance back at my bed. It's the perfect day to read. I go over to my bag and pull out a giant manuscript. Xavier asked me to take a look at the latest Si Hausen book that we just got in. Everyone at Morrow & Sons is very excited about acquiring Hausen because his last book, *Union Mist,* was made into a Jerry Bruckheimer box-office smash. Xavier was able to woo him away from his old publishing house and our archrivals, Saffron & Shultz, because they hadn't ponied up as much as Hausen had wanted for his next novel. I had heard murmurings that the new novel fell short of the first and perhaps Saffron & Shultz had made the right decision, but Xavier definitely believed that for the million dollars we paid to acquire the book, the two of us could clean it up.

Nothing appeals to me more than getting lost in a mindless book for the rest of the day, and I've always enjoyed a big task. I make a pot of coffee and settle in against my pillows with the manuscript and a red pen, but I only get about five pages into it before my mind starts to wander. I wonder what Bennett is up to right now, whether he has mentioned me to his family, when I will see him again. I envision a scenario in which our building collapses and somehow only Bennett and I are left alive, trapped in a small pocket of safety for several days before we are rescued, alive and very much in love. I drift off to sleep, thinking about what we will name our children.

"It's not like I'm totally going to stop drinking forever or anything," Skylar says, shaking her head enthusiastically. "I'm just not going to for a while. I'm going straightedge."

"Why?" Lane asks sweetly. Even Lane seems to be confused by Skylar's declaration. It doesn't seem like her.

"I just think I drink too much, and I don't really like feeling like I'm not in control, so I'm going to see what happens." She looks around, smiling proudly. We stare back. "What? It's not like I'm going to become a total loser or teetotaler or something. I'm still going to smoke and stuff."

"Cigarettes are worse for you than alcohol," I say. She rolls her eyes at me.

"I wasn't talking about cigarettes," she says, shaking her head as if I must be an idiot. "There are other things you can smoke."

"But didn't you say . . ." Reggie says, screwing up her face, then decides to drop it. "Um, so what did everyone do this weekend?"

We talk for a while, laughing about Lane's exploits showing her parents around the city on their recent visit. Reggie tells us about a friend's cast party where she had accidentally insulted the play to the director.

"Okay, Miss Hinton. Time for you to dish it up," says Skylar out of nowhere. Lane and Reggie look at me, and Skylar crosses her arms over her chest.

"Dish what?" I ask. I am no longer afraid of Skylar. At the Editorial Board meeting this week—Ed *Bored* as the assistants lovingly refer to it—the editor in chief mumbled, "Here we go again" as Skylar piped up at the other end of the table to rant about her *political and moral* objections to a new proposal that we got in, written for the "Religious Right." Once I realized that others also thought she was full of hot air, it made it easier to dismiss her when she was being shallow, meddlesome, or catty. But which was she being now?

"Yeah," Reggie says. "About Bennett. Is this true?"

"Oh." I blush. "I think so."

"So go. Tell us." Skylar is physically twitching in her seat.

"There's not much to say . . ." I start, playing it cool. "We had a date on Thursday. It was fun." At this I burst into a smile. Fun? Fantastic? Best night of my life. Ever.

Reggie and Skylar pull all of the details out of me, and Lane chimes in to help me here and there since she already knows the whole story.

"So when are you going out again?" Skylar asks.

I frown and shrug. "He hasn't called, dropped me an e-mail. Nothing."

"He's a flake," Skylar says, then adds quickly, "That's what I heard." I wince. I want to be a good influence on Lane, but I'm not so sure about Skylar. She may be beyond redemption.

"Great," I say. "I meet the one who doesn't call again."

Lane's eyes get huge in her head. "Emily! Don't tell me you let him . . . uh. Take you home?"

I shake my head quickly. "Oh no. Not at all."

Reggie laughs. "You're fine then. Absolutely fine. Boys in New York don't call the next day to thank you for a nice time. There are rules to these things."

"Rules?!" I say.

"Sure. Rules. They always wait a few days to call after the date," Reggie says.

"*If* they call," Skylar says.

"Right," I say. "If they call." I keep thinking about why he called me his *copine* at the end of the night. Lane said that it could mean friend or girlfriend in French. How did he see us? Was he bored by me? I'm not really in his league. Was he hinting he wasn't going to call, even after three days?

Lane shakes her head. "No. He's calling. I can feel it. I'm good at this stuff."

I smile at her like I just ate some bad eggs. I hope she's right.

"It's only Monday," Reggie says.

Skylar is silent.

"Right," I say with a short and definite nod. "Who cares? I'm not going to obsess about a boy." I slap my hand on the table. I need to change the subject quickly. I can't bear to think about the possibility that Bennett may never call, me, his *friend*, again. "New story. Want to hear about the awful thing I did over the weekend?"

Lane and Reggie nod, and Skylar looks at me quizzically. I'm loving this. I tell them about my escapades Friday night. When I appeared at the Locus to help Uncle Matthew serve the evening meal, I saw that awful Josie woman again. She was just down the serving table from me working the dessert section. I don't know how she gets under my skin so much. She kept laughing so loudly, like a donkey braying, Heeee-haw, and her laugh got louder and louder the longer it went on, grating on my last nerve. She kept asking Matthew over to her station for questions and insisted on calling him "Cap'n Matt" and saluting him as he walked off. I happened to overhear her tell her friend that she was going to ask Matthew to lunch on Wednesday because she had the day off for a doctor's appointment. Without thinking about it, I marched right over to Matthew and asked if he could come to lunch with me on Wednesday.

"Emily!" Lane says, laughing.

"But she's so annoying, and she's trying to snag my cool uncle. My only cool uncle. Just think of the Thanksgivings I'd have to spend with this woman!"

"If she laughs like a horse, I say she deserves it," Skylar says.

"You've got to watch out for your family." Reggie nods. "So does that mean we meet him on Wednesday?"

"Yeah. I'll bring him to the caf."

"Is he rich, I mean, cute?" Reggie asks. We all laugh at her joke.

"He's *poor*. But kinda cute," I say.

"Your uncle, huh? Won't that be fun!" Skylar says. "Maybe my grandmother can come in too. Hmm . . . I'll just need to call HR and make sure her oxygen tank won't be a problem with the security turnstiles in the lobby."

Bennett, as Lane predicted, does e-mail me. And as Reggie said, he waits until Wednesday. I had hoped it would be a long recap of his weekend full of comments like "Everyone wants to know when they get to meet you," but instead it is short and makes no mention of his family weekend. But he does ask me out again. I focus on that as a good sign. There is probably some weird rule about long e-mails too early in the relationship, I tell myself.

He wants to know if I am free for dinner and a movie Friday. On Wednesday morning, Friday feels very far away, and I almost write back to see if he wants to do something sooner, but I stop myself, determined to play it cool. Friday, I reply, sounds great, and I am so nervous with anticipation that when Uncle Matthew comes to lunch Wednesday afternoon he asks if I'm feeling okay. Lane is quick to report to him that I am "over the moon for a boy." I shush her, afraid someone at a nearby table will hear.

"What?" she asks, shrugging.

"His friends are right over there," I hiss, pointing. They must hear because they turn to see what the fuss is about.

"Emily, have I taught you nothing? Just don't make it obvious, and they'll never know. They're boys. They are naturally dense as a species," Reggie says. I shake my head.

After he gets every juicy detail from my friends and I turn three new shades of crimson yet to be invented by Revlon, I make him swear that he won't tell my parents. He recites the Boy Scout honor code, and we all laugh. I smirk to myself, wondering if Skylar misses her grandmother after all.

Jenna, Queen of the Beach,

What's up? I'm just checking in. I just got to work, a little late as usual. ☹ But it doesn't matter because tonight, I have a date with you know who, and Monday is going to be utterly fabulous. We have a book party for William Finneran at Bathhouse 7. It's a velvet rope, ohmigosh-it's-Matt-Damon kind of place. I can't wait!!! And Bennett's escorting me. I'm telling you, he is eye candy. (That's what the girls say here. Funny, no?)

When are you coming out here? I want you to see him, and I'm settled in now. I'd know where to go. And you could meet all my new friends and we could go shopping and check out the fall lines—I'll bet you haven't gone once since I left you to your own wiles. It will be good for you! Let me know what your schedule looks like.

Bisous (Bennett says this mean kisses in French, but I'm not telling you how that came up in conversation!)

Miss Emily E. Hinton

Bennett and I must leave at the same time on Friday, because I run into him in the lobby of our building after work. Skylar, Regina, and Helen, who are outside the revolving door smoking, stare at us through the glass front of the building as we talk. I smile at them, and they wave back, jaws open in shock. I fight hard to suppress the feeling of exultation that overtakes me at the joy of their recognition that I, Emily E. Hinton, am going on a date with Bennett. Bennett nods at them congenially, then takes my hand.

"So I'll see you there at eight?" he asks.

"Perfect," I say. He smiles, kisses me on the cheek, and heads out the revolving door. I watch him leave. Perfect. I shake my head in amazement. I walk outside to join the girls. When I walk up, Sklyar puts out her cigarette and mumbles a quick good-bye.

———

"Britt?" I call through the empty living room. I hear no response and shrug. "I'm out. See you tomorrow morning."

Brittany wanders in. She has a lavender mask all over her face, and her curly hair is tied on top of her head in the biggest knot I've even seen. She is getting ready for her Friday night too, which will begin at ten instead of eight like mine.

"Where you going?"

"I have a date with that boy I mentioned. Bennett?"

"Is he cute?" she asks, as though I have just offered him to her.

"I like to think so."

She nods. "By the way, a pair of my underwear is missing." She stares at me hard. "You seen it?"

I laugh awkwardly. "Uh . . . no."

"Are you sure? It's the black lace set with the little Gypsy rose embroidered on the front. I know it's missing because I only wear sets, and I still have the bra."

Brittany gets all of her expensive Italian lace underwear sets dry-cleaned. I found this out during one of our bill-paying sessions. She doesn't like paying "boring" bills (rent, electric, gas, cable) but doesn't mind the "necessary" ones like dry-cleaning her underwear or going to the spa for her monthly glycolic skin peel. What that girl does with $90,000 a year is amazing.

"Nope. But I'll keep an eye out."

"I'm just saying that if you took them but then gave them back to me, I wouldn't be mad."

I stop dead in my tracks. "What?"

"I don't know. I just want you to know that what's important is my getting them back. Not what happened to them."

"Britt, I'm not sure what you're saying here, but if I'm guessing correctly then, no, I did not steal your underwear." Just saying this out loud makes me laugh. Is she insane?

"Oh. Okay. Just checking. You can always come to me, Emily."

"Sure. Will do. All lacy larceny confessions come straight to you. Thanks, Britt." Doesn't she realize that no normal person steals underwear, let alone steals underwear that is three sizes too small for them? Oh man.

I drag a bag of dirty laundry out the front door of the building. All that talk of missing underwear makes me remember that I need to drop mine off for wash-and-fold and be at the theater by eight.

I wait on the light and then haul my giant bag of laundry across the street to Happy Clean Suds. I push open the door and greet Wi, the Vietnamese owner with a penchant for a punchy joke.

"Hello! Hello!" he says as I walk in. "Hello! Hello!"

"Hi, Wi," I say from behind the huge bag.

"Oooh. Strong woman." He takes the bag. He's still working on his English, but his humor shows through already. I laugh.

He weighs the bag—twenty pounds!—and then hands me my ticket. We chat for a little while about the neighborhood (very safe, very good) and about his family in Vietnam. His wife comes out from the back, where she does the alterations, and joins in shyly. They both wear bright, gaudy gold crosses around their necks, inlaid with jade and diamonds. I ask if they are Christians.

"Yes. We are Christian. Jesus." Wi gives Jesus a thumbs-up and smiles broadly. He uses his open palm to motion at me.

"Huh? Oh me? Yes. Me too." They smile at me with approval. I wonder if I get a discount on my laundry now. At first having someone else do my laundry for me felt a little decadent, but when I first moved in, I passed a boy in my building when I was carrying a container of powdered detergent, and he gave me a funny look. He said that *no one* did their own laundry because Wi would do it for you for a just few dollars more than it would cost you to do it yourself. And he was right. I caved in.

"I should go. Thank you for my laundry," I say. Wi chases me out.

"Face much better this time. Face much better."

I stop and look at Wi and his wife. His wife nods. My face is better? I touch my cheek. He continues to explain, seeing that I'm confused.

"Last time. The rain. Your hair . . ." He makes a spinning motion with his hand over his head. I remember suddenly. The last time I brought my laundry in it was raining, and my hair was wild so I had pulled it into a pathetic knot sticking up on the top of my head. Today it is blown straight and long for my date.

"Right. My hair is down. Thank you."

He smiles, glad that I understand his compliment. "Much better. Bye-bye."

We agreed to meet at the Colony, a tiny art house theater below Houston. Bennett said he had been dying to see this movie called *The Fort,* which was getting rave reviews for its bold use of color as an element of cinematography. There are only two characters, and they didn't say very much, so most of the movie was silent, and focuses on their struggle to build a fort in one of their backyards. I didn't think it was all that great—it actually would have been kind of boring, except that Bennett was holding my hand throughout the movie, so I wanted it never to end. My stomach had flipped when he took my hand during the previews.

"So what did you think?" I ask him as we exit the theater, navigating our way through the darkened room, past people dabbing at their eyes with tissues.

"Let's wait until we get to the restaurant," he says thoughtfully. "I need time to digest it." Digest it. Right.

He doesn't try to make other conversation, so I assume he wants to digest in silence, but he still skillfully manages to lead me to an unmarked Italian restaurant in Little Italy where all the waiters seem to know him.

When we are settled at the table and have both ordered pasta and a glass of wine, he finally announces, "I thought that was brilliant. A moving discourse on the diaspora of the human soul. Possibly the best attempt that I've seen from the film community in at least five years."

"Why do you say that?" I ask, cocking my head, hoping he thinks I am very interested, not just trying desperately to figure out what he said.

"It was clearly an examination of the struggle to recapture the innocence of mere primitive survival, right?" Of course. I nod. "And what time in a person's life better encapsulates that than childhood?" I hope I look convincingly interested. "So these modern kids, in their modern piece of subdivision, their own little parcel of urban sprawl, are clearly trying to go back to the essence of what it means to be human." Naturally. "But they can't, you see? They can't agree on anything. They fight over which tools to use. They redo each other's work when the other one isn't looking. Their friendship dissolves over an argument about how to design the ridiculous tree house. It's *Paradise Lost*, it's *Lord of the Flies*. It's a testament to the inability of the human spirit to reconcile itself with its own being. Don't you think?"

"Yes," I begin, trying to buy myself time to think of something to say. I didn't really pay attention to the movie, since I was too distracted by the feel of Bennett's arm resting against mine, but I remembered there was supposed to be something about color. "But I really thought the use of color was great."

He pauses, looks at me, frowns, and then launches into a critique of the film's palette. That element is, he declares, over-rated. "The bleak vision of the human soul necessitates a muted color scheme. The conflation of disparate iconographies just doesn't work," he says. I nod earnestly, chastened.

"You know he's a Christian, right?" he asks.

"Who?"

"Hector Vigo." I must look as confused as I feel.

"The director?"

"Oh. Right. Of course. No, I didn't realize that."

He nods. "I read it in a little independent film magazine." He looks at me like I am supposed to say something.

"That adds another dimension to the whole thing," I try. He stares at me like I'm a fool. We both sit silently for a moment.

"I'm sorry, Em. I took a lot of film in college. Almost got a minor in it. I guess I'm kind of film snob." He smiles. He doesn't seem too sorry.

He talks for most of the meal about the movie, and I listen, duly impressed by both his knowledge of cinema and his analytical skills. I will never be able to talk about a movie like that. I usually only focus on whether the stars are cute or not. Maybe whether I like their clothes.

I keep asking him questions, trying to drag out the meal so we don't have to say goodbye, but he seems to be trying to hurry things up. When the waiter offers him the dessert menu, he waves it away and makes some mention of some Grand Marnier his friend brought back for him from France. He gives the waiter his credit card before the check comes and asks him to charge it. My mind is desperately searching for something I can do to make him stay with me longer. Suggest an evening stroll? Yes. That will mean I can snuggle into his side with his arm around my waist.

We leave our table and end up staring at each other on the sidewalk outside the restaurant. I am cold so he rubs his big hands up and down my arms. He leans in to me. Is this going to be another standing-by-the-side-of-the-street kiss? I think about suggesting the walk but instead of kissing my mouth, he brushes his lips against the skin of my neck. He then puts his lips so close to my ear that I can hear him breathing. "Do you want to come back to my place for a drink?" he whispers.

My mind is racing. Yes. No. A drink? I can do that. Will he want more than that? That doesn't seem like Bennett, but then he is pressing his hand into my back firmly, and he is kissing my neck deeply. "I'd better not." I pull away slowly. What? Why did I say that! What happened to yes?

He looks at me, then leans in again to kiss my lips. "Are you sure?"

"Yeah. I have to get up early tomorrow." I don't, but I want to cover my tracks so that he doesn't think I'm afraid of coming over. What do I have to worry about? He's a Christian too.

"Okay," he says against my lips. "Maybe next time."

"Yes, next time," I say energetically. I look into his eyes, then turn. "I have to go."

"I'll call you," he says, following me with his eyes as I walk to the corner to hail a cab.

CHAPTER 7

stewed

★

The *sound of* a train rushing through the station startles me from my reverie. I stop lollygagging around, produce my Metrocard, swipe through the turnstile, and run down the stairs to reach the platform. No time for daydreaming. I am already running behind, and I don't want to have to wait for the next subway train to come through. I make it onto the train just before the doors close behind me. Running in heels is something I never thought I'd have to do, let alone get used to, but I seem to be doing it just about every day now.

Resting against the closed subway doors, I smile. Bennett is going to meet me at the big book party tonight—he is, for the first time ever, showing up in front of my friends as my date. I have invited him to join us girls for lunch, but every time he insists that he doesn't want to get the office gossip chain started and thinks it's best to keep our activities away from work.

This party, celebrating Finneran's latest release, has been the talk of the office for weeks. The point, the girls tell me, is to wine and dine the media, who will then, hopefully, get excited about the book and start talking about it to their contacts and have it reviewed from coast to coast. Lane says book parties are not to be missed. Between the swanky locale, the free food and drinks, and the chance to schmooze with the top editors, everyone is powerless against its pull. Plus, I have the added incentive of showing off who I will have on my arm.

The other girls have been paying me more attention since they realized I've been hanging out with Bennett, and Skylar even invited me to a party she's throwing with some college friends this weekend. I am poised at a crucial moment—I have been accepted as a part of the new office culture and have also actually made some friends. Plus, Xavier is really starting to warm up to me. I overheard him tell Skylar's boss, Cynthia, that he thinks I am smart. I no longer feel like the girls' nagging little sister, dressing up like them and trying to be them. And I recognize that it is my association with Bennett that has put me on their level. I have never been cool before, but this is what I moved to New York to be. To make a whole new me. And tonight is my night, I decide, to make it really happen. This is my chance to break past this apex and show them that Emily Hinton is a very savvy and world-weary New York singleton.

Clutching the paper with my scribbled directions tightly, I scan the long block. Where is Bathhouse? The street is empty except for a man huddled by the subway vent. This seems like an inauspicious place for panhandlers, but I throw a dollar into the empty hat he has placed in front of him anyway. "Oh, thank you, thank you," he says, looking up at me. He smells kind of funny, and I start to walk away. "Don't go," he calls after me. "I'm an astrology expert. Let me tell you your horoscope."

I stop and turn back. "No thanks," I reply. "I can't take the bad news."

"Oh! I never tell bad news."

What kind of a policy is that?! "Naw," I say.

"I'll just take a peek at your palm. To repay your kindness."

He's getting a little pushy. I clear my throat and try to be firm. "No thanks."

"You sure? No bad news, I promise." He then begins to stand up, lurching a little unsteadily.

Without thinking it through, I tear out of there. My feet are a blur below me. I can hear him calling after me, "I could help you! Why are you running?" But I just keep going.

I slow down after I'm out of earshot and have to laugh at myself as I turn back and see that he has happily settled back down on the sidewalk. I keep walking, looking for Bathhouse, and as my breath slows, a shiver runs through me. The weather is already cooling off for the onset of fall. I slip on my sweater and look down the dark narrow street. All I see is old abandoned warehouses, but I walk resolutely on. "Seven forty, seven forty," I mutter and then spot a small pink light shining onto a littered square of sidewalk. I walk to the door with 740 written above it in small plain numerals. This can't be right. I push open the door, a long piece of smudged glass with a metal bar in the center for a handle, and walk unsurely down a pink hallway. I can hear a vague party sound coming from somewhere.

"Emily!" comes a voice through on open doorway on my right. I poke my head in and see Regina and Skylar sitting on a long low lounge against the wall near the door. I sweep the dark room with my eyes for Bennett but don't see him. Not here yet.

"I'm glad you made it!" Skylar gushes. "Where's Bennett?"

"He's meeting me here." My, my. Aren't we anxious? "How are you guys?" I give both of them a kiss on the cheek—I've picked that up—and sit down, looking around.

I will never cease to be amazed by the décor of New York bars. This one has a cabana theme, and the walls are papered with pictures of a pool and deck chairs with straw bungalows in the background. There are potted palm trees scattered through the room, stationed by every group of couches, and the waiters (all of them really attractive, I note) are dressed in white shorts and polo shirts, white towels draped over their arms. And the best part of the venue is on display behind the long sandalwood bar. Swimming in a *giant* saltwater fish tank that contains tropical fish, coral, and a luminescent green menagerie of seaweed are two real live women in Pucci bikinis and scuba gear. I stare at them for a moment and then sink back into the comfortable lounge. It is amazing how cool and calm—almost as if we really are on vacation or in a fairy world of Swim Angels—it feels in here, especially considering what's just outside the front door.

"The margaritas are free, so grab the waiter next time he comes by and get one," Regina says, taking a sip of hers.

"I thought you weren't drinking anymore?" I say to Skylar.

"I changed my mind." She shrugs.

We chat for a while, and Reggie brainstorms what she'll serve at her upcoming Halloween party. She's planning on getting her friend Mario who does set design to convert her squat little Brooklyn apartment into a horror house of sorts.

"Let's put it this way, I'm making a serious investment in dry ice and have been shopping for fake blood in bulk on the Internet," she says.

I laugh. If I know Reggie, this is going to be a party to remember. So far, she's changed her costume idea ten times. I guess Halloween is every aspiring actress's favorite time of the year. At the moment, she's thinking of being the Bride of Frankenstein, "only like sexy not scary."

Skylar seems distracted by all of this and keeps studying the people in the room. Reggie notices and puts her arms straight out in front of herself to act like a mummy coming to eat Skylar's brain, but Skylar just gives a half-chuckle and starts talking.

"So here's the Who's Who, ladies," she says.

We both perk up. I figured there must some famous people in the room, but I'm miserable at figuring this stuff out. Skylar glances around the room and then moves to sit in front of me and Reggie with her back to the rest of the room.

"I don't want to point. Look through me," she commands. At that she points at her own chest with her index finger. I get confused but then realize that if I follow where she points with her finger through her own, now "invisible," body, she's pointing at a handsome forty-something man without his knowing it. I giggle, and she continues. "That guy in the blue shirt is the style editor at the *New York Times*," she says, turning to catch a glimpse of him and then turning back to us to confide. "He dictates what's in and out in New York, well, in the whole country really." She shakes her head in awe. "The one next to him is the entertainment editor at *New York* magazine, and the guy next to him heads up the *New York Review of Books*." I nod, assessing them. "Sadly, they're all married, but they're worth knowing anyway," she says. We are all silent, trying to look casual and inconspicuous as we stare at them. "And *that*," she says, nodding to a tall, attractive man in the corner, "is Sean Penn."

"What? Really?" I ask, at what I come to realize is too loud a voice by the shushing noise Skylar makes. She nods. "Wow," I say more quietly.

"He's a friend of William's, sorry, 'Liam's.' Sean's a big fan of his work. They say he's one of the smartest actors in Hollywood. At least the most well read," she says definitively. I keep looking around, hoping to spot some more famous people. Across the room I see Xavier talking with a man I recognize from his author photo as William Finneran himself. Helen hovers near them with three women I don't recognize, all four of them casting glances at the two men periodically.

I lift a margarita from the tray a waiter swings in front of me. It's cool and delicious, almost like a Slurpee, only less artificial and sickeningly sweet, and with a hint of something slightly warm, and I practically gulp it down, smiling broadly. The waiter makes sure we are all taken care of, then throws a smile at me that makes me dizzy. He's gorgeous.

"What's up with the waitstaff?" I ask.

Reggie laughs. "You mean, Why are they so hot?"

"Out-of-work actors and models. I think I recognize one from *Vogue*," Skylar says.

"No wonder." I whisper as a tall, tanned man with a shock of dark hair passes me.

"This needs to be the year I finally get my union card. I really want to stop talking about acting and just do it. I mean, look at the benefits," Reggie moans and then faints like Scarlett O'Hara. I take a long pull on my margarita and realize I've already sucked most of it down. Skylar notices too.

"Emily, you're joining us then tonight?" Skylar lifts her margarita and clinks it to my glass.

I cringe inwardly, remembering my first experience in a bar with these girls, but I am somehow extremely pleased by her recognition that I do drink from time to time. I kick myself for enjoying her praise, realizing that I shouldn't care what she thinks and knowing that there is a thinly veiled criticism buried beneath her approval. I promise myself that this is the only drink I'll have tonight—free or not. I've heard these parties can get out of control, and I don't want any part of that. I hear someone come in the doorway and look up quickly, hoping it's Bennett.

Lane appears, flustered, and she tells us all about her awful cab ride here. The cabbie couldn't find the Brooklyn-Queens Expressway for thirty minutes, and once they got into Manhattan, he stopped to get a slice of pizza and left the meter running. She finally ended up jumping out of the cab at a stoplight, leaving him half the fare in bills scattered on the backseat, slamming the door, and ducking into a bodega just to escape. She walked the remaining ten blocks, comforting herself with the cigarettes she bought. I place my empty glass on a passing tray, smile at the adorable waiter. Lane grabs two drinks and hands one to me. I stare at it. I see her smiling at me, and reluctantly take a sip. I'll just be very careful with this one. Nurse it.

She looks around, letting out a low whistle. "Nice place," she says, and then, turning to me, "Where's Bennett?"

"He should be here soon," I say, glancing at my watch and then at the door, realizing that it's becoming a tick. What's keeping him? I take another sip of my drink. I can't believe these little devils are free. They're delicious. Unfortunately, I am beginning to feel the alcohol and decide after this sip I'll put it down for a while. I hear a rustle at the doorway. Not him. I take another sip.

Bennett finally arrives, calmly striding through the door, spotting us immediately. He gives each of the girls a hug—why does Skylar hold him so tightly?—gives me a peck on the cheek, and then sits down right next to me.

Xavier soon walks over, and we all stand as he introduces us to *Liam*. He tries to go around the circle of assistants but accidentally identifies Skylar as the assistant to Barry Medina and not Cynthia Lederer (I'm genuinely surprised she doesn't correct him or make a snotty remark) and stumbles over Lane's name altogether, calling her "Leigh, I mean, Laurie, I mean . . ." until she sweetly offers William her real name. Xavier gets Regina right, and then it's my turn. Lucky for Xavi *and* me, he gets my name correct and positively identifies me as his "girl wonder." I breathe a sigh of relief.

"I've heard a lot about you," William says, grasping my hand between his two palms.

Ohmigosh, William Finneran! Sure, I've talked to him on the phone and faxed him reviews, but I've never actually met him.

"None of it's true," I say, laughing nervously. He's a little shorter than I thought.

"All lies," Xavier agrees, beaming at me. Then, I swear, unless my eyes are tricking me, he notices Bennett's hand on my waist. He winks at Bennett, smiling broadly. "Bennie! I'm so glad you made it out too." He introduces him to William as "a real hell-on-wheels at work."

I have a feeing I'm going to get teased about this tomorrow. The weird thing is, I realize that if I do, it will only be a good thing. Poor Lane. None of "the big bosses" can ever remember her name. I worry about her shy demeanor and future at Morrow & Sons.

Xavier and William sit down with us at Bennett's suggestion, and out of the corner of my eye I see Helen roll her eyes. Bennett calls a waiter over and gets everyone a fresh round of drinks. I take one in my hand, and we all toast, To William! while he blushes.

Xavi announces what a coup it is that he has stolen me away from the sandy beaches of California, and William begins to ask me about my home state. I tell him about San Diego (I don't mention that's not actually where I'm from) and he seems impressed. In fact, the whole group seems to be focused on me, listening to me, and for the first time since I moved here my tongue is deftly moving from one clever story to the next without fear. I even take sips of my cocktail as I monopolize the floor, never spilling once. I entertain them with my story about Wi saying my face looks "much better," and they all howl with laughter. And soon a darling waiter comes over with *another* full tray of drinks.

"I bet these margaritas remind you of home," Xavier says, grabbing and distributing a handful of drinks. I take another and place it in front of me. I'm still not quite done with the last one. How is everyone else knocking these back without being affected at all? "I hear the Mexican border is a joke, and the tequila is cheap on the other side." He pronounces it *Me-hi-can,* moving his eyebrows up and down quickly like an old-timey movie villain, and everyone laughs. Even though I have only ever gone to Mexico once and that was for a mission trip, I try to be funny and impart a native's knowledge about life near the border.

"Yep, where I'm from the liquor is cheap and the women are easy. Or so I hear," I say, winking at Bennett. When did I become so bold? I decide it doesn't matter, since the whole table laughs, and Bennett tightens his grip on my waist.

"Where I'm from, they make vodka out of potatoes," Skylar says, expertly turning the group's attention away from me and onto her. We all look at her, confused.

"Where do you come from?" William asks. The land of make-believe? Mars?

"Idaho," she says, flirting with him. "It's true. They ferment the potatoes and make a kind of potato vodka. It's great. We make everything out of potatoes in Idaho."

"Like what?" Bennett asks, laughing. I pray she says French fries.

"Oh, I don't know. Compost." She thinks. "Energy." She takes a sip of her drink. "I don't know. Maybe houses." She shrugs. "Fish." We all try to hold back our laughter. William coughs uncomfortably.

A tall blonde woman comes through the door and, seeing Xavier, rushes over and gives him a kiss on his cheek. I look around the table and most people are smirking, and Skylar is shaking her head a little. Xavier smiles at the blonde woman, gestures broadly to the group, and announces, "This is Beatrice." Then, putting his arm around her shoulders, he walks her to the back of the room. Beatrice. None other. I'm boiling with anger. Surely she knows about Laura, his wife! How could he do a thing like this? And why does nobody care? Man, does this place need God.

"That Xavier," William says, shaking his head as he stands up. "His poor religious mother is probably turning in her grave."

"Is his family religious?" Bennett asks, cocking his head.

"They sure used to be, as far as I understand," William laughs. "But then they all learned how to read, and a whole new world was opened up. That was the death of God in the Weir family. They no longer needed him, and so they killed him off."

"And none too soon," Skylar announces, completely missing William's Nietzsche reference. "It's about time intelligence wins out." She smiles at him. I smirk inwardly. How ironic that she's so concerned about the plight of intelligence. And really funny too. I start laughing uncontrollably and double over. Luckily for her, I have lost control of my mouth, and the idea of using it to say something in defense of religion seems like too much work. I sit back up and try to calm down.

Bennett, however, comes through. "Speaking of intelligence, what do you think of Barry Medina's new assistant?" he asks.

"Oh! You must mean me?" Skylar says. We all laugh and explain to William about Xavi's introductions gaffe.

"The real one," Bennett says. Skylar rolls her eyes.

I sit there and concentrate really hard. Try as I might, I can't seem to call up who the new assistant is. I can't even remember if it's a he or a she.

"Dumb as a doorknob," Skylar announces. This sets me off laughing uncontrollably again. Pot calling the kettle black, I think, and laugh some more. I take another sip of my margarita and sit back. I notice William is looking around the party. I also notice that Skylar has maneuvered to sit very close to Bennett, as if to hear him over the crowd, but it's not *that* loud in here.

"Sharp as a loaf of bread," William says, standing up. "That's what we said at our house. Listen, it was great to meet you all." He holds out his arm in a halfhearted wave, then heads over to the group of magazine editors in the corner.

I am vaguely aware, as he leaves, that I blew my chance to get to know him, but I am too busy looking at the colored lights over the bar to really care. For some reason, I can't tear my eyes away from them.

"Who wants another drink?" Lane asks, standing up. "I'll go get some more from the bar." Everyone at the table raises their hand, but I can't seem to make my arm move, so I instead tell her, "I do." Only, I realize, embarrassed, it sounds more like "ice stew." She laughs at me, then walks toward the bar. Bennett puts his hand on my knee, looks at me, and begins to caress my leg, running his hand up and down my thigh. I lean against him and put my head on his shoulder and, seeing Skylar tense up, smile.

Regina nods toward Helen's little group, then leans in to tell us a rumor about one of the other girls, who is, according to Reggie, dating a movie star. She hiccups in the middle of her story, and I laugh until she shoots a wounded look at me. I shush and sit up straight.

It occurs to me that I am a little tipsy, so when Lane comes back with the drinks, I don't take a new one but try to work slowly on the one I've still got. They all seem kind of tipsy, except for Bennett, who is cool and calm as ever. He is not out to impress his coworkers, I remind myself, so he doesn't have to do what they're doing to fit in.

They all keep talking, and though I am genuinely interested in what people are saying, I am having a really hard time following what's going on. I concentrate, instead, on my stomach, which has suddenly started to hurt. It almost feels like I have the flu, but I know I didn't a few minutes ago, so I sit still and try to focus. Listening so intently is giving me a headache, though. Maybe I *am* sick, I start to think, and decide that's what it is as I begin to break out in a cold sweat. I hold on tight to Bennett's arm, leaning my head against his shoulder. This feels better. I just need to rest for a minute.

"Are you okay, Emily?" Lane asks. "You look pale as a ghost all of a sudden."

"I'm fine," I answer weakly, burying my face in Bennett's shirt. I am not so sure I am. This is the most sudden onset of the flu I have ever had.

Lane gets up immediately, grabs my hand, and, pulling me up, leads me to the back of the room. We go down a dark hallway, where there are five doors. Each, I realize, a unisex bathroom stall. There is a line of people waiting, but Lane walks directly to the front, smiles apologetically to the line, whispers something, and leads me straight into one of the stalls that has just been vacated.

"Ooh, it's pretty," I say, looking at the mirrored walls. The endless series of reflections created by the facing mirrors intrigues me but makes my stomach lurch. "There are a lot of me in here," I mutter, as Lane closes the door behind us and leans me over to the toilet. "I don't know why we just had to cut in front of all of those people," I say, my voice going up several pitches. "I don't even have to go to the bathroom or anything. I'm really fi—" Vomit pours out of my mouth as Lane positions me over the porcelain bowl. Spitting at the water after the first wave has passed, I shake my head. Where did this come from? I think I must be done, but as I start to straighten up, I feel another wave start to come up. I lean back over, gagging, as Lane holds my hair back. I stay leaned over this time, and wait for the end.

I feel sorry for the people waiting in line since this seems to be taking a long time. Tears fill my eyes, and though I tell myself that's just something that happens when you throw up, I know they really spring from a mixture of self-loathing and self-pity.

I am drunk. I know this now. I am drunk and everyone knows it, and I am one of those out-of-control drunk girls who throws up in the bathroom. I don't want to move, can't quite fathom going back out there to face the girls and Bennett like this. Lane hands me a tissue, and I realize there is snot all over my face. I wipe it, numbly, though it doesn't really feel like I am touching my own skin. "Thank you," I finally manage to say, and she just nods, putting her arm around me and leading me to the door.

When I wake up the next morning, the first thing I feel is a deep ache in my stomach and a pounding in my head. The next is the burning warmth of shame, and I immediately try to go back to sleep. But finally I feel the ice-rush of fright, as I realize it is Tuesday, and I need to be at work in half an hour. I try to get up, but as soon as I move, my stomach lurches, and I have to rest. I sit still. A few minutes later, when I have gathered my strength, I try it again. I notice a large purple bruise on my left thigh, and I realize I have no idea how it got there. I vaguely remember having a really hard time walking in a straight line last night, and have an image in my head of getting a cab, almost as if I witnessed it instead of experiencing it. I am pretty sure I remember Bennett unlocking my door for me. I look around. He's not here, so he must have brought me home and then left. I thank God that he's a Christian as I realize in horror that anything could have happened to me in the state I was in last night, and I would have been powerless to stop it. I almost smile at how wonderful he is.

I make it as far as the bathroom door before stopping to lie down on the cold floor. It feels good to relax and be still for a moment. Enjoying the floor this much, I know I can't make it to work today, so I drag myself to the phone, dial Xavier's number, and curse to myself when he answers, quickly wondering where the voice in my head acquired such language. I had been hoping he wouldn't be in yet so that I could leave him a pathetic voice-mail message.

"This is Xavier," he says cheerfully.

"Xavier, this is Emily," I say, trying to sound like I have the bubonic plague or whooping cough. "Listen, I'm not feeling good today. I think I've got one of those twenty-four-hour bug things that are going around. Would it be okay if I took a sick day?"

"Emily," he says, sounding heartbreakingly like my father, "I knew you wouldn't be in today. Rest up, and feel better. We'll see you back tomorrow."

"Thanks," I say, quickly hanging up before he can hear me start to cry. He is so nice to me, and it is so undeserved. He knows I'm just hung over because I was drunk out of my mind last night. I am overcome with embarrassment as I realize that the whole office knows. Will I be fired? Crawling back to my bed, I bawl. I have let everyone down, and I will surely return tomorrow only to find a bright pink slip of paper on my keyboard. Will anyone ever take me seriously again? Can I ever tell them I'm Christian? They'll probably laugh uncontrollably. Then I tell myself it won't matter anyway, that my real problem will come this weekend when I will have to call my poor parents and tell them I'm coming back home because I failed. That I couldn't hack it in New York.

The worst is the disappointment I have in myself. Last night was supposed to be my big night, and I blew it. I know, deep down, that everyone will forgive me, but right now I'm just not sure I can forgive myself.

CHAPTER 8

playing dress-up

★

I *take a* deep breath and plaster a wide grin across my face, but if anyone in the lobby really scrutinizes me, they'll see the bright flush in my cheeks and my tail between my legs. I ride the elevator, devotedly applying my eyes to the floor, and slip off on our floor. Earlier that morning I had thought about calling in sick again, so it would look like I really had come down with something and actually needed to rest, but I couldn't do it. Better, I decided, to face the music. Luckily, Xavier is already yelling at someone on the phone when I get to my cubicle and sit down, so he doesn't have a chance to say anything to indicate he even remembers I have been missing. I am dreading facing the other girls at lunch, but I have already decided on my strategy for avoiding complete mortification.

Predictably, Skylar is the first to say something when I sit down at our table at lunch. "How're you feeling?" she asks, laughing. Coming from Lane, this question would have seemed extremely kind and caring, but Skylar is making it clear that they all knew how bad I felt yesterday and why.

"Oh man, was I trashed," I laugh, shaking my head. "I was so sick I got up three times to puke in the middle of the night. I haven't been sick like that in a long time." Or, uh, never. I smile, letting them believe that I am quite proud of my actions. I know this strategy has worked in frat houses for decades.

"Yeah, that sucks," Lane says. "One time, I got so drunk I was taken to the hospital for alcohol poisoning. That was the worst." She laughs, obviously a little proud of her bout of debauchery.

"When I was Lady Guinevere in college I drank a six-pack and two lemon drop shots and kissed Lancelot and *then* King Arthur at an unofficial cast party," says Reggie, crinkling her brow and looking up as she laughed. "One of them was my roommate's boyfriend." She shrugs and shakes her head, saying, not quite nostalgically, "Those were the days."

Skylar, not to be left out of the conversation she had started to make fun of me, announces, "One time I drank so much I passed out naked on the bathroom floor."

"Oh, gosh, Skylar, were you okay?" Reggie asks, laughing.

"Totally. It's really one of my best stories. I was on a college trip to Spain, and I had had so much sangria that I was singing a Beatles song at the top of my lungs on the streets of Madrid and trying to dance like a flamenco dancer." We laugh, which Skylar eats up and keeps going. "So my friends drug me back to our one-star motel and put me to bed. They said I was doing fine until I lurched out of bed and started walking around the room. They asked me what I was doing, and I just stared at them blankly. Then I went to the corner of one of the double beds and started to unbutton my jeans and pull them down. I thought I was in the bathroom. My best friend grabbed me just in time and put me in our bathroom. In the morning, they found me naked on the floor."

"Goodness," says Lane. "Did you, uh, make it?"

Skylar holds up both her hands as if being cheered by the masses and says, "I made it."

For once I am not angry that Skylar has trumped me. With her crazy story my little gaffe is immediately forgotten. I feel a little bad for allowing them to believe I think what I did was funny instead of mortifying, childish, irresponsible, disappointing, but at least the topic is buried. I promise myself to never repeat that mistake.

Bennett, always the gentleman, had called the day after the party to see how I was feeling, and he promised to take me out to dinner Friday night to "make sure I was feeling better and keeping up my health." The prospect of going out with Bennett is enough to make me feel fantastic.

Oh, to be a kid again, I think as I pass P.S. 31 on my walk from the subway to work. There are brown paper bags painted like jack-o'-lanterns and black-cat cutouts hanging in the windows. I even spy a fairy princess chasing a lion around the playground. Halloween was such an exciting time then—the fun of seeing your friends dressed up for school, the anticipation of traversing the neighborhood in search of the best treats, remembering to avoid the dentist's house because he gave out pencils instead of candy—and enjoying, for weeks afterward, a sugar-induced coma in which all was right with the world.

Some of my friends from church weren't allowed to go trick-or-treating and had to go to the Harvest Festival at church on October 31, but my parents tended to get caught up in things and loved to see us go all out for every holiday. My mom was, after all, a third-grade teacher, and observed the holiday seasons with such panache it could take your breath away. One year I wanted to be a princess on a flying carpet, and my dad actually built a wooden platform that he covered with carpet and hung from my shoulders so it rested around my waist. It looked like I was actually riding on a flying carpet. Another time, when Craig and Grant were really little, he made them Tweedledee and Tweedledum outfits from thick plastic rods and cheap fabric. My mom sewed *Dee* and *Dum* across the chests, but there were two straight weeks of fighting between them about who got to be "Dum" that ended with a parent-supervised game of one-potato, two-potato.

Though I was tempted to dress up for the office today because I rarely resist the seductive call of candy corn and hijinks, I decided that that would be decidedly unprofessional. Plus, I was convinced my credibility was already compromised by the margarita incident, and I wanted to keep a lower, quieter profile at work for the time being. But this morning as I slipped into my same-old chinos and a button-down shirt I just couldn't resist at the last moment sliding on a pair of orange socks with black cats that Mom had sent me in a Halloween care package. I had been a little embarrassed by them—if you press the cat they sing "The Monster Mash"—but no one would see them unless I pointed them out, and my Halloween spirit was just dying to escape from these business-casual pants.

I am glad I decided against the costume as I walk through the office to my desk. Except for a few bowls of candy on people's desks, no one here appears to have made any effort to make it feel like a holiday. Sighing, I switch on my computer and empty a bag of black and orange M&Ms into my candy dish. At least Xavier isn't here yet. I may have a few minutes of peace before the day really begins.

Jenna—

    I can't believe I'm coming home for Christmas in a few months! It feels like I just got here.

    Yes, I'm feeling much better. Thanks so much for your concern. I don't think it was the flu—I just needed to rest. My big worry now is not making myself sick on Halloween candy. Can you believe no one at my office dressed up? The corporate world is a scary place indeed. I bet you get to lead the kids in a costume parade today, huh? How's the new job at the day care going, anyway? Save me some graham crackers and apple juice!

How's Jacob doing? It's crazy that you ran into him after all these years. I'd love to talk with him. Did you get his e-mail address?

People are starting to get here, so I should try to act busy. Talk to you later.

Emily

I hear what sounds like music coming from behind me, and I turn around, then stop short, frozen. Darth Vader is coming down the hall toward me, stepping in time to the sounds of the Imperial March. Xavier—I know it has to be him, who else would dare?—is wearing a complete and convincing Darth Vader costume, from his authentic-looking helmet to the shiny black boots to his flashlight light saber. People all along the hallway, attracted by the music, which is coming from a child's pink Fisher Price tape player that he is carrying, are poking their heads out of their offices, some of them laughing hysterically, but the figure in black doesn't turn his head or slow his step. He walks directly to the door of his office, unlocks it, and strides inside.

I wait until a few minutes after I hear the music turn off, then poke my head into his office to say good morning and to hand him some papers to sign. I stand in the doorway cautiously. Xavier hasn't taken off the black helmet.

"I sense something," he declares in a perfect imitation of Darth Vader's voice. He must have a voice simulator under there somewhere. "A presence I've not felt since . . ." he trails off.

It's official. My boss is certifiably crazy.

"Good morning there, Darth Vader," I say, pushing the stack of paper across his desk. "Princess Leia reporting for duty. Can you drop your weapons for a second to sign these? I promise they don't come from any Jedi spies." I chuckle nervously, but I really want to burst out laughing.

"Impressive. Most impressive. Helen-Wan has taught you well," he says, lifting his hand to take them. Slowly, it dawns on me that he's speaking to me exclusively by quoting Darth Vader's lines. Nuts. But hilarious.

Grasping a pen is difficult with his giant black glove, but he is apparently going to try to do his job without coming out of character at all. It could be a long day, I think, then, watching him sign the papers without reading them, change my mind. He must not be able to see much out of that mask. It could be a good day after all.

"Oh, and the publisher's office called. They want you to give me a raise."

He says nothing, but begins to breathe heavily through his mask. I wish I could see his face to gauge his reaction. Have I gone too far?

"The force is strong with this one," he says, shaking his giant black head as he slowly lifts the *Times* off his desk and fumbles with the thin pages and his giant gloves.

It turns out Xavier is not the only one who has dressed up for the day. Skylar has shown up with little felt ears on a headband a tail pinned to her pants—she tells us she's "the office mouse, but a cute one, not like a gross rat or anything." And the copyeditor down the hall has dressed as Ned Flanders, and insists on yelling "hideleeho neighbor!" to everyone who walks by his office. For the most part, though, the day seems pretty normal, except for Xavier's occasional outbursts of Vader-speak. ("You don't know the power of the dark side!" I hear him yelling into the phone) and his insistence on playing the ridiculous music whenever he walks. And, like most days at the office, I am glad when it is over, though I have special reasons to want to run home today. I still have to assemble most of my costume for Reggie's Halloween party tonight. She finally decided what she was going to be a week ago and won't tell anyone. It's going to be good.

At five after five, I walk to Xavier's office to tell him I am leaving, but he is also on his way out the door and almost runs into me in the doorway of his office. He looks at me, doing the whole breathing thing again, then announces solemnly, "This will be a day long remembered." He pulls his door shut, nods, then walks past me down the hall. After he is out of earshot I do a low whistle. It sure will.

I wait a few minutes so I won't have to get in the same elevator as he does and try to make more conversation with the man in black, but then hurry home. I have a lot to do.

I am terrible at figuring out costumes. Hopelessly uncreative. Jenna was always so good at this kind of thing. One year she made herself into a gumball machine by putting balloons under a clear trash bag and tying it to her body, and another time she organized a large group of us to go as a pack of cards. The best costume I ever came up with was the year I tied a shoe to the top of my head, dressed entirely in pale pink, and went as gum on the bottom of a shoe, but that was only because I had stepped in gum earlier that day and it inspired me, if you can even call that inspiration. Oh well. What I have now will have to do.

I look at myself in the mirror—plaid pleated skirt, white button-down shirt, pigtails, white knee socks, and black patent leather Mary Janes, and glasses. I get a safety pin and pin my first-grade school picture of myself to my collar. I'm going as myself in first grade, and the rendering is perfect. I figure as long as my face insists on looking much younger than I am—I'm always the only one carded—I might as well take advantage of it. Plus,

I've always thought I hit my cuteness peak in first grade, anyway, and it's been downhill ever since.

I had briefly contemplated throwing together one of what I considered my "Old Faithful" costumes, both for their tried-and-true availability and for their other connotations, but I couldn't imagine what the girls would say if I showed up dressed like Joan of Arc or a nun. Besides, I already have all the pieces for a little girl in my wardrobe, and it seems nice and safe. I hate that a lot of girls use Halloween as an excuse to dress in skimpy outfits and put on sex-kitten personas they can't get away with in real life. I nod at my reflection, grab my jacket from the back of my desk chair, and walk into the living room. Glancing into the bathroom, I catch a glimpse of Brittany. She has dried and sprayed her hair into a giant pouf and is carefully twisting gold plastic snakes around sections of it.

"Uh, Medusa, right?" I venture. She turns to me, staring. For a second I almost believe her gaze will actually turn me into stone. "I like it," I continue. "You look great."

As I turn away she seems to finally understand that I am not making fun of her.

"Thanks. Have a good night," she yells, but I am already halfway out the door. I let it slam behind me.

I had thought the subway was crazy on normal nights, but tonight everyone is dressed up, in a good mood, and a little excited. As I am hurtling downtown on an express train, I see a man dressed as a ballerina admire Superman's bright blue tights. I see SpongeBob SquarePants trade candy with Gumby. And a vampire whistles at me as I walk up out of the subway stop by Reggie's apartment. I wave back.

The air aboveground is crisp and smells like burning candles. I take a deep breath. I love this time of year, particularly in New York where the weather is cool like it is in children's books. That was always the confusing thing about growing up in Southern

California, land of eternal summer. Where were the seasons from the Charlie Brown TV specials?

Reggie's door flies open seconds after I knock on it, and I am pulled into the chaos of her Halloween party. My eyes take a moment to adjust from the relative brightness of the well-lit hallway. Her apartment is dark, filled with a weird mist, and there is a track of scary noises playing. The first thing I can make out is a giant black spider, hanging above Reggie's head. The body is made out of shiny plastic, and it has eight streamer legs that stretch across the ceiling from corner to corner. There is a life-sized stuffed man in the corner with a plastic knife in his chest and fake blood on the front of his shirt. I laugh when I notice his T-shirt says *Death and Taxes*. She and Mario have really done an alarmingly good job at making this place creepy, but I do notice one minor error. Her glossy 8 x 10 headshot still hangs prominently on the wall. I smile. I'm sure she just couldn't bear to take it down. One of the governing principles of her life is an insane belief in luck. She always says you never know who'll be at a party or in the bathroom of a restaurant or seated next to you on the train. It could be your big break.

"Emily! You look so cute!" Reggie yells, pulling me into the room. "You're a naughty Catholic schoolgirl!"

"I am?" I look down and realize I sort of am by accident, and I blush. I try to correct my mistake. "No. Uh, I'm myself." I walk up to her and show her the picture I've pinned to my shirt. "See? I'm myself in first grade."

Regina looks me up and down. "Okay. But you do look pretty naughty!" I smile because I can see Reg thinks this is an awesome thing to be.

"Okay," I say. "Your turn."

Reggie's black hair is pulled into a tight bun on top of her head. She is dressed in a rich blue suit with little pockets on the front of the crop-cut jacket. She wears tights and two-inch-high power heels. They are tan with delicate blue flowers that twine around the straps. She has a briefcase and red lipstick on.

"I'll give you a hint," she says. She composes herself a moment to get into character. *"Muffins must get an appointment today!* She's simply a mess. Get Doggie Heaven on the phone right now."

My eyes get wide. I know that French bulldog's name. "You're Susanna Shriver! You're, you're—"

"The *Death Bun!*" she yells. She points at the bun on her head.

Her imitation of Lane's high-maintenance boss is hysterical. "You look perfect," I say.

Reggie pats her bun. "I even thought of putting a lot of white powder on my face but then thought, Oh well. I'm the black Death Bun! If this gets out at work, I'm so fired. *Capisce?*"

"Yes, Ms. Shriver!" I say.

"It's 'Yes, Ms. Death Bun' to you, you miserable little Regina, Lane, Emily, whoever you are!" We crack up together. Why do the editors struggle with our names so much? Reggie has really outdone herself. I hope Lane isn't feeling guilty that her boss is being parodied.

Beyond Reggie is quite a crowd of people, many of whom I don't recognize. I spot Bennett immediately, though, and I can't decide if that's because I'm hyper-aware of where he is whenever he is near or because he looks so stunning I can't help but look at him. He had told me he was coming as Socrates (*one of the greatest thinkers of all time!*), but he didn't tell me he would be baring half his chest in his toga. I had no idea he was so built. His chest looks perfectly statuesque, carved, smooth and hairless. I can't tear my eyes away. How could he possibly have a tan this time of year?

I walk toward him but am stopped on the way by Lane, who looks adorable dressed as a fairy. Her short hair is perfect for the part, and she is wearing purple tights and sparkly wings. She gives me a hug and asks if I think Reggie's Death Bun costume is going to get around work. I reassure her it won't and that even if it did, it's Reggie who will be in trouble. Everyone knows Lane doesn't talk behind Susanna's back, even though I doubt anyone would blame her if she did. Out of the corner of my eye, I see that Helen is coming toward us quickly. A little too quickly. Then I notice why—she is wearing roller skates and is out of control.

"Hey there, Lolita," Helen says, grabbing my shoulders, almost pulling me over to stop herself. "Where's Darthy . . . I mean Daddy?"

"Huh?" I ask.

"Where's Xavi? I thought you were in his coterie of girls?"

And then it hits me what she's implying. I'm tempted to tell her that my father is at home in California ruining the teeth of boys and girls in the neighborhood with the help of the Hershey's Corporation.

"I love the roller skates!" Lane says quickly. "What, um, exactly, do they mean?"

"I'm Hell on Wheels!" she announces, pointing to the devil horns on her head and the pointy red tail.

"Oh! That's very clever!" I say, really trying to be encouraging. All I can think, though, is how much sense her costume makes, and how much "Hell on Wheels" sounds like "Helen Wheels." Perfect. I smirk.

Satisfied with the compliment, she skates off to join a guy I recognize as Chris, the blond boy Bennett was eating with the first day in the cafeteria, the one who was laughing at me. I hate to admit it because he's Bennett's friend, but he's always rubbed me the wrong way. I didn't know he was close with Helen. He is dressed in baggy white jeans and a tight white T-shirt. His hair is cropped close, and *Slim Shady* is written on his shirt. I realize he is Eminem. My costume suddenly feels very lame.

Reggie swoops in and directs us to the kitchen to get drinks. Papa Smurf and Cleopatra are already there, and move so we can get to the bar. Reggie makes the first drink with half vodka and half orange juice and hands it to Lane. I sort of panic. I was thinking of refraining tonight. I don't like this drinking all the time that I'm getting into.

"Maybe I'll abstain tonight," I say.

Reggie looks at me, utterly perplexed. "I am the Death Bun! I command you to drink a delicious and refreshing cocktail!"

I laugh. "Uh, then, please only a splash of alcohol. I *am* underage, as you know." I tap my first-grade picture. She gives in and hands me a tall glass of orange juice with just a dash of vodka. I sip it very slowly and deliberately. I am going to be really careful tonight.

Drinks in hand, Lane and I go out of the kitchen back into the living room. I am still anxious to talk to Bennett and walk toward him—he smiles when he sees me coming—but a guy dressed like an extremely unattractive woman (possibly my Aunt Sharon?) gets in my way. His curly blond wig is cocked to the right, and I can see a small patch of dark hair peeking out from underneath. He is looking at my legs, leering. "Hey there," he says, placing his hand on my back and sliding his arm around my waist. "Wanna go out to the playground with me so we can earn ourselves a detention?" I try to shrug his arm off me, but he is pulling me closer. He is so gross. I look to Bennett, hoping he'll see my distress and come to my rescue. Unfortunately, Bennett is distracted.

A blonde girl in a very short, tight white dress is listening to his heart through a stethoscope. Of course it is Skylar, dressed as a sexy nurse. I tense up when I see how confidently she has placed her hand on his bare chest, pressing the listening piece against him firmly. Her other hand is on his opposite shoulder. She has carefully positioned herself so that if he looks down he'll get an eyeful of her cleavage. She is looking up at his face, laughing, and he is meeting her gaze, smiling. She leans in to him, as if she can't hear his heart and getting closer will help. I bet her stethoscope is a cheap fake anyway. Bennett keeps looking at her but slowly his gaze shifts, and he notices me across the room. What's that look in his eyes? He smiles at me, raises his eyebrows as he conspicuously lets his eyes travel over my body, and, gently pushing back from Skylar, waves me over.

I disentangle myself from Aunt Sharon and walk to him. Skylar has stepped back, but I position myself carefully between them and give him a kiss on the cheek.

"You look great!" he announces, putting his arm on my waist. That's much better. He bends down and whispers in my ear, "You must have been the teacher's pet." I shiver with delight.

Skylar smiles—is there a bit of a sneer there?—at me and says she likes my hair. I tell her the stethoscope is a nice touch, although inwardly I am seething. Doe she *have* to be so obvious about the fact that she's after my boyfriend?

I check myself. He's not, I remind myself, my boyfriend. Technically. We have never discussed our relationship, and though I keep hoping he'll want to talk about it, he hasn't ever brought it up, and I don't really feel like it's my place to do that. It is a little weird to have a relationship that is so nebulous, and to not know how to refer to him, but it doesn't seem to bother him, so I have decided not to let it bother me. He is, after all, holding me, and not anyone else, I think childishly, right now.

Though the incident with Skylar makes me a little nervous, I have to admit, Bennett stays by my side the rest of the night and kisses me at midnight—it's a Halloween tradition he just made up, he declares, but one he thinks should be perpetuated. I agree, feeling his body heat through his thin sheet.

The party goes late, but once the dancing starts to get scandalous I decide it's time to head home. We're both exhausted after a long day so we decide just to go our separate ways instead of out for coffee or dessert. Bennett walks me to the train. Standing outside the subway station, he kisses me, and I feel like I am really understanding what happiness is for the first time. He pulls back from the kiss and looks me hard in the face.

"I want you to know how blessed I feel. Whenever I pray now, I thank God for this girl that has come into my life."

I am flummoxed. He could not be more perfect. I feel myself really falling for him. What can ever harm us if God is for us? "Me too. I mean that. I never thought I'd find a guy who loved God and was cute and smart and kind." The words just run right out of my mouth.

He shakes his head and then squeezes my hand. "All those times I caved in and dated non-Christians I just never knew how happy I could be." He places both hands on my shoulders and kisses my forehead, slowly, tenderly. "Good night, Emily. Be safe."

I turn and go down a few stairs, then look back. All I see is a figure in white, walking, head down, against the black night. He looks so good. My stomach flutters, and I feel sad knowing that I will have to wait 364 days for another Halloween.

CHAPTER 9

impossible

★

"Emily?"

I'm sitting at the corner of a near-endless plank of wood, staring down at the collection of intimidating faces. Barry Medina, our editor in chief, is nodding at me from the head of the table, prompting me to go on and talk up. My throat goes dry and my voices putters out.

Even though it is intended to be instructional for us, Editorial Board is the bane of editorial assistant life. Sure it drags a little, but that's not why we hate it. In fact I find it very interesting as it invariably breaks down from its true purpose, a time for all of the editors to come together and discuss the projects they have and float new ideas to their peers, and becomes an ersatz gossip session where the editors unwittingly reveal their true opinions of famous authors, agents, and editors around town. But gossip aside, we assistants hate it because Ed Board is a shark soup for us. From what I can discern from listening to Xavier talk, in the old days of publishing, back when there were elbow patches on all the suit coats and tortoise-shell glasses abounded, editors spent a lot of time seeking out the next big authors on their own time. They went to readings in the Village, they read little magazines, they drank scotch at the round table at the Algonquin Hotel, and they injected themselves into the literati. But since the advent of the literary agent industry, editors mostly deal with the books they already have on their desks and review only books agents send in to them. Or should I say what the *good* agents send in.

Fact: The good agents don't send manuscripts to the editorial assistants.

To be an assistant is to fall in a dangerous netherworld between the editors and the agents. A world that every assistant wants to leave as soon as possible. This creates a weird unspoken competitiveness among the assistants. I never feel it from Lane or Reggie, but Skylar and Helen stink of ladder-climbing and rivalry. If I ever want to be promoted and plucked from the sea of faces that is the editorial assistant staff, I need to start coming up with my own ideas and presenting them coherently at Ed Board. The really tragic thing is, we can't all be promoted. There are about half as many slots at the next level, something we try never to discuss. I've known for a while that I must try to get my own books to edit. And since all the editors look longingly back to the old days when hot young editors were friends with the writers of tomorrow, and I certainly can't hold my breath for a manuscript to appear on my desk with a pleasant gold-embossed cover letter from an agent, there is nothing better that I can do for my career. But I have seen assistants torn to pieces in front of the board, and I am nervous.

"Uh . . . this idea . . ." I stop, clear my throat, and look down the boardroom table at all of the editors. I glance at Xavier; he is intent on unbending a paper clip to be a perfectly straight stick. "It's not like, uh, a literary idea, exactly." What am I doing?! I can present better than this. I lock eyes with Barry, who is looking bored. "But it would be a very salable idea, and if I'm correct, next year's spring list could really use a commercial book." At this Barry looks me in the eyes. He knows I'm right about the spring list. At the moment it is full of smaller, literary novels that won't hold their own without a more commercial book to balance out their sales.

"Has everyone heard of Hank Fleming?" All of the male editors look my way, and one of them smiles.

"Sure. The new guy on the Yankees."

"Right. Do you know his story? I think there's a book there." At this I stand up and pass out a sheet to everyone at the table, but I'm careful to keep talking so as not to lose my audience. "I wasn't aware of it until I started researching him. He's a twenty-eight-year-old pitcher and until winning the game last week had only had brief mentions in the news this year. He grew up with ten brothers and sisters in a one-room shack in the South and played in the farm leagues most of his life."

I hear the editors mumbling. It is clear that they don't know Hank's story. I happen to look at Helen, who is writing a note and passing it to Skylar. I avert my eyes quickly. I can't worry about that now.

"He is the eldest of the children, and when he was fifteen his parents died in a car crash. Hank convinced an uncle in town to legally adopt all of the children and allow him to care for all of his younger brothers and sisters so that they would not be split up. With a tenth-grade education and the help of the older siblings, he held them together. Now, as you can see from his stats in the past year, he is poised to become one of the strongest players the Yankees will have for the next couple of years. And he has an excellent platform. He speaks to children at New York schools about grief and the importance of family."

I see Barry nod, and even Xavier has put down his paper clip.

"But when I called his agent I learned the best tidbit of information yet. Next year, right when we'll be releasing our spring list, Hank will announce to the press that he is going back to school to finish high school. In partnership with New York public schools, he will be taking classes where his schedule allows. His agent says it's important to Hank that young people in New York know that baseball and school aren't mutually exclusive. So while he could get his GED, he's going to do it the old-fashioned way. I figured if we could get him to write his story and time the publication with his Back to School campaign, we'd have an anchor on the spring list."

I smile and sit down, exhausted but happy. I did it. And it felt really, really good. My reward? All around the table, the editors have swiveled in their Aeron chairs to look at me, sitting in the cluster of assistants hovering around one corner of the table. Some of them are jotting down little notes, some are smiling.

"Great, Emily," says Barry. "Great idea. I want you to follow up on that. Xavier, please help her get past the agent if necessary. Sometimes those damned agents think they hung the moon. Emily, if you need to, tell them I asked for you to call. I know Steinbrenner."

I lean back in my chair and tune out the gossip session that occurs about the Yankees and their controversial owner, whom Barry knows from his exclusive college. Lane nods at me and gives a thumbs-up under the table.

It's 6:00 p.m., and no one is left in the office. I forgot my cell with all of my phone numbers at home today (how did I become so dependent on it?), but I'm dying to call Matthew. I dial 411.

"City and state please."

"Manhattan, New York." I break into a broad smile. I still get a little giddy at those three words.

"What listing?"

"The Locus."

The operator gives me a number, and I dial it. A gruff voice picks up. "Hello? Locust."

"Matthew! Your plan worked!"

"What?" the gruff voice barks. "Wrong number." The phone slams down, and I jump. I call information again and get the right number this time.

"The Locus. This is Matthew."

"Uncle Matthew! I just tried to call you, but I got some weirdo."

"Oh, hey, Em. Yeah, that happens all the time. You got *Locust*. It's a New York hot spot. At least, that's what I read on the Internet."

He read it on the Internet? I resolve to get started making over my cool uncle right away. With the right look I could set him up with anyone in the company. Morrow & Sons is overflowing with women.

I tell him all about Ed Board and Hank Fleming. Matthew and I have been hanging out a lot, and I've become quite a regular down at the Locus. Last week as I was serving dinner with Matthew I told him about the difficulty of getting promoted at Morrow & Sons. The assistants call it the Impossible Dream. And I explained Ed Board. Matthew listened for a while—I believe this is what people love about him, he really listens—and then we brainstormed together a good book idea for me to bring up at Ed Board. He was the one who came up with Hank, obviously, since I don't even know if you win points or score touchdowns in baseball. Matthew knew Hank because he had come down to the Main Hall of the Locus and spoken to the community. Hank and Matthew had hung out after the engagement and really hit it off, talking about their different backgrounds. As it turns out, Hank is Catholic. The priest in his neighborhood, a tough old Vietnam vet, was Hank's father figure after his own father died. Matthew had nothing but high praise for Hank and assured me that at the very least he was a "regular guy."

"I'm so proud of you, Emily. We should celebrate, Champ. Let's get some dinner this week, my treat."

I want to repay the bottomless kindness of my uncle and see that this is my chance to coax him into shopping, the first part and very cornerstone of getting him updated. "How about lunch on Saturday instead? Didn't you say you needed to get a winter coat? We could get some lunch and then shop around. I'll help you pick one out."

"Really? Huh. I don't know. I was just going to pull one from the donation pile."

"I want to help. I love to shop. Let's try. No matter what, it will be fun to walk around and scout Christmas decorations. Some stores already have them up." I had developed a real gift for assisting even the most difficult of shoppers thanks to my mom and Jenna.

"But Thanksgiving's not until next weekend!"

"True. Of course if you're cool like my parents, your own brother, mind you, you can just leave the decorations up all year round!"

"Please tell me you're kidding. I thought I taught him better than that," he says.

"Em? You ready?" I turn around and spot Lane hovering in my cubicle. We had decided to go for margaritas at our favorite Mexican place around the corner.

"Sure. Hold on. I'll shut down my computer, and we'll go."

The bar is dimly lit, and we sit on tall stools instead of getting a table. We put our bags down to hold our seats and make a beeline for the free taco bar—the reason we always come to this place. Sometimes if we get too greedy with the free part of the free taco bar and eat four or five apiece, the owner has the bored busboys pack it up and put it away. I fix a huge plate of food. I learned quickly that what we get paid looks like a lot on paper, or in any other corner of the globe, but doesn't amount to that much in Manhattan. Now when I encounter free food, I eat my fill.

We settle on our bar stools and dig in. No one seems to be watching so I grab the little dish of complimentary tomatillo salsa, meant for the chips, and dump it over my plate of tacos. Just as I have arranged a giant bite and plunged it into my mouth, I hear an unfamiliar voice.

"Man, you girls are hungry!"

Lane and I turn around slowly and see a guy with overgelled hair. He flashes a huge grin at us. We both swallow our food and smile back. Here we go again. Men in Manhattan are so aggressive.

"Hi, I'm Chad."

"Emily," I say. I start planning our "get lost" strategy. Tell him we have foot fungus? Chew with my mouth open? Snort when I laugh?

"I'm Lane," she says. At that, Chad plops himself down on the empty stool next to Lane. Oh brother.

"Where you girls from?"

"Kansas," I say. Lane turns to me and giggles. "I'm kidding. I'm from Southern California."

"Like *The O.C.*?" he asks.

"Just like that. I drive a BMW, I'm best friends with Tara Reid, and I surf, like, every single day."

"Awesome," Chad says, nodding his head. "What about you?" he says to Lane.

"Southern girl, through and through."

"How about that accent, huh? Sexy!"

Lane and I exchange looks. "Where are you from?" I ask.

"I'm from here. Manhattan brat born and raised. Never left."

"Never?" I ask. Some New Yorkers are like this. They're so

convinced about how great the city is that they're terrified of leaving.

"Except for college. I went to Yale and then Ernst & Young made me an offer, so now I'm back to stay. Listen, girls. Bad things happen when you leave the city." He chuckles at his own joke.

I see my big chance. "My *boyfriend* went to Yale." There, now I'm safe. He won't hit on me anymore. I just need to help Lane out now. Should I make up a boyfriend for her too?

"What's his name? Maybe I know him," he asks.

I look at Chad doubtfully. I should think not. "Uh . . . Bennett."

"Benny? Benny boy?"

"No, no. Bennett Wyeth. He doesn't go by 'Benny.' " This guy is so ridiculous.

"Yeah, yeah. Bennett Edward Wyeth, the third. I totally know him. He's, like, a legend. Benny boy!" I wince at that nickname being said again.

"I can't believe you knew him," says Lane. "What a small world."

"We weren't best friends or anything, but I certainly went to his parties. Everyone did. I can't believe you're dating Benny. Benny has a girlfriend?!"

Lane and I nod. Okay, granted, Bennett and I aren't exactly using labels like that. A few weeks ago, I had asked Reggie if New Yorkers obeyed the DTR rule. She had no idea what I was talking about. When I explained that back home any couple that had been dating for a while had a "Determining the Relationship" talk, she laughed. "We should get that ratified into the New York dating constitution! How smart you guys are. But no. It doesn't exist. Until someone brings it up—try to let it be him if you can wait—you just flounder there in seeing-each-other land." But this is a desperate situation. This Chad is so cheesy. Sadly, my little plan is backfiring, and why is he so shocked Bennett is dating me?

"Oh, he's crazy about Emily," Lane says. There, guy, you see?

Chad assesses me with his eyes and then shrugs. "Hey, you're hot and everything, I'm just saying, well, no, I'm not trying to get old Benny in trouble here, but that kid was nuts! Nuts! Partied his way right out of Yale. And that's pretty hard to do when you're a Wyeth!" Chad's sick laughter echoes in my head.

Bennett,
    We need to talk. Could you do lunch today?

                                      Emily

CHAPTER 10

charms

★

We meet in the lobby, and when Bennett sees me he rushes over to give me a hug. Part of me wants to fall into his arms, but the rest of me isn't sure I ever want to see him again. I hesitate a second too long, and Bennett pulls back. "Is something wrong?" he asks, his face showing genuine concern. "Your e-mail made me a little nervous."

I can't trust myself to talk. I'm not even sure I know what I want to say. "Let's talk about it when we get to the restaurant," I say, walking toward the revolving doors. He nods and follows me through the door.

Even when we are seated, I can't bring myself to say anything. He just looks at me, trying to be patient. I'm not sure of the best way to begin. I feel like I'm going to cry, and my stomach is clenched and aching. Finally, the silence is too much to bear, and he asks gently, "Em, is everything okay?"

"Yes. No. I don't know." I pause and look at him. I take a deep breath. "I went out for drinks with Lane last night, and we met this guy name Chad." He nods, and I search his face for any recognition. I find none. "Chad Holland, who went to Yale?" Is it my imagination, or do I see a flash of panic in his eyes? "He said he knew you."

He recovers quickly, putting on a face of curiosity. "Chad Holland . . . Chad Holland."

"He said he went to all your *awesome* parties, just like the rest of Yale."

"Oh yeah . . . I think I vaguely remember him. A bit of a 'bro' if I'm right. He's probably making tons of cash on Wall Street now."

"Ernst & Young."

"Ha-ha. I was very close. Glad I escaped that route." He rips off a piece of naan.

"Yeah, whatever." I halt. I can't do this. I have to. "Bennett, he said you flunked out due to partying. He said you were a legend."

His face goes blank, but his eyes give him away. I can tell what I've just said is true, and it turns my stomach.

"Emily," he says slowly, clearly struggling to buy himself time. "I'm sorry you had to hear that." He stops, taking a deep breath, looking at me. "I didn't flunk out. It wasn't like that at all."

"But you didn't graduate from Yale?"

He shakes his head.

"You lied to me." My voice is high and shrill. The nerve!

"I did *not* lie to you," he says. "I *never* told you I graduated from Yale. I never even said I went there. You decided that on your own." I pause to think. Did he actually say he went to Yale? I can't remember. "I'm sorry if you feel misled, but please remember that I didn't *ever* tell you I went there. And I *did* go there."

"But you let me believe you graduated from Yale."

"No, I just didn't argue when you assumed it. And I didn't argue," he says, taking my hand, "because I really liked you, and I wanted you to like me too."

"But I don't care whether or not you went to an Ivy League school. I don't even know which schools are Ivy and which aren't." It occurs to me that it had impressed me, but I ignore that thought. I am not the one at fault here. "Please—look at where I went. I don't care that you don't have a degree from Yale. I wouldn't ever have even thought about it." I pause, trying to think of how to phrase what I want to say correctly. "What bothers me is that you lied to me. I—"

"I did not lie to you," he insists, leaning in.

"Okay. I'm sorry. You're right. You didn't lie. But I definitely do feel misled."

"I'm sorry you feel that way. And I'm sorry you believed something that wasn't true. But that's not my fault." I am silent. Somehow what he is saying makes sense. "I started out there. I got in, moved into the dorms, bought the sweatshirts. Did the whole college thing. My parents had both gone to Yale. My mom was in the first class where they let in women. My dad's family has always gone there. There is a dorm named after my great-grandfather." I nod. "It was always assumed I would go there too. When I got in, no one even bothered to congratulate me.

"I decided to major in chemical engineering. I didn't know it at the time, but that is one of the most time-consuming majors. I was in class or in the lab all the time. I was on the crew team too, and crew is a big sport there. I was determined to be the best rower on the team. So between school and rowing I didn't even have time to eat, let alone sleep. I got pretty sick, but I decided that if I could make it to the end of the semester, I would be okay. It was a rough time."

I nod.

"Then I hurt my back. I was rowing, and it started to hurt and just never stopped. It was the most intense pain I'd ever felt in my life, but I was determined, so I kept right on rowing. They found out later I had dislocated three of my vertebrae—just by pulling on the oar too hard. I didn't even know that was possible." I cringe. "It would have been okay, except that I didn't know how badly I'd hurt it, so I kept at it. It hurt, but I wasn't afraid of pain. I was more afraid of failure. I just didn't know . . ." His voice trails off.

"I spent most of the rest of my first semester in the infirmary. I couldn't go to class. I couldn't even move. My parents finally came and brought me home. Needless to say, I didn't finish my classes. My professors probably would have helped me work something out so I didn't fail, but I couldn't think straight, I was taking so many drugs to kill the pain."

I feel really bad for him.

"I had to take the rest of the year off to recover. I was going to come back and start over as a freshman again the next year. But since I had failed my classes, they made me take a year off before coming back." This hardly seems fair. After he had suffered so much—I want to cry for him. "So I kind of hung out at home for a year, taking it easy, going to physical therapy, spending time with my friends from high school who hadn't gone away to college. I read a lot. I slowly recovered. But when the time came for me to get ready to go back to Yale, I couldn't face it. I had a panic attack every time I thought about it. To me, all it represented was pain and misery.

"My parents were all set to have me go back, and I kind of went along with it for a while. I thought God would give me the strength I needed. But then I just couldn't do it. I was afraid to go back to the place where I had felt so much pain, where I had worked so hard, where I had failed. I went through some kind of mental thing—I couldn't deal with it all over again. I hated myself for it, but I told them I couldn't go back. They tried to make me go anyway, but I was insistent. They packed up all my stuff and loaded it in the car." He pauses. He looks like he is going to cry. "Can you imagine what it feels like to have your parents want you to leave so desperately that they would pack up all your stuff against your will?" I can't; I start to tear up just thinking about it. "When I refused to get into the car, they realized I was serious.

They finally let me stay, but they made me go to a shrink, like I was some kind of sicko. I wasn't. I just couldn't do it. It wasn't my fault."

A few minutes ago, I wanted to cry because Bennett had lied to me. Now I want to cry because his story is so tragic. He isn't to be blamed but pitied. I just want to take him in my arms and comfort him.

"So no, Emily," he says, practically spitting. "I didn't graduate from Yale. I finished up at a local state school. I'm sorry if that's not good enough for you."

I do start to cry then. "Oh, Bennett . . ." I don't even know what to say. "I'm so sorry. I didn't know . . . it's not that it's not good enough. At all. I mean . . . of course it's good enough. You're an amazing person. I'm sorry. I shouldn't have jumped to conclusions. I'm so sorry."

"No, I'm glad you know," Bennett says, wiping a tear away from my face with the back of his hand. "I didn't mean for you to be confused."

"It's my fault," I say. He says nothing. "I'm so sorry."

"At least it's all cleared up now," he says, looking at me, cocking his head slightly. "Can I kiss you now?"

I nod and lean in. I am so glad he isn't mad at me for doubting him.

"What do you think of this one?" I ask, pulling a black wool coat off the high silver rack. The hanger is caught on the bar, and I shake it loose, holding the black wool coat high. Matthew nods approvingly. It really is beautiful—the wool is smooth and soft (it must be part cashmere), the cut is clean and it falls straight, and the satin lining gleams. Matthew walks toward me, holding out his arm, and I start to hand the coat to him until I see that he is reaching for the price tag.

"Uh-uh," I say, twisting and pulling the coat away. "I don't care how much it costs. This is an investment."

"You don't care how much it costs," he says, laughing as he grasps the coat firmly and pulls it from my hands. "That's just great." He undoes the shiny black buttons. "You drag me to Saks Fifth Avenue and tell me not to worry about the price." He pulls the coat on, adjusting the sleeves and smiling at himself in the mirror. "It is nice . . ." he says, buttoning the front. "I like it." He winks at himself in the mirror.

"You look great," I say, thinking about how I am going to convince him to shave his goatee off and get a haircut that costs more than ten dollars.

He turns and grasps the tag, and squinting, lets out a low whistle. "At this price, I better," he says, undoing the buttons quickly, as if they might charge him for every second he wears it. He takes the coat off and puts it back on the hanger. "I think I may have to wait to buy this," he says, hanging it up. His self-control amazes me.

"Oh, come on," I argue, pushing it back into his hands.

"Emily, there are people starving on the street. I cannot spend this much on a coat for myself," he says, hanging it up definitively. I feel a little bit bad that if I could afford it, I would buy it in a second. I feel even worse when I remember he would have been able to buy it if he hadn't poured all of his money into the Locus. It's as if he's entirely forgotten he had thousands of dollars' worth of shoes once. "Now, let's go to a more reasonable store."

I sigh. I know there is no persuading him. "Fine," I say, stroking the sleeve one more time. "But we have to stop and check out coats I'll never be able to afford to buy first," I say, walking him toward the escalator. He humors me, letting me pick out my favorite, a camel wool coat that goes down to my knees, before dragging me down the escalator.

"Some day," I say as we walk through the breathtaking first

floor—handbags that cost more than a car, rows of dark wood counters with beautiful people fighting to put makeup on you, the smell of expensive perfume and candles filling the cavernous room—"I'll be able to afford to shop here all the time."

"Working in publishing?" Matthew asks, grinning. "I doubt it."

"Maybe I'll just have to marry a rich man."

"Sure you will. Just don't forget your poor old uncle, slaving away for peanuts," he says, pushing open the glass door and letting me walk out ahead of him into the bright clear afternoon with a sharp nip in the air.

"Speaking of rich men, how are things going with old what's-his-name?" he asks, leading me across Fifth Avenue toward Rockefeller Center. "He's got money, doesn't he?"

"Uh, I guess he does. I don't know. Things are fine. I'm going to go home with him for Thanksgiving. So good, mostly," I say quickly. Why can't I just tell him the truth?

"Have you told your parents about him yet?"

"No, which was dumb, because now I have to tell them about him and then mention that I'm going home with him for Thanksgiving. I'm nervous."

"Good luck with that," says Matthew, laughing. I punch his arm.

"So you're not going to help me serve turkey at the Locus, huh?" he says. I grin at him guiltily. "That's okay. I would go home with my girlfriend too if I had one. Just don't come back all hoity-toity on me, you hear?"

"I won't. At least I'll try not to." I pause and feel like now might be the time to mention my plan to help him. "Listen, uh, I want to . . . No. That's not what I'm trying to say. Um . . ." I wish I had planned this out beforehand. I don't want to make it sound like I think Matthew is pathetic.

He looks at me with a pleasant, curious face.

"Okay. I'll just say it. I think you spend too much time at the Locus. And I worry about you."

He nods a little and looks at his feet.

"Great. So we agree. And I always loved you because you're my uncle, but now I, uh, really like you and so I worry about you all the time. I worry that you're wasting your life."

He stares at an indefinite point in the distance, and I wonder if he's thinking back to his girlfriend, Autumn, and the life they had planned together so long ago or to any of the nameless women he has tried to replace her with. I'm trying to tread lightly.

"So I want to get you out of the Locus and update your look some and set you up with an editor from work or someone else. Whoever you want."

We are both silent. I am already preparing myself to be yelled at by my uncle or to have him just start crying, but he doesn't do anything for a moment. He turns and looks at me and says, "Fine." He nods. I wait.

"Fine?"

"Fine. I'm all yours." He pauses, staring straight ahead. "I know you're right, Emily Elizabeth, and I'd be a crazy and prideful man not to take your advice. Maybe I've let my moderation turn into a kind of monkish denial." He pauses. "That's hard to admit." He shakes his head. "I don't even have any idea what's fashionable anymore." Silence. Then, finally, "And you're right. I'm lonely."

"Really?! I mean I was thinking we'd get your hair all tidied up, and you could shave, and we'd go shopping and get some classic-looking basics and—"

"Easy now. I have a request. I'm not spending a ton of money. *Or* agreeing to any pink shirts."

I laugh. "Okay."

"And it has to be gradual. I'm not quite ready to go on a date, but I'll start wrapping my mind around the idea. I gave up the dating scene when I sold my Jaguar. It's been a while."

"Deal," I say.

"Fair enough." We stop at the railing overlooking the skating rink and watch the people on the ice. Most of the skaters are circling the small rink steadily; a few are clinging to the walls at the sides. One little curly-haired girl, dressed in a green velvet leotard with a matching skirt and headband, spins confidently in the center of the rink. She is the best skater on the ice, and she knows it. She enjoys putting on a little show for the spectators.

"You must be excited about meeting his family. The whole Wyeth crew, huh?" he asks.

"I guess so." I feel somewhat empty inside, thinking about it. I want to go home with him, but I don't want it to be like this. It was only after that creep at the bar said he flunked out of Yale and I confronted Bennett about it that he even invited me. It was almost like he felt guilty and was trying to make amends.

I stare at the girl in velvet. It must be nice to be that young and confident. I am feeling older and more weighed down than I ever have before. The conversation with Bennett was not easy, and even though we resolved everything, I have a nagging feeling that something still isn't right.

"Are you okay?" Uncle Matthew asks. I wonder how long I've been staring at the ice.

"I'm fine," I sigh. I have to be grateful for the fact that Bennett asked me to his house at all. And I am excited about spending the whole weekend with him, and it must be a sign that he thinks of me as more than just some girl he's dating.

"Good." He is quiet, then lifts his arm to point across the rink. "That's where they put up the giant Christmas tree. It will go up in a few weeks, I guess. You should come to the lighting ceremony. It's a great part of New York at Christmastime."

I nod. "You seem quiet today," he says. "Is everything okay?"

"I'm fine. Let's go," I say, pulling him away from the railing. I paste a happy smile on my face. "We've got some serious shopping to do."

"Hey. I said gradual change!"

The shopping trip wasn't a complete waste, I think as I put a spoonful of cereal in my mouth Monday morning. I did finally convince Matthew to buy a couple of nice collared shirts and a gray wool sweater, despite his protestations that wool was so itchy he would never wear it. It looked really nice on him, and the shirts would be nice to wear on a date—if I could ever get him to go on one. I even came really close to getting up the nerve to ask him about Xavier's near-legendary infidelities. Did Xavi really have both a wife and a girlfriend? Is this behavior that even Matthew had just accepted as a part of New York? But at the last moment I couldn't. I had a lot on mind with Bennett and Thanksgiving coming up. And I really liked my boss now. It would be too difficult to hear it was true.

My task for the morning, filing the huge stack of book reviews Xavier has managed to accumulate and keep in no particular order, requires very little brainpower, and I find myself brainstorming ways to set Matthew up with Cindy, the business books editor. I am so absorbed in my thoughts (and, of course, trying to recall whether W comes before X—I have to sing the song every time) that I don't see Xavier coming up behind me.

"That was really great," he says suddenly, and I spin around, knocking my knee on the open filing drawer.

"What was?" I ask, rubbing my knee through my black pants as I try to swallow my mouthful of Lucky Charms quickly. Thanks to my paltry pay, I now take styrofoam bowls of the milk they provide for the free coffee in the break room and put in some cereal that I bring from home. Voilà! A practically free meal. I've become quite a forager, especially at our almost-weekly Friday cocktail parties with cheese plates and fine wine celebrating our *Times* best-seller list success of the week. I had developed quite a taste for those stinky cheeses.

"Your presentation," he says. My presentation? He must mean my idea about the Hank Fleming book. That was five days ago, but he hasn't said anything about it since then. He can't mean anything else, can he?

"Uh, thanks," I say. "I contacted the agent last week, and he hasn't called me back yet. I'll let you know when I hear something." He nods, then starts to walk to his office. He stops suddenly.

"Are those Lucky Charms?" he asks, leaning over to peer into the bowl.

"Yeah, do you want some? I have a whole box in my—"

I stop speaking. Xavier does apparently want some Lucky Charms, as he sticks his hand directly into my bowl and scoops up a handful. Milk is dripping down his arm as he pops the cereal into his mouth. He doesn't seem to notice and nods as he walks away. "I love these little marshmallows," he says, smiling as he disappears into his office. The door shuts behind him.

I shake my head. Add that story to the rapidly growing Xavier's Antics Archive. I get up, picking up my bowl to take it to the kitchen to throw away, but I am distracted by the little white envelope that has appeared in the bottom right corner of my computer screen. I sit back down to read the e-mail—maybe I got something good.

The subject line says it's from Jacob Keller. Jacob Keller? It's that guy from my home . . .

Dear Emily,
　　Remember me? Jacob from school? I'm finally dumping you, by the way. I know. Leaving after all these years is hard,

but I've finally decided it's time to move on. I hope you'll understand. In case you don't remember, we've been dating since first grade. I also sat behind you in math class our senior year. The back of your head is quite nice, by the way. I've been meaning to tell you that for years. ☺

I hope you don't mind my e-mailing you. I ran into Jenna a few weeks ago, and she gave me your e-mail address so I could say what's up and tell you every detail of my life for the past four years. You ready? Sit back, it's a long story . . .

No, I really just wanted to see what you've been up to and how you're doing. I hear you're all alone in the Big Apple. What's it like there? What do you do all day?

I hope you'll write back and tell me all about it. I'll be here, wasting my life and my talents in the sun-drenched shores of paradise.

Jacob.

Jacob. With a period. He was always such a nice guy. A little dorky, but very nice. For some reason, I am really glad to hear from him. I look around. The office is pretty quiet. It's a Monday. I decide to write him back.

Jacob.

I didn't know you spelled your name with a period now. That's really very impressive. What am I up to? Oh, just saving the world.

Seriously. I work at Morrow & Sons. I won't explain to you, the kid who used to bump into walls because he was so engrossed in *Slaughterhouse 5*, that that's a book publisher. A lot of guys I meet here don't get it. I tell them I work here, and their faces are blank. So then I tell them I make books (see how few syllables I use to make it easier for them?) and they're still blank. Usually then they confess that they haven't read anything since *Lord of the Flies* in high school. Ha ha. But I really like the job. For instance my boss enjoys dressing up as Darth Vader, eating cereal out of my bowl with his hands, and gossiping about all of his old girlfriends from college. And the other day I caught him eating peanut butter out of the jar with his finger. This would have been weird enough if he was alone; it was even stranger because he was having a meeting with an author at the time. I don't think he even offered the poor destitute writer any.

What about you? Saving the world too? What do you do with yourself now that you don't have the school newspaper to single-handedly run? Have you stopped tapping on everything with those infernal drumsticks?! I think I still have a headache from when you sat behind me. It is a nice head though, isn't it? My mom gave it to me.

Write me back and tell me something. No more of this mysteriousness, eh? We're all Jenksians here.

Emily?$#!^&

I spell-check and reread it. I am surprised this time to see that I made myself sound kind of single. It's true about the boys, but maybe I should take it out. I read it again and shrug. It's harmless. And, I tell myself, since Bennett hasn't officially asked me to be his girlfriend, who cares if Jacob, who lives three thousand miles away, thinks I'm single? I hit send.

Jacob. There's someone who could use a makeover. Who knows? Maybe he learned in college that blue and black shouldn't be worn together and that sometimes, on very, very special occasions, one can wear something besides a T-shirt bought at a rock show. I laugh, and then hope he writes back. I'm curious to hear his reaction.

The phone rings. From the caller ID I see that it's Jenna and smile. I look over my shoulder, don't see anyone around, brace myself, and pick up.

"You're going to Bennett's house for Thanksgiving??? Have you told your mom?? She is going to fuh-lip on you, Em!" she belts into the phone.

"Hi Jenna. Easy now. I haven't had my coffee yet." I laugh. It's ten in the morning here, and there is a three-hour time difference. How can this girl be so peppy at seven in the morning? She'll never change. She probably ran five miles already.

"I mean . . . you write me this e-mail, and you don't expect me to be curious. This is big. I'm mean *huge*. When are you telling them?"

CHAPTER 11

supervision

★

As *the bleach* stings my eyes, I know it is time. With Thanksgiving coming right up I have to face calling my parents and telling them the big news. I don't normally put things off, but the Saturday before the big weekend I find myself at the bottom of my shower scouring it with some bleach and a scrub brush.

I hate to clean.

I finish up, clear a place for myself on my bed, and dial home.

At lunch last week, I broke down and asked the girls' advice.

"I need your help," I said.

"Shoot," said Reggie.

I took a deep breath. "Do you guys tell your parents about your boy . . . I mean when you're dating someone?"

"No," said Skylar.

"Sometimes. If it's serious. I have a six-month rule," said Lane. Reggie was chewing a mouthful of lettuce, but she shook her head no. Okay, good. I felt better.

"I need to tell mine about Bennett because I'm going home with him for Thanksgiving."

"So tell them," said Skylar, a little bored and making sure I knew it by the tone of her voice. "What's the big deal? Aren't you an adult? What are they going to do? Come and get you?" She wiggled her fingers in the air at me like a witch or a goblin. We all laughed.

I sighed and tapped my foot under the table, thinking about it. I *was* an adult now. It wasn't really their business.

"I know," said Skylar. "Why don't you ask Xavi for permission? He'd *definitely* write you a hall pass for this one."

They all laughed. I frowned. I didn't know why Xavier insisted on being so open about keeping Beatrice on the side. At Ed Board this past week, the cookbook editor was talking about a certain restaurant when Xavier broke in with his usual aplomb and declared it very fine, for he had taken "his Beatrice" there. Ugh. I had really come to respect him, and it made me a little crazy to have to confront this failing all the time. The company, as a whole, loved to joke about it.

"I'd just tell them, Em. It's all on the up and up and if they have a problem with it, I bet they'll get over it pretty quickly. And better to do it now than wait until you're telling them about him as you're moving in together," said Reggie.

I knew she was right about telling them, but the idea of moving in together made me want to giggle. Yeah right.

"Hello?"

"Mom?"

"Hi sweetie! It's good to hear from you. Preston, it's the girl professional calling from New York."

"Hi Manhattan," he yells in the distance.

I laugh. "Tell him I said hi back."

"Hi back," my mom says. "Guess what? We got one of those web things! Now we can use the Internet at home! We got it just so we could e-mail you. Isn't that great?"

"It's about time, Mom. Geez, we must have been the last family in California. But that's great. Now I expect to hear from you more."

"And maybe you will. So what's up?"

"Um . . . I need to talk to you guys about something. It's not really a big deal."

I try to give mom the shortened version. She is elated that I have been dating someone, but I sense she is a little hurt that I waited so long to mention it. Since I had been in New York we had been growing apart in weird ways, and sometimes we both felt it. I still couldn't get them to call me. I had to call them. They were too afraid to rain on my parade and were trying to give me my freedom. This was noble, considering how hard they had fought against it. Unfortunately it sometimes felt that they had forgotten me.

The conversation is taking quite a while because my mom keeps relaying all the highlights to my dad in the background.

"Is Bennett a Christian?"

"Oh yes. I think we're the only two in the company, in fact."

Mom thinks the whole thing sounds like Happily Ever After. I find myself wanting to tone down her enthusiasm a little. Why didn't I agree? Certainly this relationship was everything that I had always said I wanted. But her excitement about it does give me confidence to tell her the other part of the story. I mention that I'll be meeting his parents and that I wish they could meet Bennett. I explain I'll be going there for Thanksgiving and declare it very convenient since I can't come home. Didn't she think so too? The phone goes silent.

"What?!" my mom asks. Her tone is the sharpest I have heard since leaving home. "Preston, will you go pick up the phone in the bedroom? I want the three of us to have a discussion."

I gulp.

My parents are shocked that I would even consider such a thing. Did I know what the sleeping arrangements would be? I try to reassure them that Bennett's home has something like ten bedrooms and that I'm sure I'll have my very own. My mother wants to know if there will be a lot of people around. She basically hints that she felt that Bennett has invited me home for Thanksgiving as a thinly veiled excuse to have me shack up with him for the weekend. I try to remain calm. I reassure them that I am the same girl I have always been and that my value systems have not changed. The entire situation is legitimate, and I insist Bennett has no knavish plans. I tell them all about his upstanding family and how they are pillars in the community. I even say he went to Yale. I pinch myself as I leave out the other part of the story, feeling like an awful person. Finally, my parents both calm down. My father says it sounds fine and even recognizes that it will be nice for me to be with a family on the holiday. My mother decides she will feel much better if I can just give her Bennett's mother's phone number to call.

"Oh no!" I beg. "You just can't. I'll die of embarrassment."

"Why? If they're as nice as you say they are, I'm sure they'll appreciate a call from me. I just want to introduce myself and hear the plans for the weekend. And maybe the sleeping arrangements."

"Mom. I love you. And I know I don't need your permission anymore. But I really want you to feel comfortable, which is why I told you all of this, but I just don't think calling Bennett's mother is a good idea. It's going to make us seem like crazy country folk."

"Oh, Emily. You shouldn't be so easily ashamed. I think it's perfectly customary, and I promise to be good. I won't pry too much. Just a friendly chat."

"I think your mom's right, Emily. It's a nice gesture, and Bennett's parents will probably appreciate it."

My mind is racing. They can't do this to me. "Oh. Why don't you call Uncle Matthew. He's met Bennett before. He'll vouch for Bennett."

"Great idea, sweetie. I will. But I still want to call Mrs. Wyeth."

"Manhattan. Just let your mother do this. I promise you'll be glad you did."

Jenna, Oh sane one,

Argh! I want to kill my parents. So I finally told them about Bennett and Thanksgiving. They want to call Bennett's parents and talk to them. Mom wants to know the "sleeping arrangements." Ick. Why won't they trust me??? You trust me, don't you? I'm outraged that they think so little of me. I'm the same Emily who left Jenks.

Seriously. Were they this crazy when I lived there? I'm thinking about taking that scholarship I got to study on the moon. Forget planet earth. It's too frustrating.

One Mad Little Emily

Em,

Good to hear from you, but what's the big deal, kid? Problems with Vera, eh? I mean, yes, your mom does like to have scrapbooking parties (I think we all remember the Crop Till You Drop blowout she threw) but this isn't that big of a deal, is it? Just talk to Bennett. From the way you talk about him, he'll understand. After all, he's a Christian too. He's in the same boat.

Trust me. His mom will adore you if you let Vera talk to her. I've got to run. I just saw one of my wards looking at the paste with that certain sparkle in her eye.

Jenna Marie

Lane, Skylar, and I sit at the cafe in the park, sipping our chai tea lattes and hot chocolates, each of us bundled up in every layer of clothing we have. The sun is out, thank goodness, but when the sharp breeze blows it stings my eyes a little.

Janelle Meister, our publisher, sent out an e-mail at ten this morning saying that in light of the holiday season, we were all allowed to leave at noon. I grumbled at first because Bennett and I had already bought our train tickets for Wednesday so this extra time was wasted. But then Lane popped her head in my cube and suggested a girls' afternoon—even the Death Bun said she could leave early—and I was suddenly very excited, even if Skylar was going to come along. Reggie of course went straight home. We hadn't seen that much of her lately. She had been dating a boy, a fellow actor, and she was quite taken with him. They were always going to do karaoke or trying out to be extras in soaps and movies together. It was pretty cute.

Lane is stuck with Skylar for the entire Thanksgiving vacation. In true Lane fashion, last week she sent out an open invitation for all of us to join her at her parents' house for the holiday if we had nowhere else to go. I was floored when that night Lane called me and said that Skylar had accepted.

The cafe is in front of a little pool where children sail toy boats in the spring and summer. Today, however, there is only one chubby toddler, dressed in what my tacky Aunt Sharon would call "John-John style," slapping the water with his hand and splashing his nanny.

Lane sighs, shuts her eyes, and lifts her face to the sun. It's really one of those perfect New York fall moments. We all sit in the silence of the park for a while, happy to be away from the ringing phones at work.

"Skylar. So what happened with your plans?" I ask, since I can't stop wondering what would possess her to go home with Lane for the holiday. "I thought you were going somewhere."

"Nope. No plans. My family's not from TV Land like yours.

My mom's going to be at her new boyfriend's parents' house, and my dad is cutting turkey with the witch and her children, who I hate, as you know."

"Oh," I say. What does one say to that? "Lane's house should be great then."

"It will be! There's going to be this huge spread of food, and all the cousins will be there. You'll love them, Skylar," says Lane. Lane is always enthusiastic about her family in the way that all good Southerners are.

"I don't change diapers. That's all I'm saying," says Skylar.

We settle back into silence, and I feel a great respect for Lane. It could be a long Thanksgiving. I also wonder if Skylar's parents invited her home at all. I recently learned that Britt's parents don't celebrate Thanksgiving. There had been no question of her going home, especially since her father, the oilman, was still in the Middle East. I found a "turkey loaf" in our freezer labeled "Brittany ☺ ", which she told me she would cook and then eat while watching some of her favorite movies on DVD. Her new boyfriend, a medical student, had to work the entire weekend.

I look up at the blue fall sky; I see the moon, out in the middle of day like it sometimes is this time of year, and I sigh. At least my weekend looks bright on this perfect fall day. I decide I'll just stay here on earth after all.

home again, home again

★

The train ride to Westlake, Connecticut, only takes a little over an hour, but it transports us to a whole different world. We watch the grime and cramped spaces of the city slowly give way to suburbs with tree-lined streets and, eventually, large expanses of green interrupted only by towns every few minutes. The leaves had all fallen from the trees, and the bare, claw-like branches of the naked limbs stood out sharply against the bright blue sky. It feels like we're in the middle of the country, except that every once in a while the train stops at a quaint little old-fashioned train station. They look like they were modeled after the stations I've only seen at Disneyland, though I suspect it happened the other way around.

I'm so engrossed in the scenery—it's unlike anything they have in California, that's for sure—that I forget to be nervous about meeting Bennett's family. Until, that is, the Westlake station is announced, and Bennett stands to take our bags off the overhead luggage rack. I start to panic. Seeing my face screwed up in agony, Bennett puts down the suitcase and takes my hand.

"It'll be fine," he says, smiling at me. "They'll love you."

I nod, put on a smile, then grimace as he turns to carry our bags to the door of the train. I follow, focusing my eyes on the back of his head to keep from feeling woozy.

The doors open, and we step out into the cold air of the train platform. My light jacket is not warm enough for this weather, but I've never owned a real coat. I intended to find one in January in all of the after-Christmas sales, but I suddenly wish I had just put it on my credit card and worried about paying for it later.

Bennett is looking up and down the platform, searching for his parents. The station is crowded the day before Thanksgiving, but Bennett spots a tall dark-haired woman at the other end of the platform and begins to walk toward her. I follow, and she steps forward to meet us.

Bennett puts down his bag to give his mother a hug, which she returns briskly and kisses the air next to the curly hair covering his ear. "It's good to see you," she says, pulling away. She turns to me. "And you must be Emily," she says, leaning in to give me a hug. I return the hug awkwardly, trying not to crumple her dark pantsuit. She smells like Chanel No. 5. "It's wonderful to meet you."

"It's nice to meet you too," I say, straightening my back to match her perfect posture. She leads us to the car, a shiny black Mercedes, and opens the trunk so Bennett can put our bags in. I blush at my Wal-Mart–issue rolling black bag next to Bennett's top-of-the-line elegant Tumi matching two-piece set. I linger and make sure Bennett takes the front seat with his mother and then climb in.

"How was your trip?" she asks, backing the car out of the narrow space. I notice that her nails are perfectly manicured as she slides them over the leather steering wheel cover.

Bennett tells her about the hassle of getting to Penn Station amidst the crush of holiday traffic, but I can't tear my eyes away from the car window. Westlake has to be the cutest little town

I've ever seen. We are driving down what looks like the main street, lined with colonial buildings housing shops and cafes. It looks like a Norman Rockwell painting—there are antique stores and old-fashioned ice cream parlors, picturesque street lamps and a grassy town square. The streets intersect at strange angles, and in the middle of one of these places where five streets intersect, an old copper statue of a man on a horse has turned green in the wet East Coast weather.

As we drive out of the center of town, we pass stately houses, set back from the road and surrounded by lush green lawns. Though some of the houses are wooden clapboard and some are stone, they all look old and expensive. We pass a graveyard and turn off onto a side street, lined up and down with oaks. These houses are larger than the ones downtown, and the street is immaculate. I can practically see the old money hanging from the trees.

"Ahh. Home again," his mother says, stopping the car in the long shaded driveway that runs along the side of the house. Bennett's house is a large wooden colonial, set back from the road and surrounded by trees. The trees stretch so high that I figure they must be two hundred years old.

"Wow" is all I can stammer, and then kick myself. Try to act as natural as possible. I didn't want them to immediately realize the brown-shag-carpet truth of my own background.

The house is imposing, not because of its flashiness—at home people demonstrate their wealth by building big ostentatious houses of pink stucco—but because of its understated elegance. It is old and valuable and they know it, but they would hardly point it out.

"Excuse me, will you, Emily? I must go freshen up," says Mrs. Wyeth. I smile and nod.

Bennett leads me inside. "Leave your bags there," he says,

pointing to a spot on the floor by the door. I feel a little weird about leaving my bags on the floor in such an immaculate home, but I do as he says. "I'll give you the grand tour. I've heard my mother do it a million times so it should be no problem."

I stare at him. "You're kidding, right?"

"Nope." He starts to laugh. "Our home is on the National Registry of Historic Buildings. Between bridge at the club and her service with the Junior Women's League, and, once in a while, seeing her psychiatric clients, Mom has found it in her heart to give tours."

I still just stare at him. He takes my hand and leads me into a room full of dark, heavy furniture. "The grand parlor," he says, affecting a snooty accent, gesturing widely and rolling his eyes. He drops his arm. "We never use this room. Don't ask me why we even have it." He puts his hands on my shoulders and angles me through the side parlor and living room into the kitchen area. The kitchen is a traditional farmhouse affair but with such tasteful attention to detail and such refined materials that instead of looking homey and warm, it is impossible to picture anyone cooking in here. Off of the kitchen is a large side room that seems be a pantry, though it's roughly the size of my living room in New York. "This," he says, pulling me into it, "used to be a tavern. This very house was the town post office, bar, and stopping place for the early mail system more than three hundred years ago." He laughs. "But it's been the private home of my family for at least a century now." He leans in conspiratorially, and I know immediately I'm about to learn something that's not on his mother's tour. "We used to sneak down here and pretend it was still a bar when we were teenagers." He winks at me, pulling a bottle of dark liquid out from under a counter. "Gentleman Jack! Want a swig?" he asks, unscrewing the top.

"Uh, no thanks. I mean, not right now," I say, and he shrugs, putting the bottle up to his lips.

As it goes down he makes a face. "Mmm. Divine!" he says, once again affecting his mother's snooty accent, wiping his mouth with his sleeve and putting the bottle back.

He leads me back through the kitchen, where his mother is beginning to prepare dinner, somehow miraculously without a making mess on the counter, and upstairs, where there are eight bedrooms—*eight, Jenna*, I reiterate as I compose an e-mail to her in my head. She's going to die. Outright die. I better remember to wear earplugs.

My favorite part is the dumbwaiter in each room. I can't get over how clever it is, all built in like that, and how great it would be to never have to carry your food upstairs or your dirty plate downstairs again. I can just see Craig and Grant transporting things—most likely each other—up and down it. Bennett just laughs at me: "You've never seen a dumbwaiter?" he asks.

Bennett's bedroom surprises me. It is practically empty. There are a couple framed diplomas on one wall and a poster of a man sculling on a placid lake at sunset. His full-sized bed is covered with an off-white bedspread, and the matching dresser and night table are plain and free from clutter. There is nothing out of order, nothing to indicate anything about the personality of its old inhabitant. "Isn't this the room you grew up in?" I ask, sliding my arm around his waist. "Where are the GI Joes and trophies?"

He just shrugs. "My parents cleaned all that stuff out when I went away to college." I think of my own bedroom at home— the peach flowered wallpaper, the books I had loved as child still cluttering the bookshelves, the posters from every phase of my life. I would probably be embarrassed for him to see many relics of my childhood still featured prominently in the décor, especially considering how recently I had moved out, but I am surprised, and somehow extremely sad, to see this bleakness.

I am also surprised to see my bag sitting next to his at the foot of the bed. I step forward to pick it up, bending over to take the handle. "Where should I put this?" I ask, hefting it up onto my shoulder. I can't believe how heavy the bag I've packed for just a weekend is.

"You can just leave it right there," he says, pointing to the spot where it has just been.

"But wouldn't it be easier to just put it where I'll be sleeping now so it will be there when I need it later?"

"I was thinking," he says, drawing me into his arms and putting his lips close to my ear, "you could sleep in here with me."

"With you?" I am confused. "But there's only one bed. It's your parents' house."

"They don't mind. I've brought home a couple of other girls over the years, and they've always slept with me. It's not like we're going to do anything—we'll just sleep and cuddle. It's really fine."

Bennett had asked me to stay at his apartment before, but I thought we had agreed that while we both trusted each other and knew that nothing would happen, it was better not to tempt ourselves and to be above the reproach of our work colleagues. It had already come up at lunch that I didn't stay over, and the girls just stared at me in shock, but I felt like it was really setting an example for them. Plus, I certainly didn't expect this, after the whole phoning his mother episode. Bennett had thought the whole thing was nuts and had very reluctantly given me his home phone number and made me wait to pass it on until he had prewarned his mother. "But didn't your mom say we would be sleeping in separate rooms? There is no way my parents would have let me come if they knew—"

"I don't know what our parents talked about," he whispers, his lips brushing my skin, the reverberations of his voice tickling my ear, "but your bag got here somehow."

I pull away and turn to face him. I don't know what to say, so I just stare at him.

"There are plenty of other rooms," he says, thinly veiled irritation in his voice, "if you're going to be like that." He bends over to pick up my bag and walks with it to the hallway.

"No, Bennett, wait," I stammer. Please God, don't let him be mad at me. Maybe I'm being too square. Maybe there's nothing wrong with this. "I think . . . I wouldn't mind . . ."

He stops at the doorway and turns to me. "I'll put your stuff in the next room. I don't want you to be uncomfortable." His voice is cold. "You're welcome to join me in here at any time." He turns. I practically run after him, desperate to make him happy.

"I'm sorry, Bennett," I say as I catch up with him in the doorway of the next room. He puts my bag down on the narrow twin bed, covered with a colorful quilted bedspread. There is little space for anything but the bed in this tiny room, and the yellow walls and the framed pictures of sheep make me think this was once a child's bedroom. Everything about it feels diminutive, extraneous.

I don't know what to say, so I just walk up and kiss him, and he seems to forget his irritation.

We hear footsteps coming up the stairs and pull apart. His mom is coming down the hall, and, seeing us in the small bedroom, gives us a weird look. "Your dad just got home with Blair, Bennett," she says, brushing past us into the hallway. "Why don't you go down and introduce Emily?"

"Come on," he says, taking my hand and leading me to the stairs. "I'll introduce you to the rest of the family." He leads me down the front stairs (the back stairs are all the way on the other side of the floor, and Bennett confides in me that that was so that in the old days the real residents could avoid having to watch the comings and goings of *the help*) and down through a series of rooms that look only vaguely familiar to me. I think I may never figure out the layout of this labyrinth. Finally we come back to the side parlor, and, walking in, see a gray older man sitting on a well-oiled leather couch and a blonde girl across the room curled up like a cat in an overstuffed leather chair. Both are reading books and look up as we enter.

"Well, hello there, son," the man says rising to his feet. He sticks out his hand to Bennett. "Good to see you." Bennett takes his hand and shakes it, then gestures to me. I look around for his pipe and smoking jacket. He seems to have misplaced them.

"Dad, I'd like you to meet Emily," he says, gesturing toward me. His father takes my hand as well, shaking it firmly. "It's good to have you here," he says almost warmly. "Please make yourself at home."

"Thank you," I say, bewildered. Bennett's father just shook his hand to welcome him home. My father would have scooped me up in a gigantic hug and, in his excitement, hugged everyone, Bennett included (if he didn't run away). He then would have turned up the John Denver on vinyl and done what I call his Happy Dance. I think of my father just stepping back and forth in place to the music and waving both hands in the air, as if he's fanatically greeting someone—and giggle a little. My near-inaudible giggle seems to echo in the quiet of Bennett's home, and I stop. Suddenly I wonder what's going on at Lane's house.

"And this," Bennett said, gesturing to the girl getting up out of her chair, "is my sister, Blair." Blair is tall, willowy, and as she advances toward me, I notice her blue sweatshirt has a gray bulldog on it. I assume this must be the Yale mascot since *all* the Wyeths go to Yale, but I make a note to double-check later. "Blair's a freshman in college this year," Bennett explains, and she takes my hand, welcoming me. "It's nice to meet you, Emily," she says. Her voice is high and raspy, but her words are kind.

"Have a seat," his father says, gesturing to the old-fashioned high-backed loveseat across from the fireplace. We sit down—the loveseat is much harder than it looks—and Mr. Wyeth begins to ask Bennett about life in New York. Bennett answers quickly, as if talking with his father makes him uncomfortable. When Mr. Wyeth turns to ask me about my job and where I come from, Bennett gets up and walks across the room and stands in front of a giant mahogany sideboard. From the crystal decanter on top, he pours himself a drink of dark liquid and throws it back quickly. He refills his glass, and, picking up another, fills it and brings them both back to the couch. He hands one to me as I tell his father about the nuances of my job. I take a sip. Ick. Scotch.

Mr. Wyeth asks a lot of questions, barely giving me a second to breathe between answers. He comes across as gruff, confrontational, and imposing; he never seems to let his guard down, but he isn't unwelcoming. I get the odd feeling he's putting me through some kind of test. Bennett and Blair sit there and listen to the two of us with blank faces, but all the same, I can't help feeling that we are getting along pretty well. It seems like he is honestly interested in learning about me. And I am really uncomfortable only once, when he asks why I haven't gone home to have Thanksgiving with my own family. It's clear he isn't insisting that I'm not welcome here, but he just seems to think it is curious I wouldn't fly home for the weekend. Apparently it doesn't occur to him that a flight to California on a holiday might be a pricey thing, and I can't tell him that I couldn't afford it, so I mumble something about not wanting to bother with all the crowds at the airport, which he seems to think makes sense.

We have a good long chat, but Mr. Wyeth seems somewhat distracted. Then I hear a dinging sound from the dining room, and he gets up so quickly that it becomes clear why—he had been waiting for the dinner bell. *Yes, Jenna, an actual dinner bell.*

Thanksgiving at my house had always been a loud, boisterous time—all the relatives would come over, we would watch the big parade on TV (and I would dream about someday living in New York watching the parade in person all bundled up in a hat and a scarf), and we would laugh and make fun of each other. And eat, oh yes we would eat—we never got up until we were so stuffed we could barely move.

Thanksgiving at the Wyeth house, by contrast, is pretty reserved. No one turns on the television to watch the parade; instead, we all get into the Mercedes to drive to church.

The church, as I suspected, is old, ornate, and beautiful. The service is formal, carefully orchestrated, and seems very removed from the people's lives. It is certainly distant from them physically speaking, as the preacher stands on a high pulpit raised up from the stage, which is already a good distance from the first row of pews. It is, as we would have said at home, very high church. There are no frayed jeans here like at our church in the city, and no tank tops and flip-flops like back home either. These people are serious about their ceremony, and hats and ties abound.

After the service, I am introduced to about half the congregation, who all seem to be related to Bennett. I manage to remember the first few names, but they quickly begin to meld together in my mind. Aunt Carol with the navy blue suit and pearls is very hard to distinguish from Aunt Catherine, in the black suit and gold dangly bracelets, and Aunt Margaret, in the brown suit and the hat with the fake white bird on it. There are a couple cousins in there, but Bennett and Blair seem to be the youngest of the family, and there aren't any children to fawn over.

I had been hoping I could impress Bennett's family by showing them how good I am with kids.

And then, after some uncomfortable lingering in the foyer, to my surprise the families just start saying goodbye to one another. There is no talk of seeing each other later, and I realize that each family will be having Thanksgiving dinner on its own, though they live just short blocks from one another. When I ask Bennett why they aren't all getting together somewhere, he shrugs. "That's the way we've always done it," he says, which seems to satisfy him. Although it seems strange to me, I find I am actually kind of thankful for the isolation, since I have just started to feel comfortable around the immediate family—at the very least, I knew their names—and would feel overwhelmed by the entire Wyeth brood.

I get into the back of the Mercedes to go home and put my fingers to my temples. Is that the start of a headache? Can you get a headache from boredom? I try to look on the bright side. The trip certainly hasn't been an entire waste. The Thanksgiving dinner tonight will most likely be splendid, and I loved the train ride up here with just Bennett so that I could pretend that we were older, on our own, and on some sort of fabulous vacation by rail in Europe. But definitely, I think to myself, the highlight so far has been seeing Bennett walk around last night getting ready for bed without a shirt on. Just seeing that almost persuaded me that it might be okay to sleep in his bed, holding him. And, true, I did spend a little longer than I intended saying good night to him in his doorway, but I *had* ended up going back to the kid's room. I smile thinking of it. My mother's anxiety was unjustified.

By the time we sit down to Thanksgiving dinner at the Wyeth house, I am pretty sure I know what to expect—china, crystal, candles. I even knew I would be expected to wear a dress to the table, since Bennett had graciously warned me in advance to bring something nice to wear. But I am not prepared for the extreme level of formality that they all seem to accept. There is no joking or laughing.

We all gather in the dining room at the appointed time and sit down stiffly. Instead of turkey and mashed potatoes, there is veal and foie gras. I don't like the idea of eating baby cows and goose liver, but I'm certainly not going to say anything about it. Thank goodness Mrs. Zuwickie, my Home Ec teacher in high school, forced us to learn what all the different spoons and forks are for. The only thing I can't remember from her otherwise useless class sits at the head of my giant, antique, hand-painted china plate. In front of each person's plate there is a small silver angel holding a dainty tray of white powder and a tiny silver spoon. I look around. No one is touching theirs. I shrug and begin to butter my roll carefully.

Bennett volunteers to bless the meal and recites a prayer I believe I once heard in a movie. The Wyeths all seem to know it by heart as they say amen in unison at the end, but I miss the cue. It doesn't get better. From there, the conversation, quiet, stilted, easy for me to stay out of, is fine until Mr. Wyeth turns to me and asks, "So, Emily, what does your father do?" I swallow hard. I don't want to lie, but I also don't want to tell him that my dad works at a cement plant. That would cast me as a country bumpkin for sure.

"He's in sales," I say evasively. He was, sort of. The concrete plant did sell the concrete they made. "And my mom's a teacher," I add.

"Of course she is," Mrs. Wyeth says, smiling. I must look as confused as I feel, since she follows that up with, "I just guessed she might be. She seemed like the kind of person who deals with children when I talked to her on the phone."

"Oh, I'm really sorry she called you like that. I tried to keep her from bugging you, but she—"

"That's fine. It wasn't bugging. It was actually very cute," she says, taking a sip of wine—another thing that would never end up on a Hinton Thanksgiving table. "She was just so earnest and concerned, I couldn't help but think it was darling. She was so worried about you." Blair lets out a little laugh, and Mrs. Wyeth glares at her.

"We told her we'd make sure you were well taken care of," Mr. Wyeth says loudly, winking at Bennett.

"Yeah, they're funny people," I say, trying to laugh, but inwardly feeling a bit guilty. "They're a little old-fashioned." As embarrassed as I am by my mother's phone call to the house, I don't like the idea of Bennett's family laughing at her, thinking my parents are quaint. It feels like betrayal to sit here and join them in the joke.

"Oh, that's quite all right," Mrs. Wyeth says, placing her napkin on the table. "Who wants coffee?"

When she disappears into the kitchen, Blair and Mr. Wyeth begin talking heatedly about James Joyce (Mr. Wyeth thinks *Ulysses* is overrated; Blair disagrees), and I kind of zone out—food coma always hits hard on Thanksgiving. I notice that everyone else has placed their utensils side by side in the middle of their plates, and I quickly move my silverware to the appropriate position. A small cup of coffee is placed in front of me. Taking it, I say thank you to Mrs. Wyeth and sit up to wait for the small silver pitcher of cream they're passing around the table. Desperate for caffeine, I decide to speed up the process of coffee consumption by adding the sugar to my coffee while I'm waiting. I look around for the sugar bowl when it dawns on me what the little angel is offering in her dish. Perfecto! Quite proud of my deduction, I lift the little spoon and dump a large mound of sugar in my cup, then pick up my coffee spoon and begin to stir. Looking up to see if the cream is coming my way yet, I see Bennett staring at me, a look of horror on his face. Before I have time to wonder what the problem is, a squeal comes from the other end of the table. "That's salt!" Blair exclaims.

I stop stirring instantly, and I feel my face go red. I have never wanted to disappear as badly as I do now. They just stare at me, not sure what to do. Finally Mrs. Wyeth gets up. "That's okay, dear," she says, picking my saucer up. "We'll just go get you another one."

I start to argue, to insist that I really don't mind salt in my coffee, even start to wonder if they'll believe me if I say I always drink it that way, but I don't have the strength. Suddenly, I am exhausted and all I want to do is go up to my room and cry. I hang my head. "Thanks," I say quietly.

Alone in my little room that night, I pull out my cell phone and call home. I am so glad to hear my mom's voice I start to tear up. When I talk to Grant, who tells me about the game of street football they played that afternoon, and Craig, who tells me about the fake spider they put on our grandmother Nanna's chair and how loudly she yelled when she saw it as she sat down to dinner, I can't help but think how somber this house felt today. And when my dad gets on and tells me there are exactly nineteen days left until I fly home for Christmas, I have to bite my lip to keep from bawling.

He's been counting down the days.

Suddenly I can't wait to be home.

Mom passes the phone around to all the relatives, but ends up with it again to say goodbye to me. She has told me she loves me a thousand times before, but as she says it this time before she hangs up, I let go. I hang up the phone sobbing. I don't care about anything right now except how much I love them all. I'm so absorbed in missing them, so desperate to feel them near me, I don't even mind when the door to my room slowly opens and Bennett walks in, pulls back the quilt, and slides into bed with me.

CHAPTER 13

wobbly

★

"Morning, Emmie!" *Emmie? What?*

I am hunkered over my desk staring at my e-mail screen. It's Xavier, looking better than I do after his long weekend. I couldn't sleep on the train home. I had a lot on my mind and Bennett's incredibly heavy head on my shoulder.

"Good morning, Xavier. How was your Thanksgiving?"

"Fine. Fine. Although you should say my *Thanksgivings*."

I cock my head at him. There should be a law at Morrow & Sons. Everyone must act normal until ten thirty or until we've all had two cups of coffee, whichever comes first.

"I got to have two Thanksgivings. One for each of my girls."

What does one say?! "Oh."

"They were just marvelous." At that he walks out of my cube, whistling. I shake my head. I want to yell down the hall that mine was marvelous also, but I know he won't hear me. Darth Vader at Halloween, sure, but Space Cadet the rest of the year.

I look at my screen and see a curious little e-mail from Jacob and click it open. In the background, I can hear Xavier whistling an old AC/DC song.

Emily,

How was your Thanksgiving? I got to ride a harvester with my redneck cousin who is inexplicably called Mondo. Needless to say, some of my uncle's crops lost their lives. Don't you miss old Jenks? I must admit, I was always trying so hard to earn my ticket out of there, I did take it for granted. *Not* that I'm moving back. I'm very happy in San Diego.

What am I really up to? I'm an aspiring journalist. I just landed my first job at the free weekly here. It pays so little that I also teach kids to drum—no, I have not stopped tapping on things!—but I love it. And guess what they let me cover? Shows! I can see as many bands as I want now . . . it's free!

By they way, here's a picture of me and my family. I hear girls like guys who are "about family." Did it work for you? Are you a victim of my charms yet?

Jacob.

P.S. As you can see from the picture, I've stopped letting my mom cut my hair.

I can't believe I'm even able to smile through this Monday morning fog but I am. There in front of me is the entire Keller family, sitting on hay bales. The picture seems to have been taken at Thanksgiving this past weekend. Jacob looks about three inches taller than I remember, very tan, and his hair is brown and styled sort of messy on top. He's also not wearing a band T-shirt. But it was Thanksgiving, I remind myself, and old habits often die hard. I guess his mother made him dress up for his grandmother. I close the e-mail out and go for some coffee.

I stare down at my giant cup of coffee—the size I lovingly refer to as the "medical dosage." I don't know why I'm having such weekend lag. After all, I survived the Wild Wyeth Weekend, as I have come to refer to it. I make a quick list of things to look forward to in my head to get me through the brief month of December: going home for Christmas in about fifteen days, lunch today outside the caf with Lane (her request, I guess we each missed the other), and two weeks in the serene California countryside to catch up on all my manuscript reading and eat my mom's famous Santa cookies. I take another sip of coffee and move on to work. I'll write Jacob back later. He deserves a good one back, and I can barely think at the moment.

We snag the last table at the Thai place down the block and talk for five minutes straight about work. Both Lane and I are suddenly very busy at our jobs. Xavier accidentally overloaded the current span and is using me to pick up the slack. I am "helping" him edit one of the smaller books on our upcoming list, which basically means offering suggestions so he doesn't have to give it his full attention. Lane is dealing with a diva cookbook author who keeps demanding that her cover be redesigned. That would be enough of a nightmare on its own, but her boss, Susanna, also sprained her ankle running in Central Park, so now Lane is stuck being the Death Bun's "other self" and has to get Susanna's coffee, lunch, cigarettes, *W* magazine, and dry cleaning.

"Okay," I say, putting my glass of water down like a gavel. "I'm stopping us right now."

Lane giggles.

"First of all, my dear friend Lane, I want to say that I missed you over the break."

She gives me a wobbly smile. I'm not sure what it means but brush it off. I tell her all about the Wyeth weekend. She looks greener and greener as I continue. I take it as a sign that she understands my pain.

"They're a little crazy, right?" I ask with a laugh.

"Uh. I don't know. I guess," she says and pushes her food around with her fork.

"What's up with you, Lane? Is something wrong? Oh. How did it go with Skylar?"

Lane looks up as if she suddenly remembers something really important to tell me. She tells me about the whole weekend with Skylar, who is apparently a completely different person away from work. I can't believe her, but Lane just keeps on talking about how great she was. She says Skylar was the first person up from the table to help with the dishes. Skylar tied her grandmother's shoelaces without anyone mentioning it. Skylar rolled around on the floor with all of the baby cousins. Skylar wore beat-up sneakers and ratty jeans. My mouth gapes open. Lane laughs.

"Listen, though, there's something you should know that I found out this weekend from Skylar."

Lane says she was so fascinated by this brand-new Skylar that they stayed up late talking one night, slumber party–style, complete with Skylar in a sleeping bag on the floor. Skylar confessed that she was envious of Lane's family and that she worried that her own unstable family often made her lack self-confidence. But, Skylar said, she at least had her brother Tyson, whom she was very close to. In fact, that was how she met Bennett. How they started dating.

"What?" I gasp. "She didn't mean my Bennett. Did she date my Bennett? Did you know that? Does everyone know that? Why didn't you tell me?!" It is safe to say I am talking too loud at this point. Lane makes a "lower-lower" gesture with her flat palm and then signals to our waiter for the check.

Lane says it was the first she had heard of it, but yes, it seems to be true. Bennett and Skylar would have broken up right before Lane was hired. And I was hired three months after Lane.

I have my head in my hands. I have already been filled with guilt about letting Bennett sleep with me in my bed and now I am finding out that all those weird vibes I felt between him and

Skylar are real. And she isn't even a Christian. "Please tell me there isn't more."

Lane wrinkles her nose. "You want me to stop?"

"No. Get it over with," I say.

We walk out of the restaurant and start heading back to the office. Lane slips her arm through mine to steady me. Apparently not only have they dated at Morrow & Sons, but they met much earlier than that. Skylar went to stay with Tyson when he was a sophomore at Yale and she was a senior in high school. She met Bennett at a party then, but nothing came of it. That was all before Bennett flunked out of Yale. Then they met again later at Morr—"

"Oh, he didn't flunk out. He had to quit because he got really sick," I say.

"Uhh . . . That's not what Skylar said. She said he had something of a reputation for being a party guy. That he basically got kicked out for never going to lectures and failing his classes."

I know I don't want to hear any more but will never be able to sleep until I have the whole story straight. Lane and I make plans for coffee later. I need to get every last morsel of information she got from Skylar over the weekend and then hear Lane's advice. But should I talk to Bennett? I hate to rock the boat again after we just got back from Thanksgiving together, when I feel closer to him than ever.

Sitting at my computer again, I shake my head, and my heart pounds fast in my chest. Why doesn't he just tell me the whole story?! Not knowing is worse than the facts themselves. Why does he think I will care? What is he hiding? How can he be so wonderful on the one hand and so shifty on the other? Perhaps if I can just get him to crack and tell me everything? He must think I will judge him. People often hide their sins from me because they assume I will judge them because I'm a Christian. It stings to be left out, and I at least like to think I'd be understanding and supportive. I'm not here to judge. I do believe that's someone else's job.

My job is to try to send e-mails to nutso authors while my heart races about something Bennett may or may not have done.

not just some suitor

★

"W*i?*" *I ask* above the loud din of the dryers. It's so cold outside that I don't mind waiting inside for a moment with the heat from the dryers warming my back. I look around at the interior of Happy Clean Suds. It has been decked to the gills in tinsel and greenery, giving even my mother's year-round obsession with Christmas a run for the money. There are paper cutouts of Jesus in the manager with Mary looking down from above and long ropes of silver garland woven in and out of the cheap ceiling tiles that are so popular in public schools.

"Wi?" I call again.

He appears from the back and upon seeing me beams a giant smile. "Emily, Emily, Emily."

I laugh. It's been a month since I've done my laundry. He runs over to me and gives me one of the most awkward hugs of my life. I pull back and smile, wishing I were a more touchy-feely person.

"It looks great in here."

"Yes. Thank you. It is our first Christmas in New York City."

I'm suddenly very touched and sad at once. It's also my first Christmas season away from home, even though I'd be flying out to join my family any day now.

"What will you do on Christmas?" His wife, Nan, comes out from the back. She still does not speak English, but she likes to come and listen. I smile and wave hi to her. She smiles and nods back to me.

Wi puts his arm around her. "We will go to church."

Right. Of course. But I couldn't help but feel like they'd be missing out on the big family, is-that-a-nose-ring-please-pass-the-mashed-potatoes-magic of it all. "You should go here." I hand them a brochure for the Locus from the stack Matthew gave me to hand out. Wi looks at it and then looks confused.

"For dinner. All kinds of people go here after church on Christmas to eat, together."

He nods and smiles.

"It will be a big American Christmas."

"Big Americans. Big Americans." He nods and winks at me. He thinks he's got the gist. I shrug. Who knows if they'll end up there, but it might be fun for them to be with people when the rest of their family is so far away. Also Matthew has had the mayor and several New York celebrities, including Hank Fleming, who is now officially our author, give their word that they will be joining in the big family meal. At any rate, I think, turning to head out to the street, I tried.

As I walk downtown, I can't help but be thrilled by the lights and the decorations in every window. Although the air itself is so frigid that I have to wear two sweaters, and I finally broke down and bought a pair of cheap gloves when my hands started to chap, the city seems warm and bustling. I am meeting Uncle Matthew for some authentic New York cheesecake before I "head back out west and forget to come back." I had hoped to serve one last meal with him at the Locus but ended up getting stuck at the office, since for some reason everything there is urgent all of a sudden. Xavier is swamped and trying to get himself ready to go to Hawaii for the break, so I have taken on a lot more responsibility. Unfortunately for me this means a lot more hours at my desk. Of course, on the other hand, I don't want to be an assistant forever. Maybe I'm flattering myself, but I feel like I'm really starting to "get it," as Xavi likes to say.

Matthew is already sitting at a table in the crowded little restaurant when I get there, drinking a cup of coffee and huddled over a newspaper. I don't recognize him at first—apparently he has gone through with the haircut appointment I set up for him at Coiffuse, the chic salon near our office. He looks great, as he peers up at me and smiles, practically ten years younger with that heavy mop gone. The shorter style looks much more modern, and, is that . . . ?

He cocks his head as I walk toward him, laughing. "What do you think?" he asks, standing up to give me a hug.

"Is that gel in you hair, Uncle Matthew?" I say, giving him a bear hug. "You look like a racy version of your old self. The ladies aren't going to be able to resist you!"

He winks at me. "That's the plan."

We both sit down, and I start to tell him about the authors Xavier had asked me to stay late to contact. "They're all crazy. I swear! Not one of them is normal. We should do psychological testing before we sign any of them on to write a book."

"How is Xavier? What's he up to for Christmas?"

"He's, uh, going to Hawaii and then skiing. Must be nice, huh?" I laugh. I can never decide how much Matthew knows. I am so close to asking, but the waitress comes over just then and Matthew orders us two pieces of "gen-u-ine cheesecake with extra strawberries on top."

"Yeah, that Xavier," Matthew continues as the waitress walks away. "He's always up to something. I'm sure he'll have a great time and come back with all kinds of crazy stories. I always wished I could be more like him."

I feel a little sad. So much of Matthew's life, at least since Autumn's death, has been lived for other people, quietly slaving away in the shadows. "Yeah, he's great, I guess," I say, "but you don't want to be like him. One of him is enough. I like the way you are much better."

He laughs. "Of course. Who wouldn't? Have you seen my new haircut?" He takes a sip of coffee. "I'm really not jealous of him, but you have to stand in awe of his ease with women. He doesn't need a new haircut to get up his confidence. As long as I've known him, he's always seemed to have two or three women around at any given time."

"So I hear," I say. So, he does know? Interesting. "But *you* don't need two or three. What we're looking for for you is The One."

"The One, huh?" he asks, taking another sip. "Wow. I don't know about The One. It's just a new haircut so far. But I had a really good conversation with Josie yesterday. You remember Josie from the shelter, right?"

"Sure, sure," I say. I try not to let my irritation show. "She's sweet, I guess. But I was thinking I might try to set you up with this woman named Cindy at work. She's really cute and blonde— and she edits business books, so she's serious enough for you. She's really fun and nice, too. I think you guys would really hit it off," I say.

"Business books?" he laughs. "I wonder if she could help me find a way to turn the shelter into anything but a financial black hole."

"Probably. And I also hear she can cook really well. Did I mention she's really cute and blonde? And about your age? Oh, and she can walk on water too," I say.

"Is that so, little enthusiastic one?" He's chuckling at me.

"Maybe. You can call her and ask her yourself," I say, pushing a paper across the table. He laughs as he sees that it has Cindy's phone number written on it.

"Em, I don't know about that," he says. "I'm not going to call up some stranger and ask her on a date." He laughs.

"Suit yourself," I shrug, hoping I've at least piqued his interest. "But maybe this will help," I say, pulling a wrapped present out of my bag and sliding it across the table.

"Oh, Emily, you shouldn't have," he says, picking it up. "It was so nice of you to get me a present. You shouldn't be spending your hard-earned money on presents for your dorky uncle," he says, carefully pulling the paper off.

"Don't thank me until you see it," I say.

"*How to Find and Marry Your Soul Mate in Six Months or Less*, huh?" he says, reading the cover.

I can't take it. I start laughing.

"Isn't it a scream? This is the sort of thing we publish when we're not improving the lives of the American public through great works of art. But I hear it's supposed to be really good, actually," I say.

"Thank you," he says. "I appreciate it. I'll read it over Christmas. Does the six-month timer start now, or does it wait until I've actually finished it?"

"I think you can start counting when you're done with it," I say. "But if it will get you moving, I'll start it now."

"That's okay. Please don't." He smiles at me. "But while we're on this topic, how are things going with Bennett?"

"Oh, we're fine. I mean, great." I say, pasting a big smile on my face to cover the uncertainty I am afraid to let my words convey. The truth is that I'm not sure we are. I haven't told him I know anything about Skylar, and in fact have gone out of my way to avoid even mentioning her name, nor have I said anything about what really happened at Yale. It's as though there are suddenly two Emilys; he's split me apart. One Emily won't believe he could lie to me, but the other sort of knows it's true. Whimsical Emily is still crazy about him and sure she'll never meet anyone who's as perfect as he is and a Christian to boot, but the other Emily is looking forward to having some time away to think. "I'm sure going to miss him when I go home."

He nods. "You're flying home Saturday?"

"Yeah. I can't wait to be back in the land where the sun shines all the time and it's never thirty degrees."

"You're really not going to come back, are you? You're going to get used to the perfect weather and having your perfect family nearby and forget about us out here—"

"No. No way." I say. "Of course I'm dying to get back there— I mean, people out there just make more sense to me. But I love it here. I have no intention of not coming back. I'm changing the world, remember? Look at all I'd be giving up—"

"Like what?"

"Noisy subways. Dirty streets. Tiny apartment. Frigid winter. And everything else that makes New York great."

"Then I did the right thing. I don't trust you for one moment, young lady. This is my insurance to get you on a return flight to New York," he says, pulling a shopping bag out from under the table. He puts it on the table and pushes it across to me.

"Think that bag is big enough?" I ask, laughing as I pull a large wrapped box out of it. I begin to unwrap the paper. "I bet it's a watermelon. Or a stuffed Care Bear. A sprinkler?" He just smiles at me. "A chainsaw." Then I see the writing on the top of the box. "A chainsaw from Saks Fifth Avenue . . ." I lift the lid off the box and gasp. "Uncle Matthew, you didn't. You couldn't," I stammer as I pull out a camel wool coat. "It's beautiful! You can't give me this. This is . . . oh my gosh, this is the one I picked out, isn't it?"

He nods. "You should have seen me in that store by myself."

"But I didn't need this coat! You can't afford this. I can't accept it."

"I'm tired of seeing you shiver. You needed a coat."

"No, Matthew. *You* don't even have a proper coat."

"Emily Elizabeth, I'm not just some suitor you can reject. I want you to have it. Besides, you won't get to wear it in California, and if I know you, you'll come back just for the chance to show it off."

"But—"

"Emily?" I stop and look at him. "Merry Christmas."

Xavi is frantically rifling through his papers Friday evening at 4:45. I drum my fingers on the desk. I had hoped he would already be gone so I could go home and finish packing. My flight is early tomorrow, and I am supposed to try to meet up with Bennett sometime tonight, but I am never going to have a chance if Xavier doesn't get out of here. He's been here, so I've been here, late every night this week, as he has been trying to get four manuscripts edited before he leaves on his vacations. I don't know why he can't take the manuscripts home to work on them while he's gone, but I guess he thinks he'll be too busy "with his girls." I roll my eyes. I need to go. I'll write one more e-mail and hope he'll be done then.

Jacob.

My life is crazy. My boss is crazy. I don't have time to explain right now, but I'm really looking forward to seeing you when I get home. Which will be in about eighteen hours, assuming my crazy boss ever gets out of here so I can go pack. I'll give you call when I arrive. Got to go light a fire under the boss-man.

Emily

Without explaining to myself why I'm doing it, I open Jacob's last e-mail and reread what he wrote and chuckle. Then I look at him in the picture again. I use the little magnifying glass to zoom in on his face. Definitely cute. Not exactly New York cute, but definitely cute. Or was it just a good picture? I shrug and close it out. What's Xavier doing?!

"Are you okay in there, Xavier?" I say, trying to sound helpful. Please say yes. Please say you're leaving. A stack of papers hits the window and slides down the glass, a few loose papers fluttering down slowly.

"I ain't had this much fun since the hogs ate my brother," he yells, slamming a desk drawer shut.

"Just checking." I sigh and return to my cube. I close all the open programs on my computer, except for my e-mail, of course, which goes off when and only when the computer itself goes off, so I can be ready to run out the door as soon as he's gone. This week has been completely exhausting—not only have I worked longer and harder than at any other time, I feel emotionally drained as well. The Bennett conundrum has me worked into a ball of mush. I've decided to ignore my confusion and enjoy my last night with him before I go home, but I am afraid of the end of the evening. Twice since Thanksgiving Bennett has tried to get me to spend the night at his place, but I have made excuses both times. I just don't know what to do—no matter how much I remind myself that nothing happened and that there were extreme circumstances, I can't stop feeling weird about Bennett sleeping in my bed at his house. Though I wasn't sure how to react at first, I had to admit I had enjoyed having his arms around me all night. And I had loved waking up next to him. And I hadn't even tried to fight it when he slipped into my bed the next night. It was so nice having him so close—and yet . . .

And yet Jenna freaked out when I told her. Freaked out. My head still hurts thinking about the number of Bible verses she had quoted to me over the phone. How she had reminded me three times that even though "nothing happened," we were supposed to be above reproach, and it could confuse people about what my values really were. How she kept insisting that the way things look to the casual observer is just as important as what's really going on inside if I wanted to convince anyone of the sincerity of my beliefs. I shake my head, thinking about how I got defensive and started arguing back. Part of me thought she was just being old-fashioned and narrow-minded and told her so. The worst was that at least some corner of my mind, a portion from back home, knew she was probably right. The phone conversation ended up with her saying she needed to go, something was on TV. I tried to tell her I'd see her when I got home and we'd talk about it more, but she had already hung up.

So now my best friend thinks I am headed down the wrong path and is mad at me. I had thought about asking the girls at work what to do, but I was pretty sure Reggie would shrug and change the subject, or Skylar would laugh at me for being such a prude. Even Lane, who would be really nice about it, just wouldn't understand what the problem is. Caught between two poles, I didn't know where to turn and couldn't wait to get home and have some time and space to think.

I need to get out of here.

I hear Xavier mumbling something about missing a flight and something about Mongolia. I sigh and look back at my computer screen.

Dear Jenna,

I'll be home in a few short hours. I can't wait—and I really can't wait to talk to you. If you don't e-mail me back, I'll be forced to just come by. I know where you live! Ha ha.

Seriously. I understand that you're disappointed in me,

and I know we need to talk. I trust your opinion more than anyone's. We'll get this sorted out.

Love, Emily

A loud thud tears me away from my e-mail. I turn around quickly to see Xavier locking his office door. He walks toward me holding a large stack of papers.

"So you want to be an editor?" he asks, slamming the stack down in front of me. "Here's your big break. Edit this over Christmas, and we'll see how you do," he says, pulling the strap of his bag onto his shoulder, already walking away. Without another word, he begins to run down the hall to the elevators. I look after him, trying to clarify what he wants me to do with the manuscript, but he is gone. This is the stuff they never tell the authors. I roll my eyes. I guess I'm ready.

I look down at the manuscript. It's called *The Marine Corpse*. I shake my head. This isn't exactly what I had hoped my first editing project would be. I flip through the first chapter and am aghast by the number of times the word *bodybag* is used. Shaking my head, I turn to put it in my tote and am startled to find Helen standing behind me.

"He gave you the military thriller to edit?" she asks. "He said he might give that to me." Does she look disappointed? I almost feel bad for her, until I see her start to sneer. "I wouldn't wish that book on a dead horse. I guess he does like me after all."

Is it pathetic to miss Bennett already? I ask myself when I am buckled into my airline seat thirty thousand feet above the ground. Yes, I decide.

I have been through a lot in the past few hours. I need my boyfriend—geez, or whatever he is—right now. I decide to write him an e-mail. It's about the only thing that will make me feel better. I suddenly feel so alone. No New York friends. No Jenna. No Matthew. I slip my laptop out and turn it on.

I feel bad about just leaving Bennett last night—he was begging me to come back to his place with him because we'd be apart so long, but I told him I had to get up for an early flight, and I couldn't tell when I left if he was mad or just disappointed. Either way was not good as far as I was concerned.

I open up my e-mail program. Of course, I can't send it until I get home and hook up the computer, but I can write it now while my thoughts are fresh and save it to send later. I briefly consider just taking out a pen and writing a letter, but I dismiss that idea. No one writes letters anymore. Besides, why not take advantage of the fact that approved portable electronic devices are now okay to use.

"Bennett," (I begin)
When you look out your window and all you can see is Kansas, you know you're in for a long ride. What's a girl to do? No phone and only a really bad manuscript involving hand-grenade murders to read, so I decided to write to you. Charming, no?

I pause. This feels weird. I'm in the mood to write a really happy e-mail and just relax and tell someone about my zany airport adventure this morning, how much I'm looking forward to my father's Happy Dance, and how much I'll miss Lane (and maybe even Brittany), but unfortunately, I'm so mad at Bennett, or just confused, or worn out, that I can't do it. Maybe it's because I'm not sure how he feels about me. I don't want to write some dopey e-mail to a boy I'm clearly obsessed with who I'm possibly just another Skylar to.

"Ugh," I say aloud, accidentally. I look around to see if anyone heard me. One lady who has made her knuckles blanch from holding the armrest and her own knee is looking at me. I smile at her in apology and turn back to the computer.

Maybe I'll just send this to Jacob. I owe him a funny e-mail, and I'm too conflicted at the moment to write Bennett. It will sound fake if I try to write Bennett, I tell myself. I make good use of that delete key and try again.

Jacob. King of California!

I deliberate for a second and then keep what I've written so far about Kansas. Is that an e-mail foul? I add a little flourish before it to make the text seem new.

I figure I owe you a good e-mail, after that hilarious one you wrote me complete with an illustration and everything. Plus, I did send you that mean, cranky one from work saying I couldn't write. You = awesome. Me = knave. Wait, can a girl be a knave?

I smile at this. He's going to love this e-mail if I have him pegged correctly.

So I had to leave really early to catch my flight home. I was going to take the subway, but I packed so many pairs of shoes (you're not the only one who hasn't changed) that I decided I should just call a car to take me to the airport. No problem, I figured. Only, of course, I didn't wake up when I was supposed to and had to scramble to get myself together. And then the car started honking outside my window. I stuck my head out, while brushing my teeth mind you, and begged the driver to wait just a minute or two longer. Five minutes later, I ran down with my suitcases, and we were off!! To La Guardia, I cried!

Thanks to traffic we got there only about an hour before the flight. Whew, I thought. Just enough time to check in my baggage and grab a bacon, egg, and cheese delicacy. I gave the ticket guy my ticket at the check-in counter, and he stared at it, and then me. "You're at the wrong airport!" What?!!! "Go get a cab to JFK right now."

I ran outside, flagged down a cab, nearly in tears, and told my cabbie, "Quick, JFK, I'm at the wrong airport." He said, "I am Russian. We will make it." I nodded. What was that supposed to mean?! I had very little faith (although he certainly was driving like a madman) so I called the airline and asked about alternate flights that still had seats open. "Nothing," the guy said. "You've got to make this or you're not getting home for several days." "What?!" I cried. "Hey, lady," he said. "It's Christmas. You know, Christmas?" I just hung up. You know that thing your mom says about not saying anything at all if you can't say anything nice? Yeah, that.

I arrived at JFK a half hour later, just enough time for me to check my baggage for my hop to St. Louis and then from there to San Diego. I flew in the door and just made it. I grabbed some quick food and put it in my belly so fast that I had a stomachache. Then I waited to board. Any second. Any second.

My flight was canceled!!!

The airline was forced to rebook all of us on a later flight directly to California. Oh man.

I went to get coffee at a cafe on the second level. By then, I deserved it. While drinking my coffee, my wallet fell out of my bag and onto the level below. The next thing I heard was someone saying, "Ma'am? Ma'am? You dropped your wallet."

Needless to say, once I got on the flight to California, I collapsed. Maybe the government should make you pass some kind of test to travel alone.

Oh, and airline food . . . I mean, it's free, so normally I'd be okay with it, if not exactly excited by it, but guess what they served us for lunch? Potato salad. I know! Potato salad! Who does that? So I tried to pawn mine off on the people sitting next to me, but they were too smart. They realized I was offering them potato salad and declined. I can't wait to get some Jamba Juice.

I reread it. Oops, I think. It's really long. I'm sort of embarrassed. But I can't help but feel it's a cute e-mail, one that Jacob will love. It seems a shame to waste it, and I can't send it to Bennett. He prefers the phone, with its free nights and weekends. I know he'd make a crack about it. Hmm . . . But if I do send it to Jacob, then certainly he'll write me a really long e-mail back, which will probably split my sides it'll be so hilarious. I think of home and the bratty twins and my parents singing in harmony. I'll need the distraction.

I put on my headphones and sit back and close my eyes. I feel so much better now, as if I was able to share my harrowing event with a friend. I let out a sigh, and even start to think about pulling out *The Marine Corpse* to do some work. But then I can't fight it. My lids slide down.

The next thing I know, I am being asked by a flight attendant to put my computer away, my tray table up, and raise my seatback to its full upright position. Somehow I have missed all of the drink runs, two rounds of snacks, and a bad remake of *The Parent Trap*. I shake my head, trying to clear my thoughts.

I feel like I have been hit by a truck—exhausted, confused,

my head pulsing. I am in a daze the entire time the plane is on its final descent, trying to get it into my head that I am really about to be in Jenks. I am not in New York anymore. I am about to see my parents. And the goons.

I get really excited when the wheels of the plane finally touch down on the pavement. We are on California soil. I can't wait to run off the plane. I start bouncing my left leg up and down, up and down, in anticipation. I didn't think I would be this excited, but when the captain comes over the loudspeaker and announces that he would like to be the first to welcome us to San Diego, California, I start to cry. The old man next to me turns to stare, but I don't care that there are tears running down my cheeks. I am home.

CHAPTER 15

christmas paradise

★

Craig *leaps up* from the table and goes to the stereo center in the living room. I see him find a cassette tape covered in dust and put it in.

"Christmas, Christmas time is near, time for toys and time for cheer . . ."

Craig wails right along with the Chipmunks the lyrics to the number-one Christmas classic of the Hinton household, "The Chipmunk Song," but he must now use a falsetto voice that wasn't necessary last Christmas when we all sang this together. As he pulls up his chair and sits back down, Grant makes a horrendous farting noise. Nanna, seated in between the twins for the sake of peace and elbow room, twists Grant's ear, and he howls.

"Mom? Nanna's hurting me," says Grant.

I see my grandmother feign shock at Grant telling on her. My mom tries to look stern, but she's cracking up. When Pops passed away a few years ago, Nanna was inconsolable. But ever since she moved to La Jolla and comes over all the time, the mischievous twins have restored her spunky attitude.

"Nanna, please don't pull on Grant's oversized ears. Grant, please don't be a tattletale. And Craig, please spare us all your singing. Those poor Chipmunks," says Mom, shaking her head, acting like it's shameful to insult the creative work of such talented rodents.

It's been so long since I've been at a family meal with everyone—complete with good old Max, our lovable one-ear-up, one-ear-down mutt that followed the boys home one day, planted right by my chair because he knows I'll slip him some food when Mom's not looking—that I'm incapacitated with laughter. I used to be the life of this party, but I'm not up on all the inside family jokes. For one, Craig has a girlfriend. Her name is Kate. Now everyone, even my father, who isn't particularly funny unless dancing, teases him about her. They spend hours rhyming her name, saying "Craig is going on a date with Kate," or "Did Kate make you late?" or "Kate—isn't she great?" This makes Craig go crazy, and then he swears she's not his girlfriend. And even though they're identical twins, Grant is now half an inch taller than Craig, and inordinately proud of this fact. Grant likes to tell his older brother (by ten minutes and forty-five seconds), "You stay there, brother. I'll get that cup for you. It's waaaayyyy up on the top shelf." I'm picking up all the jokes pretty quickly, but I'm shocked at how much has changed in six short months. I feel an empty hollow inside of me when I realize that my brothers are growing up without me. I can't even bear to imagine them in their matching tuxes going to their prom without my being there to straighten their bow ties and tell their dates they look fabulous.

"This is all I wanted for Christmas this year. I wanted Manhattan home again and everyone to come together and just eat dinner like we used to," says Dad.

The boys, tearing into their rolls—the only thing they can get away with eating before grace—ignore Dad, but Nanna and I smile at each other.

"It's good to be home," I say. Mom and Dad bought my ticket

to California as my Christmas present. I want them to know how happy I am. "I've missed the insanity and chaos."

Mom raises her eyebrow at me.

"No, really. I have. Bennett's family was so . . ." I start to say it before I even think about it. My whole family is listening all of a sudden. There's been some gentle teasing about Bennett, but for the most part they've left me alone about him, which I was surprised by. Now I realize it's just because I've been gone, not because they're not dying to know about it. I cover my tracks. "Bennett's family is just a lot smaller, and their meals are a little quieter." Breakout conversations resume immediately when Craig and Grant both reach for the mashed potatoes.

I look at my Nanna across the table. She puts both her hands in the thumbs-up position and rests them on the table in front of her plate. She winks and me. I quickly put my fists on the table with my thumbs up. Then Grant and then Mom and then Dad. Craig sets down the mashed potatoes and looks at everyone with their thumbs-up sign shown.

"Ah man!" says Craig.

We're dying laughing. He says the same thing every time when he loses the thumbs-up race. I get *this* joke. Whoever puts their thumbs up last has to say grace. We've been doing it at big family meals for years, and unless there's an unwarned guest at the table, Craig always gets stuck. It's just so funny that he can't remember. Ever.

At ten o'clock that night the house is disturbingly quiet. Even though I should be tired because New York time is three hours ahead, I'm not. I guess I've gotten used to the energy on the streets of Manhattan, the rumble of traffic at all hours, the clusters of people always walking somewhere. In Jenks, the sound of the silence is pressing in on me. The boys have already wandered off to bed, Craig with the portable phone in his hand and Grant with a Kate rhyme on his lips. My parents conked out together on the loveseat shortly after their favorite sitcom. And Nanna, she's hopeless. She went to bed at eight. So here I am. At home. Alone. Doing nothing.

Max comes and sits next to me on the couch. He lets out a very contented doggie sigh and puts his chin on my thigh. Well . . . mostly alone. I pat him on the head.

I had gotten in that morning at eleven because of the time change just two hours after I took off from New York, and crashed immediately, sleeping away most of the day. Plus, weeks ago my mom had requested that tonight, my first real night at home, I stay in for a big family meal. I had already written Jenna that I wouldn't be able to hang out until the following day. Luckily for me, she's still answering my e-mails. I am definitely ready to see her. But what am I supposed to do until tomorrow morning? I look at my watch: 10:08.

I decide to call Bennett on my cell phone. After all, I got the more expensive plan so that I wouldn't have any long-distance fees, and it's only one in the morning there. I figure he'll still be up.

"Hey Emily," the familiar voice greets me.

"Hey there. How's the Wyeth Family Christmas going?" I ask, smiling to hear him.

"Whatever." He sounds really bored.

"Oh. You're such a spoilsport, Bennett. I'm having the best time. And guess who says hi?"

"Who?" he asks drowsily.

"Max! The man in my life before you."

"Oh."

"Now if that doesn't make your spirits bright then you are the Grinch himself."

He gives a weak laugh. "I am the Grinch. I don't like Christmas all that much to be honest. It's just a holiday that Hallmark took advantage of. There's nothing to do but sit around and watch *It's a Wonderful Life* again and again and again and eat too much."

I can't pretend that his intellectual wet-blanket routine doesn't bother me. He is such a drag when he's like this. "Oh," I say.

There is a long, awkward pause. I pull at a thread on my sweater. I think about recommending he watch the old version of *Rudolph the Red-Nosed Reindeer* with the weird puppets, but I am not in the mood to crack jokes.

"I'm sorry, Emily. You're right. I guess I just miss my girl, and I'm not coping well," he says.

I smile weakly. "That's sweet."

We hang up shortly thereafter. With all the questions I have for him hanging between us and his disenchantment with my favorite holiday, I have little to say, for the first time in my life.

After the call I feel worse than ever, full of nervous energy, staring at a wasted evening in paradise. I need to physically do something if I am going to prevent my mind from turning into mush. In desperation, I excuse myself from Max and go to check my e-mail. I see him sleepily make his way down the hallway, no doubt going to bed like any sane person, uh, dog. But I can't. I've got the jitters. Maybe Jacob responded to my message.

I open my e-mail. There is a message from Reggie, wishing me a Happy Holidays and a kiss under the mistletoe. There is one from Brittany, wishing me a safe trip and telling me when she is returning to the apartment. She also asks if I would please make sure the pine wreath I bought for our door is gone and "cleaned up" by the time she returns because she suspects she's allergic to the oils in its needles. I just shake my head and close out my e-mail, feeling lower and lower.

"Hmph," I say, sitting down in front of the TV, which never seems to be off in this house. In fact, the puppet version of

Rudolph is on. I know it is my evil fate after all and begin to watch it, even though I sense it is depressing me further and has always creeped me out on some level. My cell phone rings.

Bennett, I figure. I hope he is in a better mood this time, but when I look at the screen I don't recognize the number on the caller ID. His parents' line?

"Hello?" I ask.

"Uh, Emily?"

I pause.

"It's Jacob. Uh, from home? I mean, Jenks? From e-mail?"

"Oh." I am startled.

"You were sleeping, weren't you? I'm sorry. I knew—"

"No! No, no, no. I'm not doing anything. I'm just surprised."

"Hey, lady. You gave me your number."

I laugh. "Guilty, guilty. I just thought I had scared you away with that nutty e-mail."

"Are you kidding me? Why else do you think I'm calling? It was a work of art. Emily, you get an A. First in class. And I'm also calling because the only thing on TV is *Rudolph the Red-Nosed Reindeer*, but not like the good *Rudolph*, the scary one where he's a puppet and that weird elf wants to be a dentist. You know the one I mean?"

We talk for three hours. At separate times both Craig and Grant come in to ask me to "Shhh" and "Go outside," respectively, because I am laughing so loudly. I finish my conversation in the backyard, lying on the old trampoline, looking up at the stars. Every time I try to go, Jacob asks me to stay because he swears when he closes his eyes, he can still see that evil reindeer puppet coming after him. How can I say no?

CHAPTER 16

comfort and joy

★

Despite getting to bed around two in the morning, I wake up bright and early the next morning. I mumble a curse about time zones, then hit myself. When did I start cursing?

There's no one else up this early, and I try to fall back asleep, but I finally realize it's no use and get up to make coffee. I look on my floor and see that Max has come in and curled up on a giant pile of my dirty clothes, just to be near me. As I stumble through my room, he wakes up and drowsily starts to follow me around. I get dressed while the coffee's brewing and then we walk quietly back into the kitchen. As I'm putting sugar in my coffee, I gaze out the kitchen window. There are birds fighting over a seed in the birdfeeder my mom has hung outside. I take a sip and decide I might as well get some work done. I go back to my room and grab my manuscript, then head out to the back porch, mug in hand. I sit down and then hear a quiet whimpering and some light scratching. I see Max on the other side of the door with his head turned to the side, trying his very best to be cute. I get up and let him out with me. I sit back down on one of the patio chairs my dad so lovingly refinishes every year, Max jumps into my lap, and I sigh. I would never be able to edit while sunbathing with a lovable little furball in my lap in December in

New York. My building doesn't even allow pets, and I chuckle thinking of Brittany around an actual animal.

Max passes right out. Ahh . . . the life of a dog. Luckily for me, the plot of *The Marine Corpse* is not very complicated, and the reading goes pretty quickly. I have a few suggestions about tense shifts and the limits of the first-person narrator that the author seems unaware of, but for the most part, the book is in pretty good shape. I even start to get engrossed in the story and am slightly startled when Mom pokes her head out the back door to ask if I want eggs for breakfast. Yes. Of course I do, and not just because they're free. Someone else is cooking them! I put the pages back in order, slip a rubber band around them, shoo Max down, and bring them and my empty mug into the kitchen while somehow managing not to trip over Max in his excitement that everyone is up now. It's nice to be where you are taken care of. I had forgotten how good it feels. Also the dishwasher is a real marvel of modern technology. If only my New York friends could see me now.

As much as I'm looking forward to seeing Jenna, I'm also dreading our lunch today. Jenna suggested we get together at the all-you-can-eat salad buffet we always loved, and I decide it is as good a place as any for what is bound to be an awkward meal. It feels weird to be fighting with her—sure, we've had our differences over the years, but we've never had to have a meeting with the express (though unexpressed) purpose of reconciliation.

My parents have kept my car in the driveway the whole time I've been gone. It is an orange station wagon with peeling wood paneling on the sides that my dad bought to haul everybody around after Craig and Grant were born. But when I got my driver's license, they officially bequeathed it to me and bought a newer used car for Mom. I smile as I slide into the driver's seat—

it feels just right. The seat is pushed way up to the steering wheel, just the way I like it. The radio presets are all tuned to my favorite stations. The hula girl I stuck on the dashboard and the fuzzy dice I hung from the rearview mirror are exactly where they are supposed to be. This car is old and ugly, but it is mine, and I love it.

I turn the key and static comes on where one of my favorite stations used to be. I suddenly remember I haven't driven once in six months.

I tune it to a real station and back down the driveway nice and easy. It's just like riding a bike. I drive toward the freeway entrance. Freeways are something else I miss, I think. Traffic goes quickly, and they take you everywhere you need to go. Pulling into the parking lot, I realize that I would never admit it in New York, but I also miss malls. Of course they sell the same thing as in every other mall in the country. Who cares? What makes them fun is the good, old-fashioned thrill of buying some candy, walking around with your friends, spying cute boys, and running into half your town. I pull expertly into a narrow parking space, turn off the engine, step out of the car, and slam the car door. No need to lock it—no one is going to steal this car. I walk across the parking lot to the restaurant. From a ways off I can see that Jenna is already waiting outside. Punctual to a fault. She hasn't changed.

"*Emily!*" she yells. She waves both her hands frantically.

My heart swells. She's wearing baggy blue jeans, a big T-shirt she got at orientation week at San Diego State, and white tennis shoes. Her sandy brown hair hangs straight down her back. That's my Jenna, I think as I walk toward her. I'm so happy to see her that the dread and the embarrassment fall away. I give her a big hug, and we hold each other for a few seconds.

"I've missed you so much," she finally says, pulling back. "You look great!"

"I've missed you too," I say, dropping my arms. "You have no idea how much."

"Oh, no. I can imagine. I would miss me too," she says, laughing.

"Yeah, well, not as much as I missed Fresh Express," I say. "Let's go eat."

We both walk in and move to the end of the infinite salad bar. "You'll never guess who I talked to last night," I say as I reach for the arugula.

"Who?" she asks, taking a big spoonful of iceberg lettuce. Jenna thinks anything else tastes like weeds.

"Jacob! We've been in touch since you ran into him that time. He's doing really well these days." I place tomato slices, peas, and carrot slivers on top of my lettuce. Jenna reaches for the grated yellow cheese.

"Oh yeah?" she asks, pouring about a gallon of ranch over her lettuce. I get a neat little cup of Italian vinaigrette and put it on the side of my plate.

"Yeah. He's so funny now. I don't remember him being that fun to talk to in high school."

"Annoying is how I remember him. Do you remember the youth group trip to Mexico where he held your pillow for ransom?" she asks.

"Yeah. And he demanded a bottle of pineapple soda to get it back. Instead I just told on him, and he got in so much trouble."

"Oh yeah. He was so mad!"

"He seems to have forgiven me. We talked for three hours last night."

"Three hours!"

"He says we should all get together this week to reminisce."

"That sounds great to me. Now that you're gone, I really need to meet more sane people who still live around here."

We finish loading up our trays with breadsticks and soup and baked potatoes, then sit down at a table in the corner. "So tell me all about New York," she says. "What's it really like?"

"It's really . . . great," I say. How do you sum up six months in a big city? "It's fast-moving and exciting. It's very stimulating. There are great museums and parks, and so many interesting people. There is always something new and exciting to do. There are people from all over the place on this little island, and no matter where you go you can get good food from anywhere in the world."

"So when you have a special occasion, you must have a hard time deciding where to go!" she says. "What's your favorite?"

"Oh, I don't know. I really like this one little street that is just lined with Indian restaurants—they're all basically the same, but these men stand out front each one trying to convince you to eat in their restaurant. They're all decorated with millions of colored lights and mirrors and most of them have live sitar music. It's really quite an experience," I say, looking around at the drab white walls with framed prints showing baskets of fruit. "But we don't just eat out for special occasions, really. I almost never cook now. I don't have time, and everyone eats out there. It's just what you do."

"Emily! That's so expensive. Eating out every meal?"

"Not every meal. I eat cereal for breakfast," I say, realizing how lame that sounds.

"But how do you afford it?"

"It's just another expense. Food is food—you need it anyway. That's easier to justify than some of the other things you have to spend money on out there. Like alcohol. And clothes. You are expected to look nice and be stylish all the time."

Jenna looks down at her salad and then over at me. "I noticed those were some fancy jeans you were wearing," she says.

"I'm not even going to tell you how much they cost," I say, spearing a piece of lettuce with my fork.

"I don't think I want to know." She uses her bread to push some lettuce onto her fork. "Why the alcohol? You don't need to spend money on that."

"But I kind of do, see? That's what everyone does. You go out for drinks after work to bond with your work friends. You drink when you go out on a Saturday night. You have to—to be at all socially acceptable, you drink. I could sit at home by myself, or I could go to the bars and make friends. It costs money."

Jenna doesn't say anything for a minute, but I can sense her disapproval. "So do you like the church you've been going to?"

"It's really good—everyone is young and artsy, and sincere." I look at her. "And don't worry—I go almost every week. I'm not falling away like you seem to think I am."

"Oh, Emily . . ." she begins. I take a deep breath. "I didn't mean to imply that you were falling away or a bad person or anything. I really didn't," she says, taking a sip of water. "I'm just worried about you, is all. I care about you so much, and I want what's best for you."

"I appreciate that, Jenna. Seriously. You have to know that I love you for that, and I am glad to have you concerned about me. But," I say, pausing, "how can you know what's best for me? You live three thousand miles away. New York is a different world, and one that I am dealing with adjusting to."

"I know you are, Em. I know you really want to do what's right, and I can see that you're trying to walk the line in a very unforgiving place. But you have to admit you've changed. You care about different things. You spend your time differently. You're making different decisions."

"Jenna, I . . ." What do I want to say? How can I explain to her that of course I've changed, but deep down nothing at all is different? "Look, I appreciate your concern, but I'm still the same. I dress a little differently. I have different eating habits. I have made some new friends. But I am still a Christian, and that's never going to change. Nothing is ever going to take that away from me."

"You're still a Christian, but are you living like one?"

I am not sure whether to be hurt or angry at this.

"Jenna, yes! If only you knew how much ridicule I took for not drinking as much as everyone else, for going to church, for not staying over at my boyfriend's apartment. It was just that once at Thanksgiving, and I've already told you I'm not sure that it was right." I'm getting emotional and defensive. My voice raises an octave. I bite my lip, hard, and hope I don't burst into tears.

"Okay. I'm sorry. I don't mean to sound judgmental. But what about this boyfriend? Is he trying to make you do things you don't want to do?"

"No, He's just . . . not really. He's just—"

"He's a Christian, right?"

"Of course he is. He brought me to church. He—"

"Okay. Then if he really is, and he really cares about you, he should want what's best for you spiritually."

"He is. And he does. Like I said, he brought me to church. He introduced me to the pastor."

"But he *is* trying to get you to sleep with him?" It's kind of question, kind of an accusation.

"Not like that, Jenna. He just wants me to stay over sometimes. He doesn't have any bad intentions or anything. He just wants to be with me. Which," I say, taking a bite of my breadstick, "I find extremely flattering. He's a really good guy. He's amazing, in fact. If you could just meet him, this would all make sense. You would adore him. Everyone adores him."

She nods. "Maybe."

I stare at her for a minute. "Jenna," I say. "I know what's important to me. That is not going to change. I know what I believe, and I am going to stick by that." I think about telling her about the time I got drunk and how guilty I felt about it afterward to prove that I knew how bad things turn out when you go against what you think is right, but I am not sure I can deal with what I know will be a bad reaction to that little story. "I am a Christian, and I'm living in a place that doesn't take too kindly to Christians. It's not like here. At all. I'm doing the best I can."

She stares at me. "I know you are. And I admire you for making the effort to try. I just worry about you because I care."

"Thanks, Jenna. Please continue to care. And please pray for me as I try to walk the line."

"Oh, I will," she says, laughing. "Believe you me, I will. You're sure going to need it."

"Yeah," I say. "I probably will." We're both quiet for a minute. The silence is awkward, and I'm uncomfortable with the idea that we're both pondering my spiritual well-being. Say something to make this less awkward, Emily. "So now that we've got that out of the way, let's go get some dessert."

Jenna smiles broadly. "I'll race you to the frozen yogurt!" she says, already getting out of her chair.

We build swirled yogurt towers in our bowls.

"Know what the girls in New York call this? Fro-yo."

"Emily," Jenna says, "is there no end to how weird those people are?"

Jacob's parents, it seems, have been keeping him pretty busy over the holidays at their wine and cheese shop. I vaguely knew that his parents owned some kind of business, but I guess I had never been curious enough to ask about it. He tells me they have two locations, both called Burgundy & Brie. One is located in La Jolla, and they have just opened a new store in San Diego. His parents are originally from Jenks and were high school sweethearts. They still love the country and therefore see no reason to live anywhere else. They are ex-hippies, like most of our parents, only, from the sound of things, they traded in their tie-dye not for Kiwanis Club and the Junior Women's Service League T-shirts, but Kenneth Cole and Diane von Furstenberg.

He's been he?ing them with the Christmas boom, working late and closing the San Diego location almost every night. He said in an e-mail that when he wasn't working, he was looking up child labor laws. I was trying to be our group's social coordinator. I'd attempted to get all three of us together several times, but I finally gave up hope that Jenna, Jacob, and I would ever find a hole in all of our schedules at once. Jenna said to just go ahead and hang out without her and get Jacob's phone number so that they could get together once Christmas was over and her life calmed down.

We decided to go to a movie and then maybe grab some coffee to catch up, but the day of our little get-together, Jacob called to say he was swamped at the shop and wouldn't be able to go home to get his car so he couldn't meet me at the theater like he had been planning. Would I mind just picking him up at the store so we could head over to the theater together?

I ask my parents if I can borrow their "new" Volkswagen for the evening. It was minted a mere five years ago, making it the youngest car at the Hinton household. My mother raises an eyebrow and asks, "Jacob? You always said he was a pest. Isn't he the one who made you cry in third grade when he wouldn't stop talking about how he beat you at Bible drill?"

I shrug and say, "I don't know. No one else is home. Jenna's busy. Besides, he lives here." I shrug again. I don't really know what I am doing either. Am I that bored or that intrigued? Is this a date? No. Do I want it to be? Probably not. I have a boyfriend already. I live in New York. And Jacob can't have changed that much, no matter how bored I am.

I sigh as I turn the key off in the ignition. It seems presumptuous to assume Jacob might get the wrong idea, but I can't help feeling like I should have told him that I have a boyfriend. This is what I've always hated about dating. I can't really tell him I have a boyfriend unless we are on a date. If we are just "hanging out" as Jacob said in his e-mail, my confession about Bennett will be apropos of nothing, and I will look like a fool. I shake my head and get out of the car. Maybe I will try to slip a reference to Bennett into the conversation at some point.

I pop my head in the door and see fifteen or so people crowded in the quaint Burgundy & Brie. I enter, look around for Jacob, and finally spot him behind the cheese case. He looks a little older, a little more defined, somehow. He sees me, bends in half with a sweeping bow, his left arm extended and his right folded at his waist, and then smiles. I laugh.

"Sir Lancelot? May I try the chèvre when you're done?" a customer asks. He shrugs a silent apology to me and begins to help the woman with her sample. There are several other people at the counter also wanting samples. I notice he's a little red after his good-natured scolding.

Jacob's mother, Catherine Keller, is behind the cash register. I smile and wave at her. She was always active in the church nursery, so I remember her. She drags her hand across her brow, laughs a little at the chaos, and smiles back. I decide to look around the store for a minute and see if the closing rush dies down a little.

The interior is intended to look very European. The shelves are lined with bottles and bottles of pricey wine, arranged by region on rough-hewn wooden shelves. I notice there are little display cards next to some of the bottles proclaiming employee favorites. I scan the shelves and eventually find Jacob's favorite, a French wine.

Inky, full-bodied red from the village of Beaune. Excellent when paired with beef or lamb. Also recommended for a romantic evening of Scrabble.

I laugh out loud. His parents must be pretty cool to allow him to get away with that. Also, I can't help but be impressed by his wine knowledge. Of course, Bennett is good at that stuff too. Was I the only twenty-something who never became an oenophile? Perhaps that's what they teach at the good schools. I hear something behind me.

"I hadn't planned on us playing Scrabble tonight, but you should try this anyway."

I turn around and see Jacob standing behind me in a crisp white apron, extending a glass of deep red wine to me. I take it and smile. He leans down and kisses me on the cheek. I see that a few of the people in the store notice and smile at us.

"Hi, Emily."

"Hi yourself," I say. I kick myself for being such a flirt, but he laughs.

We stand there looking at each other as the busy clusters of people swim around us. His hair is dark brown and perfectly disheveled on top. His eyes are still shockingly green. His long white teeth gleam through his huge grin, and he is so tall. I finally look down. He doesn't even look like the same person. That bothersome little boy. I can feel that my cheeks are very hot, and I say a silent prayer of thanks that I decided to put on my nice jeans and the boots after all.

He shakes his head. "You look great. Just like I remember."

"If I look so great, why are you denying me my game of Scrabble?" I ask, turning my head up to him. Why am I flirting?

"It's simple," he says. "You'll lose." I open my mouth to protest, but he speaks first, cutting me off. "You're still a pain, I see. Good. That was always my favorite part about you. Come say hi to my mom. Wait. First, taste my wine."

I have a sip. It trickles down my throat and feels warm and strong. "Wow. It's really good."

"Hey, hey, Miss New York. Don't sound so surprised. We know a thing or two about city living out here too."

"I just didn't know *you* knew about wine."

"Are you kidding me? I was raised in the La Jolla store. I know everything about wine and cheese, whether I'd like to or not. How to tell if a cheese was made from goat's or sheep's milk doesn't come in too handy when writing about music, but I think the ladies like it."

A little prick hits my heart. What ladies? I regain my composure. Two can play at this game. "Oh! Are you as sought-after as all that? My congratulations, sir. Mercy. The things women will do for a man who knows his cheese." I deliver this little speech with layer upon layer of sarcasm, something I have really gotten a lot better at lately.

He winks at me and puts a hand on my back, urging me across the room to his mother.

We don't talk with Mrs. Keller very long, but she asks about my family and tells me to call her Catherine, which feels weird after a lifetime of Mrs. Keller.

She looks at the crowd swarming Abby, the one employee on staff tonight besides herself and Jacob. "You guys hurry up and take off before the looting hordes get you. Have a wonderful time. I want a full report."

Jacob kisses his mom on the cheek and watches as she helps Abby with the crowd. They are swamped, and the customers waiting in line are looking impatient. He looks torn. He turns to me. "We should go. You ready? Bottom's up!"

"Jacob, we can't leave your mom like this. You stay. She'll never get out of here. I'll take a rain check. I'll be here a few more days."

He looks a little relieved and glances at his mom. And then

he turns back to me, screwing up his face. "No. I will not agree to that. I'm harder to get rid of than that, Emily Hinton. Nice try, bucko."

I try to protest again, to convince him that another day is really fine with me, but he walks away. He is back in an instant with a giant white apron. He puts the neck-loop over my head and pulls me to him. He grabs my shoulders, spins me around, and ties the strings behind my back. It's thrilling in a weird way to be so close to him. I can tell he's done tying the strings, but he lingers for a moment. I fight the urge to lean into him.

"You're stuck with me. The good news is, you can have all the fine wine and cheese you want. And, maybe, just maybe if you're really good at the end of the night, we'll have a pizza party."

I'm cracking up.

"What do you say? Everyone loves a pizza party."

I don't look at my watch until ten thirty. The evening flies by. Instead of closing at the normal hour, we stay open until the crowd dies out naturally. Jacob mans the cheese, his mother the wine floor, Abby works the cash register, and I bag and wrap things to go. After the last customer leaves, Catherine disappears into the back. The background music in the little store soars. It is a lively merengue band that I've never heard. While I help Jacob shut down the cheese case for the evening and Abby counts down the "reg," his mother sings in Spanish and mops the floor like a seasoned professional. At one point, Jacob strolls out onto the floor, grabs his mother, and the two waltz around. He spins her out, and she grabs the mop back. He then turns to me and beckons me to join him. I refuse. I don't know how to dance. At that, he fakes being stabbed in the heart, which makes Abby and me laugh.

Finally the whole place is shut down. Eleven o'clock. And I

am exhausted. I give Catherine a hug. She thanks me for my help and makes Jacob promise that I'll take home one of the expensive gift baskets to my parents. Abby leaves while Jacob and I are on the phone with the only pizza place that is still delivering at this hour.

Jacob turns off all the lights in the store and locks the front door. I know now we are definitely on a date in his eyes. But I suddenly don't care. I don't want to have a boyfriend anymore. I put Bennett in the back of my mind while Jacob goes into the storeroom in the back. And then I hear a man singing in the most beautiful and pained voice I've ever heard. I can't place it. It's definitely American and soft but somehow still what my mom would call rock and roll.

"This is one of my favorite bands," he says, coming back out.

I roll my eyes at him. Of course. It all comes back to bands.

"What did you think? I was going to put on some jazz and romance you? Miss Hinton, you still underestimate me." While he's tsk-tsking me, he spreads a blanket on the floor. "I stole this from our Tuscan display. Remind me to put it back. The housewives really think it's precious." He grabs a bottle of wine from the French section and goes behind the counter to open it. "You like the reds, right?"

We talk for two hours, laughing so much I can't breathe. Maybe it's the wine, but we're having the time of our lives. We wonder what makes pizza so good. Is there some magic involved? We discuss his career in music journalism. He calls it "nonprofit work." We laugh about high school. I can't believe we survived. I tell him stories about New York, about being a Christian in the city.

"It's really hard being a Christian at work. But it's a great opportunity to be able to influence the lives of people who've had very little contact with the church and God. I feel like a freaka-zoid when I say that I go to church every Sunday and look at communion as more than an opportunity for a snack and a swig of wine."

"Try being in clubs every night of the week. It's almost impossible. But mostly it's lonely. I ask myself, how will I ever find a girl? My requirements essentially eliminate the entire human population."

We are quiet at this. He reaches out, tugs gently on my hair, and shakes his head a little.

"Emily, Emily. Tell me. Why is it that you live in New York again? To ensure that I have a miserable life?"

I'm so excited to hear him betray his feelings for me. Then I remember Bennett.

I feel Max licking my face and can sense two bodies standing over me.

"*Merry Christmas!*" the twins yell. They give each other a high-five and Grant burps.

I fumble for a pillow to throw at them, but they are already off to wake up Mom and Dad. I had hoped that maybe this year they were old enough to sleep past seven on Christmas Day, but I guess not. Max keeps putting his wet nose all over my face, and for a moment, I actually miss New York. Britt never disturbs me when I'm sleeping. Some things are sacred.

As I sit up and join the land of the living, a smile spreads across my face. It's Christmas! Christmas! And I'm sure Bennett will call today. I hadn't heard from him since I hung out with Jacob the other night, and I really need him to call. And if I'm honest with myself, it's partially because I stopped Jacob from kissing me. It had been a weak moment, but I persevered for Bennett. For what we had. And I am glad. Bennett is not perfect, but he is gorgeous and charming. And, I remind myself, a Christian. Plus my life is in New York now, not California. Jacob was very classy about the whole thing, but he told me it was a shame. I agree, actually. He is an amazing person, but it will never work.

I focus on the present. This year it's really special being home with my family again, particularly at church last night. Mom somehow managed to talk Craig and Grant into suits for the candlelight Christmas Eve service. Although it's the same every year, I am always moved to tears when we sing "Silent Night" in the dark, and then the pastor lights one candle and passes the flame on to the ushers. The ushers ignite the candles of the people surrounding them, and slowly, the room lights up, physically demonstrating what it means to have and share the light of the world. This is always my favorite part of Christmas, a chance to remember why we celebrate and come together.

"Emily?" I hear my mom calling from the kitchen. I swing my legs over the side of my bed and head straight for the coffeepot to get my dark lethal brew going. Mom makes us eat breakfast before any of the presents get touched, which always drives us crazy but adds to the excitement of the morning, and this year is no exception to the rule. She says she doesn't care how old we think we are, tradition is tradition. There are loads of presents under the tree—most of them small, but Mom likes to wrap everything separately so that the sheer abundance of them is an impressive sight on Christmas morning.

Mom and Dad bought Craig and Grant the latest video game system, and they almost knock each other out trying to get the paper off. It doesn't seem to bother them one bit that they are expected to share, and they spend most of the day trying out their new games, discussing secret moves. I try to ignore the obnoxious sounds from the thing and dive into a book until Aunt Sharon and her brood come over to spend the day.

Eventually the *Muppet Family Christmas* comes on, and the whole kit and caboodle gathers round for yet another Hinton family tradition. Dad swears it is the funniest Christmas movie ever made and ends up on the floor with tears rolling down his cheeks in laughter and Max barking in all the excitement and licking his face. I've seen it so many times that I know it by heart, so I feel no guilt zoning out and turning back to *The Marine Corpse*. I can still laugh at all the appropriate jokes without even paying attention.

Toward the end, the doorbell rings, making Max go nuts until my mom promises him it isn't a burglar. Mom makes me grab one of the emergency fruit baskets from the living room, afraid it is a neighbor that we don't have on our Christmas list bringing over a present. But it isn't a neighbor—it's the FedEx man.

"FedEx delivers on Christmas?" Grant asks after he flings the front door open.

"We sure do," the man says, smiling. He is dressed in a regulation uniform but has on a Santa hat. "And I have a package for a . . . Emily Hinson."

"Hinton," Grant corrects him. Craig kicks him.

"It was close enough," Craig explains to the smarting Grant. I set down the fruit basket in the foyer and rush to the door to retrieve my package and relieve the poor delivery guy of my brothers.

"Thanks so much for bringing it by today," I say, taking the small box into my arms.

"Enjoy. And you all have a merry Christmas," he says, waving as he turns to walk back toward his truck.

"Wait!" I say. I don't know if it's just the season or the unexpected gift, but I am feeling great. The FedEx man turns back and looks at me, puzzled. I put down my little box and grab the basket. I run out on the driveway to him with the fruit. "Merry Christmas." He chuckles and thanks me, and I run back inside.

"Open it!" Craig says, slamming the door shut.

"Who's it from?" Mom yells from the kitchen.

"I don't know yet. It doesn't say on the outside," I yell back. I hope it's from Bennett. Sure he gave me a gift, a silver bracelet from Tiffany's, before I left, but I can't help but hope this is another little surprise he sent just to show how much he cares. I tear open the box and find a smaller box covered in thick, shiny red paper. It's tied with a wide silver velvet bow. Bennett really went all out. I shake the styrofoam peanuts off the paper, slip the bow off, careful to preserve it, and slit the tape on the side with my nail. You can't just rip into a package like this, although Grant is ready to do it for me if I don't hurry it up. Inside the box is a layer of thin tissue paper, and when I lift that up I find a brown leather wallet. The leather is shiny and soft, and the pockets are lined with a crimson silk.

"It's beautiful," Mom says, leaning over me from behind. "It's from Bennett, isn't it?"

"A wallet?" Grant asks, disappointed.

"And pretty darn expensive, by the looks of it," adds Dad. "Whoever got you that is a friend you need to hold on to!"

"I think it's from . . . oh, wait. There's a card here in the bottom of the box," I say, spotting a little white envelope. I pull out the small square of white cardboard.

Emily,

Sorry I didn't get this to you before you left. I didn't get to do my Christmas shopping until Christmas Eve! I hope it gets to you in time for the big day and that you're enjoying your time with your family. Thanks for being a great roommate.

Brittany

"It's from my roommate," I say quietly. Brittany got me this wallet?

"Your wacko roommate sent you this?" asks Craig, laughing. "I hope you got her something good."

"Yeah, like etiquette lessons," Grant says. Have I really complained that much about how crazy she is? I feel a little green.

"Wow," I say, fingering the leather. "Actually, I didn't get her anything. I just didn't really think of it. I sure wish I had."

"Maybe she's thanking you for putting up with her craziness," Dad says.

"Preston, that's not nice," Mom says. "But that really is very sweet of her. To have it arrive all the way across the country on Christmas Day and everything!"

"Yeah" is all I can muster. I am dumbstruck by her unexpected generosity. Maybe Brittany is human after all.

Christmas dinner is the culmination of all things Christmas each season, but I'm not enjoying it as much as I'd like because there is still no call from Bennett. With my family, Aunt Sharon and Uncle Philip, their two kids, my cousins Sophie and Brent, and Nanna, the table is full and loud. Much of the meal is spent questioning Sophie, who has recently decided to become a vegetarian. Earlier, I winced for her when I spotted the "Tofurky" she brought over to eat. I knew she was going to catch some grief, both good-natured and not, for going over to the dark side. Nanna doesn't approve but controls her tongue, and Grant only has to be kicked once when he asks, "If God didn't want us to eat animals, why did he make them out of meat?" before he remembers his manners. Craig, just to be different than Grant, pronounces it "cool."

After dinner, I try to read, but I can't focus on the words on the page. I sigh. Bennett (I'm trying to project to his subconscious back in Connecticut), call me. Call me! He's probably busy with his family. I ignore the voice in my head that wants to remind me exactly how busy the Wyeth household is at holidays. It doesn't mean anything. It doesn't matter. But I can't help feeling that it really does.

more fish in the east river

★

The apartment phone rings, and I nearly drop my toothbrush trying to get to it before the caller hangs up. It's the lobby calling; Bennett is here. I tell the doorman to send him up to my apartment, then rush back into the bathroom to rinse the toothpaste out of my mouth. I am both excited and terrified to see Bennett. I just got back into town this afternoon and am exhausted, but he was so sweet when he called. He said he was really excited to see me again, so I caved in and told him to bring over dinner.

I don't get him. I'm glad he can't wait to see me, but if he missed me so much he should have called a few times while I was gone. I smooth my hair, checking in the mirror one last time before he gets to my door. At least I have a tan.

I hear a knock and rush to open the door. Bennett is standing there with a bag of Chinese takeout in one hand and a bottle of wine in the other. A few flakes of snow cling to his dark hair. He steps forward and wraps his arms around me, pressing the wine into my back. He pulls back, looks me in the eye, then leans forward to kiss me. We stumble into the room, and I kick the door closed. He manages to put the bag down on the table without moving his lips away from mine. Slowly he backs me into the living room, still kissing me, where he gently pushes me down onto the couch. "I've missed you," he finally says, propping himself up on his right hand.

"I've . . . I missed you too," I say, looking at the curve of his shoulder. I start to move away, but he starts to stroke my hair, and I try to relax. I start to move again as his hand slowly moves lower, but he pulls me back. We're both quiet, listening to each other breathe, and he begins stroking my stomach. I twist away, but he pulls me back.

"The food is going to get cold," I whisper.

"I don't care," he answers, kissing me again. I hear the clock ticking. I hear the refrigerator humming. I feel him pressed against me and remind myself how lucky I am to have a boyfriend who would come through the snow to my apartment to welcome me home, but as he slips his hand under my shirt and begins to work it up past my stomach, I pull away again.

"No," I say, pulling my shirt down defiantly.

"Emily," he moans. "Come on. I missed you so much," he says, sliding it back up.

"Bennett," I begin, but he covers my mouth with his and presses his weight down on top of me. I push against him, but he is stronger and heavier than I expect. I twist underneath him, trying to sit up.

"What?" he asks, pulling back. "Why are you making this such a big deal?" He leans in to whisper in my ear. "I'm just trying to show you how glad I am to see you."

"I think we should eat dinner now," I say, sitting up quickly.

"Emily, you're always stopping things when I'm getting romantic with you," he says, more than a hint of irritation in his voice. "Why do you do that?" He sits up.

"We've gone through this," I say, burying my head in my hands. "I just think we need to be careful that things don't get out of control."

"They've never gotten out of control before. Not with any

other girl. They're certainly not going to with you," he says. He uses his fingers to brush his hair back into place.

I bristle. I am not sure how to take that.

"Other girls like Skylar, you mean?"

"Yes," he snaps. "Other girls like Skylar. I wasn't sure if you knew about that or not, but apparently you do. Yes, I went out with Skylar."

"Were you going to tell me about that? She's my friend," I ask. My voice fails.

"Eventually, yes," he says. "But I don't see how it matters. I went out with her. We broke up. Now I'm with you. What more do you need?"

I have gone too far. Now he's mad. But at this point I have to push on. "I thought you only dated . . . well, uh, why did you break up with her?"

"Emily," he says, taking my hand and looking me in the eye. "That was a long time ago." I just stare at him. He sighs. "Okay, here's the whole story. Skylar's brother was a friend of mine at Yale. She came up to visit him one time, and we got along really well. But obviously nothing was going to happen, since she lived so far away and she wasn't a Christian. But once she started working at Morrow & Sons, we ran into each other and started hanging out. We had a great time, and we were obviously very attracted to one another. So we started spending more time together than we should have. And pretty soon we were going out all the time. I knew it was a bad idea, but I thought it wouldn't matter too much." He takes a deep breath. "Only it did matter. And the more I cared about her, the harder it was. So I broke it off—she wasn't what I needed. And then I met you, and you were."

I try to absorb this, but I can't figure out what I'm supposed to think. All I know is this doesn't sound right. "So I'm just convenient to have around because I happen to go to church?" A tear leaks out of my eye.

"No, Emily, it's not like that. I mean, yes—at first I asked you out because you were a Christian. You were exactly what I was looking for, what I really thought I needed. I really felt like I could make myself stop caring about her if I started caring about someone I could end up with."

My stomach turns. I wait a minute until I'm sure I'll be able to speak without being overcome by tears. "You wanted to go out with me to get over her? Because I happened to be a Christian?"

"No. I mean . . . no, not at all. I liked you for who you were, but I wouldn't have gone out with anyone who wasn't a Christian at that point. I was really trying to do the right thing, and you helped me. You were exactly what I needed."

His words hit me in the gut, knocking the wind out of me for a moment. "So . . . you used me," I whisper. "And you still care for Skylar—"

"Emily, I am not going to go out with Skylar ever again."

"We're so different. I mean, she's so . . . But you would if you could?"

"Any guy would jump at the chance to go out with Skylar, Emily. But I feel so conflicted—"

"And you lied to me about Yale," I interrupt. He stops and looks up at me, bewildered.

"I thought we cleared that up. I told you I had to leave."

"But you didn't tell me that you were flunking out when they *asked* you to leave."

"I . . . where did you hear that?" I can see from his shocked expression that it is true.

"It doesn't matter where I heard it. I can't trust you at all, can I?"

"We have so much in common. We're both standing on the same solid rock, for starters. We can work this out because of that." He has once again pulled out his faith when it is convenient for him. I don't buy it anymore. He's so spiritual right now, but most of the time it feels like he's just going through the motions.

"Bennett?" I say. "I think you should go now. I'm really sorry. I like you a lot, but this is obviously not working."

"You can't just throw me out. We need to talk about this. Don't be a child, Emily."

This stings. I stare him directly in the eyes, wanting to burn a hole in the back of his head with my gaze. I might be inexperienced, but I am no child. "Out." He can just take his conflicted self out of my apartment.

"But Emily, come on," he says, trying to pull me back down onto the couch. I walk to the door and open it.

"I'd appreciate it if you'd go now," I say carefully.

He rises, then walks slowly, measuredly to the door. "Okay. I'll leave. I'll call you tomorrow so we can talk about this some more," he says, leaning over to kiss me.

I lean back to avoid his lips. "No," I say. I am surprised how sure my voice sounds. He stares at me. I don't blink. He slowly leans back, turns away, and walks out the door. As soon as he's out, I close and lock the door, and then burst into tears. I run to my bed and crawl under the covers and cry. I cry for more than an hour, sobbing, shaking. I wipe my nose on my sheets and brush the tears out of my eyes with my throw pillow. Finally, when I have no more tears left, I lie quietly in my bed and slowly drift off to sleep.

I awake a few hours later. I expect it to be morning, and my heart sinks to discover that it's still Sunday night and that I've just broken up with Bennett. I want to go back to sleep and forget everything, but I know I need to get up, get ready for bed, and turn off the lights. I have to go to work in the morning.

I pull back the covers and walk into the living room. The

Chinese food is still on the table. I start to put it in the fridge, but then decide that even if it is still good and I'm poor and starving, I won't ever be able to eat this food. My stomach lurches just looking at it. I should give it to someone who's hungry, but I can't muster the energy. I walk to the trash can and open the lid, but then reconsider. I turn and walk to the kitchen window and lift up the sash. A blast of cold air hits me, but it feels good. I stand in front of the window for a few minutes, then take one of the small white containers, and, carefully opening it, put it out the window and turn it upside down. The sweet and sour pork slides out slowly in one glutinous mass, then disappears from my line of vision. A second later, I hear it hit the pavement with a satisfying splash. I grab the chow fun noodles and do the same. I take the small container of rice and put my head out the window so I can watch it fall in a solid block and break apart on the pavement. Lastly, I take the fortune cookies and throw them at the brick wall of the building next to us. I hope to hear them shatter. They don't even come close. I quickly shut the window, walk to the table to get the bottle of wine, and open it. I pour myself a nice tall glass, then sit down on the couch to think. I know it's going to be a long night. So much for sleep.

I wake up feeling awful—my head pounds, and my stomach churns. Consciousness is so painful right now. The idea of getting out of bed and going to work sounds impossible. I put a pillow over my head. I hide from the day.

I contemplate calling in sick, but as I think about it, I realize that it might be good for me to be in the office, busy and distracted. Surely I will be swamped all day after such a long break. Slowly, I sit up and lower my feet to the cold floor, then stumble to the bathroom. My eyes are practically swollen shut. Maybe that's better. I can't really see how awful I look this way. I throw on some wrinkly clothes from the suitcase I haven't bothered to unpack yet and make it out the door. The snow has turned to sleet and made the streets slippery and the air heavy. Everywhere there are black puddles that look like the asphalt, until you step in them and the filthy water rushes over your shoes. The subway stairs are slick and the platforms are crowded with grumpy people, unhappy about returning to work after a long vacation.

I sit down at my desk, feeling like I should get an Olympic medal for Urban Nightmare Commute After Rotten Breakup, and switch on my computer. I see the verse Jenna made for me, still hanging there on my corkboard, and tear it down. I miss him already.

I have 287 unread e-mails waiting for me when I switch on my computer. Just perfect. Sorting through the spam will take me all morning. At least it will keep me busy and help me avoid facing my undoubtedly well-rested and annoyingly chipper coworkers. I am not sure I can deal with anyone in a good mood right now—nor anyone who might ask me about or remind me of Bennett. I am not ready to talk about it yet.

I sigh and scroll to the bottom of the screen. E-mail number one is from an author, sent the evening of the last day the office was open before Christmas, demanding to know when he was going to see a copy of the cover of his book. Delete! Deleting never felt so good.

Fortunately no one else seems to be in the mood to chat either. Reggie comes by to drop off a stack of papers and asks how my vacation was. I'm friendly, but I try to keep my back turned to her so she can't see how puffy my face is, and she walks away. E-mail number thirty-four is from my credit card company, alerting me that I am within one hundred dollars of my maximum balance. What else is new? I hit delete. Xavier doesn't even say anything when he comes in but walks by my desk in a huff and goes straight into his office. An official e-mail from Morrow & Sons outlining some recent database updates. Delete.

I am on cup of coffee number three when I get to e-mail number 279—it's from Jacob. My heart idles. I click on it twice, and my computer has to think a couple of seconds to get it open. In that small space of time, I don't breathe.

Emily,

I guess you're probably back in New York now, but just in case—I got two free tickets to the Sweet Torture show tomorrow night. Do you want to come? They're a pretty small band, but they've gotten some good press recently, and I hope to give them more. I'm casually letting it slip that the lead singer is really cute in case that will motivate you to say yes. So what if you're in New York? Fly back. We're talking about torture here! We're talking about an evening with *me* here! Torture with me!

In other news, I had a brilliant idea. I have a few friends with birthdays coming up in the next few weeks, and I had a dilemma. I want to get them gifts that are a) unique, and b) cheap (hey, I'm poor!). Where do you find something like that? Three somethings like that? But I remembered that I have this old silk-screen kit (from the days of making T-shirts for the Happy Few, the band I started in college), and I know that I can get some blank T-shirts for pretty cheap, so I thought about making them all T-shirts. I was trying to think of the perfect thing to put on the shirts when it hit me (get ready, this is the brilliant part)—what's more perfect than me???? So I drew my own face, wrote Jacob Is My Friend! underneath it, and silk-screened T-shirts for my friends. Is there anything more wrong than that? I hope not. I think I'm going to make a bunch and use them as presents from now on. Maybe if you're lucky you'll get one.

.Let me know about tomorrow (tonight? It's 1:00 a.m.) and whether you're actually even in town. If you're smart, you'll pretend you're in New York even if you're not.

Here's hoping you're dumber than you used to be,

Jacob.

P.S. I'm trying to reestablish a jocular tone in our e-mails à la pre-Christmas. How'd I do? I haven't forgotten our talk, and I respect your decision to pass me up, although I still maintain you must be crazy. But seriously, I can't live without your e-mails. Okay, I could. But it would be a narrow existence. Also I thought for the first time in my life, I'd take a girl up on her promise that we could "still be friends." So you have to keep writing me. My hope for the honesty of all womankind rests on your shoulders!!

I can't help but smile, though it's a little weak. I'm relieved that we're still going to be talking via e-mail. Frankly, I don't feel like I can face work without his humor at the moment. He put his face on a T-shirt? That's fantastic. Should I tell him I broke up with Bennett? I decide I'm not in the mood yet. I have to read the e-mail again. After the third read through and even some audible laughter, I move on to number 280, which is from the *New York Times* and contains the day's headlines. Delete.

Jacob's e-mail, coupled with three cups of coffee, cheer me enough to make the morning go quickly. I duck into the bathroom at lunchtime, though, so I don't have to face whoever comes by to ask if I am coming to lunch. I am not hungry at all, and I certainly can't face the cafeteria, and the possibility of seeing Bennett, today. I go back to my desk when I'm sure the coast is clear and start writing an editorial letter to the author of *The Marine Corpse* to let him know what needs to be changed in the manuscript.

The afternoon drags, but I don't cry at all, which I count as a major victory. The closer it gets to being time to go, the less I want to leave. Going home to an empty apartment sounds too miserable to bear. I think about staying really late at work, but I decide what I really need to do is stop feeling sorry for myself. I'll go to the Locus and serve tonight—it won't be fun, but it will better than going home and finishing that bottle of wine by myself.

Somehow the trek downtown seems drearier than usual, as if I'm in some strange Dorian Gray parallel and what's going on inside me is made evident in the sky itself. Dark, heavy, oppressive. I watch a woman on the other side of Broadway slip in the slush and fall into a puddle. I can barely hold back the tears.

The Locus is bright and bustling, and seeing Uncle Matthew is like a breath of fresh air. He compliments my coat and asks if he can take me out to dinner afterward to celebrate my triumphant return. Still, though, the place is packed—there is no one begging on the streets tonight, as even the most troubled and destitute have sought shelter in this weather—and the serving lines are long, thick with impatient, hungry people. I man the dessert table tonight, and try to be happy passing out the chocolate cake, but the sight of it almost turns my stomach. I just feel awful—tired, sick to my stomach, and my abdomen is all cramped up for some reason.

Oh no. I instantly know. I turn to the volunteer at the roll station and ask her to cover for me for a few minutes. Picking up my purse, I slip into the bathroom.

Of course! Of course I don't have anything with me. My period coming was the last thing I was thinking of this morning. Feeling more and more sorry for myself, I dig through my purse, desperately hoping to find a quarter to buy a tampon from the machine on the wall. There aren't any in my wallet but after several minutes of rifling through that scary jungle of lipstick tubes and scraps of paper in the bottom, I find one. It's too bad I don't have any Advil, either, I think as I put the quarter in the slot. The cramps are going to get worse pretty soon. This is the last thing I need right now.

I pull on the silver handle of the dispenser. Nothing happens. I pull it again, straining to hear the sound of something inside the machine moving, looking into the metal tray to see if anything has dropped onto it. Nothing. Oh no. Please God, I pray. I can't deal with this right now. I just need this thing to work. Just this once. Please. I try the handle again. Nothing. There is no coin return slot. Grasping the handle in my right hand, I pull it really hard, then push it back in, and pull it out again. Suddenly I'm yanking on the handle, angrily pulling and pushing it to let it know exactly how I feel about it swallowing my quarter. And when I am done yanking, I start to cry. I give up. I take a seat on the brown metal folding chair by the sinks and bury my head in my hands. I've been holding it in all day, and now that I'm going, I can't stop. I'm crying for my quarter, for my cramps, for Bennett, for the loss of my idyllic New York life. I know now everything isn't going to be perfect just because I want it to be.

I am so concentrated on my good cathartic cry that I don't hear the door opening and don't know anyone has come in until Josie is standing in front of me. I reconsider. *This* is the last thing I need right now. I shake my head in disbelief.

"What's the matter?" she asks sweetly, concern on her face. Why do I want to sneer back?

"The machine ate my quarter," I say, pointing at the dispenser on the wall.

"Oh, sweetie." She crouches down to look at me. Her face says she can tell that's not really what I'm crying about, and I expect her to say something obnoxious about turning that frown upside down, but all she does is reach into her bag and pull out a tampon. She hands it to me, and I grasp it uncertainly. "There you go." As I stand up, she leans over and puts her arms around me; her hug is strangely comforting.

"Thank you" is all I can muster.

Lane and I decide to have a good old-fashioned slumber party that Friday. I jump at the chance to spend the night on her futon to avoid my lonely apartment and the prospect of hiding my sadness behind a cucumber and mint face mask. I need some girl time.

Over a tube of raw cookie dough and a bag of barbecue potato chips we found in the cupboard, Lane drops some big news on me.

"I'm leaving Morrow & Sons," she says.

"What?! No. I can't handle this right now. I dump my hot boyfriend and now my closest friend is deserting me?" When was this life going to cut me a break? "Wait. Why?"

She shrugs. "I don't want to be an editor, and Susanna's no walk in the park."

"I mean I knew you had your problems with the old Death Bun, but I thought you liked working on books." I guess I'm also surprised because I *love* my job.

"Yeah, I like working in the food world and I've always loved to read, but I don't enjoy the editorial side so much. Besides, I think I want to be a teacher."

At first I try to talk her out of it, knowing that things will inevitably change when she leaves the company. Sure, she'll still be in New York, but I won't see her that much. Then I realize I am being really selfish. I start listening to her talk about how much she loves kids and how wonderful it will be to introduce them to Roald Dahl and Beverly Cleary for the first time. She is glowing as she talks, and I realize that her plan is right for her.

"Go for it," I say.

"Yeah?"

"Absolutely. You look really happy. Like you have it all figured out now. Also, just think. No more errands to pick up Miss Muffins from Doggie Heaven and bring her back to Susanna just because she's malingering with a twisted ankle."

Lane laughs. "Susanna and all her neuroses I will miss in a weird way, but I'm going to tell Miss Muffins not to write. But you're right. I think I do kind of have it figured out now, and it feels good, but, you know, scary also. This was my first job after college. And I'll be responsible for all of those kids!" She sits across from me in a green face mask, smiling from ear to ear. I am happy for her but feel all the more lost. My life couldn't be more undecided.

"What's wrong, Em? I'm not leaving. We're still going to be able to see each other all the time," she says.

I nod and pause. I decide to just have it out. Even though all the girls now know the official story of the breakup, I haven't yet just spilled my guts to anyone about it. And though they knew I went to church with him sometimes, they don't know why. I decide to confess to Lane that I am a Christian.

"Lane. I guess with you leaving and the breakup with Bennett and everything . . . Ah! My life is such a mess. I used to have it all figured out, you know, because I'm a Christian and I believed, I don't know, that it would all be so easy for me with God on my side. But now, it's just so hard. And I feel like some kind of freak at work."

There is a weird pause. Is she shocked?

"Oh, Emily," she says. "I don't think you're a freak. And obviously I knew that about your beliefs. It wasn't hard to figure out. But then, I did grow up in a religious family, it's just my parents who don't go to church." I feel like a dolt. All this time I thought she didn't know, and it turns out she put the pieces together herself. And she *still* likes me.

"I'm sorry, Lane. I sort of denied it to you once, during our first lunch together when we were talking about Bennett. I just didn't know how you'd react."

"Emily. You're being too hard on yourself. It's okay. Everyone does stuff like that when they're unsure of themselves. And that helps explain why you liked him so much! I was always a little wary of him."

"He was the only datable Christian around. It stinks that it didn't work out. Now who will I date? I'm in a total slump. With boys, with God, with work, with everything," I say.

She tilts her head to the side and gives me a concerned look.

"You know, I'm glad I broke up with Bennett, but now, well, I don't have that much to do. He was a major part of my social calendar. It's making me feel like that awkward little girl who moved here again. Even my Uncle Matthew is dating."

"What?" Lane asks.

"I know. I made him over, you know, and then he got up the confidence to ask out this woman at the center, Josie."

"Oh no. The one you hate. Maybe it won't last."

"I've actually decided she's all right. Not great, but I guess I can see it. It's a start. I'm really happy for him."

"But what about you?" Lane is one of the best listeners I know.

"I don't know. I used to be so happy with Bennett. And then I wasn't. How can doing something you know is right make you so miserable?" I start to sob a little. I feel awful for so quickly raining on Lane's big, happy parade.

"Yeah. That's another reason to leave publishing. There are *no* guys," says Lane. She touches my shoulder and smiles, hoping to brighten me up.

I nod. Most of the men in the company are married, older men. We both silently consider how bleak our prospects are.

"Emily. I make a motion that we start dating. We'll go to bars together, and we'll make a conscious effort to meet new boys. Why, I'll even join some kind of recreational sports league if I have to."

I start cracking up at the idea of sweet, Southern Lane on a basketball court in Brooklyn. I extend my hand to her with all of my fingers in a fist except my pinky. "Deal. I will if you will. Pinky swear."

Jacob.

Oh my, where do I begin? With an apology, I suppose. I know I shouldn't have waited a couple of weeks to get back with you, but things have been insane out here, as usual. I was actually thrilled you wanted to keep writing. Or maybe I'm just doing it to maintain your faith in womankind. You'll never know!!!

This just in: I broke up with Bennett right after I got back. I think hanging out with you over Christmas made me realize that I could be happier. Interpret that as you will. I finally decided that there was no sense in continuing to date him when there wasn't really a future, and there are other fish in the, uh, East River.

Unfortunately, so far all I've found are really flashy smelly fish. Two or three days old, sitting-in-the-sun fish. I went on the worst date of my life the other night. He was a friend twice removed who my coworker said was perfect for me. We decided to meet at this big cube sculpture on

Astor Place, and as I was walking over, I could see that
there was one cluelessly dressed boy on the near side of the
cube (facing me) and one other person whose feet I could
just barely see on the far side. I was hoping that maybe
Brad was the person on the far side. No such luck. So, for
starters, from ten feet away, Brad is four inches shorter than
I am, wearing a black trench coat and some weird kind
of blue pants with white sneakers. As I stepped closer, I
realized that he bore a startling resemblance to my father.

So he'd chosen a bar, run by monks, which I actually
thought sounded kind of cool. Until I arrived there, got my
drink, sat down (across from my father at twenty-seven),
and was overwhelmed by a tidal wave of shushing. Like,
Shhhhh! Shhhhhh! Apparently, they don't allow talking at
this bar. Allow me to repeat: The bar that this guy picked
for a first date did not allow talking, only quiet whispering!
And there was frequent shushing from not only the monks
(who were actually dressed in robes), but from the other
patrons! Oh, and did I mention the name of this fine
establishment? It's called Burp Castle. Seriously. Happily, I
had made dinner plans with Lane and got out of there after
an hour. At least he paid. Shudder. I'm hoping he was a
fluke. As you know, I never really dated that much and so
far I think I used to be wise beyond my years. You were
right. I am getting dumber.

Your turn.

Emily

CHAPTER 18

figs and dates

★

I *walk into* the Thai place Brian had suggested and look around. There is only one guy with blond hair and blue eyes waiting.

The girls had all been trying valiantly to lift me out of the funk I had slipped into since coming back from Christmas, and everyone seemed to have a friend they thought would be just perfect for me. I'd gone on a couple of blind dates, and so far they'd all been awful, but hope springs eternal. I decided to give this one a try when Reggie told me her friend from college had an extra ticket to the Winged Chariot concert and was looking for a date. At the very least it would be a good practice date, and he seemed nice enough when he called. Once we got to talking on the phone together we agreed that it would be a little awkward to go to a concert with someone we'd never met, trying to get to know one another by yelling over the loud music, so we decided to get dinner one night after work.

"Brian?" I ask, walking carefully toward him. Tall, preppy, athletic. Pretty cute. He'll do. He sees me and smiles, looking me up and down, slowly. Suddenly I am feeling very self-conscious, but he comes forward and greets me with a kiss on the cheek.

"You must be Emily," he says. "Wow. Reg said you were cute, but she didn't tell me you were hot!"

"Um . . . it's great to meet you too," I say, stumbling over my own words. How does one respond to that? I decide the best plan is to match his forwardness with flirtatiousness. It will make the evening less awkward and more fun anyway. Besides, maybe Bennett was right. Maybe I need to loosen up a little and enjoy the attention of men without assuming that bad things are going to happen. "You're not so bad yourself," I say, smiling. He just keeps looking at my legs, then puts his hand on my waist and steers me toward the hostess.

"Two," he says. She nods and leads us to a table the back of the restaurant. As I glance over the menu—he always gets Pad Thai, he says, so he doesn't need to look at the menu—he begins to talk about himself. He is in consulting, which isn't *that* bad. He works a lot, travels a lot, and gets a lot of *cashola* for it. When he does have spare time, he likes to hit the gym. A lot. He lives on the Upper West Side in an apartment with some of his "buds" from college and is really involved in the Manhattan chapter of his alumni association.

I just nod to most of this and feel like an alien. I realize that my upbringing, while quite common in Jenks, is exotically backwoods and simple here. But I can't help but feel more authentic in a way. I try not to make these snap judgments I love so much, but he sure does love to talk about his own dull life. A lot.

As the meal wears on, I become less concerned that he has plans to take me to an abandoned warehouse and kill me and more and more worried that he has plans to try to get me into bed with him. I can't help but notice that several times when I start to say something he has to tear his gaze away from my chest to look me in the eye. And when some sauce splashes onto my shirt, he immediately dips his napkin in water and reaches across the table to help me blot it.

When the food comes, he starts talking about an article he read about Jennifer Lopez in *Maxim*. "I bought it because it had her on the cover, and she looked really sexy," he confesses, "but it turns out it has great articles too. Who knew?" I laugh, cringing. Did he really just tell me that? "I'd buy anything with J Lo on it," he says, laughing at himself. I have to laugh with him, but for a different reason. "I have posters of her all over my bedroom. But you'll see those," he says. When does he think I am going to see the inside of his bedroom?

"Jennifer Lopez? Whatever. She's not that great. But I'd run off with George Clooney in a second if I had the chance," I say, laughing. He begins rating all the female starlets he can think of, so I counter with ratings of all the hot Hollywood men. It's fun at first, but he gets so detailed in his rating system (face, breasts, butt, legs, and overall sex appeal as a bonus category) that I begin to be concerned he might be a little off his nutter, as Nanna liked to say. But I play along, and he seems to think we are really hitting it off, although I am becoming more and more guarded. I imagine myself at the concert with him and keep picturing him as some kind of octopus. I will have to spend the entire evening extricating his wandering hands from my body. I'm kind of glad when the check comes and reach eagerly into my purse to take my wallet out.

"Oh no, I've got this," he says, whipping out a credit card and placing it in the black tray.

"I've got money," I say, pulling out a twenty and laying it in the tray.

"No way am I going to let you pay," he says, pushing it back toward me.

"That's not fair," I say. "I ate too—let me pay my share."

"I've got this one," he says, moving his eyes from mine back down to my chest, then back up. "I'll let you do me this weekend."

"You'll let me what?" I ask, laughing flirtatiously to mask my fear and hoping he did not mean what I thought he meant.

"You heard me," he says. He winks.

I paste a smile on my face as I rush to put on my coat and scarf. My head is whirling, but I try to appear calm. Apparently this has gone too far. I need to back up immediately. We step outside, and he turns to me to give me a kiss. I move my head so his kiss lands on my cheek.

"Thanks for coming. I'll call you about this weekend," he says as I turn to go.

"Okay. Thanks," I say. I won't be answering that call. I pull my hat down and start to walk away, my head whirling. Does he really think I am going to sleep with him? Is he a complete boor, or did I go too far in encouraging him? Can I tell him before Saturday that I won't be going home with him? Can I put up with his fascination with sex and his roaming hands all night anyway? The more I think about it, the more I dread the concert. I will call him. Yes, I will call him and cancel, but will Reggie be mad? I'd fake a cough. It isn't cold season anymore, I realize because I have to unbutton my coat, but he will buy it.

Thank goodness New York finally seems to be warming up a bit after the abysmal depths of winter. I have just gotten the last button undone and am still reeling down the sidewalk with my mind racing about Brian when I hear a familiar voice.

"Emily! Is that you?" I look up sharply and am surprised to find Xavier standing in front of me. With a woman who is not Beatrice.

"Hi," I say stupidly, stopping short. It feels more than a little strange to run into my boss outside of work. What should I say to him? "I was just having dinner with a friend." Way to impress him with humor, Em.

"Oh? We're just on our way to dinner now. This is my wife, Laura. Laura, this is my faithful assistant, Emily," he says. The dark-haired woman smiles warmly, her eyes crinkling in the corners, and sticks out her hand. "Emily, it's great to finally meet you in person," she says. Her voice is very familiar from her phone calls, and it is good to finally have a face to put with it. Although I can't say anything, my heart goes out to this poor woman. I wonder if she knows about Beatrice or if she just assumes Xavier works late a lot. *I'm sorry*, I tell her telepathically. I nod and smile, tongue-tied.

"Emily is doing a bang-up job," Xavier explains to Laura. "She edited her first manuscript recently."

"Oh yes," I laugh. "I'm on my way to the top. Watch out, Xavier, I may take your job soon." I guess it's better to laugh at how slowly people—even people who clearly deserve it, like me—get promoted than to complain about it, and I know Xavier will appreciate it.

He laughs and shakes his head. "Who knows?" he says.

"Honey, we've got to get going," she says, smiling up at him. She looks so innocent, so happy, so unaware. *Oh, Xavier.* "We'll never get to the show on time if we don't make our dinner reservation." He nods.

"I'll see you tomorrow, Emily," he says.

"Have a nice time. It was great to meet you," I say to Laura, who returns the sentiment. They continue down the street, and I turn and resume walking toward the subway. I don't know who to feel more sorry for—Brian, Xavier, Laura, Beatrice, or myself. All I know for sure is that romance seems to have gone completely awry in this city. While Xavier has so many catches he is letting them flounder on the decks, I just keep pulling up spare tires and octopi.

I scan the caf, looking for Bennett's telltale head of dark curls, and don't see him anywhere. Maybe he's avoiding me too. Maybe he's out to lunch with a new girl. Regardless, I'm glad he's not around to make me lose my appetite. It still feels like a cold poison coursing through my veins when I accidentally run into him in the building. And last week he made my heart stop altogether when I spied him chatting up Skylar at our receptionist's desk. I darted into the stairwell and let the tears pour out for a while. To compose myself I walked down the twenty-three flights of stairs to the lobby and then climbed all the way back up again. Exercise always clears my head.

I get my tray, put a slice of pizza on it, check out, and head over to our usual table.

"You'll never guess who I ran into last night," I announce as I sit down. Lane is looking at me expectantly, and Reggie is carefully spreading peanut butter on celery sticks, making it even and smooth. She's trying to lose ten pounds by next week for an audition. Sklyar looks bored. "Xavier and Laura! I've never met Laura before."

"What's she like? That's the wife, right?" Reggie asks.

"Yep. She seemed pretty nice, I guess. Very pretty. Long dark hair. I don't know. I didn't talk to them for very long. It was uncomfortable, of course."

"Has anyone else ever seen her? I can't remember Helen ever mentioning seeing her. You may be our only source on this. What else can you tell us?" Lane asks. The private lives of the editors are endlessly fascinating to us, much like the lives of our teachers were in elementary school.

"Not much. I was just feeling so bad for her and trying not to look her in the eyes," I say. "I kept worrying I'd crack under pressure and say something about Beatrice."

"Too bad," Skylar says. "I would love to have some dirt on Xavier." We're silent for a while. Since I have attended lunch less lately I feel a little out of things and don't know what to say, particularly to Skylar. Every day I tell myself it's not her fault that

Bennett is so hung up on her, but it kills me when I look at her. She's just so blonde and cookie-cutter. I thought he wanted something more original than that. Something special. Something like me.

"Speaking of Helen, have you guys read that proposal she got in?" Reggie asks. "It's great."

I'm thankful for Reggie interrupting my destructive chain of thoughts. "What's it called? What's it about?" I ask, trying to perk up.

"It's an argument for why marriage is an outdated custom and should be dissolved as a legal status. The author is trying to get the laws changed from the antiquated, Judeo-Christian–based system to one that's more fair for everyone—eliminating the debate about same-sex marriage and trying to make it legally and socially acceptable for couples to live together without a piece of paper legitimizing it. It's sort of based on the idea that religion used to structure our society, but since no one believes in God anymore it's illogical to keep imposing the old rules and standards on society. We need a new system. It's really smart and very well done."

Lane looks at me, cringing. I keep silent, watching Reggie.

"It's supposed to be a big project, and she really wants to do it, but she's worried about getting it past the bigwigs here, so she's trying to keep it hush-hush," adds Skylar.

"Why?" asks Lane. "It sounds smart."

"Because they're a bunch of bottom-line bottom-dwellers, that's why," chirps up Skylar, caustically. "Helen told me she's just nervous that they won't want to buy it because the schlubs in Middle America won't go to bookstores and buy it. It's pretty anti-God in parts. You remember how that treatise for the elimination of government did that we published last fall. It sold about six thousand miserable copies, all in California and New York. That's why I hate this job. It's all about profit. They'll turn down Helen's book and then go for the touchy-feely memoir by a hard-luck baseball player who can't even write," Skylar says.

I am fuming mad. Skylar's diatribe is definitely a dig at my Hank Fleming baseball book, which probably will sell really well in the heartland because of his fame and his positive message. I say my next sentence with more anger than I mean to let out. "So how is it that she's going to slip this one past, I don't know, everybody?" I ask. It seems like a dumb plan. It will never work.

"I'm not sure she's figured that out yet," Reggie says, giving me a weird look. "But you guys should check it out. Ask her for a copy. It's really convincing. It will change your thinking, I swear."

I keep forgetting that Lane is the only one who knows. I know the rest see I'm a little different, but I suspect they assume I'm from a small town, that I'm behind the times, that's all. Everyone else seems to think that it's a good project. I keep silent and decide to read the proposal myself. I always hated when Jenna rejected things she'd never even investigated. It might be interesting. But change my thinking? I doubt it.

I get back to my desk and check the weather in San Diego: 75 and sunny, no humidity.

I see I have a new e-mail, and open it.

Dear Emily,

I'm so sorry to hear about your parting with Bennett. Okay, no I'm not, but I'm trying to be supportive here. I trust you're doing okay? You were too good for him anyway. Him and his dumbwaiter.

Did you know that Jacob is the most popular name for baby boys in America? It's true. It finally unseated Michael, which had been reigning for the past thirty years. What makes this beautiful story all the more compelling, though, is that the most popular name for baby girls is *Emily*! We're number one! Seriously. The fact that this pleases me so much is evidence that I have OCD, which I have been trying to control all my life.

Also, I've decided to take up curling. You know, the sport? It's played on ice. You've seen it on TV, I bet. It's an Olympic sport, and it involves brooms. What more could you ask for? It's true that the average age of players is sixty-four, but I figure that just gives me an advantage. Those old guys may have forty more years of experience than I do, but I have youth and vigor going for me. And trust me: in a sport that makes shuffleboard seem like child's play, that counts for something. I'm not sure what, though.

Now, why, you may ask, would you take up a game that's played on ice when you live in Southern California? To that all I can say is this: I decided I needed a hobby, and I narrowed it down to either curling or learning one of those African clicking languages, and since I was voted "Most Likely to Be Attacked by an Angry Woodpecker" in my dorm in college, this just seemed less likely to cause severe bodily harm.

Speaking of dates (you were), I went on one last night. She asked me out, if you can believe it. She was the bartender at this place I went with guys from work last week. She heard me talking about the Cold Pastoral concert I was writing a review of, and she told me she'd been at the show too. So we got to talking, and, hey, she was cute, so when she asked if I wanted to get dinner with her sometime, what could I say? Am I making you jealous yet? How's this? We had a great time. Really fun. I know, I know . . . she's a bartender. Not exactly the kind of girl you can bring home to meet the folks. Probably not the kind of girl I should even go out with a second time. But she asked again . . . so what could I do? I'll let you know how it goes.

At this point, I can't help but think some actual dating would be good for me. Forget waiting for someone special. I just want to have some fun, hang out. Meanwhile my girl friends all tell me that if they're not married by a certain age, they're going to marry me. Lowest bid so far is thirty-two! I can't wait.

Jacob.

P.S. I've decided that it was high time you were gifted. Keep your eyes out for present. I haven't decided what it will be yet, but the wheels are a-turnin'.

P.P.S. How do you feel about figs? I tried one for the first time yesterday—I never knew what I was missing. If you've never had one, try one immediately.

Reading Jacob's e-mail back at my desk, I start cracking up. Hmm . . . a gift, I think. I'll bet it's a crate of figs. I better tell him I'm allergic in my next e-mail. Better yet, it's probably a Jacob Is My Friend! T-shirt. He's crazy. But what's this about the bartender? Part of me wants to be happy for him, but mostly I'm just annoyed. Jacob, I want to yell, you're better than that. Why are you going out with a girl you know you shouldn't? And I hope he's not actually considering marrying one of those other girls as a consolation prize when they don't meet the man of their dreams. But why do I care so much? Because I want what's best for him, I decide. Because he can—and should—do better. Because, I have to admit, I am a little jealous. Because I do care.

I decide to put it out of my head and go get that proposal from Helen. I walk to her office, but she's on the phone and holds up her finger to tell me to wait. She says something under her breath, then says goodbye and hangs up.

"Hey Helen," I say, standing in the doorway. "Reggie was talking about a proposal you had in that we should all read. I'd love to take a look at it. Can I make a copy of it?"

"I guess," she says, somewhat reluctantly. "But keep it quiet. Don't mention anything to Xavier about it in your little hang-out sessions."

"I won't, I promise . . . But why wouldn't Xavier like it? From what I understand, it's the kind of thing he might like."

"You know how he is. He has no backbone. If the big bosses don't like it, neither will he. He doesn't stick his neck out for anyone. He just says 'I agree' to whatever upstairs thinks."

I know she's right. Xavi is in this business to make money, which is probably what drew him to mass-market thrillers. Still, sometimes I have hope for him. Look at his work with Finneran. "Okay. My lips are sealed. I just want to know what it's about."

"You won't like it," she sneers. "Here you go." She hands me a stack of papers. "Bring it back when you're done copying it, please." I start to thank her, but she has already turned back to her computer.

I have been slammed at work all day. My body physically aches from running around the twenty-five floors of Morrow & Sons, trying to coordinate a book on terrorism by an author whom I love but who happens to be very disorganized. I had asked Hugh, the author, repeatedly to please send in a map for the book, but even though he was a reporter for the *Washington Post*, he couldn't seem to figure out this task. He kept sending me a map of half the globe. I tried to tell him a detailed map of the Middle East was what we needed, but he claimed he couldn't find one anywhere. I had told Xavi about Hugh's incompetence, and he said, "Fix it, Emily. I'm swamped in here."

So I spent the rest of the day locating the perfect map in the atlas in another imprint's art department and filling in all the labels for him. Thank goodness I had read the book already. Hugh said he owed me a margarita and would take me out when he came to New York. He really owed me nice chunk of that $100,000 advance check he got.

At nine in the evening, when I am still at work, I reread Jacob's e-mail one more time and am now officially bent out of shape about it. I know it's wrong to care because we aren't dating, but I realize that in the dating wasteland of New York, I pin a lot of my hopes for boys in general on him. He represents what I want in a New York boy. I guess I feel like if he had found an amazing girl like me in San Diego to date, then all would be right with the world. But for such a great guy to be wasted on another flake, well, it just depresses me. I am mad at myself for feeling this way and resolve that I have just gotten frustrated too easily after a couple of bad dates recently. I'm sure out of the 8 million people in New York I can find one who is as good as Jacob if not better.

I research churches in the area with singles activity groups. That is where I will meet someone with my interests, and I need a new church anyway. I have stopped going to the Greenwich Village Church because I can't bear to see Bennett there. I resolve to try Parkside Baptist next Sunday, particularly because they boast four thousand active members and one of the most extensive young professionals outreaches in the city.

I shut down my computer and pack it in, but out on the slushy streets of a dark and haunted Manhattan, I nix my plan of going straight home and decide to go to a coffee shop in my neighborhood for a latte to warm and cheer me up. Even though it isn't in my budget to do this sort of thing all the time, I need to treat myself.

I sit down with my steamy, frothy vanilla latte and am feeling better already. I have deftly scored a nice tall table for two in a dark corner of the funky shop and settled in, leaning my back on the exposed brick wall. The music is soft and down-tempo and reminds me of a CD Jacob played during our night together in the Tuscan display of Burgundy & Brie. I start to think about him and get frustrated about my own dating situation again, so I decide I'd better do some reading to get my mind off things. I find Helen's proposal in my bag.

It is a long proposal with a full outline of the book's structure and three sample chapters. I start into it. I am immediately struck by the power of the writer's voice. Her name, Martha Heggler, sounds vaguely familiar to me, and her CV is longer than my arm. Harvard professor. Studied at Oxford. I skip straight to the first sample chapter.

Dr. Heggler has a winning presence on the page. I can't deny that her argument is soundly researched, and she has a gift for persuasion. And she is right on her twin premises that most people are no longer religious in our country and that our family structure is taken directly from the Bible. I find it sad but true, and something about her narrative voice is appealing and makes me want to keep reading.

I look at the next sample chapter, called "The Family." I take a sip of my latte and realize how wise my plan to unwind had been. I am feeling better already. I just needed a little downtime after the chaos of work. But I also wonder about this proposal. If I had read it eight months ago, would I have felt differently about it? Would I have even read it? I think I would have rejected it outright. Is this change in my perceptions what my friends and family have been so worried about? I guess yes. But I also doubt that I am wrong now, questioning the things I used to accept blindly. Surely God doesn't want us to stay in a place that is safe and unchallenged. Doesn't he call us to go out into the world and be among people of all backgrounds and religions? I shrug and pick up Dr. Heggler again.

I feel the blood rushing to my face and keep pausing from reading the proposal to compose myself. What is she saying, exactly? The second chapter debunks the entire concept of the family, calling it unnecessary. Dr. Heggler proposes that once monogamous marriage has been dissolved, then couples can begin to live with one another freely, reproducing for the joy of having children and not to fulfill some bourgeois concept of family. What? Her findings in this chapter, unlike the first chapter, feature very little research, and her tone is laced with bitterness. I put the proposal down, lost, thinking of my own family. Where would I be without Nanna's mischief or my mother's examples of how to be kind and good? What about the boys and all the laughs they brought to my life? And my father and all his goofy ways? Or how he never once complained about rising before the sun every morning to be down at the plant, working for us? Without my family, I would not be where I am. I would not have known what love and sacrifice was. Dr. Heggler is wrong, and it is really getting to me. Well, my parents loved me. I don't know what was going on at Martha's house. The nerve.

I finish the chapter on the family, and I look down to find my right hand clenched in a fist. I also realize I've been grinding my teeth. I polish off my latte and decide to read the final sample chapter another day. Whatever relaxing I have done after my hectic day is now shot.

CHAPTER 19

not!

★

I*'m sitting at* the table in Ali Baba's, chewing on a piece of hot pita. Jihan keeps filling my water glass and talking to me about how her junior year of high school is going. Matthew is now officially twenty minutes late for our dinner date. I'm a little nervous. It's not like him. And, to make matters worse, I'm starving.

Another ten minutes go by, and I go ahead and order the lamb shwarma platter to go. I can't bear to hold up their table during the dinner hour, although I doubt they'd mind too much. They love Matthew, and I suspect he's their most regular customer. When the check comes, I pay Jihan, give her a bigger tip than normal, and leave her with a note for Matthew in the event he ever shows up. She smiles at me, and I can't help but wonder if I look as pathetic as I feel. My own uncle is standing me up now. What's this world coming to?

I call him on my walk to the subway.

"Emily! Hey!" He sounds very upbeat.

"Uh, hey, Matthew." I begin to wonder if maybe I was mistaken about what night we were getting together. "Weren't we going to—"

"Huh? No, it's Emily. Is that okay? Okay. I'll just be a second. Wait. What did you say, Em? I'm out to dinner with Josie. Sorry about that. I wanted to tell her who it was. You know, not like my other girlfriend calling."

The wind is knocked out of me. He's totally forgotten. And he's with Josie. Girlfriend?

"What were you saying, Emily? Speak up. The garden area of the restaurant's kind of noisy."

"Oh. I was wondering if you were all right. I waited for you for half an hour at Ali Baba's. I guess, though, you're fine." Okay, I'm being a little petty, but this was a painful blow to my ego and just about the last thing I needed right now.

"Oh no! Em. I'm sorry. Your bumbling old uncle is sorry. Oh no. Really sorry. Are you okay?"

I start to answer, but I can hear him explaining everything to Josie in the background, and I just get more frustrated. I decide to hang up as soon as possible. I'd talk to him about this later, without his little girlfriend present. I pull out my happiest voice possible. "Ha ha . . . No, these things can happen. I totally understand. We'll get together soon. You guys have a great dinner and tell Josie I said hi." And tell Josie thanks for stealing my dinner date.

"Emily? I feel awful. Are you sure?"

"I'm fine. I've got some lamb shwarma now, and I need to do some editing anyway."

"Yeah?"

"Yeah. Hang up now. Eat your greens. Have fun. I'll call you soon. I'm just glad you're okay."

After a little more convincing and apologies from him, we hang up.

I arrive home on a perfectly nice Friday night with no plans and find I'm no longer hungry. I put the takeout box in the fridge. Instead of getting anything productive done, I turn on the TV and find an old eighties movie to watch and settle in.

The movie ends at about midnight, and I'm still not tired. In fact, I have a lot of things on my mind. Part of the reason I wanted to get dinner with Matthew is I need his advice. This Dr. Heggler proposal is really bothering me. I feel in my bones that it's wrong, and I don't want to see it published. But, if I'm honest, I don't hate it for any professional reason. I hate it because it goes against what I believe. Against God. The final sample chapter is a prediction from Dr. Heggler about how society will be structured after the breakdown of the construct of family. She takes many cracks at God, whom she calls "that old bearded white man who frowned a lot," and she celebrates the fact that he is now "dead." Could I really continue to work for Morrow & Sons and look myself in the mirror if this gets published? Am I being too extreme? I need to talk to Matthew, but it has been impossible to get a hold of him lately. He seems to always be out with Josie. I am happy for him on the one hand, but on the other, he reminds me of a friend in high school who only called me when she was between boyfriends. I hope that I wasn't that way when I was dating Bennett. I can't quite remember.

But I remember, gleefully, that I owe Jacob an e-mail and go fetch my laptop. I hack into my work e-mail, reread his to me, and then settle in.

Dear Jacob,

I'd like to say first and foremost that I like figs just about as much as I like Bennett Edward Wyeth III at the moment. Ick. How can you eat those things? My best theory is that you have more in common with your curling teammates than you let on. You can tell me, you're really a senior citizen, right? This is actually Jacob Keller's grandfather who is e-mailing me? Seriously, I thought only old people ate figs.

I'm excited about getting a present. I do love me some presents. Speaking of presents, I do sort of miss Bennett. Ha ha. I'm kidding, and for me to be kidding about it is definitely progress. I'm fine, and you're right. I deserve better. I know I did the right thing, but it's tough because he goes to my (old) church and works at the same company.

Yeah, I've decided to try to find a new church, although just the idea of looking exhausts me. I'm sick of being "the new girl" everywhere I go. But the church I'm trying out this Sunday is supposed to have a lot of young professionals activity groups. I've declared a moratorium on dating boys I meet in bars and through friends. Manhattan is a weird place. But I have high hopes for this new plan. I want to meet someone who will turn my life upside down, which, I guess, makes me the opposite of you, Jacob "I just want to have some fun" Keller.

What's up with you, huh? I sort of thought more of you than this. I know I'm being kind of hard on you, but you were giving me a lot of hope for mankind. Why date beneath yourself? I don't even know Cold Pastoral, but I'll bet they're overrated. But, hey, it's your life, bucko. If you don't see how cute and smart and different you are, then I don't know how to tell you. Well . . . I'll try. Let's put it this way, in a city of 8 million people, I haven't found anyone who could even hold a flashlight (or should I say lighter?) to you. But! I'm going looking this Sunday. Wish me luck!

I ate pizza a couple of days ago, and I thought about you. It was smart of you to throw me a pizza party because I eat it all the time out here so I'll probably be thinking of you all the time. You are wise beyond your years. And crafty.

Emily

"We need to talk."

I jump a little in my chair hearing the male voice behind me. I didn't know anyone was in my cubicle. I turn around. It's Xavi. "Oh. Okay. Now?"

"Yeah, now." He walks to his office, and I rise to follow him as my insides shift around. This can't be good news. He's never this serious.

"I just got out of a meeting with Barry Medina."

"Oh?" I say. He lets his pause draw out longer, meanwhile my stomach is lurching about.

"He's not happy with *The Marine Corpse*."

Forget my stomach, my heart has turned to stone. I don't know what to say. I worked really hard on it over Christmas. I thought I did a good job. I'm so confused.

"He thinks the characters are really flat, and in particular, the romantic side plot has no narrative arc."

"But . . . but . . ." I stammer. "I thought that at least some of that was the genre, you know? It has great pacing and dialogue."

Xavier stares at me. I know he's upset, not about my editorial decisions but about Barry being disappointed in him. In me. Well, I guess, in us. Did Xavier tell Barry I edited it? "All the same, you should have given me a draft to look over before you transmitted it to Production. Now it's too late to make the kind of changes he wants. I reassured him that with this kind of book, these flaws were expected, but he's not convinced."

I am outraged. I tried to get Xavier to look at my work on *The Marine Corpse* a thousand times. I only transmitted it to Production when they called and threatened that I was about to cost the company a lot of money for being behind schedule.

"I'm sorry," I manage, choking back all the things I really want to say. "I didn't mean to get you in trouble."

"Oh, you didn't. I told him you were the one who worked on that book."

At this, I'm so angry that I consider giving my notice. We'll just see how Xavier manages without me for one day. Let him call the insane authors and calm them down. Let him find the perfect map of the Middle East or stay up here till midnight sifting through a backlog of proposals. Let him edit a book with exactly zero instruction. And let him do it all for just a few pennies above the poverty level. Helen is right. Xavier takes no one's side. Only his own.

"It was my first book," I say lamely. "And I wasn't sure. Besides, I think it reads fine for the genre. When's the last time he read anything like that that you've published? It's not William Finneran, and it's not supposed to be."

Xavier stares at me. I think he's possibly going to say I'm fired. I wait. Finally he talks. "All the same, Emily." And then he picks up his pen and starts reading a proposal. I'm apparently dismissed.

When I get back to my desk, tears start rolling out of my eyes. The injustice of it just kills me. I often cry when I get angry. I think my head must be wired wrong. Aren't I supposed to yell back? Defend myself? Instead I'm just reduced to a blubbering mess. Man. I pull out some napkins I have stashed in my desk for when I spill my coffee and try to carefully blot my face. I make sure to keep very quiet as I cry and try to distract myself with e-mail. Luckily, it's my turn to e-mail Jenna. Thank you, God, I murmur. I need her right now. I'm so confused.

Jenna,

I'm e-mailing you right now because I just got in trouble with Xavier. I sense that everything will be fine eventually, but you know how I am when people yell at me. I sure wish you were here now. Or I there.

So. I'll move on to cheer myself up. Hm . . . how about the weather? It's *finally* starting to get warmer. That's good.

But all I want to do is go to the beach. It will be several months before I can do that, I'm afraid. People here don't go until June! Did you know that Memorial Day actually marks the start of summer out here? Crazy. It doesn't matter, though, since it's pretty hard to get to a beach anyway. Just about the only place you can get to by subway is Coney Island. Famous, yes, but from what I understand, not exactly what you'd want to go swimming in, unless you're a hypodermic needle. I thought I missed California this winter, but the prospect of a whole summer without taking a dip the ocean is almost too much to bear.

Did you ever get that kid out of the bathroom stall he locked himself in? I used to always be afraid I would get stuck in the bathroom and die there. Here's hoping that doesn't happen.

See ya, Emily

Xavier is still testy on Thursday. Apparently he does not react well to criticism. And although I have chosen to move on and tried very hard to get over it, I still haven't. Late in the afternoon, he calls me into his office.

"Emily?" he yells. I get up, running to see what's wrong. I don't want to bear the brunt of whatever this is.

"Yes?" He has his hand in a jar of peanut butter, scraping the empty sides.

"I'm out of peanut butter!" he yells.

"I'm sorry?" How is this *my* fault?

"Fix it, Emily."

"Fix it?"

"Yes! Fix it," he says, throwing the empty jar against the wall.

"How do you want me to—"

"I want you to go to the store and buy some for me," he says slowly, as if I'm an idiot for not understanding. I start to protest, but I give up. I turn, walk to my computer, and grab my purse. "Expense it!" he yells after me. All I can do is shake my head as I walk to the elevator.

That evening, after I have Xavi taken care of and have stocked my cabinet with a every kind of peanut butter sold, I look up and see it is 6:15. I don't remember why this sounds familiar. Was there something I was supposed to be doing? I have really been trying to double-time it at work so that Xavier can see what a hard worker I am. Not that it has been helping. I pull out my daily planner and flip to Thursday. I see the word *bowling* written really big with a bowling alley name and address.

I start packing things up in a hurry. I'll only be about a half an hour late if I hurry, subway time included. And this is serious. This is not like my job that I was going to get fired from for no apparent reason, this is my chance to meet a boy who isn't a monk or a sex fiend.

I had gone to Parkside Baptist on Sunday and had had a pretty decent time. They were well prepped for people my age stopping by alone. I had worried about who I would sit with or if I could even bring myself to talk to anyone, but the greeter at the door, a strikingly tall blond boy in his late twenties, had me fill out a name tag and gave me an orchid corsage to wear.

"This orchid is pretty and all that, but it's really so you'll be easy to spot," he said.

"What?"

"On any given Sunday we have about thirty new singles dropping by to check us out. Odds are they came alone, which takes a lot bravery. So we decided that once they're here, they shouldn't have to make the effort. If you wear that corsage, the other people your age will come by and introduce themselves. And you can also spot the other visitors."

I was impressed and relieved by this system. It was different than what I was used to but certainly took the pressure off me. I thought I might try to flirt a little with the handsome greeter. "So what do the male visitors wear?" I asked. I laughed thinking of them in corsages.

"My name's Jeremy, by the way."

"Emily."

"Nice to meet you. Get to work on that corsage. As for the guys, I campaigned for ten-gallon hats, but everyone else said I was insane. So they get a name tag and a dumb bracelet that none of them even wear. I can't blame them. But ten-gallon hats—"

"Ten-gallon hats would have definitely been a hit," I said, the two of us laughing. I was still fidgeting with my corsage. I've never been able to do these.

"Here. Let me help. I've been a greeter for two years now. I've gotten good at this."

I liked the way things were going at Parkside Baptist already. Jeremy seemed perfectly normal, he believed in God, and best of all, he was adorable. My fears about attending church alone faded with the hope that perhaps this was where all the people like me in New York had been hiding.

"Jeremy, let me help you."

The next thing I knew some red-lacquered fingernails were clawing at my chest, and Jeremy's hands faded away. I looked up, way up, to see a gorgeous, but rather traditionally pretty girl. She kept working on the corsage while she talked. "I'm Jeremy's fi-ancée, Anna. He's all thumbs when it comes to these things so I thought I'd come bail him out. So you're new here? Are you also new to the city?"

Anna was clearly very territorial, and I wasn't sure she was wrong to be. Jeremy was a big flirt. I was thankful he wasn't my fiancé, even though she did have quite a rock on her finger. I made small talk with Anna and then told them both goodbye and went to sit down in the middle of a pew in the back of the giant church.

Pretty soon two girls about my age came over and asked if they could sit with me. Their names were Susan and Sherry. I couldn't help but wonder if Parkside had paired off their entire singles program in twos, preferably with people whose names started with the same letter, so that they could divide and conquer. At least the system worked. I couldn't deny that I was happy not to be sitting alone.

Susan and Sherry were very talkative about the church and all of its programs. I could tell we weren't going to be best friends, but I was thankful for their warmth and friendliness.

The service fell somewhere between my church back home and the Greenwich Village Church. It was traditional but not dull. They still sang hymns, but there was a band and, thankfully, no organ. Organs were meant solely for basketball games and country churches where the youngest member is fifty-five and their favorite song is "One Day at a Time." But at Parkside the children's choir sang a cute song about "fishies in the sea" with lots of hand motions, and the youth group all sat together, a trend I remembered fondly from that age. I thought I might even be able to start babysitting again. I really missed kids. Plus, I scanned the crowd, checking out people my age. Jeremy was right, I saw a number of girls with orchids and boys with name tags, and I was pretty sure I spotted some interesting prospects, both some cool girls I could be friends with and some cute boys whom I might allow to buy me dinner sometime. I was intrigued, so when Susan and Sherry begged me after the service ended to come to Bowling Night that Thursday, I reluctantly agreed.

I've always hated bowling. Always. In middle school, I went on a bowling date with Calvin McRae, my hot next-door neighborhood, ran out too far in the lane, and slipped on the slick surface, falling flat on my back. I just lay there, bemoaning my parents for deciding to have children, when I heard Calvin yelling uncontrollably. Apparently after I slipped, my ball had kept rolling down the lane and knocked all the pins over. I had gotten a strike. I stood up, recovering a little, and strangely excited about my strike only to have the very serious bowler in the next lane tell me I was distracting him and that I'd better behave or he'd call the manager. He thought I was sliding down the lane on my back for fun.

And I hate bowling alleys. They smack of small-town boredom and doom. But this was Parkside. Parkside seemed to do things in style, I reassured myself. And this was my dating future. I couldn't keep trying to meet boys the old-fashioned way, and I desperately needed to reassure myself there was life after Bennett.

I arrived fashionably late at Bowlmor Lanes down in Union Square. I had read about this bowling alley in *Vogue*. Apparently, if stars ever get an itching to strap on some rented shoes and eat chicken fingers in Manhattan, this is where they come. That, at the very least, seems to make the fact that I am bowling in a city where there are thousands of other fun things to do okay. The bouncer—yes, bouncer—at the door snarls at me and says, "Twenty dollars. Let me see your ID." I am taken aback. In Jenks, bowling runs you about five dollars. I produce my California ID and fork over the cash. With his pudgy fingers, he puts an armband around my wrist. "This means you can drink. Don't take it off, or they won't serve you." And then he motions to the elevator. There is so little space in this city that everything seems to be in the basement or upstairs.

The elevator opens into a sleek retro paradise. This isn't bowling like I knew it in Jenks. This is the ironic affectation of bowling. I shake my head in wonder and amazement. Manhattan. It's better than Disneyland sometimes. To my left are dark lanes with fluorescent benches at the back and Day-Glo pins lined up at the front. They have black lights on and a disco ball going. The music is blaring some electronica Madonna remix. The only familiar thing about Bowlmor is the thunderous crash of the balls slamming into the pins. I have to laugh. I make a quick sweep of the lanes and don't see any group that looks definitively like Parkside, and I don't see Susan, Sherry, or Jeremy and Anna, so I head over the bar area on the right, kicking myself for not getting one of the S girls' phone numbers.

The bar area matches the rest of the alley while mimicking a fifties luncheon counter. There are tall metal stools that spin around anchored to the floor and pleather booths behind them. It looks like the old soda fountain in downtown Jenks, but instead of chocolate malts and grilled cheese sandwiches they are selling chicken satay and Brooklyn Lager. I take a seat on one of the stools and order a beer. I had learned in Manhattan that when you're alone and waiting for people to arrive, you look cooler if you have a drink. It gives you something to do with your hands. I pay the bartender and take my plastic cup of beer back to the lanes, looking to see if anyone looks familiar or if any of the display screens say Parkside or something funny like God's Generals or Bowling Baptists as a team name.

As I weave through the lanes, I spot, wait, could it be? Yes, oh my, it is, it really is Drew Barrymore! I stop for a quick second and then tell myself to *act natural* and keep moving, staring at her the whole time. It really is her. Wow. Wait until I tell Jenna, and Mom and Dad, and Jacob, and the work girls, and Mathew and and and . . .

"Emily?" I hear a vaguely familiar voice behind me.

I turn. Oh. Is this Susan or Sherry? Oops. "Hey! There you are," I say, trying to sound confident.

"Yeah. Sorry. I was trying to keep an eye out for you. Come over here. We've got two lanes."

In my Drew Barrymore state of mind, I had walked right past the Parkside crew. I still can't remember her name. "So, uh, where's—"

"Oh . . . yeah, Sherry's still finishing up class. She's in med school."

Okay. I have Susan on my hands. "Oh. Cool. Hey, Susan," I drop my voice really low, "did you notice that's Drew Barrymore over there?"

Susan looks behind her and then back at me. She has a confused look on her face. "Who?"

"You know, Drew Barrymore. She's been in a ton of movies lately? She's really famous? Cover of *Vogue* last month. And she's usually dating a rock star or two?"

Susan looks behind her again. And then back at me, shaking her head.

"She was the little girl in *E.T.*?" I say.

"Oh. I liked that little girl. I love *E.T.*, only it scares me."

It scares her? Wow. I'll have to remind myself not to invite her to my Halloween Horror Film Extravaganza. "Yeah. She was, uh, cute in that. Whatever. She's famous. It's kind of cool to see her."

Susan looks at her score on the screen. "Well, she's not much of a bowler, I'll tell you that."

"Yeah, who is, though?" I laugh.

A guy in pleated-front khaki pants turns to us. "Susan, your turn. Bring it home."

Susan smiles at me. "Hey, C.J., this Emily. She's new."

He comes over and takes Susan's seat while she bowls. "What are you drinking?" he asks.

I look quizzically at my telltale clear plastic cup containing a dark liquid capped with a frothy top. Is he kidding? "A beer. I like one now and then."

"Oh. That's, uh, great."

I look around, and sure enough, no one else is drinking. My heart sinks. Isn't this bowling? Isn't this bowling in New York? I find myself feeling defensive for some reason. "I'm not, like, addicted or anything, you know."

Addicted? What was my mouth saying? I did not give it permission to say that. Addicted?

"Oh no. I'm sure you're not. I just don't. It's a personal choice. I think it makes witnessing to the guys at work harder."

I want to get off this topic, immediately. This C.J. character does not need to hear my speech about being the salt of the earth and really relating to non-Christians on their turf. And he especially should be spared my skewering when I ask him what Jesus's first miracle was. Oh, turning water into wine at a party, right. Don't tell me he didn't drink. I hold my tongue and decide to try out my Drew Barrymore sighting on him but have no luck.

Thankfully, Susan returns right then. I look at the screen, but her score is just a bunch of slashes and Xs.

"What's up with your score?" I ask. Something must be wrong with the computer.

"Susan's the best bowleer we've got," says C.J.

Susan blushes. "I was on a pretty serious league back in Kansas."

Oh. I realize she's doing so well, she broke the machine and that's why she doesn't have a score yet. Who's good at bowling? I shake it off and try to mix with some of the other people.

When I get home, I thankfully find a little bit of white wine left in my fridge. I pour myself a glass and sit at the kitchen table, flipping through *Vogue*. Whenever I need a pick-me-up—all the time, lately—I look through it and dream of a fabulous life like the models have in the fairy-tale photo shoots.

I try not to think back to the Parkside Bowling Night, but it is unavoidable. I even hold C.J.'s card in my hand. I should be excited, really, that I met a group of Christians and even a Christian guy like C.J., but I am just not. The whole group struck me as being, well, out of it. One girl, Lacey, who grew up in Tennessee, seemed really sweet. The two of us were talking and really hitting it off. She taught at a private Catholic school in Brooklyn. She confessed that she had been having the hardest time meeting non-Christians, and that, in fact, she didn't know a single non-Christian. My jaw hit the floor. I tried not to act shocked and recovered by telling her I was the opposite and didn't seem to know a single Christian in the city so we should be friends.

And then there was C.J. He was nice enough and certainly many girls would find him attractive, but it irked me the way his slang was about ten years behind. He kept saying things that weren't true and then saying *Not!* gleefully. Perhaps he should just watch more television. Also, he talked quite a bit about his mother and his church back home. It turned out that he lived an hour from his childhood home in Long Island and went there most weekends. To help out, he told me. I guess it didn't strike me as that weird until I realized he was twenty-seven years old. When I left he pulled me aside, awkwardly, interrupting a conversation I was having with Susan.

"Emily. I think you're really nice. I'd love the pleasure of getting to see you again."

"Oh, uh, thanks, C.J. That's sweet. Yeah, we should hang out," I suddenly felt like a boy, trying to keep things vague. No promises this was a date, buddy.

"Why don't you take my card and shoot me an e-mail about what night is good for you."

"Sure. I'll do that. What'd you have in mind?"

"Not to tip my hat too much, but if you're free next Wednesday I get together with a bunch of people and we play Trivial Pursuit at someone's house. It's really fun and usually we all bring takeout."

Nothing sounded worse to me. I knew immediately I was busy that Wednesday.

I take a sip of my wine and enjoy it as it trickles down my throat. I can't help but think of Jacob again, and a little of Bennett, too, if I am honest. Bennett might have had trouble telling the whole truth, so help him God, but he was really cool. And worldly. I never felt like he was out of touch or condescending to non-Christians. We both wanted to really get out in the world and live. And Jacob too. Jacob is so amazing. I guess he is the kind of guy you'd only realize was Christian if you hung around him enough and observed his kindness and selflessness. Jacob is the kind of guy you could take anywhere, and he'd fit in. It was too bad he had to fit in so far away.

I throw C.J.'s card in the wastebasket and clean up the kitchen. I know I can't go back to Parkside. I am different than those people. I climb into bed and hope to drop off to sleep, but toss and turn all night, wondering where I fit in this world.

what are we doing

★

"Lane?" I ask. I know she can hear the tremor in my voice because she swings around in her chair really fast.

"What? What? Are you okay?"

I just shake my head and tears start pouring out of my eyes. My Tuesday morning has really started off with a bang. She gets up, puts an arm around my shoulders, and hauls me off to the bathroom. It's only nine thirty. It's empty. She opens a stall, kicks down the lid, and sits me on it.

"Emily. What's wrong?"

"My mom just called from the hospital."

"Oh no!"

"My Nanna fell and broke her hip." I start sobbing, thinking of Nanna.

Lane bends down and takes me in her arms. "Oh Emily. I'm sorry."

I nod. I know Lane's sorry. She's the best friend ever. I'm so glad at a moment like this that we work together. I am sobbing big loud sobs and coughing intermittently.

"So what's the report? Is she going to be okay?"

I swallow hard. "My mom says that after a rough night, she's stabilized now. She has a really weak heart so they have her in ICU. And she has to have hip replacement surgery this week."

"Oh no. That's awful. But it sounds like she's in good hands."

"She is. I'm so glad she lives just down the road from us so that my mom could be there, but the worst part is, um, the statistics. My mom said the doctor told her that seventy-five percent of all senior citizens who get hip replacement surgery die within the year. Their bodies are just too old to bounce back from it."

"I didn't know that," says Lane. "I'm so sorry."

"I know I'm freaking out about this, and I should be thankful my grandmother's alive, but it's just weird to think that even if she does recover completely that she might not have much time left. And I'm so far away."

"Emily. Don't be so hard on yourself. It sounds like she's going to be just fine, and I'm sure your whole family is really thrilled with everything you're accomplishing. I mean, they call you Manhattan. That sounds to me like they're proud of you. And you can't just run home every time something goes wrong. You know?"

"I know you're right," I say, mopping up my face with my sleeve. Lane hands me a roll of toilet paper, and I blow my nose. "And if I know Nanna, she's going to come back fighting. It's just weird, you know. She's never really been ill before. I see her as the model of good health. It's hard to face that she's getting older. And my mom, she sounded like she really needed me. I would have been at the hospital with her. We have to stick together. There's a lot of guys at our house."

"I know. I know. But at least you talked with her. And you can do what you can from here. You know, send a care package and call relatives for your mom. It will be fine. I promise."

I hang up feeling so much better. Nanna was spry on the phone, and I got to tell her how much I loved her. My mom said that all the hospital staff had started to fawn over her and call her "Nanna" themselves. Nanna had even drawn up mock adoption papers for her favorite nurse, Callie. Callie had cried and signed them immediately, posting them on the wall above Nanna's bed. And apparently her room was overflowing with flowers.

Now I can pack up and go home. I had stayed late that day because we were still slammed at work, and I had not been able to multitask like the madwoman I normally was, so it just seemed easier to call from work. Nanna had been in the hospital several days now, and though the surgery had been a great success and she was doing a little better, I still hadn't been able to talk to her. Mom said they hoped she would get moved out of ICU sometime next week. All afternoon, I had jumped when the phone rang, but Mom hadn't called with the latest update.

I tell the night security man good night on my way out and step into the brisk air. New York is really taking its time to get warmer. I try not to think about how beautiful the weather would be in Southern California right now. As I am walking to the subway, a couple catches my eye. Maybe it is her white-blonde hair, maybe his tall frame is familiar, I don't know. But there they are, Bennett and Skylar, lip-locked in front of a little bistro across the street from work.

My blood boils. At first I am tempted to walk up and kick Bennett in the shin. But then a weird calm comes over me. I realize that they make sense together, and I don't care. It was a breakup. No one died or anything. These things happen. And, I roll my eyes as I think about it, forcing myself to walk on, breakups would continue to happen if I wanted to keep dating. There are a lot of things I'm not sure about in my life, but the one I am sure about is dating. I really still hold out hope for dating. Perhaps I am delusional, but at least I'm not delusional about Bennett anymore. And I wasn't insane for being jealous of Skylar. He *did* have feelings for her, the entire time we dated. And she wasn't just mean to me for no reason. She was, in fact, jealous of me.

"Hmph," I say. I have to laugh a little. It's kind of funny. And then I think of Nanna. I laugh again. I know she'd have *hated* Bennett's family. Or would have rolled her eyes if he had gone off on one of his "Yale" stories. Ha ha. He wouldn't have lasted a minute at my house. The more I think about it, the happier I get.

Staring at my closet and listening to the rain outside—could the weather be more miserable?—I am waffling between going out and staying in. Friday nights are always such a toss-up. On the one hand, you are exhausted from your week at work and probably several weeknights when you stayed out later than you had intended. But on the other hand, it is officially the weekend. Since New Yorkers believe that any night of the week is just as good as any other to go out until the early morning, the weekend often becomes a time to catch up on sleep and have lazy brunches. The girls are all meeting for a movie and drinks, and I just can't decide if I'm going to join them or not. I am looking to my closet for inspiration when my computer dings to tell me I have a new message.

"Get your act together," I tell my closet and then throw myself on my bed, pulling my laptop over. I see immediately that it's from Jacob and am thrilled. He didn't write right back like I had wanted after my scolding e-mail. I'm dying to know his response.

Dear Emily,

Hi! This is Jacob Keller's grandfather, here. My name is Cecil. I'd like to thank you for all the lovely e-mails you've been sending me. In fact, I've become rather addicted to them. So between that and my fig addiction, my life is pretty fulfilling. Oh yeah, and then there's the couple of hours every week I get to spend beating my grandson at curling. Have you ever heard of a twenty-something curling? He's a bizarre boy.

Ha ha. My grandfather loves you, Emily. He told me so. So how did your quest go to find someone as great as me at the new church? I'm going to tell you I hope it went well, but I'm not sure how much you should trust that sentiment. I'm glad I'm giving you hope for mankind because I'm making me lose hope in mankind.

Okay. So I can't lie to you. Not even a sin of omission, so I think you should know that I went out with the Cold Pastoral girl again and things went a little too far. No, not that far. I'm still not sure how I feel about it. Compared to my friends, I'm still in the dugout, as they say, but I know I'm not thinking long-term with this girl and only followed her lead.

I don't know. Something about it feels bad. What do you think? And take it easy on me, Emily. Your last e-mail smarted a little, although I had to admit you are right, on some level. I don't know. I'm pretty turned around.

Jacob.

I slam the top of my laptop shut. "Argh" is all I can manage to say to my empty room. What is he doing? I lie back on my bed and a thousand thoughts go through my head. This boy is making me crazy over the Internet! What is the world coming to when Jacob Keller is making Emily Hinton insane through technology?! I curse him. I curse the little date, or whatever it was, that we had. I curse him for turning out so cool and then flushing it all down the toilet. I curse myself and all the boys in Manhattan.

I sit up and e-mail him back.

Jacob.

If you're home, call me. Cell phone.

Emily

I hit send and spend the next fifteen minutes wondering exactly how long an e-mail message takes to travel to California. What if my connection is down? It was acting funny last week. After about fifteen minutes, I realize he's not going to call. He may or may not have gotten that crazy e-mail from me, but regardless we aren't going to talk tonight. I force myself to sit up and go see if my closet has anything to say for itself. I pull shirts and slacks around on their hangers, but I can't get my mind to focus. What was I going to say, anyway? I don't have some kind of master plan. I just . . . I don't know, we need to talk. I haven't confessed to anyone how much Jacob and I have been e-mailing, and I begin to wonder if he has.

The phone rings. It's on my pillow. I stare at it, holding my breath. Will it ring again? Or did I imagine it? It rings again, and I pounce on it. The screen says Jacob. I'm instantly nervous, my mouth goes dry, and I must swallow hard to answer.

"Hey there. You *are* home," I say to him, trying to sound upbeat, nonchalant.

"Yeah. Sorry it took a minute. I'm staying in tonight and trying to cook so I was in the kitchen wrestling some rice into submission. Have you ever noticed how hard it is to cook that stuff?"

"Rice cooker. That's what I use. They're foolproof and usually have a tacky floral design that really brightens up your kitchen."

"I'll write that down. How about some more advice for my life, Emily?"

I laugh nervously. Wow, he likes to get right down to business. "Jacob. You don't really want to hear my opinion."

"I do. We might as well just have it out, I think."

"It's going to be harsh, and I can't help but feel like I have no business telling you these things. I mean, who am I? I'm just some girl who e-mails you." I know I'm testing the waters here.

"Emily," he says. "You know that's not true. You're some wild girl who I am fascinated by and who already told me no once. Your opinion means a lot to me. I feel like, well, if I'm honest, we're twins. Or, at least first cousins, which is most likely why you wouldn't let me kiss you back in December. Or at least that's what I'm telling myself right now. So spill it. I'm asking you. I don't care what a lot of people have to say, but I want to know what you think."

I start gently, but after about five minutes, I just start laying it out there for him. Why were his standards suddenly so low? I ask. How could he pretend to be one way with me over e-mail and then fail the first time he's tempted? I tell him that he could be such an excellent example for other guys because he actually is cool and is out there in the world living, but instead he's just one of them. "I just think the world doesn't need another typical guy. Or another typical Christian guy. Those two types have been well covered in my experience. You could really be something fabulous that lands in between there, something really fresh and powerful, but you're falling flat on your face," I say. Okay, so maybe that is a little harsh.

There is a long pause. He groans. "Ouch, Emily. Ouch. It really kills me to know you're disappointed. But what does it matter? I mean, to you? Why the personal interest, may I ask?"

I look at my window at the rain streaking down it in long threads and then pace over to my closet. "I . . ." I don't know what I should say. What do I have to lose? "I guess, you know, um . . . if I'm honest—"

"Yeah?" he asks. I can tell he's pretty hurt and browbeaten. I don't want to lose him.

"I'm just saying, that's all. It's just useless what you're doing when there are girls like me who would die to date a guy like you." I am standing in front of my mirror, staring wide-eyed at myself. Oops.

"Emily. You know I like you. You've been my ideal since first grade. And now that we're e-mailing all the time, I only like you more. But you told me no."

I am grinning like the cat that got the mouse. "Jacob. Please. You must know I like you by now. Hello? Do I strike you as the kind of girl who has made-up Internet boyfriends? There are plenty of dumb guys I could e-mail out here. But I e-mail you because I like you. And I told you no at Christmas for a good reason. I'd be lying if I said you didn't have some small part in my breakup with Bennett. You're definitely my ideal. That's why it kills me to see you dating some girl you met in a bar." It feels so good to finally admit these things to him and wonderful to hear his voice again. We sit in silence awhile.

"I don't know," he says finally. "I'm really confused. You live pretty far away. I guess, you know, I hope someday we get to be together, but I don't think it's right now. You said yourself you were really happy in New York, and I just got this job."

His reminder of reality crushes me. It's true. He couldn't possibly live farther away. "I know" is all I can muster.

"Maybe I could move to New York in a year, you know, but in the meantime, I've got to keep living my life. Wouldn't you rather I date girls I'm not excited about? I mean, at least that way, I'll still be able to move in a year for you once I get some good clips and make some contacts."

My mind races. Are we talking about him moving? Yes? Wonderful. Wait, scary. But the thought of Jacob dating other women makes my stomach lurch. I want to ask him to not date anyone. How can he keep dating? Isn't he feeling this, this thing I'm feeling? If he isn't, why is he talking about moving? Isn't a connection like this rare? I decide to be nonchalant. "Do what you decide, but don't look for my approval for dating beneath yourself. Low standards are appalling." With this statement, I realize that he is the only boy I want and that my New York dating

hopes are now dead. In fact, they probably were never real because my standards for dating were set sky-high by Jacob at
Christmas.

"Emily. Don't take this so hard. I really care about you. And
I'm not a bad guy. In fact, I'm a great guy. I know I am. It's just a
weird situation, you know? I think we should be prudent. I'll bet
in a year I'll be there in New York, calling you up and begging to
take you out."

"Who says I'll be here in a year?" I say it without thinking. I
can't wait around for him while he dates half of the girls in bars
in San Diego.

"Ha ha. You see? This is why I like you, Emily. You're so smart
and sassy. You take no prisoners."

I roll my eyes. Then stop dating. Or move to New York. Or
stop e-mailing me and making me insane. "I know I'm great. I'm
perfectly confident in that."

"Oh man. I swear I'm great too. This situation is just not
bringing out the best in me."

"Then tell me something you've done that you're proud of,"
I say.

The hours begin to fly by. Jacob tells me about the week his
mother and grandfather both had major surgery, and his family
flew him out to be the one who took care of his gramps. He had
to stay with him in the hospital, drive him home, cook his meals,
feed him, change his diaper, the whole bit. I cave. It's a beautiful
story, and I like how he tells it. He clearly loves his grandfather.
I tell him about Nanna, and he reassures me she will be fine. We
chat about work and San Diego and about New York and about
Jenks. He tells me about the people from high school he bumps
into, and I tell him about the girls at work. Three hours into the
conversation, we finally pause. I realize I'm smiling again. I'm not
happy about his decision to keep dating this girl, or really any girl

but me, but I've calmed down about it and must admit that after Bennett, it's pretty cool to have a guy who is so honest and forthright that he'll even tell you things you don't want to hear. He speaks up first. Moans, really.

"Emily . . ."

It's really cute. He's in some kind of pain or something. "Yes?"

"Emily . . . what are we doing here?"

"You tell me, bucko."

I hear him sigh. "I just feel like a fool. You know, we've been on the phone for over three hours, and it feels like five minutes, but when, uh, Karen talks, I have the hardest time paying attention. I get bored."

Her name is a little hard to hear, but I'm so proud of myself that I put it in the back of my mind. He finally sees my point, I tell myself. "Yeah. It does feel like five minutes. I guess I'm staying in tonight."

He laughs and then goes quiet again. "What are we doing? Oh man. What am *I* doing? Wow. This Karen thing is really a problem. And you? You're a problem. Emily . . ."

I smile from ear to ear. "I think we've definitely gotten ourselves into a little mess for sure. Of course, I'm not dating anyone, so I think it seems a little clearer here in New York."

"I'm just going to move. I mean, how great would that be, right? We could hang out all the time. And we'll just talk and agree on stuff and go to shows. I should move out there to give you a proper one-on-one music education."

I love this game immediately and join right in. "You definitely should move to New York. We'd just sit around smiling like dopes all the time. I'd have to parade you all over town and show you off. And you could kick Bennett if you saw him."

He laughs a little and then goes back to groaning. We finally hang up an hour later, as the sun is coming up in New York and my cell phone is beeping to tell me I'm about to lose my battery. We say an awkward goodbye, I plug my phone in, and I settle down for my rest, at last.

I sleep like a baby.

act now

★

Sunday night I tossed and turned all night in my sleep, never really achieving REM, but that doesn't stop my alarm from going off at 6:45. It's the most faithful pest I have. I hit snooze, remembering during my five extra minutes of peace the bizarre dream I had had. I dreamed that I was trapped inside a glass bottle with a cork in the top in some kind of science laboratory, and I was really tiny. All I could see were two sets of giant human hands. They kept tapping on my glass bottle, making a *thump, thump, thump* sound. I could hear their muffled voices saying something. And they were observing my every move.

The third time the alarm goes off, I decide to just get up and hopefully free myself from this eerie dream. I get in the shower— Brittany must be sleeping late too—and then towel off. As I pass back through the living room to my bedroom, I hear the thumping again and realize it is someone at our door. I freeze. Who could it be? A neighbor? I'm not dressed yet. A UPS man? I'm not dressed yet.

"Emily!" I hear a muffled familiar voice say in desperation through the door.

"Brittany?" I ask. What is she doing? I open the door a little to see Brittany looking very cross and rumpled in her clothes from the day before. She pushes past me and slams the door behind her. She has to be bipolar.

"I am so mad at you right now. In fact, I don't even know if I can look at you," she says.

I have gotten used to Brittany's ways so I am not all that upset by this proclamation. I ignore it. "Why were you outside?"

"I was outside because you were too rude to answer the door. *Why was I outside?*" She repeats my question to herself and shakes her head as if I were the dumbest creature she's ever come across. "What? Did you have some boy in here and not want to let me in?"

"Britt. That's you. When have I ever had a boy stay over? What time were you knocking on it?" I ask.

"It was like midnight or something."

"That can't be right. I was still up then."

"I guess it was more like two in the morning."

I think for a moment. "Were you banging on the door all night? Did you sleep in the hall? Where were your keys? Why didn't you just go over to John's house? Doesn't he have spare keys?"

"John and I broke up last night, thank you very much. And if you hadn't ignored me when I knocked on the door, I wouldn't have had to sleep in the hallway. Now I'm going to have to go and get a massage because my back is all out of alignment."

Even for Brittany this is surprising. Was I really getting blamed for her getting locked out? I realize she doesn't actually think I was ignoring her. She is just taking out her frustration on me. And on a Monday morning, after taking this sort of abuse for months, and with all the drama in my life of late, I decide I can't take it anymore. "Brittany! Snap out of it." I storm over to the table next to the door and pick up her Cartier key ring. "Here are your keys! *You* left *your* keys here. I go to sleep every night at about midnight. I sleep soundly. *You* locked *yourself* out. I had no part in this melodrama." I turn and walk toward my room. She isn't going to make me late too.

"Wait. Why didn't you just have the doorman let you in?" Britt's face sweeps with regret. She didn't think of that. I stifle my smile. Clueless, she's so clueless.

"I shouldn't have needed to do that, Emily. You should have let me in. Thanks for all your help, Emily. You're a great room-mate," she says, her words laced with sarcasm.

I slam my door.

I place my tray down at the lunch table, slide into a chair, and wonder if I'll even be able to feed myself I'm so exhausted.

"Where in the world have you been?" Lane asks.

I just shake my head. "I'm so tired. Sorry I haven't been to lunch lately, but there's just a lot going on in my life." I think about mentioning the Jacob thing and finding out if they think it's insane, but then I think better of it.

"You haven't missed much," says Skylar.

I sort of chuckle internally. It strikes me as a very funny thing for her to say to me. In fact, I haven't missed much. Bennett wasn't much, just some smoke and mirrors. I practically made him up. I am missing nothing.

"I got a part in a really big play!" says Reggie, gleefully.

"That's great," I say. I mean it. While I'm not the biggest musical theater person, she's been trying so hard all year. "What's the part?"

"I'm a soldier in a fight scene. I, um, die. Dramatically. And then I lay on stage all through the second act!"

"Good for you." I smile at her.

She starts laughing. "It's a start at least," she says, her spirit undampened.

"How's it going with Alex, Lane?" I ask. Even though I haven't been around much lately and I flaked on the girls' Friday night to stay home and talk to Jacob on the phone, I have tried to keep up with Lane.

"We're going on our fourth date this weekend. On Saturday."

"She's been upgraded from weeknight dates," says Reggie.

I'm very happy for Lane, and she catches me up on all the latest gossip about Alex, who loves to read biographies, is a fabulous chef, and can fix things around the house, like Lane's toilet, which makes Lane swoon.

Listening to Lane, I realize I'm dying to know if Skylar and Bennett are official yet. I don't care anymore and have in fact received three e-mails from Jacob this morning alone, calming me down about the Brittany fiasco, so I decide to ask. "Skylar. Are you and, uh, Bennett dating now? I'm just curious. It's really fine if you are. I know about the past and everything now."

She stares at me like I'm a fool. "No."

I wonder why she's even bothering to deny it. What's her problem? She must really think I care. "I promise. I don't mind at all. And if I'm honest, I saw you guys together."

I had assumed this was common knowledge and that no one was talking about it with me to spare my feelings, but I see Reggie lean in to hear Skylar's response and Lane's eyes get wide.

•Skylar is flummoxed. "When? We're not together, Emily. I wouldn't lie to your face."

Was I wrong? Was it another couple? A wave of regret sweeps over me. Of course I had thought it was them. I'm probably hypersensitive. "I'm sorry. I guess I was wrong. It's just that I saw this couple kissing in front of the bistro across the street, and it looked like you guys."

Skylar laughs. "At La Petite?"

"Yeah," I say.

"Last week?"

I nod.

"Oh. Then that was us."

Reggie's mouth falls open, and Lane makes an audible gasp. I feel vindicated. I don't know what Skylar's story is, but I'm not insane. Not at all.

"So then you *are* together . . ." Lane says in a quiet voice full of shock.

"No," says Skylar.

Reggie starts laughing. Lane and I look at each other, confused.

"Listen, Emily. I don't *really* like Bennett. He's hot, sure, so sometimes I let him take me out, and sometimes we even end up kissing a little. But I'd hardly say we're dating," says Skylar.

My eyes are wide. Lane laughs nervously. I feel a little bad for Bennett, even. I say, calmly, "I think he really has feelings for you."

"I don't care," says Skylar. "Sometimes I let him take my cute self out. Period. That's our arrangement. I don't see why you guys always think in terms of one boy for every girl."

I'm still recovering from the shock. Skylar is more duplicitous than even my wild imagination had thought. She continues.

"You see. This is why I love Helen's proposal by Dr. Heggler. If you'd read that you'd see that monogamy is not a natural state for humankind. I don't lie to any of the boys. But I also don't date exclusively. What's the point? I might someday settle down with one boy, but in the meantime, I want to keep getting free drinks and dinner. What's so wrong with that? I'm not sneaking around."

I don't feel like arguing with her and just poke at my food.

It'd be too difficult to explain all of my reasons to disagree with her and Dr. Heggler. I simply say, "I guess I'm just a hopeless romantic, that's all."

"I agree, Skylar. Good for you," says Reggie. "You're an inspiration to us all. Why limit yourself to just one boy? You'll never know what you're missing if you do that." We all sit and digest this.

"By the way," Lane asks. "Has Helen thought of a plan yet to get that proposal by the Ed Board?"

After lunch I come back and find an e-mail from my mom about Nanna. I am engrossed with the details of her recovery. She has finally been allowed to go home and is now living in my old room. Unfortunately, she's taking longer to heal than doctors expected, and my parents have hired a hospice nurse to sit with her around the clock. I worry about my parents' finances. I know this is a great strain on things. I let my eyes go out of focus and sit there thinking about home and Nanna. I can't help but feel so completely helpless stuck way out here in New York. I resolve to send her a package.

"Ms. Hinton?"

I turn around in my chair to see Carl from the mailroom. I've told him a thousand times to call me Emily, but his unfailing politeness will not allow him to comply. I smile. He hands me a clipboard to sign for a FedEx package. As I'm signing I get a rush when I see the sender is Jacob Keller. I hand the pen back to Carl and start tearing open the hard letter-sized envelope. What could this be? He's written all over it "Please do not bend" and my favorite, "No Squish!!!" I laugh. I see a piece of beige, high-grade paper inside and pull it out. It's a coupon of some sort, the size of a certificate or a diploma. I read it:

SPECIAL OFFER

Jacob Keller—Total Happiness
GREAT CELL PHONE SAVINGS
Preserve Your Sanity through Dating

Right Now the City of San Diego is offering you, Resident of said Cubicle of Morrow & Sons, a Once in a Lifetime Offer to immediately release its most-beloved resident and famed music critic, Jacob Keller, to live in New York for your personal happiness!

ACT NOW

Sign this coupon and send it back to the address below, and one Jacob Keller will soon be on his way to New York (please allow 6–8 weeks for delivery of first issue). The cost to you is FREE (your heart will be billed later, rates good in U.S. and its possessions only).

Free Consultation 617–555-LOVE

www.Jacobmovestonewyork.com

My hand covers my gaping mouth. My heart races. I knew Jacob was mulling over the idea of moving to New York in a year or maybe six months because he could be with me and because New York would be a great place for him to pursue his career in rock journalism, but I didn't know he had been considering moving immediately. I just don't know what to say. The coupon is so sweet, complete with sloppy but earnest calligraphy, a faux seal made of tin foil, and fake trademark symbols. I run a finger over it and think about how great it would be to have him here, to be able to just grab some Thai food on a Friday night and stay in to watch a DVD. But there's a knot in my stomach. I wonder if it's nervousness, but I know it's not. It's something else. While I want nothing more than to be able to really date him and hold his hand, I feel in my gut something is wrong with this plan. It stinks of disaster.

I frown. This is not going to be easy to explain, and it shouldn't be done via e-mail. I jot him a quick Thank You Thank You Thank You e-mail and ask if I can call him tonight. He responds immediately. He's not out of the office on an interview, thankfully, and I should definitely call tonight. He asks if anything's wrong. I gulp. I write him back a vaguely reassuring note without directly answering the question and tell him I have to run to Ed Board.

The editorial meeting that week is long. So long. Or maybe it just feels that way, since I am distracted and hate being stuck in this meeting when I want to be at my desk, obsessively checking my e-mail. I worry Jacob is freaking out.

Xavier talks about a new apocalyptic thriller he has in. "The body count is higher than my cholesterol—it's amazing!" he announces. Everyone laughs. I manage to crack a smile, though under the table I am tapping my foot.

Susanna brings up a book of recipes for cooking for your cat. Recipes include Meow Munchies, Whisker Whispers, and Feline Fancies. Are there really people who have so little to do that they cook for their cats? Somehow the editors seem to think this is a good idea. They tell her to make an offer on the book this afternoon. I cross and recross my legs.

I have brought up a few more ideas in the past couple of months and am currently researching a young writer who is at a smaller house now, but this week, I have nothing. Thankfully. I don't think I could focus enough to string a coherent sentence together. And I am so worn out I almost feel like I could fall asleep here.

Someone brings up a new diet book. We've seen too many of these. A new kind of yoga. Passé. How to better understand your mate. We already have more of these than we know what to do with. Please end soon.

Helen speaks up. "I have in a proposal for a book by renowned Harvard law professor Martha Heggler," she begins.

I perk up. She begins to walk around the table distributing a copy of the proposal to the editors. She has one copy for all of the assistants to share.

"It's a fascinating study on marriage and the family in the United States. Dr. Heggler has been researching this project with other leaders in her field for the past three years, and her results are remarkable. Her claim is that marriage mores in the U.S. need to be revised or revisited because they were originally based on the teachings of the Bible, thus leading astray any person who does not buy into the outdated biblical model. Her writing is engaging, and her point is solid. It's really well done and will probably get a lot of media attention."

Barry Medina nods. "Has she written a book before?"

"No. She's only written articles so far, one of which was published last year in *Time* magazine and caused quite a stir, if you all remember. The good news is, we could probably get it for very little money." I watch Helen carefully. Is she going to continue on and say that after the first chapter in the book, where Dr. Heggler's point is valid and well researched, she falls away and begins to ruminate on God and the family? That this book is in fact a treatise celebrating the death of God and the end of the family? That it isn't well researched, and the tone becomes petty and conspiratorial? I reach over to Lane and ask to see the proposal copy we have down at the end of the table and flip through it. Do I say something? I hate this book.

"It's a good idea," Xavier says. "It could do well."

"Sounds like a no-brainer to me," says Barry. "Give the agent a call and see how much they want for it."

"Good," she says, making a mark in her notebook. "I'll do that."

As I flip through the copy of the Heggler proposal, I see that

she has taken out the two latter chapters where Heggler skewers
the family and God. Also she has attached a copy of the *Time* article that focuses on the dissolution of monogamy. It's so misleading. Indeed, this proposal *would* be a good book, but this is not
what Dr. Heggler intends to write or Helen to publish. The two
women are basically conspiring to publish their personal, caustic
opinions. I swallow hard.

I am there before Uncle Matthew, which is becoming quite a
trend these days, and walk to a booth at the back of the pizzeria.
I shake the water off my umbrella, hang my raincoat on the back
of the chair, and sit down, grumbling to myself about the rotten,
rainy spring. I pull out a manuscript and a pen and get busy
editing, paying extra careful attention. Once again, I had intended to go down to the Locus to help out but got caught up
at work.

I look at my watch and thank God California is three hours
behind us. I need to be home by eleven to call Jacob. We
e-mailed the rest of the day, but we didn't discuss the coupon.
This evasion alone makes me think he knows something is
wrong. My stomach hurts. I wonder if I'll even be able to eat. And
then there's this Martha Heggler problem. I've been thinking
about it a lot since Ed Board. I don't know what to do. I don't
want to ignore it—something like this should not be published—
but I'm hardly in a position to speak up for it. Barry likes it. That
means Xavier will say he likes it. And I know for a fact that Helen is basically lying to them. But then, my place in the company
is a little rocky after my editing skills were questioned on *The
Marine Corpse*. And I'm just an assistant. I've *got* to ignore it.
There's no question. If I speak up, I'll reveal that I'm a Christian.
What will Xavier think of me? Clearly he believes the traditional
family is bunk. His lifestyle proves that.

Still, I don't like that I haven't been to the Locus in three weeks. I do some quick math and realize I've spent eleven hours shopping in that time. I make a mental note to go soon before my priorities get completely out of whack.

I get into the manuscript. It's not bad, though I find several grammatical errors. I find myself getting involved in the story—it is a mystery involving a serial killer and his architectural marvel of a house. I get so involved, in fact, that when I look up forty-five minutes later, I realize for the first time that Uncle Matthew isn't here yet. I roll my eyes. I think I know where he is. In a word, Josie.

I return to the murder currently taking place in the basement—the killer has a giant built-in oven and has just locked a woman in it. Ten minutes later, and halfway into the manuscript, Uncle Matthew comes rushing through the door. His hair is tousled by the wind, but even from where I'm sitting I can see the twinkle in his eye and the grin on his face.

"I'm so sorry, Emily," he says, unbelting his raincoat. "I got caught up talking with Josie after we finished serving and didn't realize how late it was."

"That's okay. I got a lot done while I was waiting. Uh . . . how is Josie?"

"She's doing well . . . she's . . ." A pink blush creeps over his face. He grins. "She's great." He smiles guiltily. "She's been busy, though. Out past her bedtime more than she should be."

"So things are going well between you two?"

"Yeah," he laughs. "Really well."

"Uncle Matthew, I'm glad to hear it. At first I wasn't sure about Josie, but seeing you so happy makes me really glad it's working out." I want to be mature about this.

"What's wrong with Josie?"

Oh no. I forgot he never realized how I felt about her. He

looks a little hurt. "Oh, I didn't mean . . . She's great. Really. She kind of annoyed me at first. She's just kind of, um, full of life, I guess. It bothered me a little. But that was before I saw how sweet she can be. I think she's a fine person." As I finish my little speech, I realize I actually mean it. Mostly. Maybe Josie always will have an annoying sense of humor, but she clearly cares about my uncle, and he seems to like her back. He's happier than I've ever seen him.

"I'm going to get the three of us together for dinner. You guys are a lot alike. I just know you'll like her," he says. He still looks a little hurt.

"I shouldn't have said anything. And really, I do like her. Now."

"Really?" he asks.

"Really."

"Good," he says, smiling sheepishly. "So do I." I look at him and can't help but smile. He won't hold my gaze, and his face is bright red. He looks down at the menu. "But I'm still getting us together for dinner soon. It's my fault that you feel a little conflicted about her. I know I've been really flaky lately, and I've been keeping her all to myself."

"Don't worry about it, slugger. You're in love," I say. "And I'd like that. Let me know when you guys want to go out."

"Thanks, Em. Will do. So do you want to split a pizza?"

"With mushrooms?"

"Perfect." He's silent for a few minutes, and I gather up my papers and start to put them into my bag. "How is work going?" he asks.

"Oh, it's fine, mostly. Really busy. But it's going well. The Hank Fleming book is coming along. The manuscript should be in soon." I pause. There's so much going on at work, in my life, I don't even know where to begin.

I take a deep breath. "Uncle Matthew?"

"Yes?" he asks, leaning in. He seems to be able to tell this is serious.

"Is Xavier having an affair?"

"Whoa . . . What makes you ask that?" I look at his eyes. Is he really asking, or is he hedging? I can't tell.

"Everyone at the company seems to think he is. And they joke about it. Two different women call him all the time, and I've seen him out with both. Plus, he's been on vacations with both of them. I know one of them is his wife, but this other one is always around."

"I don't know, Emily." He pauses. He begins speaking, very slowly. "That's a serious accusation to make." He stops again. "The answer is that I don't know. I've known Xavier for a long time, but our paths just don't cross very often anymore. I guess there's a lot about him I don't know. And I guess . . ." He pauses again. "My guess is that if he is, he would hide it from me anyway. That's not something you tell your missionary friend." I nod. "He's always had girls around, but—"

"But what?"

"But I think he really loves Laura. That's the impression I've always had. Though I guess it's possible. He loved his first wife too, I guess." His first wife? Xavier is divorced and still has two new women? "I don't know, Emily." He gives me a crooked smile. "But either way, you're not going to let that interfere with your work, are you? It doesn't really concern you, right?"

"No, I know it doesn't. It's not that at all. It's just . . ." How do I explain this? "There's this editor at work, Helen. She used to be Xavier's assistant. She got in this proposal for a book that argues that we should change the family structure that we have now, because it's based on the Bible, and we no longer live in a primarily Christian country."

He nods. "I think I've heard of that before. It may happen."

"Right. That part is well done. But then the author goes on to say once people don't have to get married anymore, then God will officially be dead and the nuclear family will completely dissolve."

He shakes his head. "That's not right."

"I know it's not. And I don't think it should be published. And Helen took those parts out of the proposal and just left in the part about the current nonreligious society in which we live. She thinks publishing a revolutionary book will change the minds of society and also make her career. So she's been really sneaky. I just figured out what she did this afternoon, and I don't know what to do about it."

"She's definitely misleading them," Matthew says.

"And I want to tell Xavier about it so she won't get to buy the thing, but I'm not sure I can. If he is having an affair, surely he's going to get angry when I tell him that I think a monogamous marriage is not only a gift from God, but also the glue that is holding our fragile society together. He's going to get angry and fire me." I don't even mention the thin ice I'm already walking on at work.

Matthew is silent. Brooding. "Surely he'll notice that she's trying to slip it by them."

"I doubt it. We really need some more books for our upcoming fall list so they're in this buying frenzy. They'd have to go and ask Helen for the complete proposal, but no one's going to do that. It's so busy at work, and they have no reason to believe she's lying. And besides, Xavier lives on Planet X most of the time. Plus his boss, Barry Medina, said he liked the idea. Xavier doesn't *ever* challenge what Barry says."

"I see." He waits. "That's a tough place to be in, Emily. Wow." The waitress places the pizza down between us, and Matthew waits until she leaves. He slides a slice onto his plate. "So what do you think will happen if you tell him?"

"Best-case scenario? Helen gets a slap on the wrist and is forced to tone down the proposal. I'll get dismissed as a fanatical and paranoid member of the Religious Right and relegated in their minds to the 'Never Promote' pile of assistants, essentially flushing down the tubes all the hard work I've done to stand out. And the book will get published anyway."

"What's the worst-case scenario?" Matthew asks.

"Xavier will have one of his moments of insane rage, take my stance personally as a condemnation of his life, Helen will get promoted, I'll get fired, and the book will still see publication."

"Okay. So what happens if you don't do anything?"

"Then it definitely gets published, as is, and people will be misled by a lie."

He just looks at me.

"What do you think you need to do?"

"I don't know," I whine. "I've worked too hard to give it all up now. I can't be fired over this. And yet—"

"Yes?"

"And yet I feel like I should stand up for what I know is right." He is quiet. He looks down at his plate. I play with the wrapper from my straw.

"It sounds like you've already decided what you need to do."

"But how can I?"

"Emily?" He pauses again. "The truth will be made known. We serve a God who will not be thwarted by some book. If you don't speak up, he will still win in the end." He stirs his water with his straw, clinking the ice against the side of the glass. "And yet, how many people will believe it? How many people will be deceived? Maybe you are here for a reason—to stand up, to stop it." He takes a sip, swallows. "Who knows? Perhaps you were put in this spot for this very reason. Maybe that's why you're here."

I have nothing to say to this.

I come home from dinner with Matthew weighed down with the pressure of indecision. Should I stand up for my beliefs? Let them all know that I am a Christian? Would it really change anything? Probably it will just get me fired.

I open the door to my apartment and see Brittany on the couch alone. It all comes flooding back to me. I had completely forgotten about our fight. About her breakup with John. I try to act like everything is normal, but she just ignores anything I say. I even go so far as to half-apologize that she had to spend the night in our hallway and try to reassure her that I never heard her knocking. She just turns up the volume on the TV. I don't have time for this, I think, and go to my bedroom to call Jacob.

I am not able to keep to small talk for long.

"Thanks so much for my coupon, Jacob. It's great."

"But," he says, prompting me. There is a lot of hurt in his voice.

"But I don't know if I can redeem it. Are you sure about this?" I ask.

"I *was*."

This hurts. I know he had expected me to be thrilled, call him crying, sign it, and send it right back to him. He had expected tonight to be our night of joy and excitement, when I told him thank you a thousand times, and we planned all the fun things we'd do in New York together. I really want all of those things with him, but I just can't picture it. I don't know why. I don't know how to explain it to him. "Jacob. There is nothing I want more than to be your girlfriend. I really want to sign this and send it back to you. But something's wrong . . . I just can't picture this whole us–in–New York scenario yet. I don't know what to tell you except that I need some time to think. This really took me by surprise. But I care about you so much. I really do. I wish you knew that."

"Emily, I can't help but feel like you're just toying with my emotions. I'm sorry, but after Christmas when you didn't even tell me you had a boyfriend until I tried to kiss you and now that you don't want me to move to New York, I can only assume that you like me, but you don't really want me around. There's no other ex-planation."

"*No.* That's just not true. I know it looks that way, but you've got to see how much I care about you. I was just thinking you might move here in a year. I'm just surprised. I need to think. This is really big."

"I hate to tell you this, but I'd never move to New York for you now. I just think if I did, you'd freak out. You'd want me there in theory, but I'd uproot my life and arrive there only to have you realize that you couldn't handle the pressure of dating. Emily, I'm sorry. It's not going to happen. I needed you to take this leap of faith with me, but you didn't."

At some point in the conversation I just begin to weep. He is so upset, and I know I can't fix it. I understand why he thinks I am just toying with him, but I also know my heart. He is the only boy for me. And I have ruined it. He is slipping away, and I can't stop it.

The conversation ends pretty quickly because I can't talk through my tears. He tells me he still cares for me and will be thinking about me, even if he isn't e-mailing. That part hurts the most. I am losing him entirely.

I hang up the phone and let the hot tears fall into my ears. My nose is running. The TV is still on, which means Brittany is still up and can probably hear me sobbing, but she will never come in to comfort me.

At one in the morning, my phone bleats in the darkness, but it doesn't wake me. I'm still trying to fall asleep. I run over and pick it up. The screen says Bennett. I shake my head and read it again. I am paralyzed. Why is he calling me? I let it go to voice mail. I check the message. He says he is eating some cold take-out and drinking a bottle of wine, thinking about me. I shiver in the cold of the apartment and erase the message. I leave my phone to charge and go back to bed, more confused than ever. Sleep never comes that night.

CHAPTER 22

i could change it

★

Bleary eyed, exhausted, and completely stressed out by my life, I am still at work. This is a victory. But I can barely focus. And people keep bringing me things to do. I don't mind the work so much, but I'm just about up to my limit with people. I'm out of relationship energy. I can't both be pleasant and do my job this morning, so I've decided to just do my job. Although every time someone comes into my cubicle to drop something off or to check the candy dish, they seem to want to chat. I start just not turning around when they say hi. I continue typing while they talk to me. And yet more people keep coming. So when I hear a quiet "Emily?" from behind me, I don't even look to see who it is. I continue typing.

"Hi," I say back quickly, not taking my eyes from the computer screen.

"Uh, I just wanted to let you know that I gave my two-week notice to Susanna this morning." I swivel around. Lane.

"What!?"

"I haven't found a teaching job yet, but since summer is when schools do their hiring, I wanted to be available for interviews during the day. So I have two more weeks."

"Lane, you can't leave me right now! Go tell her you were just kidding. Tell her—"

"I'm sorry, Emily. You know, now that it's official, I realize I really will miss working here. It's weird . . . but I'll still see you guys tons. We'll still hang out. Nothing is going to change about our friendship."

I know it will. I also know she's really excited about her new opportunities and relieved about having the conversation with her boss out of the way, but I can't bring myself to be happy for her right now. I give her a weak smile. I'm trying.

"That's great, Lane. Really." She doesn't look like she believes me, but then I guess she shouldn't. I try again. "Wanna go out for drinks tonight to celebrate?"

"That'd be great." She just stands there, looking at me. "So where should we go?"

Oh. Right. I should say something about organizing it. I'm trying to make my mouth work when Lane says, "I'll send around an official announcement to the girls, and invite them all to happy hour at the margarita place."

"That sounds great. I'll be there," I say. That's about all I can manage right now.

"Cool," she says, turning to walk out of my cube. She's gone for less than a second, then pops her head back in. "Wow, it's a party out here," she says, then goes back into the hallway. I stick my head into the hallway and immediately see what she means. The whole company seems to be in the hallway, and she has to thread her way through two clumps of people to get back to her desk. Susanna, her soon-to-be-ex-boss, is standing in the doorway of the office next to hers, talking with the editor inside. Reggie and Skylar are standing at the other end of the hallway, laughing. Xavi and Barry Medina stand outside of Helen's door, closest to me. This looks interesting. I roll my chair to the opening in my cube to see if I can hear what they're saying.

"She's really fantastic in person," Helen is saying. "And her platform is amazing. She could probably get half of Harvard to give us quotes for the front cover." My stomach churns as I realize they're talking about the Martha Heggler book. "We'd be able to get a ton of publicity. We could probably get her on the *Today* show." I inch out a little farther into the hallway.

Barry nods. "I'll bet we could get a ton of copies into the chains. Big displays in the windows. With her contacts, if the sales department really got behind this, we could have a best seller on our hands." Oh, dear. I hope not. I inch out more.

"The idea is great," Xavier says. "Nice work, Helen."

"It's bound to spark controversy, which could be really good for sales," Barry continues. I am practically all the way into the hallway now, and I am starting to sweat. I don't want them to talk about this anymore. I'm suddenly furious. They are already being misled by a lie.

"It sure will," says Xavier. "I can't wait. She does such a good job of convincing the reader that the end of religion and the end of marriage is a really good thing. She's really pushing for acceptance and tolerance." I can't take this. Not today. "What she's saying only makes sense," he continues. "She's saying that abstinence until marriage is ridiculous. You want two women? Heh! That's okay!" He laughs. "Who wouldn't love that book?" They're all grinning.

"I wouldn't." Oh no. Did I really just say that? Xavier, Barry, and Helen turn and look at me, eyes round. I immediately cower, but then realize I'm sitting in the middle of the hallway. There's nowhere to go.

"Why not?" Barry asks, his face very serious all of a sudden.

"Because it's not true." They continue to stare. I have to go on. "For one thing, what Helen showed you is not the whole proposal. The book is only partly about marriage." Helen's eyes open wider than I thought possible. She takes a step toward me. "The book goes on from there to attack the concept of families.

Heggler laughs at people who buy into such quaint notions as true love and self-control." Helen's face is red. "It ends up being a celebration of the death of God and all things associated with him." Wow. I can't believe I just said that.

"Is there more to the proposal?" Barry asks, flipping confusedly through the papers in his hand. Lane pokes her head out of her cube to see what's going on.

"I just gave you a section of it," Helen says quickly, "so you could see her writing style and her main points."

"So what's in the rest of it?"

"Well, it's kind of like Emily said," she says, raising her voice, glaring at me. "As a logical extension of her main point, she shows why our concept of family is flawed." Barry nods. A few people in nearby offices have stopped working to listen in.

"That doesn't seem so crazy," Xavier says to me. "What is it that you have a problem with?" Reggie and Skylar have started walking down the hall to hear what's going on.

Here I go. I know that I have to do this, and, honestly, right now I am so angry I want to. "I have a problem with the fact that if this book gets published, millions of people are going to be misled by a lie," I say confidently. "It's based on the idea that God is not real, that he could somehow lose his relevance in our society." Xavier is staring at me with his mouth open. I press on. "I believe that he exists, that he's active and very much alive. That he set up the family in the Garden of Eden and uses the family model as a way to demonstrate his love for us. He uses monogamous marriage to illustrate how much Christ loves the church." I am getting louder now.

"You actually believe that stuff?" Helen asks, aghast.

"Yes, I do," I say. She screws up her face as if to say, It figures.

"So why do your beliefs mean we can't publish this book?" Barry asks, looking me in the eye, his face cold.

"If we publish these false ideas, people might believe them." I look at Xavier. His face is blank. "And I can't support that."

Why are they all just staring at me? What are they thinking?

"I'm sorry you feel that way," Barry says quietly.

The hallway is silent for a minute, everyone staring at me in my little chair. I feel so exposed, but I won't move. I'll let him fire me here, in front of everyone.

Finally, Xavier breaks the silence. "Helen, can you get me a copy of the entire proposal please?" he asks, then quickly turns, brushes past me without taking his eyes off his shoes, and walks into his office, slamming the door.

"I'd like to see it too," Barry says to Helen, before turning on his heel and walking the other way. People scurry away as he comes, trying to pretend they didn't see what just happened. Helen glares at me before turning and going back into her office. And suddenly I am alone in the hallway. Even Lane has disappeared. I bury my head in my hands, then realize I have to force myself to stand up.

I don't know what I'm doing. My thoughts leap and lurch all around. I'm surprised I even remember to breathe. I wander, bewildered, over to my desk and consider sitting back down. But my chair is still in hallway, and my cube looks oddly ridiculous to me. Why would I do this when I'm clearly going to be fired? I look around at my pencils and pens and think I don't even know how they are used anymore. My stacks of manuscripts in different states of pre-publication look like wastes of paper. I glance at my computer screen with several unread e-mails from people in different departments in-house. It strikes me as funny, suddenly, that half of my job is sending and answering e-mails.

Without understanding why, I pack up to go home. It's only eleven in the morning, but nothing else makes sense. I think of taking things with me, of shutting down my computer, but then decide against it. What's the point really? I just grab my purse, push my chair under my desk, and make my way to the elevator bank, aware that the office is completely quiet. Everyone I pass on my way either boldly stares at me or consciously tries to look away. I smile at Lane as I pass her and give her a wink. She winks back, and it makes me feel better.

Outside I am suddenly hit with the realization that it's a beautiful day—finally—in New York. The weather must be in the upper seventies, and the trees are beginning to bloom. Spring. How did I not notice it coming on, not notice it this morning as I came into the building? It is glorious. The sky is filled with white puffy clouds, and the sun is warming the pavement and my cheeks as I break into a wide smile. I stand on the sidewalk in front of Morrow & Sons for a moment and take in a breath all the way to the bottom of each lung, filling them both with air. Behind me the cold behemoth hunkers down, but before it lies a glorious new day. I smile and start walking down Broadway. I don't even know where I'm going.

I reach Times Square, and it's thrilling with all of the people bustling around. The world beyond the doors of work is exciting. It's a completely different crowd on the streets today than on a weekend. It's the unemployed, either temporarily or permanently. There's the homeless man playing the saxophone with a plastic milk jug in front of him and the family of plump tourists from the Midwest all wearing the same red T-shirt saying *Farquar Family Reunion—New York!* I pass a couple on their honeymoon tightly holding hands, staring at the lights, and the Chinese art student drawing names in highly ornate letters for a price. The world is tacky and fun. I'm so excited to be outside and away from the endless "concept" of Morrow & Sons. The backbiting, the intellectualisms, the ladder climbing, and ego clashing.

A giant red double-decker bus pulls to a stop at a little sign in front of me, and people begin to get on. I file in line behind them. I've always wanted to ride around the city on one of these, sitting in the open-air top section like Mrs. Dalloway. I buy a ticket from the driver and climb aboard. The driver tells us the bus will make many stops around the city and, if you get off, another bus will come by every fifteen minutes. The city is your playground.

There are only a few people sitting with me up on top since the weather is still a little cool once the bus starts moving, but I am having the time of my life. We go through Times Square and then circle up Madison Avenue. I see the glitzy housewives shopping with their darling babies in strollers, and the decadent old mavens in their thick tights and dripping jewelry, and blue, swirled hair. We pass the quaint shops of Madison Avenue and drive downtown. The driver stops the bus.

"Empire State Building," he says.

The Empire State Building! Without another thought I stand up and get off. I've lived in New York almost a year and have never once been to the Empire State Building. What have I been doing all this time? Why had I not thought of this before? I skip to the entrance, beating most of the rest of the passengers from the bus, pushing the revolving door confidently. I wait in line to buy my ticket to go the top, and then uniformed doormen usher us all into a large elevator. A woman in front of me asks her son a question, and I hear a pronounced Southern accent. I am surrounded by tourists, and I am loving it. The doors open, and we are led into a glass room. I practically run through it, and I am outside. It is a little chilly so high up, but it doesn't matter. What matters today is life. I am a million miles up, away from Martha Heggler and Xavier and Brittany and Bennett.

The whole city is spread out before me, and I relish the opportunity to watch instead of participating. I grab hold of the heavy iron bars that keep you from falling, and I stick my head through the space between them to look down. The yellow cabs are moving resolutely through the streets, the people on the sidewalk almost too tiny to see. They're all going about their business like it's a normal day. I laugh. I wonder how many times someone in a high building has watched me walk down the street. Those people have no idea that I am watching, and they can't see that there's a huge world they're missing. If they could step back to where I am they'd see so much more than the little piece of sidewalk in front of them. Maybe no one wants to think about how insignificant we all really are, how small a part we actually play in the life of this crazy city. I sniff. I had really thought I could change it.

I walk to the south side of the building and look downtown. The tall towers of the financial district block most of Brooklyn, but I can see the Hudson River flowing toward the sea. I can just barely make out the Statue of Liberty, her proud green form dwarfed by the distance. There is so much more than this, just beyond the bend in the river. I feel, somehow, free. The breeze tosses my hair, and I start to pull it down, but then just let it go. A single tear rolls down my face. There's a big world out there, away from this place.

I spend more than an hour walking around the observation platform, noticing the view from every angle, trying to gauge if the sky looks any closer from so high up, watching the people on the lower rooftops. Drinking it all in so I will never forget. Eventually, slowly, I descend and am an ant on the sidewalk once again.

I walk immediately to an Internet cafe and log on to the web. I click to a website I have heard Reggie talk about, where you name your own price for a plane ticket, and if an airline accepts your price, you must fly when they tell you to. I type in San Diego, the departure and return dates today and Sunday, and give it the price of $225. I laugh. No way will it find me a ticket. The computer thinks for a moment and then makes me an offer. If I will agree to fly back Monday instead of Sunday and leave in three and a half hours from New York, I can go to San Diego for $245. I reach for my wallet instinctively and then panic. I think of calling Lane, or my mom to see if she'll be home this weekend, or Jacob to see if he even wants to talk to me anymore, but then I realize that I must go home. I have made a decision, and I need to tell my loved ones about it in person.

I find myself sitting in the San Diego airport at eleven o'clock on a Friday night utterly alone. I had just barely made my departing flight. I packed in such a hurry I was pretty sure I didn't even have a toothbrush on me and hadn't been able to check my small weekend bag. Now I walk through the sleek terminal, past the baggage claim and out through the automatic doors, a little dazed. My stomach is churning. What have I done? I hadn't had time to think about what would happen when I arrived because I had collapsed in exhaustion upon getting on the plane. I was just overwrought with all the pressure lately. I take a breath of the California air. It is a nice warm night and more than anything, it feels great to be home. I dig my phone out of my purse to call my poor mom and wake her from her sleep but then change my mind at the last second.

It rings and rings. With each additional ring, my heart sinks further. Jacob's voice mail picks up.

The tone beeps, and I panic. I clear my throat. "Uh, Jacob, hi. It's Emily. I know we're not really talking right now but, uh, I really need you to call me back if you get this. It's pretty important . . . I guess that's all. Thanks." I hang up. Thanks? Oh man. He's going to think I'm dead in a ditch but still remembering my manners. I roll my eyes at myself and have to laugh. What kind of day was this? I fly to an airport at almost midnight and call Jacob, who hates my guts? Oh yeah, I add, let's not forget the part where I walk out on my job after telling my boss I don't approve of his lifestyle. Oh man.

As I scroll through my phone book looking for the word *Home* to call my parents, my phone rings with an incoming call, and I see it is Jacob. I punch the button twice instead of once in my excitement, both answering the phone and then hanging up on him by accident.

"Hello?" I ask. I hear nothing. I punch the button again. "Hello? Jacob? Hello?" I realize what I did and curse myself and then scold myself for cursing. I call him right back. Thankfully, he answers.

By Sunday things have calmed down enough around my house that I have a chance to e-mail Xavier and tell him I'm not going to be in until Tuesday. I am glad to put off, even if by one little day, my return to Morrow & Sons to face the music. I must have told the story of my imminent firing a thousand times this weekend. Even Jacob can tell it now. At the moment, I can hear him in the living room playing cards with Nanna. She is trying to cheat by swearing that the queen of spades is the best card in the deck and that in Hearts you want to get a lot of points. It makes me laugh. He hasn't left my side all weekend. Ever since I told him I was moving to San Diego.

Nanna was ecstatic when I told her my new plan. I apologized about never sending her a get-well-soon package, but she said my surprise trip home was better than a box full of brownies. She actually cried when she saw me on Saturday, and I cried too. It had been a rough season for her.

I wondered how my parents would take the news that their daughter had gotten emotional at work and become a martyr for something that probably wouldn't matter and had gotten fired. I was the first person anyone could think of in the family who had gotten fired, but they listened to my story and told me they thought I'd made the right choice. Dad even said he was proud of me. Mom was a little nervous, of course, about what kind of job I'd get in San Diego, but I assured her it would be fine. Nothing could be as hard as Manhattan.

Plus, they were thrilled about having me home again. Not to mention they seemed to really like Jacob. My mother was won over when I told her that on the night of my arrival he left a concert for me at eleven thirty, got me some dinner, calmed me down, and then immediately took me to his married sister's house in San Diego to stay the night.

Jacob and I talked all night at Bryn's place. Her husband, Michael, seemed really nice, and Bryn clearly thought my adventure and Jacob's affection for me the sweetest thing she had ever seen. They made me a nice bed on the couch, and Jacob gave me a kiss good night when my eyes were shutting. He promised me he'd be back in the morning with croissants and coffee to drive me home to my parents' place. I fell asleep and slept soundly, knowing I had made him happy, that I had gotten him to see how much I cared, thinking of our future together.

The longer I am in California, the more right my decision feels. I only wish I hadn't left New York in such a wreck.

I arrive at the apartment early Monday evening, refreshed. I remind myself as I turn the key in my lock that Brittany is mad at me. I walk into our living room, and the entire apartment looks so foreign to me. I'm really ready to move. I don't see her, but I hear voices in the kitchen.

"Britt?" I call. I wonder if she's been worried about me. Lane called over the weekend to find out where I was, but she was the only one. I didn't see Matthew enough anymore that my absence for a weekend would alarm him.

She appears, all smiles, with John, who is holding a bowl of popcorn. "Emily! There you are. We're about to watch a movie. You want in?"

I shake my head. She can really be very sweet when she's not being evil. "No, uh, thanks though."

I decide to tell her everything right away, just have it all out as soon as possible. John is very patient and listens while we talk. I agree to pay the rent for another month, which gives her enough time to find a new roommate. And she seems genuinely sad that I'm leaving. Or maybe she just has gas.

"I guess I just thought you'd be here forever. That you'd be my maid of honor, and I'd be yours," she says. Her sentiment is real so I stifle my laugh, realizing I will miss her in some bizarre way.

Walking into work the next day is weird. I try to hold my head up in case anyone is looking, but the floor is quiet. My desk is exactly as I left it, the colored lines of my screensaver dancing away. The lamp above my desk is still on. I sit down, and place my bag under my desk. Xavier's not here yet. Good. Maybe I'll have time to tie up some loose ends.

Jenna didn't even know I was home over the weekend. She'll definitely yell at me about that one. I e-mail her to let her know I'll be coming home. I can't wait until she reads that. She'll go nuts.

I e-mail Lane—I'm sure she knows I'll be gone from Morrow & Sons soon, but I want to tell her that I've decided to go back to California.

I e-mail Uncle Matthew to see if he can fit me into his schedule to meet me for dinner in the next few days.

I make a list of all the things I need to do—figure out how to ship my stuff back across the country, drop my laundry off one more time with Wi so I'll have something to wear when I get home, remember to cancel my dentist appointment next week. I hear footsteps behind me. I take a deep breath.

"Good morning, Emily," Xavier says as he quickly walks past and opens his office door. He looks pale, and there are dark circles under his eyes.

"Hi Xavier." I try not to sound sheepish, but I am afraid that's exactly how I appear. He just goes into his office.

I'll give him a few minutes. I e-mail a few more people, and I even start to write a message to Bennett, but Xavier calls out, "Emily, can you come in here for a minute?" I take another deep breath, stand up, adjust my skirt, and walk into the lion's den. "Please close the door behind you," he says.

I sit down in the chair in front of his desk and look him in the eye.

"Emily, I have to admit I've never seen anything like what happened here on Friday," he says, playing with a paper clip. I nod. "Your behavior was, shall we say, unconventional." I nod again. "And your leaving for the day was extremely unprofessional." I start to apologize, but he cuts me off. "I'm afraid we can't have that kind of childish behavior around here, and, unfortunately, we're going to have to do whatever it takes to make sure it never happens again." I nod, silent. Here it comes. I am ready.

"That said, I need to tell you that what you did was also very brave." What? "Helen is very smart but very cunning, and she holds grudges. She wants to climb to the top. Unfortunately, as we just found out, she is willing to do whatever it takes to get there." He puts down the paper clip and picks up a fountain pen, rolling it in his fingers. "You were right about the proposal she gave us. She was trying to tell us the book was one thing when it was something different. Lying to your bosses does not speed your climb to the top." He sighs. "We realized we couldn't trust her. Because she's been with us for so long, we couldn't let her go, but this is not the kind of thing we will quickly forget." He taps the pen on his desk. "All this is to say thank you for chiming in. We would have bought that book, and probably lost a lot of money on it."

"So you're not going to buy it?"

"No, and I doubt another publisher is going to either, if they've read the whole proposal. It's gibberish. But here's the point. You showed us on Friday that you really get this job. Your instincts are good, you've done a fine job editing books, and you've done good work. You've also put in your time." He looks at me and smiles. "Congratulations, Emily. You've just been promoted. Welcome to life as an assistant editor."

What? Promoted? I can't make my mouth work.

"You don't seem as excited as I expected," Xavier says, laughing, then rising from his chair and holding out his hand for me to shake.

"Excited? I'm, well, I'm completely shocked," I stammer. "I thought you called me in here to fire me."

"Fire you?" He seems genuinely baffled.

"Yeah, fire me. You know, for unprofessional behavior. For voicing my religious beliefs in the middle of the office." I might as well say it. It doesn't matter at this point anyway. "For condemning your choice to have a wife and a girlfriend."

"My choice to have what?" he exclaims.

"Yeah. I couldn't help but notice you bringing your wife around sometimes, Beatrice others. They both call all the time. But don't worry. I don't judge you for it or anything. You're welcome to do what you like. But, well, I don't necessarily think it's the best way, and I kind of announced that to everyone within earshot on Friday."

"You thought Beatrice . . . oh my." He starts to laugh. "Emily, Beatrice is my . . ." He is laughing really hard now, almost doubled over. Tears are starting to run down his cheeks. Why is this so funny?

"Emily, Beatrice is my stepdaughter. She's my first wife's child. I adopted her, and since Elizabeth's death I have been her guardian and, well, friend. She's all grown up now, obviously, and we are very close." He wipes his forehead. "Oh, God. Beatrice. Is that what other people think too? That explains so much," he chuckles, then sits up straight and looks at me. "Family, Emily. It's really important to me too."

I don't know what to say. I guess I just kind of stare him because he looks at me and starts laughing again. "So we'll get some business cards printed up with your new title," he says, "and maybe we'll even be able to move you into that empty office on the other side of the floor."

"Oh, about that," I begin. "You probably shouldn't put in that card order. I'm, uh, well . . . I've decided to move back to California."

"You've what?" he asks, his mouth hanging open.

"Yeah. So, um, if you're not going to fire me, I guess I'm putting in my two-week notice."

"But why? Don't you like it here? Is it the money? Because of course you'll get a raise with your new title."

"No, it's not that. I just . . . well, I realize I left home looking for something I had all along. And I decided I need to be where the people I care about are. You know, family." And Jacob.

He sighs. "You sound like your mind is made up."

"It is." I nod. "I'm really sorry. You've all been great to me. I sure wish California and New York were closer together."

"Me too," he says. "Well, then, I wish you the best. I'm going to miss you, that's for sure. And now I have to find a new assistant, which is going to be a royal pain in the butt." He laughs. "But I'm happy for you."

"Thanks. Me too."

He nods. "If you're leaving me, you've got a bunch of projects to finish up before you go." I nod. "Well? Get on them," he says, laughing again. I stand up to go, and he stands too. He puts out his hand. "Are you going to shake my hand this time?"

I put out my hand, and he grips it firmly. "You did good work, Emily," he says, then turns away quickly. He's pretending to adjust his glasses, but it looks to me like he's wiping away a tear.

It is hard to say goodbye to the girls at work, but since Lane and I end up leaving at the same time, they throw us a big going-away party at Reggie's. As I crack open my second beer, Skylar reminds the group of the first time we went out and I ordered a Diet Coke. Everyone, including me, thinks this is hilarious.

It is kind of weird that Bennett is at the party, but Skylar brought him. Actually, I am really glad he came. He had been a huge part of my whole New York fantasy, and I need to say goodbye to him along with the rest of it.

Late in the evening, after everyone has had a drink and is relaxed and laughing, Reggie announces that they have prepared a little performance for us. Skylar and Reggie get up and read a funny poem they have written about the two of us. Reggie starts with,

Well, darn it all, they're leaving,
Our little Lane and Em,
But though we are bereaving
We've had good times with them.

Skylar continues:

We've had our daily lunches,
Our laughter over victuals,

We've rolled with the punches
Dealt by manuscript transmittals.

They go on for several more verses apiece, making fun of our quirks and laughing at what they like about us. It is really sweet, and very funny—it means a lot that they would put it together for us.

When Bennett gives me a hug at the end of the evening, I don't even flinch. Goodbye forever, Bennett. Good luck getting over your blonde vixen.

As we are finally leaving and I am looking for a taxi—I decide I deserve one last cab ride home on my last night here—Lane hands me a card and gives me a hug.

"I'll sure miss you," she says. I can't tell her I feel the same because I am too choked up. On the cab ride home, I read her note.

Dear Emily,

I am so thankful I got to know you this year. You've meant so much to me—I'm sure you have no idea how much of an impact you've had on me. Thanks for teaching me about what real faith is. I'll miss you. Keep in touch.

Lane

I am crying too much to be able to see the money in my wallet, so I just hand the driver the first bill I find and tell him to keep the change. He smiles so broadly I can tell it must have been a twenty. Oh well. It is my gift to the faithful cab drivers of New York City.

When I get home I finish packing and sleep a little, though I have to wake up early. Uncle Matthew and Josie are driving me to the airport in Josie's roommate's car, and I don't want to be late. It has been a busy two weeks, but I can't wait to get home. For good this time.

Brittany gives me a hug on my way out the door. She's never up this early, and I am touched that she dragged herself out of bed to say goodbye. Until she hands me a bill for the remaining utility fees I owe her. I promise to mail her a check.

On the way to the airport Uncle Matthew makes me promise to come visit. Just to make sure he gets his money's worth out of that coat, he says. I promise I will. Josie tells me she will miss me at the Locus. And, I have to admit, I just might miss her too.

The announcer calls my flight number, and I stand up. I give Uncle Matthew a weak smile. "Thank you for all that you've done for me this year," I say, leaning in to hug him.

"Oh, Emily," he says. He returns the hug, then pulls back and takes Josie's hand. "Thanks for all you've done for me this year."

I bend down to pick up my carry-on bag, then start to walk to the gate. I have made it.

Reaching into my pocket to pull out my ticket, I feel Lane's note. Maybe I haven't changed New York, I think as I take one last look over my shoulder at Uncle Matthew and Josie, but I have left my mark.

© Wayne Adams

about the authors

ANNE DAYTON graduated from Princeton University with a B.A. in English and is currently working on her M.A. in English literature at New York University.

MAY VANDERBILT graduated from Baylor University with a B.A. in English and went on to earn a master's degree in fiction from Johns Hopkins University.

Hired within a month of each other, they both work in the editorial department of a major New York publishing house and live in Brooklyn.